PLANT THEM DEEP

Also by Aimée and David Thurlo

PLANT THEM DEEP

✖ ✖ ✖ ✖ ✖

AN ELLA CLAH NOVEL

AIMÉE & DAVID THURLO

A Tom Doherty Associates Book
New York

PLANT THEM DEEP

Copyright © 2003 by Aimée and David Thurlo

A Forge Book
Published by Tom Doherty Associates, LLC
175 Fifth Avenue
New York, NY 10010

www.tor.com

Forge® is a registered trademark of Tom Doherty Associates, LLC.

Library of Congress Cataloging-in-Publication Data

Thurlo, Aimée.
  Plant them deep / Aimée Thurlo and David Thurlo.—1st hardcover ed.
    p. cm.
"A Forge book"—T.p. verso.
  ISBN 0-765-30478-3
1. Clah, Ella (Fictitious character)—Fiction. 2. Mothers and daughters—Fiction.
3. Police—New Mexico—Fiction. 4. Navajo Indians—Fiction. 5. Navajo women—
Fiction. 6. Policewomen—Fiction. 7. New Mexico—Fiction. I. Thurlo, David.
II. Title.
  PS3570.H82P57 2003
  813'.54—dc21

                                                          2003009216

First Edition: November 2003

Printed in the United States of America

0 9 8 7 6 5 4 3 2 1

To the Navajo Plant Watchers,
who protect and honor the Plant People.
This book is for you in appreciation of the
wisdom you shared with us.

PLANT THEM DEEP

ONE

✖ ✖ ✖

The midmorning sun cascading across the Chuska Mountains filtered downward into the wind- and water-carved canyons, revealing the stark beauty of the *Dinetah*, the land of the Navajo people. Rose Destea stood by the open kitchen window, a cup of herbal tea in hand, enjoying the sweet scent of sage and piñon pine that drifted into her warm kitchen.

With her granddaughter Dawn at day-school, and her daughter, Ella, a police officer, at work, mornings at home were quiet these days. The peaceful hours had become her time to think, to remember, and, most important of all, to reinforce the *hózhq*—everything that was good, orderly, harmonious, and beautiful in her life.

Rose stood alone in the silence, at peace with herself and her surroundings. She'd spent most of her adult life here, in this house that Raymond, her husband, had built for her almost fifty years ago. Memories whispered from every corner. These walls had seen life, and endured the emptiness and loss a death always left behind.

Their marriage had been stormy. She'd remained faithful to the Navajo Way as a traditionalist, while as a Christian preacher, only the Anglo God had held Raymond's complete respect. But after his murder, the fire at the center of her world had given way to a coldness that nothing could penetrate. Lena Clani, her lifelong friend, had helped her crawl out of the deep abyss of sorrow that had almost destroyed her.

Raymond's passing had signaled the end of an era for her. Not really needed anymore by her adult children, Rose had known that she'd need to find a new purpose—something that would sustain her and give her direction—a reason to get up every morning.

She'd found herself again through her love for the tribe. The *Dineh*, The People, defined her and centered her. Now Rose frequently spoke on behalf of Mother Earth, which had been devastated by the various mining companies that had come to their land with promises of new jobs and a better life. The *Dinetah* was a sacred place given to the Navajos by the Holy People. To honor Mother Earth, harmony would have to be restored—to the land and to the tribe.

The phone rang, interrupting her musings. Rose picked it up, knowing who it was even before she heard the voice of Jennifer Clani, Lena's granddaughter. Jennifer took care of Dawn, Ella's daughter, before and after day-school.

"Thanks so much for calling back so quickly. I need you to come in early today," Rose said. "I'm going to be leaving shortly and I want to be sure that someone will be here when my granddaughter gets home. They're getting off early."

Getting Jennifer's assurance that she'd arrive in a matter of minutes, Rose went outside. She'd heard a truck coming up the road and suspected that Herman Cloud would be pulling up to the house in a moment or two. If she was there to greet him, he wouldn't have to wait by his car.

Herman always honored traditionalist ways by never approaching anyone's front door unless invited to do so and

Rose appreciated the courtesy. Having a modernist daughter meant that the old ways got swept aside often. Although she'd grown to accept it as inevitable, she missed the small courtesies The People had extended to one another in times past.

Seeing her wave at him, Herman came up to meet her. Herman, whom she'd teasingly named *Bizaadii*—which meant the gabby one because he was usually so quiet, stood around five-foot-seven and had broad, erect shoulders. His face was leathery and rough, and marked by a multitude of deep lines that attested to a lifetime of hardships and the spirit of determination that had kept him strong through the years. His deep-set eyes sparkled with intelligence and alertness. Although a man of few words, he was easy to talk to and cared about the tribe as much as Rose did.

"Good morning," he greeted. "Are you ready to go gather the medicinal plants you wanted?"

"Almost. Come in while I prepare a jug of iced tea. It's going to get hot outside quickly today."

"We all keep hoping for some rain, but the clouds come and go without so much as a drop."

"The rains will start later this month. The Plant People have learned to be patient," she reminded, referring to all plant life in the traditionalist way. "We have to do the same."

Rose brewed some mint tea and cooled it quickly with ice cubes, then poured it into a large thermos. They were almost ready to leave when Jennifer arrived. Today she was wearing a long, full denim skirt and a vivid red cotton blouse.

She gave Rose a bright smile. "Is there any special job you want me to take care of today?"

"Could you water my herb garden, Boots?" Rose said, using the nickname Jennifer had been given as a child. "I'm running a little behind and didn't get a chance."

"I'll do it now while I'm waiting for your granddaughter."

"Her friend's mother is bringing her home today, but it's possible my granddaughter will want her little friend to stay and visit," Rose advised.

"That's fine."

As Rose and Herman got under way, Rose gave him directions to her favorite collecting site near Pinedale, a rural community north of Fallen Timber Ridge. It was about one hundred miles southeast of Shiprock. "I know the journey is a long one," Rose said, "but 'blue pollen' grows there in abundance, and also 'wondering about medicine.' "

"I know 'blue pollen.' Outside our borders it's called wild larkspur. I remember that from an essay my son did for school once."

"That's the one. The blue flower petals can be dried and ground with other plants and used for sacred pollen. I like carrying some in my medicine bundle." She pulled out her *jish*, a small leather pouch that contained soil from the sacred mountains, white shell, and other items of power. "I also carry a rock crystal in here. The crystal stands for the prayer and the power of the spoken word, and the pollen signifies well-being. Together, they work to make all prayers come true," Rose said.

Herman nodded in approval. "What's the other plant you mentioned?"

" 'Wondering about medicine.' The Anglos call it silvery lupine, I believe. My son needs it for a Sing he's doing for a patient, and I'd like to transplant a healthy plant or two into my own garden. The lotion we make from the leaves is a good treatment for poison ivy. With my granddaughter going everywhere these days, I think I should have a supply on hand."

As they traveled south toward her plant-collecting site, Rose gazed with concern at the familiar upland desert country they were passing through. These days the Rez seemed more barren than the *Dinetah* she remembered from her youth and could visualize so easily in her mind's eye.

"The reservation has changed so much since we were young," she said sadly. "When I was a girl, we'd see sheep grazing almost everywhere. We could eat sumac berries and *hashk'aan,* the fruit of the yucca, when we were hungry. Now look at that old rusted-out drilling equipment. Everything around it is dead, even the earth itself. Mining has destroyed so much of our land." She exhaled softly. "I wish I could make my daughter and others of her generation understand what we've lost in just their lifetime."

He nodded. "It's the same with my two nephews, the ones in the same profession as your daughter. To them life goes by fast, and sometimes it seems that the moment is all that really matters to them. But I believe, deep down, they *do* know that change isn't always for the better—that you have to pick and choose what you give up and what you allow to take its place."

"All things are connected. That's why I'm so worried about all our Plant People. Some of the areas near the mines, not far from where we're going, used to be filled with Indian rice grass and there was goosefoot as far as you could see. Yet nothing but snakeweed grows there now. I know snakeweed has its place—it can cure snake and ant bites—but it also poisons livestock. The imbalance caused by mining is making many of the Plant People leave, and without them, livestock grows weak and dies. Eventually, without the animals, The People will go hungry too."

Off the interstate east of Gallup, they traveled down a graveled road through the piñon-juniper-covered hills adjacent to Fallen Timber Ridge. At long last they pulled over, and Rose walked with Herman across a large field. Herman carried a small shovel, while Rose brought the soluble fiber plant pots they'd need.

"Blue pollen" plants were plentiful. Rose left an offering of white shell beside the plants she'd be leaving behind, and explained why she'd be taking two of their neighbors. Then, after a brief prayer, Herman dug up the plants and she potted them. Afterward, she buried the plant fragments that remained and said a final prayer.

Carrying the pots, they continued their search for "wondering about medicine" for another hour, but, despite their efforts, the plant was nowhere to be seen.

"It should be growing all around here," Rose said. "The flowers are grayish lavender in color, and the mature shrubs should be almost two feet tall by now."

At last, in an area where Rose remembered having seen the shrubs once, they found two sickly plants barely a foot tall. Rose studied the ground, puzzled. "There are several holes around here," she pointed out, "and they're not the work of prairie dogs. I think someone must have dug up the other 'wondering about medicine' and left only these two little ones behind."

Herman crouched down. "Whoever it was used an entrenching tool."

"A what?"

"It's something originally used by soldiers to dig foxholes and trenches—a short shovel that folds up and can also be used like a pick. The business end is pointed."

Rose nodded toward the marks on the ground. "That seems about right. But who would harvest the plants so indiscriminately and without leaving any offerings? Our people know to take only what they need and leave the best and strongest behind so there'll always be a supply."

"It's undoubtedly someone who wasn't taught that there's a right way to collect plants," Herman said.

"Some are saying that the Plant People are moving away

because they don't feel we honor them," she said softly. "Maybe they're right."

"This was probably done by someone in a hurry and willing to cut corners."

Rose looked at the small plants. "I'll take the smallest of those two. Maybe with some natural fertilizer and proper watering I can help it grow strong again. If these plants are becoming scarce, we need to try and save some."

"Agreed. I think if you leave that one there it'll die, so by taking it, you're giving it a chance. Its neighbor has better odds of survival left on its own."

Once she finished transplanting it, Rose patted the earth back in place with her hands, then looked up. "The earth smells strange. I've never noticed that before around here." She held up a small clump of sandy soil and sniffed it closely. "Maybe that's the reason all the plants around us look so weak and spindly."

"Could be," Herman answered, looking around. "We've walked farther than I realized. I can't see the truck from here. Let's start heading back."

Herman helped Rose to her feet and they began walking back, carrying the plants they'd collected. "That sure is an odd smell. What do you think it is?"

Rose considered it silently, not wanting to alarm him. But it was clear to her what it was. Here, the earth itself was dying.

Herman looked across a low spot where a few underweight cows were grazing. "I don't think they should be grazing livestock here," he added.

"What other choice do they have? Animals have to eat what's available."

They headed back slowly, each immersed in thought. Suddenly Rose heard a low, rapid scuffling close to her right, followed by a soft, plaintive cry. "There's something in trouble over there, near the arroyo. I'm going to see what it is."

As she drew near, she heard the mournful cry of a calf. Rose looked around, but she couldn't see the animal anywhere.

"It must be down in the arroyo," Herman said, having heard it too. "Maybe it wandered away from the others and got trapped. We should try and help it out."

Rose set down the plants, but Herman held on to the shovel as they walked down the slope into the arroyo, which meandered as far as she could see in a north-south direction. As they reached the bottom, Rose discovered a half-starved calf on the floor of the trenchlike wash. The hoofprints along the steep rim of the embankment told the story. The animal had fallen in and was now lying on its side, obviously exhausted from repeated attempts to climb back out.

"From its condition, that poor animal must have fallen in here some time ago. With the lack of grasses around here, my guess is that it went off looking for better grazing and ended up where it is now," Herman said.

"I know the woman who owns this animal and the others we saw. She has four or five cows and probably double that in goats, and lives about a half mile from here. But I don't think she has a truck or a horse she can use to get this animal out. Last time I saw her, all she had was an old station wagon that was barely running. I think we should try to get her calf out of this arroyo before it dies of exhaustion or lack of water."

Herman walked up to the animal, and it turned its head, letting out a sad cry. "You're right. It's young, and it may still survive if we can get it out. I'll walk back to the road and bring my truck. I have a tow strap, so maybe we can find a way to pull or lift the calf out."

While Herman hurried back to his pickup, Rose began trying to figure a way to get the stranded animal out of what was essentially a ten-foot-deep, steep-sided ditch. A cave-in had toppled a section of embankment, probably the same spot where the calf had fallen in. The mound of soft earth had blocked off the arroyo in the direction that apparently led downhill, and tracks showed where the calf had walked back and forth several times. The arroyo was probably blocked at both ends.

Rose decided that the best bet might be to try and carve off more of the sides, shaping a slope gentle enough to allow the calf to climb out with their help—if it could get on its feet again. Getting closer to the edge, she found a crack in the ground where the embankment was starting to break away. It would eventually topple into the wash.

The sound of Herman's pickup got her attention, and she waved to him as he pulled up within ten feet of the bank, the front of the truck facing her.

"Don't get any closer. The sides have been breaking away, but that gave me an idea," Rose called out. "Do you have anything we can use as a lever to pry off more of this embankment?"

Herman stepped down out of the cab of the truck. "Thinking of making a wide enough ramp so we can walk the animal out?" Seeing her nod, he added, "It could work, if we plan it right."

"There's a sturdy-looking branch over there"—she pointed toward a juniper—"that we can use."

It took about ten minutes and two branches, but together they managed to carve off enough earth and sand to fashion a gentle slope leading into the arroyo.

Rose went down and walked over to where the calf was. It had managed to stand up on its own. Using the tow strap like a lead, they coaxed and pushed the weary animal back up to the surface.

"Can you load her into the back of your truck?" Rose asked.

"Yeah, she's small. I think I can lower the tailgate and we can help her up," Herman said. Moments later, with Rose pulling and Herman pulling, the task was accomplished.

"I'm sorry to put you to all this trouble, but Sara Ahasteen is a widow and would have had a lot of trouble handling this by herself. Although her daughter comes to help from time to time, she's pretty much on her own."

"Her daughter lives off the reservation?"

Rose nodded. "She works in Albuquerque. That's where she got her job after college. She's asked her mother to come join her many times, but that's hard on the older ones, you know? All Sara's ever known is the reservation, and she feels that she belongs here between the Sacred Mountains."

"What about her clan?"

"Most of them live in Arizona. She could join them, but she wants to stay here where she raised her family."

Ten minutes later, after loading up the plants they'd collected, they pulled up in front of a small stuccoed, wood-frame house. The pine-branch corral next to it was in good condition, but it now stood empty.

They waited in the truck, and soon saw a Navajo woman about Rose's age walking in their direction from over a low hill. She was wearing a long skirt and a loose blouse. Her skin was weathered and dark, but there was an agelessness about her that attested to a spirit as tough as the land itself.

Rose climbed out of the pickup to greet her as Herman went around to the back of the truck to lead the calf out.

"*Yáat'ééh*," Rose greeted.

Sara Ahasteen smiled as she saw the scrawny calf that Herman led out of the truck.

"There she is! I've been searching for that poor animal since the sun came up," the woman said. "I can't afford to lose any more livestock. All I have left are a few cows and that calf."

"Something has happened to the land around here, hasn't it?" Rose asked.

Sara nodded. "There was an old settling pond from the uranium mines near here at one time. After the water evaporated, they buried the waste chemicals that were left over. That was about thirty years ago, but I still remember the man telling us that the chemicals would never leak out of their containment area and harm the soil. But now it looks like they were wrong. Near as I can tell, some have seeped into the groundwater."

"Have you reported it?" Rose asked.

Sara shook her head. "Most of the families who used to live here had so much trouble with the land that they just moved away. I'm the only one left these days and no one's going to do anything for just one person."

"I'll report it for you anyway. Maybe someone can help," Rose said as Herman led the calf into the corral.

"All right."

Rose watched Sara take a bucket of water to the animal, then give it a small handful of grain and a flake of old hay. When she looked up again, Rose recognized the emotion she saw mirrored in Sara's eyes. It was the *ch'ééná*, a mourning for what could never be part of their lives again. When the land cried, Navajos like Sara cried with her.

TWO

✖ ✖ ✖

Two hours later, not far from home, Rose stretched in her seat, trying to loosen her seat belt a bit. "Do you think they'll send someone who can figure out what's wrong with the soil over there?"

"Probably," Herman answered. "They may even run some tests. But I doubt anything will be done to fix all the damage. You can treat the water when you pump it out of the ground, but that won't help the plants, or the animals who happen to feed on them."

Rose had rolled down her window to let in some fresh air. As the midafternoon sun beat down on them, the temperatures had risen to the low nineties. "Are you still planning to go with me to the ceremony at the Navajo Forestry Department later this afternoon?"

"Of course, but this trip took longer than we planned. We're not going to have much time to rest up." Herman stopped the truck in Rose's driveway, and they both began unloading the plants they'd gathered.

"I know. I'll prepare a small good-luck plant to present to the new director of the nursery, then shower and dress up." She thought of Henry Yazzie. He was a modernist, but he'd been raised in a traditionalist family. The small plant would be a gift he'd appreciate and value.

"Okay. I'll go home, clean up, and meet you back here in forty-five minutes. How's that?"

"All right."

Rose went around the side of the house carrying the potted plants they'd brought to her small garden of medicinal plants and herbs. She set them on top of the soil, intending to give them a day to acclimate, then went into the house.

Jennifer and Dawn came into the kitchen from the living room just then. Seeing her grandmother, Dawn ran over and gave her a hug. "I'm going to ride Wind. Come watch, *Shimasání!*"

Dawn was nearly four now, and always used the Navajo word for grandmother, something which pleased Rose a great deal. "I can't, little one. But you can tell me all about it later." Looking at Jennifer, she added, "Remember that I may be late tonight. You're prepared to stay until my daughter or I get back?"

"Yes, I'll be happy to do that. And please don't worry. She and I will play games and after she goes to bed, I'll watch some television or read until one of you returns."

"Thank you. I appreciate it. Of course, you'll get paid overtime, as usual."

As Dawn and Jennifer went out the back door, Rose smiled. She approved of Jennifer wholeheartedly. Her granddaughter couldn't have a better sitter. To make things almost perfect, Jennifer was a traditionalist.

Ella would never be traditionalist, but having Jennifer around almost made up for it. In a lot of ways, Jennifer—Boots—had become like another daughter to her, one who shared her beliefs. Maybe their combined influence on Dawn would persuade her to choose the old ways someday. The possibility never failed to cheer her up.

Rose went out to the storage shed, picked up a small clay pot, then added water to a wash pan full of her homemade soil mix. Mixing the muddy soil with her hands, she squeezed the excess water out of a handful, then placed the soil loosely into the pot.

Taking a small hand trowel, Rose went out into her garden and walked to the far row. "Oak under a tree" was a small shrub so compact that it was barely six inches tall. She'd always liked its clusters of small yellow flowers. To the Anglos, it was just creeping barberry, but to the *Dineh*, the plant was believed to remove bad luck, and its pollen was considered a general cure-all.

Rose transplanted the hardy young plant she'd grown from a cutting early in the spring, placing it in the prepared soil already in the pot. Once finished, she went back inside to clean up and get ready.

Thirty-five minutes later Rose stepped into the living room wearing her long indigo skirt and a velveteen blouse of the same color. It was fastened at the waist with a silver concha belt that her son Clifford had made for her. An impressive-looking silver and turquoise squash blossom necklace hung from her neck.

"Wow, you look great, Mom. Hot date?" Ella Clah, Rose's tall, slender daughter asked from the kitchen doorway. The sandwich she'd obviously grabbed as a quick snack was still in her hand.

Rose rolled her eyes. "Hot date? Only if you're referring to the fact that the temperature outside will be one hundred by sundown."

Ella laughed, then stepped back into the kitchen. "Touchy."

"You have the strangest sense of humor, daughter." Rose shook her head, joining Ella and pouring herself a glass of water. "What are you doing home at this time of the day? Caught your share of criminals earlier than usual?"

"I wish. Actually, I was hoping to catch my daughter and say hi, but she and Boots have already gone out riding. That pony is hard to compete against," Ella added with a smile.

Hearing the deep rumble of Herman's pickup approaching, Rose went to the porch to greet him.

Ella followed. "Where are you off to?"

"To the ceremony at the new tribal plant nursery. As a Plant Watcher, I have an interest in how that's run."

Ella sighed softly. "Mom, I really worry about you," she said softly. "I know you're doing what you think is right, but tread softly. You made enemies by campaigning against gambling, then you placed yourself right in the middle of the controversy surrounding the nuclear power plant."

"I've only spoken the truth, daughter, and they all know it."

"The fact that you're right ticks them off even more, so watch yourself. Bad enemies have long memories and they'll strike back at you when you least expect it."

"I'll be careful, daughter, just as you are," Rose said gently.

As Herman came up, Ella smiled at him, then, with a quick good-bye, walked to her tribal police unit.

Rose gazed at her agile, athletic daughter as she climbed effortlessly into the unmarked blue Jeep. "My daughter still doesn't understand why I stopped being the stay-at-home mom she's always known."

"You're wrong about that. She does—she just doesn't like it. I think she wants things the way they used to be." He paused, then added, "We all do that to one extent or another—wish for what has past, what was familiar. Can you blame her?"

Rose smiled. "You're a wise man."

"Are you ready?"

Rose went back for the potted plant, then joined Herman at his pickup, where he was holding the door open for her. As they set out, Rose ran her fingers lightly over the large squash blossom necklace. The sterling silver and turquoise piece was adorned with ten squash blossoms fashioned of silver, five on each side, and at the bottom was the Naja, a horseshoe-shaped design worn by early Spanish horsemen. The Naja held seven turquoise stones set in silver bezels spaced evenly around the horseshoe shape. Each of the squash blossoms also held matching stones set in silver, separated from one another by two rows of large handmade silver beads. Like many of the things she treasured, it was a link to her past.

"That's a beautifully crafted necklace."

"Thank you. It's been in my family for generations. Someday I'll give it to my daughter, and eventually she can pass it on to her daughter." She paused, then added, "This necklace is much more than a piece of jewelry. It's a link that connects the women in our family. That's why I've always treasured it."

Forty-five minutes later, Herman parked outside the large new facility located near Toadlena, southwest of Shiprock and in the foothills of the nearby mountains. There were at least two hundred people touring the nursery, which was spread over several acres.

"I'm glad to see so many people supporting the tribal nursery," Rose said. "I understand they'll specialize in native pines and other varieties that can be replanted to take the place of the trees we harvest for lumber."

"It's a sensible plan," he answered, "replacing what we use."

They were walking toward the main entrance to the facility when two men she recognized came up to her. One was her granddaughter's father, Councilman Kevin Tolino, and the other was Councilman John Begay.

"*Aqalani*, greetings," Begay said, using both the Navajo word and the English equivalent.

"I speak Navajo, Councilman," Rose said, amused.

He nodded. "Oh, of course. Force of habit, that's all." He

cleared his throat and continued. "I know you're probably in a hurry to get out of the heat, so let me get right to the point. We need your help. The tribal council has been receiving complaints from several of our medicine men and herbalists. They claim that native plants needed for rituals and medicinal purposes seem to be quickly disappearing from the Rez."

"Sometimes the Plant People move on."

"This is more than plant succession or natural selection, although the extreme weather we've had the past few years is definitely a factor. We've been told that there's evidence that someone has been indiscriminately harvesting our ceremonial and medicinal plants—just digging them up and carrying away as many as he can. Whoever is doing this leaves only the weak or diseased plants behind. This is making a serious situation even worse. Some of these plants are already endangered. Naturally the tribal council shares the concern of our medicine men."

"Earlier today, east of Gallup, my companion and I saw where holes had been left by someone digging up plants. Perhaps this is another incident. What is it you want from me? Do you need someone to investigate these reports?" Rose asked.

"Yes, and we naturally thought of you, not only because of your knowledge of plants, but also because of your active interest in matters that concern the tribe's welfare. We also want you to take it a step further," Kevin said. "We want you to conduct an official plant survey for the council and determine the status of these plants around Shiprock and the Four Corners area. Then we'd like you to draw up a plan we can use for the entire Navajo Nation to ensure that any endangered Plant People are given the chance to reestablish themselves and increase as they've done in the past."

"Our ultimate goal is to restore our Earth Mother to the way she was before overgrazing, industrial activities, and the population explosion among the *Dineh* took its toll," Begay added. "As a longtime leader of the Plant Watchers, you're ideally suited for this job, and we hope you'll accept. Of course, you'll be paid for this," he said, quoting her a salary, "and your traveling expenses will be covered."

"We'll also assign someone to assist you in case you should need a driver or require technical help with anything," Kevin added.

"It's a very tempting offer," she said. "How soon do you need to have my answer?"

"As soon as possible," Begay said. "We want to make sure we don't lose any of our native species completely."

She could see no reason to turn it down. It was the kind of work she would love doing for the tribe. "Then I can give you my answer now. I accept."

"Wonderful!" Begay said. "Come by my office tomorrow. I'll answer any more questions you may have, then give you the list of plants we've been told may be endangered. You may discover there are more. We'll also have an instruction sheet—really a form—that will show you how we want the reports structured. You can start as soon after that as you wish."

As the two councilmen walked away, Herman glanced at her, a serious expression on his face. "I have a feeling your daughter will be very upset that you didn't consult her before accepting this job. If someone is stealing the tribe's plants, you could be stepping into the middle of some nasty business."

"Yes, I'm aware of that. But as a Plant Watcher, there's no way I could have turned this down."

"I understand, but I just don't trust politicians. I can't help but wonder what their real motive is—you know, the one they aren't telling you about."

Rose laughed. "Oh, I thought of that right away. I'm sure that this appointment is designed to keep me from bothering the tribal council for a while. Otherwise, they could have picked someone else equally qualified for this work. I can think of a few right now in the Plant Watchers group. But with my public campaigns against gambling casinos, power plants, and mining, I've become the burr under their saddle. They want to give me something to keep me busy."

Herman chuckled. "You hold them publicly accountable for the decisions they make, or don't make, and that's as it should be."

"By offering me this job, they're officially saying that I'm a respected authority and expert in the field. If the time comes when they get angry enough to want to label me an extremist or discredit me in any way, they're going to have a tougher time doing that without making themselves look bad."

"Good thinking, woman," he said. "I wish you luck."

"I'll need it—but not as much as a new pair of comfortable walking shoes," Rose answered with a smile.

Herman spotted Henry Yazzie standing beside a forestry truck. "There is the one you were looking for. While you go talk to him, I'm going to say hello to some friends of mine."

Rose went to meet Henry, and presented him with her small gift.

"Thank you," Henry said after she explained the plant's significance. "It'll be perfect right outside my office." He glanced around. "I'm glad you came. I think you'll enjoy what's ahead. A *hataalii* will soon arrive and do a Song of Blessing for us. We're trying to get things off on the right foot."

Rose nodded, privately disappointed. There had been a time when nothing less than a Blessing Way would have been considered, but a Sing that would take several days no longer fit in with those who always seemed to be in a hurry.

Looking over her shoulder, Henry smiled, then glanced back at Rose. "There's someone I'd like you to meet."

Henry waved at a young Navajo woman examining a row

of pines that were probably a year old now. Seeing him, the woman smiled and approached. She was wearing jeans, lace-up hiking boots, and a short-sleeved cotton shell, and looked like many of the young people on the Rez these days.

"Have you two already met?" he asked, then continued when Rose shook her head. "You both have the same interest in plants, though you have different viewpoints. Why don't I leave you two to get acquainted?"

The young woman gave Rose a cold smile. "I know who you are, ma'am, but I don't think you know me. My name is Maria Poyer," she said, adding, "That's my Anglo name, so I don't guard it. Feel free to call me Maria."

Rose nodded. At least the girl knew something of her own culture. These days, Navajos who honored traditional beliefs only guarded their secret war names, keeping the power inherent in those intact. Anglicized names were commonly used now, put of necessity and habit, to avoid confusion.

Rose still preferred to avoid the use of proper names, but she could see that in today's world that wasn't always possible.

"I've heard you and I are on opposite sides of the plant issue," Maria said. "I studied agriculture at college and came home to teach others how to use the latest research and technology. I believe we need to bring in genetically engineered crops that will give us higher yields and better results. Some of our people rely too much on traditional methods and native plants for medicine and animal forage."

"Of course we rely on what the land provides. It's our way," Rose said. Maria reminded Rose of the many Anglos who'd come to the reservation over the years promising to make things better. They seldom, if ever, did, and often made the situation even worse. Then they left.

"But we can make things so much better for ourselves,"

Maria said eagerly. "One option is to replace native grasses with genetically improved high-yield varieties that will produce more nutritious feed for our livestock."

"But how many poor Navajos will be able to afford what's needed to accomplish these high goals you propose? Even alfalfa is expensive. We've seen many ideas like these brought here before. Do you remember hearing about the new, improved breed of sheep they forced on us? The Navajo churro sheep thrived in our desert for nearly four hundred years. Its wool glistened and made our blankets beautiful. Then the government came in and killed two-thirds of our sheep, saying we had too many—that was the mandatory stock reduction. The poorest Navajos paid dearly for those losses. Then, when we were finally beginning to recover from that, they came back and decided to *improve* our stock. The government brought us other kinds of sheep. But they didn't do well here. They became sickly and needed a lot of attention and care. Our four-horned sheep had been a gift the gods gave us so we would prosper. Without them, things didn't go well. Recently, programs have begun to bring back our churro sheep. What we'd had at the beginning was found to be the best after all."

"Mistakes certainly have been made in the past, but we can't let that stop us from trying to make things better. We need to compete with the Anglo world economically if we ever intend to stand on our own as a tribe. I want to bring methods I'm certain will work for us here and teach The People how to become first-class farmers and herdsmen. I've applied for a grant to establish demonstration crops in previously uncultivated areas so I can prove that what I'm proposing really works under our particular conditions. I know that's the only way I'll ever really convince people."

Rose smiled, admiring her determination. If enthusiasm was a building block to success, nothing would stop Maria.

"The Plant People given to us by the gods are hardy and can survive here. They come back year after year. Designer crops don't usually make it past our baking heat or droughts."

"Substandard grazing promotes malnutrition and disease. We have to introduce more nutritious plants as quickly as possible. They'll crowd out the low-yield native species, and in time our animals will be grazing on quality feed. That, in turn, will improve the health of The People who depend on their animals for food."

Rose considered saying more, but the look on Maria's face stopped her. The young woman was a selective listener, choosing to hear only her own words. But Rose knew they'd meet again. She'd fight anyone who wanted to do away with the Plant People here on the *Dinetah*.

Out of the corner of her eye, she saw Herman saying good-bye to his friends and coming over to join her, and was relieved.

"The ceremony's about to start," Herman said, greeting Maria with a nod.

"John Joe is a great medicine man," Maria said. "He's really into our culture, and has his own style. Everyone I know is really impressed with him."

"What do you mean his 'own' style?" Rose asked. The Sings depended on exactness to work. A chant litany allowed for no deviation from the formula. Theirs was not a religion in which one pleaded with the gods. Navajo prayers were meant to compel the gods to obey. Some prayers were so powerful that they could never be repeated in the same day, or be done in part. Unlike the shamans of other tribes who relied on visions and dreams, Navajo medicine men relied on symbols and knowledge. "Either the prayer is right or it isn't."

Maria shrugged, then, seeing a friend, hurried over to meet another woman her own age. Rose gave Herman a worried look. "A modernist *hataalii* who is 'into' being a Navajo? That makes no sense. What on earth does she mean by that?"

"I'm not sure," Herman answered. "But now I'm curious. Let's go find out."

The *hataalii*, a handsome, energetic-looking young Navajo man, came out of one of the small buildings in the middle of the nursery grounds. The moment he appeared, Rose was reminded of a movie star making a spotlighted entrance at a film debut. There was something flamboyant about him and that put her off instantly. A proper *hataalii* should have been humble in appearance and manner.

"John Joe is so impressive, don't you think?" she heard one of the younger women whisper. "If I ever needed a *hataalii*, I'd go see him in a second. Wouldn't you?"

"That depends," her companion answered, brushing back her long black hair, which hung down to the seat of her jeans. "I admit he's good-looking—and single too. But if I were sick and really needed the Sing to work, I'd go see Clifford Destea. John Joe looks good, but image isn't everything. Clifford's Sings work."

Rose nearly laughed out loud. As Herman caught her eye, she had to bite her lip to remain quiet.

As the ceremony continued, the *hataalii* stood beside a cluster of young pine trees, surrounded by the crowd, which had formed a loose circle around him. All eyes were upon the *hataalii* now, and, sensing it, he began a Song to the Sacred Mountains, beginning with the one to east, where the gods first appeared to man.

With a flair that reminded her of a magician onstage, John Joe brought out a pinch of pollen from his medicine pouch, touched the pollen to the tip of his tongue and his forehead, then threw the rest upward. It caught in the breeze and sailed up as he said an invocation.

Last of all, his voice rose in a Song of Blessing, and when

he finished, an unearthly stillness settled over them. Not even the birds marred the silence.

John Joe smiled to those gathered there, turned, and walked away, disappearing through a doorway into the main building.

A heartbeat later, a loud cheer rose, and the celebration started. People moved quickly toward a row of long tables filled with refreshments.

Waiting in line, Rose had to admit silently that the young medicine man had done everything right. Her only objection was the blatant showmanship.

Soon, friends came to greet Herman and Rose. Everyone, it seemed, was talking about the new *hataalii*.

Lena Clani came over with some punch for Rose. "That certainly was an interesting ceremony," she said. "I'm not sure I like his playacting, but he's certainly rekindling interest in the Old Ways among the young ones. That's a good thing."

"Yes, that is," Rose admitted. "I suppose I can overlook his cockiness in exchange for that."

As Lena greeted another friend who'd come up, Rose excused herself and went to meet Ron Charley, one of the young workers at the nursery. She'd known his clan almost all of her life, and felt comfortable advising him on the best ways to get the nursery's pine seedlings to grow and propagate.

"Thanks for the information. I appreciate it," he said after she'd offered her advice.

"And you might consider setting aside a section of the nursery for growing native grasses. We could make them available to the mining companies and ask that they use our own plants to reclaim the areas their operations have damaged."

"I've made that recommendation myself," Ron Charley said. "The area where my grandmother used to take her sheep to graze is barren land now. Strip-mining has taken quite a toll. I'd like to see that land restored the way it once was."

Eventually Ron excused himself and Rose took her own tour of the nursery. When Herman caught up with her at last, people were already starting to leave.

"I think it's time for us to go too. We've both had a long day," he said.

Rose nodded. She could tolerate the heat better than most, but late afternoons were meant for the indoors—unless it rained. Then, like most of her neighbors, she preferred to sit on her porch and watch the rare event that always cooled as it blessed the parched ground.

THREE
——— ✖ ✖ ✖ ———

The next morning, Rose waited in the reception area of the tribal offices in Shiprock for Councilman John Begay. She'd been looking forward to this meeting and beginning her work for the tribe. Her daughter seemed to support the assignment, at least in a backhanded way. Ella had said, "This should keep you out of trouble for a while," then smiled.

Ella hadn't fooled her, though. It was her daughter's way of showing respect without seeming sentimental.

As she glanced down the hall, she saw Maria Poyer arguing with someone. The man had his back to her, so she couldn't make out who it was, but it was clear that the young woman was pressing the issue. Rose thought about straying in their direction, curious to find out what they were arguing about, but just then Begay came out of his office. Seeing her there, he smiled and invited her to join him.

Moments later Rose took a seat in his sparsely decorated office. Already inside, seated at a small table, was a young woman who was clearly Indian, though Rose was sure from her skin tone and facial features that she wasn't Navajo or Ute. Although young, she wasn't wearing slacks or blue jeans, what seemed to be the uniform for young Indians these days. Instead, the Native American girl was wearing a long, dark blue skirt and a loose cotton blouse. Her only jewelry was an inexpensive watch, and she had a small book bag beside her on the floor.

"*Yáat'ééh*," she greeted, then smiled. "And that's the extent of my Navajo."

Rose laughed. There was something engaging about her easy smile. "That's all right. You already know as much as many New Mexicans, and your pronunciation is much better than the yacht-tuh-hay I usually hear from non-Navajos."

"I'm Sadie Black Shawl," she said with a nod. "I'm Oglala Sioux from the Pine Ridge Reservation, and I'm here on a work-study program at the college. I'm going to be your helper."

"Sadie's a very competent conservationist," Begay said. "She'll advise you on the scientific and technical matters you'll need to include in your reports." Begay reached into a folder, then handed Rose several documents, which included topographic maps and a list of plants that were of special concern. "You probably won't need the maps, since you've lived here all of your life, but your helper might find them useful."

Rose suspected that Sadie's job was also to keep an eye on her and make sure she stayed out of the council's hair for as long as possible. With the nuclear power plant issue coming up for debate again in the council, they wanted to make sure she wouldn't be around to interfere. Of course, that wouldn't be necessary now, since she'd already made her position clear. "How soon will you be ready to start working on this, miss?"

"As soon as you are," Sadie answered. "And please, just call me Sadie. Our tribe uses names."

"Okay . . . Sadie, let's go, then. We have a lot of work to do."

As they went outside, Sadie saw Rose's old pickup and hesitated. "Your truck has obviously served you well, but if you'd like, we can take my Jeep and that will free you to watch for specific plant types."

"You're very diplomatic," Rose said with a tiny smile. "But if you're worried about breaking down somewhere in the hills, you're underestimating my truck," Rose said. "On the other hand, it would probably help if you drove your Jeep so I could keep an eye out for the Plant People. You're right about that. So let's stop by my house first. I'll leave my truck there, and we can pick up a jug of iced water to take along with us at the same time. Summer is never easy on the reservation—on any reservation, I'd expect."

Sadie smiled and nodded. "You should see our winters."

When they arrived at her home. Rose invited the young woman inside. Sadie seemed very easygoing and calm, and Rose had a feeling they'd work together well.

"To really understand the crisis we're facing, you need to see for yourself one of the reasons why the Plant People are moving away," Rose said. "Have you visited any of the areas that mining has affected?"

Sadie shook her head. "All I've seen are photographs in books and magazines, and a few films. Most of the latter were very out-of-date."

"Then I'd like to start by showing you stretches of healthy desert land, then taking you to the areas that have not been successfully reclaimed," she said, offering Sadie a glass of iced herbal tea. "Then you'll be able to see firsthand how fast our plant populations can sink to a critical level, particularly if someone is harvesting what's left."

Sadie accepted the tea while Rose went to the back room to change. She returned a few minutes later wearing a long skirt and a smooth flowing cotton blouse with sleeves that would keep her from getting scratched up.

"This tea is good."

Rose smiled. "It's made up of common herbs like chamomile

and brook mint which I gather just for this recipe. But I also have a secret ingredient," she added with a smile. "It gives it just an extra tangy taste."

"My mother has her own herbal tea mix too. She won't even give *me* the recipe," Sadie said with a chuckle.

"You're far from home . . ." Rose said, purposely leaving the sentence hanging.

Sadie nodded. "I'm the youngest of six girls. All of my life I've had to compete with my sisters. No matter what I wanted to do, they'd done it before me, and usually better than I could. I needed to go out on my own someplace where my work would be judged on its own merits, not compared to whatever my sisters had done." She paused, then continued. "But it's more than that. I came here to learn my own strengths and weaknesses. That was something I could only do away from my family."

Rose smiled. "There was a time when my daughter felt the same way you do about that. She left to find herself too, and was gone for many years before she returned."

"I expect I'll go back home someday too."

Once they were under way, Rose gave her directions to an area near Narbona Pass, which was farther south from Shiprock than the new nursery she'd been at yesterday. That forested area, named for a Navajo warrior, was one of the few places on the reservation that still looked just as it had when she'd been young. As far as Rose was concerned, the hour-long trip would be worth it.

"How did you get involved with this kind of conservation work?" Rose asked.

"I like to fix things. When I was younger, I'd collect stuff people threw out—from old garden tools to hair dryers. I'd fix them up, then sell them or just give them away. I've never liked discarding things, but I hated having old junk just lying around.

It still makes me a little crazy when people abandon a car or haul out an old refrigerator and leave it outside to rust."

Rose nodded thoughtfully.

"These days, I'm still doing the same thing, but on a larger scale, and what I'm trying to fix now is something much more important. The land is at the heart of all the tribes. It provides food for us and our animals, and gives us minerals. But if we don't take care of the gifts as well as the gift giver, we'll lose it all. My goal is to repair the harm that's been done—both here and on my tribe's land."

Rose smiled, in complete agreement. "It's a worthy goal. I fight hard to protect life here, because this is our home." Rose looked out her window. "If this isn't worth fighting for, I don't know what is."

"Tell me about the place we're going to visit."

"It's southwest of here where the piñons give way to the ponderosa pines. I used to go there as a young woman, herding sheep and goats. It's a place of peace—wonderful during the summer, and so much cooler than it is down by Shiprock. The Plant People who live in the great mountains are tough enough to survive the hardships of the Navajo Nation."

They fell silent the rest of the journey. There was no need to talk. Even without further words, they understood each other now. To fix—not discard. With those words, the alliance between them was formed.

The first place they visited was everything Rose had described. Sadie visibly relaxed as she walked with Rose, who pointed out some clusters of Indian rice grass, "That plant grows much more abundantly at lower altitudes, and can even be found on sand dunes. Long ago, the grass was picked, and the chaff burned off so that the seeds would come free. Those would then be gathered and ground into cakes or cooked with water to make mush," Rose said. "We all knew how to live from the land back then, even though it was hard work to do so."

They walked around the dry western forest for what seemed hours. Rose checked the list of endangered plants, but found none of the rare species in that area. At least there were no spots where it appeared plants had been uprooted

"This really is a place of peace," Sadie acknowledged as they returned to her SUV.

At the second site, farther north and in the foothills, Rose showed Sadie land that had been ravaged by uranium mining. Few things grew here, though the mines had closed many years ago. Settling ponds that had once been filled with contaminated water had been left uncovered like open sores. "Children still swim in those during the rainy season, and livestock drink the runoff where it collects," Rose said. "The land here is cursed. Our people believe that knowing the name of your enemy gives you power over him, so we named the uranium dust *Yeetso,* yellow monster. Once it was freed and allowed to roam our land, all *Yeetso* has done is cause us pain."

"It's all so sad. If death had a face, I think it would look like this," Sadie said.

"This is at the heart of many of our problems. Collection sites for herbs and important plants are diminishing because so much of the land is no longer well," Rose said, "Things will get worse in a hurry too, if someone is harvesting the Plant People and taking them away."

"We have a big job ahead of us," Sadie said.

"The first thing we need to do is examine the collection sites very carefully and verify which plants are the most endangered. Once we know that, we can take whatever steps are necessary to protect them."

Sadie took a deep breath. "We'll also want to search for new, untouched collection sites for the plants that seem in shortest supply. If we can't find any new sites, then we'll need to present the tribe with some plans that will help them remedy that situation."

As Rose and her helper walked back to the Jeep, they went through an area filled with open mine shafts. Suddenly someone yelled out a warning, and Rose stopped in her tracks. She reached for Sadie's arm and pulled her back, looking around for the person who'd called out to them.

A moment later, she spotted a tall, sunburned Anglo man wearing a cowboy hat, jeans, and boots, and large metal-framed sunglasses. "What on earth are you two doing wandering around here?" he asked, hurrying toward them. "This is a dangerous place. Go home."

"We *are* home," Rose answered firmly.

"Then you might consider fixing up the porch." The man stepped in front of Rose and Sadie and, using his walking stick, hit the ground before him hard. Wood splintered, then an instant later the pieces of rotting wood fell into a dark shaft that seemed to go on forever.

"This place is a disaster. The aboveground uranium tailings left behind have contaminated this entire area in a way that'll take a miracle to fix. Not to mention the open mine shafts just waiting for someone to fall in. I can't understand why the tribe allowed this to happen."

As he strode off angrily, Sadie glanced over at Rose. "It looks like you may have found a reluctant ally. I know that man. He's an ecologist for Southwest Power Company. If he's out here, you can bet he's surveying the site to see if there's a way to reclaim this section of land at the same time that they fix the parcel over by Fruitland that was ravaged by coal mining."

"So he's one of their 'experts.' Maybe my letters and meetings with their people are finally paying off."

"One of the endangered plants mentioned in the list is

blazing star, what your people also call 'tenacious.' According to my research, it's supposed to grow in this area—that is, unless the mining operations have wiped them out."

"Let's see if we can find some around here before we leave," Rose suggested. "But look where you step."

Although they searched carefully, this time being extremely careful where they placed their feet, they only found a few poor examples of "tenacious" near a hillside.

"This plant is scarce under the best conditions, but we should at least have been able to find some growing near the road, where moisture tends to drain. Now, to make things even worse, we find this," Rose said, pointing to spots on the ground where something had obviously been dug up. "Someone uprooted plants here. My guess, from the proximity of the other 'tenacious' plants, is that they took the hardiest ones of that species—those with the best chance of surviving a transplant. I think it's the same person who's been stealing the endangered plants too. He used what a friend of mine called an entrenching tool," she said pointing.

"Yes, the old GI shovel. I bought mine at an old Army/Navy store. It's great for camping because it folds up."

" 'Tenacious' is a very good eye-wash medication, and the seeds can be ground up and used as food. This particular plant is important to the heritage of our tribe. It's considered one of our Life Way medicines and it's used for prayersticks in several ceremonies. If it's no longer available . . ."

They spent nearly two more hours searching for "tenacious" along the roads and embankments, but finally they were forced to give up. "I have a class this afternoon, so I have to get back," Sadie said apologetically.

"All right. We've searched long enough. This place always depresses me."

Sadie nodded, and soon they were on their way. "You might

want to talk to Bradford Knight, the man we saw back there," Sadie suggested. "If he's going around to the different areas that need reclamation, he's probably also taken notes on the plants he's observed at those sites. He may be able to help us find some of the Plant People that are so scarce right now."

"That's a good idea. I'll follow it up," Rose said.

It was late afternoon by the time Rose got ready to leave for her appointment with the Anglo man. She'd just climbed into her truck when her old friend Lena Clani, Jennifer's grandmother, pulled up. Her ancient sedan had traveled more miles than a reservation school bus, but it still ran, and as far as Lena was concerned, that was all that mattered.

Lena walked up to Rose's truck and peered in through the passenger's side, "I thought I'd come by and visit," she said.

Lena's hair was a salt-and-pepper color, her skin deeply tanned and rough. Though Rose could have made a guess, no one really knew how old Lena actually was. Birth certificates hadn't covered everyone on the reservation until recent times.

"I'm on my way to see an Anglo ecologist who works for Southwest Power," Rose said, and explained what had happened earlier.

"Let me come with you. As a Plant Watcher, I may be able to help a little, or, at the very least, I can be there for moral support."

"I'd be glad for your company," Rose said.

"Why don't we take my car? The seats are a lot more comfortable," Lena said.

Rose tried not to cringe. Lena had to be the worst driver on the reservation. She seldom went over thirty miles an hour, no matter what the posted speed limit was. This was probably a good thing, considering Lena usually drove down the center, except on the highway, of course. "I think we'll be more comfortable in my pickup," Rose said diplomatically. "It has air-conditioning that actually works now since my friend fixed it."

"Then your truck it is."

As they set out, Lena glanced over at her. "I've been asked to give a few classes on native plants at the college. Well, not classes, really. They've asked me to come in and talk to the students."

"Are you going to do it?"

"Yes. Why don't you join me? You'd still be working for the tribe—in a way—and it's safer than what you're doing."

"What do you mean?"

"Didn't you tell my granddaughter that you almost fell into a mine shaft this morning at a site that needs reclamation work? I spoke to her a while ago and she mentioned it to me. I don't want to lose a friend."

"There's nothing to worry about. I have a woman helper from the Oglala Sioux tribe who'll be with me."

Lena shook her head. "Your helper may be very trustworthy; I won't speak ill of someone I've never met. But you need to be careful who you trust. People with interests linked to those responsible for the damage to our land might want to try to scare you away or discredit your work."

"What could happen?"

"Between the enemies you've already made and the ones who don't want to face up to the environmental disasters we've suffered here, you and your helper may find it's very dangerous driving around to remote areas."

"We'll stay alert," Rose said, mostly to appease her.

"*Bizaadii* and I have already decided to help. You're going to need someone around to watch your back, so he and I are going to take turns riding shotgun."

FOUR
✴ ✴ ✴

Rose looked at her old friend in surprise. "You're kidding. Are you sure my daughter didn't put you up to this?"

"Not at all. If you need help, we'll be close by. That's what friends are for."

Rose sighed. She hadn't wanted Lena involved in this, but there seemed no way around it now. "All right. We'll all look out for each other."

Once they arrived at the power plant on the east side of the reservation, they went inside the offices of the massive facility and approached the reception desk. The young Navajo girl who greeted them knew Rose.

"When I heard Mr. Knight talking about the tall, sturdy-looking Navajo woman he'd seen wandering around near the open mines and examining the plants, I had a feeling it was you. I wasn't surprised when you called and asked for an appointment." The girl lowered her voice to a whisper. "But if you think he's going to support your way of reclaiming the land, forget it. He's missed a lot of work the past year, and probably can't afford to back any action that doesn't fit company plans."

She started to say more, but seeing someone coming down

the hall, her expression changed and she became all business. Rose turned to see who had caused the abrupt change, and saw Maria Poyer approaching with Bradford Knight.

"I hope you don't mind if I sit in on the meeting," Maria said, looking at Lena and nodding politely.

"Since she's a Navajo scientist and you're here to speak about our reclamation work, I thought it would be appropriate to have her present when you and I met. I see you've brought someone along too," Knight said, then looked at Lena.

Rose introduced Lena as a member of the Plant Watchers.

Knight gave her a nod. "You're welcome to take part in this meeting, of course." He led the way to his office, then offered them all comfortable seats, "Now, how can I help you ladies?"

Rose strongly suspected that Maria and Knight shared the same philosophy about replacing native plants with introduced species. Forcing herself to concentrate only on the business at hand, she began. "I understand that your job is to advise and take part in the reclamation work that needs to be done at the various sites."

"That's right, Mrs. Destea. I've been speaking to Maria and she and I have discussed various techniques that will practically guarantee good results. As you know, in the past we've had problems because we've introduced whatever generic seed stocks happened to be available at a good price, and those died just as soon as we stopped babying them with excess water and fertilizer. They were clearly the wrong plants in the wrong place."

Rose nodded slowly. "The focus should have been on selecting the appropriate plants. We are in agreement on that," she added, trying to ignore the fact that the Anglo was saying her name aloud. "Some plants aren't meant for our desert, especially under the altered conditions that exist after the miners have moved on. One of the first things that has to be done is to restore the water-trapping nature of the soil, and that takes more than a rich layer of topsoil. We have to make sure water is held where it will do its job—at the roots."

"That's exactly what we're trying to do now," Knight said, his voice sounding disinterested, or weary. "We're experts at this, Mrs. Destea. You'll just have to let us do our job."

Rose tried to keep her expression neutral, but it was obvious that Lena was skeptical. "I came to you today because we've recently discovered that some of our most important ceremonial and medicinal plants are becoming very scarce. We're searching for blazing star and silvery lupine, among others," she said, using the Anglo terms, and handing him a copy of the complete list. "If we can find some of these varieties and use cuttings, seedlings, or even seeds to replant more in areas that have to be reclaimed, it would be a great service to the tribe."

"Not many native species are easily propagated, and as you probably know, transplanting them doesn't always work either. In the long run, it's usually more expensive and less productive than using sturdy nursery stock and commercial seed stocks, but I'll certainly keep what you've said in mind."

Rose nodded, though she could swear Lena was about to roll her eyes in disbelief. "As you walk around studying the various sections of land, I'd also like to ask that you keep an eye out for the varieties on that list—most have the common Anglo name listed beside them—and if you happen to see any of them, please call me. My telephone number is written at the top of the page."

"I'll be happy to do that for you," he said, walking them to the door.

As they walked outside and headed to the truck, Rose and Lena remained quiet.

Once they were in the truck and on their way, Lena finally

spoke. "He has no intention of doing anything to help us or the tribe. You know that, right?"

Rose nodded. "He was giving us what my daughter calls the 'party line,' " Rose said with a shrug. "But pointing it out to him wouldn't have done us any good. I just hope he and Maria aren't joining forces," she said, telling Lena about her.

"The Plant Watchers should know about this situation. It's their duty to help the Plant People. You need to use the allies you have. And it's also very possible that, with their help, you'll be able to find the endangered plants."

"You're right, but it's going to be awkward for everyone. Collection sites are sacred knowledge that's inherited in the same way Good Luck Songs are and other family treasures. It's not right to ask them to divulge their secrets."

"How they help is up to them. They may know or be able to find new collection sites for you. There's an information meeting going on today. Maybe it's already begun. Why don't we both go?"

"I'd been so busy thinking about the plant survey, I'd forgotten about the get-together at *Gishii's* house," she said, using Reva Benally's nickname. She was called "the one with the planting stick" by almost everyone who knew her. It was said that when she wasn't working outside in her garden, she was cultivating plants inside her house.

"Let's go," Rose said.

Already in the general area, they arrived a short time later. They walked to the back of the yard, where everyone had gathered around a large buffet table, and were greeted by six women. The youngest of the largely traditionalist group was Jane Jim, who was in her late forties. All the Plant Watchers had welcomed her eagerly, hoping more women of her generation would come join them.

Gishii came forward and offered Rose and Lena glasses of

iced tea. Rose had tried to duplicate the special-blend recipe several times but had never quite managed to get it just right. *Gishii* had claimed to have given her the recipe, but it was obvious that she'd left at least one ingredient out.

"Welcome," *Gishii* said. "We were hoping you two would join us today."

Rose looked at her and then at the others. "I came as the bearer of bad news, I'm afraid. We have a serious situation on our hands, one we felt everyone here should know about." Rose quickly explained what she'd been hired to do, then read off the list of plants that were believed to be endangered. "My first priority is finding these plants and determining just how low their numbers have become. Also, I'd like to be able to direct the medicine men to new locations where they can still be found."

Soon Rose was fielding all kinds of questions, taking suggestions, and offering answers and responses regarding native plants in the area. The other ladies kept turning to her for the last word, and Rose slowly began to feel the weight of responsibility that had been placed on her shoulders when she accepted the tribal council's job. She silently wondered how often people became leaders simply because no one else stepped up to do the job.

"The Plant People are moving away because they don't feel appreciated," Clara Henderson said. "The modernists and even the new traditionalists think they can go to the closest drugstore and buy the right pill or potion to cure whatever ails them."

Rose looked at Clara, who had to be close to ninety-five. She'd outlived all her children, and was one of the most respected members of the Plant Watchers. Clara always had time to help anyone who came to her, and seemed graced with boundless energy.

"The Plant People want to be among friends," Clara continued. "They were treated with respect once and they grew to like it. Now they don't feel loved, so they've started to leave us. Maybe if we search for them, they'll understand that they're a part of us, just as we are a part of them."

Rose placed her hand on Clara's shoulder. "Well spoken, old friend," she said softly. "We need the Plant People and we now have to find and take care of them so they'll become plentiful again."

"Some of us may not want to share the exact locations of our own collection sites," Jane said, "but we can at least let you know if we find any of the plants the medicine men are searching for." She paused thoughtfully. "I've heard that the new traditionalist *hataalii* has his own garden of native plants and herbs. My sister-in-law told me that another medicine man had to go to him for some 'brittle grass' that he needed for an Enemy Way Sing. You might ask him if he's seen any of the plants we're looking for."

After getting directions to John Joe's home, which was just east of the river but close to Four Corners, Rose and Lena set out. The directions were complicated, first requiring them to go north on Highway 666 nearly to the Colorado state line, then west down a series of dirt roads back toward the river, roughly parallel to a natural gas pipeline.

The roads most of the way were nothing more than ruts, alternating between rocky and sandy. "Try to miss at least some of the major holes," Lena said.

Just then they hit a rocky stretch that bounced the truck around hard, then a sandy stretch that forced Rose to keep moving or risk bogging down.

Lena yelped as the rear end of the truck fishtailed from side to side. "You drive like a crazy person. Slow down!"

"If I slow down, we'll get stuck for sure. That means digging out the tires and lining our path with branches to get traction."

"What branches? All there are around here are a few stubby clumps of grass," Lena said.

"Right. So let me drive."

"Why? I know I can pick better routes than you do. I certainly couldn't do any worse."

"I don't agree. Making up your own lane—that's worse." Rose glanced over at her and then promptly hit another hole. Muttering under her breath, she made a concerted effort to keep her eyes on the road, such as it was.

They arrived at the medicine man's home, on a low wooded bluff overlooking the San Juan, ten minutes later. There was a horse in the corral, and two goats keeping it company. A new-looking pickup was parked next to the main house, a simple wood-framed structure with a pitched shingle roof. There was a sizable garden in the back, fenced in with chicken wire. About twenty yards from the house was a traditionally designed eight-sided log medicine hogan. The entrance, on most hogans covered by a blanket, was fitted with a regular house door, which was open just a crack. "It must be really hot in there right now," Lena mumbled.

They sat in the car, doors open, waiting to be invited.

"Look," Rose whispered. "There's an extension cord leading from the main house to the hogan."

"What did you expect? There's probably a TV in there, he's a new traditionalist. They choose to follow the old ways—as long as they don't have to give up cable. Do you think he'll know what we're doing, waiting out here?"

Before Rose could answer, John Joe came out of the medicine hogan and waved at them. He was wearing jeans, a cotton shirt, and the blue sash medicine men often wore around their foreheads.

"Forgive me for not inviting you in sooner, " John Joe said.

"I was trying out my new air conditioner, seeing how effective it was this time of day." He pointed to a portable evaporative cooler on a wheeled stand just visible inside the hogan. "They work better when you open a door or window a tiny bit, you know."

"An air conditioner in a *medicine* hogan?" Rose said.

"It won't make the Sings any better if we're all half dizzy from the heat." He invited them to sit on sheepskins on the floor. "What can I do to help you two ladies?"

"We're members of a traditional group of herbalists. Perhaps you've heard of the Plant Watchers?" Rose asked, and, seeing him nod, added, "We're looking into reports that some of our native plants are quickly disappearing, and some no longer available at all except by chance discovery."

"I know. I've seen some evidence of that myself. It looks like somebody is digging up and hauling away the good plants. Twice, I've had to sell herbal supplies I've collected from my garden to other medicine men who haven't been able to find what they needed."

"We may have to come to you to purchase some starter plants too, if we can't find the varieties we're searching for. May we see your garden?" Rose asked.

"I only sell the parts of the plants that are needed to conduct a ceremony or make an herbal infusion for a patient—not the plants themselves. Those I keep for my professional use."

"I understand. But may we still see which plants you have in your garden? Some native plants are so scarce, they're endangered, so it would help us to know what you have here and could make available to others."

He stared at the hard-packed clay floor several moments, then looked up. "I hope you won't take what I have to say personally, but I don't show anyone my garden. The Plant People need to be left alone in order to thrive. I don't even go to my own garden unless I need to collect something, or care for the plants themselves. The Plant People appreciate that extra courtesy. That's why I've never had a shortage of plants, and why I'm now in a position to help the other medicine men."

"Then would you please give us a list of the things you grow? That would help." Rose tried to keep her voice level and unemotional, but the man was starting to irritate her.

"My garden is not nearly as extensive as people think," he hedged. "However, if you need a specific plant or herb, I can usually find what's required. What my garden can't supply, I usually locate at my special collecting sites. But I don't choose to share any of that information with others, because, like our ways teach, to share all knowledge is to deplete yourself."

"Then I guess we'll be going," Rose said coldly.

Lena stood up and faced him. "The plants belong to all."

"But the knowledge of them is something we have to work for as individuals," he answered easily.

Rose shook her head, but said nothing as they walked back to the pickup. Soon they were on their way.

"What an annoying man," Lena said after they'd both fumed for several minutes.

"I wonder why he didn't want us to see his garden," Rose said thoughtfully. "His explanation sounded like lawyer double-talk, not the words of a medicine man. I wonder if he has something to hide and, if so, what that is."

"Now you're thinking like your daughter, the cop," Lena said. "But I can't blame you. He certainly wasn't much help, and obviously very selfish with what he considers his."

"He's probably afraid we'll cut into his business. He's selling herbs that The People can't find, and that can become very profitable for him. Notice the new truck and air conditioner? He can set his own prices and others will have to meet them or

PLANT THEM DEEP ✳ 53

do without. But I definitely don't care for his attitude. I expect more from a *hataalii*. I'd ask my son to talk to him, one healer to another, but I doubt it would help."

The bumpy, dusty journey back to the highway exhausted both of the women. By the time they reached the paved road. Rose felt as if she'd permanently dislocated every bone in her body. She stopped, and tried to get a tiny grain of sand out of the corner of her eye with a tissue.

"That's a road that only should be traveled on horseback," Lena said with a long sigh after they pulled back out onto the highway.

Rose drove carefully, never increasing her speed past forty-five, afraid that she'd stress her truck even more. It now had at least two new separate rattles.

As the road curved to the left, she noticed a tan pickup she hadn't seen before about four car lengths behind her. Knowing how slow she was going, Rose stayed to the right so the driver could pass. But a couple of minutes went by and the pickup remained with her, matching her speed.

When Rose glanced back for a third time, Lena turned around in her seat. "I think the driver of the pickup is a man," Lena said, "but he's too far away to identify. If he keeps following us, then drive straight to the police station. We'll see what he does then."

"Good idea. I'll do just that if he's still with us by the time I reach the hospital turnoff," Rose said.

A heavy silence fell between them. Some people talked incessantly whenever they were afraid or uneasy, but Lena and she had always reacted in the opposite manner. It was one of many traits they'd shared all their lives.

When they reached the hospital turnoff, the truck was still there. "The police station it is," Rose said, making a right turn at the next intersection, then circling back to the highway. The truck stayed with them, but always kept its distance so they couldn't see who the driver was.

Four minutes later, as Rose approached the police station, she slowed to make the left turn, but the pickup suddenly turned right onto an adjacent side street and headed off in the opposite direction. Relieved, Rose exhaled softly and continued going instead of pulling into the station.

"You don't want to go in and tell your daughter about this?" Lena asked.

Rose shook her head. "I'd rather not, if it's okay with you. She'd worry, and there's nothing she could do about it now. It's not a police matter, because nothing illegal was done. I have enemies and this was probably an attempt to scare me. If he'd wanted to harm us, he would have done more than just follow us. This is nothing I can't handle," Rose said firmly, amazed at how certain she sounded. The truth was that, deep down, she wasn't very sure at all.

FIVE

✘ ✘ ✘

Ella joined Rose for breakfast the next morning. Dawn had already eaten and was outside with Jennifer, feeding the pony and adding water to his trough.

"Mom, twice this morning Boots has started to say something to me, but she keeps changing her mind. Something's bothering her. Do you have any idea what's going on?"

Rose realized instantly what must have happened. Lena had probably mentioned the incident with the tan pickup yesterday when she got home, and Jennifer had learned what had happened. Avoiding Ella's gaze, Rose poured cold water into the teakettle, then began selecting herbal teas from the cupboard to make her own blend.

"I wouldn't worry about it," Rose said, keeping her tone light. "If she has something to say, Boots will get around to it eventually." Then she made the mistake of looking up at her daughter.

Ella's gaze sharpened, and she gave Rose "The Look." "Spill it, Mom. What's going on?"

Rose sighed and told her everything about the trip and the pickup that followed them. "It's not a big deal. All I can tell you is that it was a tan pickup and we think the driver was a man. That doesn't narrow it down much."

"True, but you should have told me this last night."

"Told you what? That it was *possible* someone followed us into town? I'm not even completely sure that it was a deliberate thing. He may have simply been traveling in the same direction we were. That's the most direct route from Colorado, you know."

"Is it possible someone may be hoping you'll lead them to different collection sites?" Ella said. "The fact that someone's digging up certain native plants already worries me. Can't you let someone else handle this survey for the tribe? I have a bad feeling about this."

"As a police officer, you're in danger all the time, daughter, and I've learned to accept it. This is something *I* have to do."

"Okay, Mom, you win—for now." Ella gave her a hug, then reached for the pistol and holster that she kept on the high shelf in the kitchen out of Dawn's reach. "I better get going."

The telephone rang and Ella stopped in midstride. Rose shook her head. "It's for me."

Accepting that her mother's instincts were as reliable as caller ID, Ella hurried outside.

As she picked up the receiver, Rose had a feeling that the caller would be Bradford Knight and she wasn't wrong. She listened to what he was proposing while watching her daughter hurry to her police vehicle.

By the time Rose finished the call, Herman pulled up in his truck, waving at Ella as she drove away. Rose welcomed her old friend inside and offered him a cup of coffee. She didn't drink coffee herself normally, but she always kept some on hand for her daughter and visitors.

"So what's on your schedule today, *dzání*? I came to help."

Lately, he'd taken to calling her *dzání*, the Navajo word for woman, whenever they were alone. Although it was old-fashioned. Rose liked it.

She sat at the table across from him. "I made an appointment early this morning to meet Mr. Knight, the ecologist from the power company, at the old mines south of the power plant just past Hogback."

"Yes, I know that area. The mining company tried to reclaim the land after they'd removed all the coal, but they picked a lot of plants that don't normally grow here. Although it looked really green the first two years, everything in that first try except the tumbleweeds and snakeweed died."

"Knight called to say that he thinks some of the plants on my list are growing there now," Rose said. "I hope he's right."

"I'm surprised to hear the Plant People are moving back in. That area was not contaminated with poisons in the soil, but strip-mining took a heavy toll there. The layers of bedrock that held the rain close to the surface are gone."

"Maybe some of the organic matter from the plants that they tried to introduce retained a little moisture in places," Rose suggested. "I wanted to go and check things out right away. We can take my truck."

He shook his head. "I don't think that's going anywhere this morning," he said ominously.

"What's wrong with my pickup?"

"Besides two flat tires? It's leaking so much oil, your oil pan much have been punctured."

"I had a feeling about that," she said dejectedly. "The red light was on by the time I got home yesterday."

"I'm sure it can be fixed as long as you made it home with most of the oil still in the crankcase." He stood up and rinsed out his cup. "You ready to go? My truck's right outside."

"Let me make a phone call first. My daughter knows the mechanic who maintains the police cars and I want to arrange for him to come by and fix my pickup."

Herman nodded. "You better tell him to come out in the tow

truck, then. I think he's going to need to haul it back to the shop."

"Good idea," Rose replied, reaching for the telephone.

The sky was a vibrant blue as they set out toward the southern tip of the Hogback rock formation, a place that had held much coal at one time. Once past a few scattered homes near the highway south of the town of Shiprock, the dirt road they took alternated between rocky and sandy stretches, the former jarring their teeth and the latter stirring their stomach contents as the vehicle fishtailed back and forth like a mud puppy in an inch of water. Heading east, they soon descended into the old flood plain of the San Juan River, where there was more of a mixture of clay, sand, and water rounded boulders.

When they were still a quarter of a mile away, Rose spotted a shiny new Jeep parked in the middle of a field. Here in the sediments of the river valley lay what was regionally known as the bosque, the forested areas that bordered the rivers. Grasses and herbs had once been plentiful, as well as trees such as the cottonwood. Now there were vast stretches of barren land dotted with tumbleweeds, and in some places alkali left white deposits where water had pooled and evaporated. Scraggly salt cedars, not native to the Southwest but now widely distributed, sucked up precious water with their deep root systems and gave little in return to The People.

"Help me look for 'tenacious' and 'sweet cattail,'" Rose asked Herman as they parked, then walked over to where Knight stood.

He nodded. "I'm familiar with *Teel'likanii*," he said, using the Navajo name for "sweet cattail." "A *hataalii* I knew used it for a Shooting Way my mother had done once. That was many, many years ago," he added with a rueful smile. "All I remember is that it had a central, leafless stalk with greenish flowers."

"It's probably not quite flowering yet, so just look for something with long, cattaillike leaves, kind of like big-bladed grass or mariposa lilies, but larger."

"Without the flower and stalk I'm going to have a hard time spotting it, but I'll try."

"Head towards the marshlike areas, and look around where you find saltbrush and saltgrass. If we split up, we'll be able to cover more ground faster."

"Done."

As Herman walked away toward lower ground, she met Knight, who hadn't moved. "Thank you for calling me this morning, Mr. Knight."

He nodded. "I went over the list carefully. I was able to identify most of what you're searching for by their latin or common names, but I wasn't able to come up with anything for 'frog tobacco' or 'salt thin.' I searched quite a few books and spoke to some of the professors at the college, but I haven't made much headway."

"I don't think there's a common name for either. Some plants are familiar to us, but not to everyone else," Rose said.

"I did find a few campanula plants for you. They're not in very good shape, but they're there."

Rose didn't recognize the name, but when he led her to where a few of the plants were growing, she knew. "We call this 'sweet cattail.'" Once again, she could see signs that the person with the entrenching tool had been here. "Someone has taken the best—and as many as they could." She looked around, trying to spot Herman, and wondering if she should call him back or let him keep looking in case there were other "sweet cattail" plants nearby.

"Maybe he's trying to cut his losses by making up with volume," Knight said with a shrug.

The casually spoken words made her cringe. The Plant People were alive. They were gifts from the Holy People, not nuts and bolts in the hardware store. "This person doesn't understand what he's doing. It's the only way to explain what's going on. Our method of collecting plants is very specific, and respectful to the plants and our people. We don't just bring a shovel and help ourselves," Rose said.

"Apparently not everyone around here shares your respect for nature," he said. After a brief pause, he added, "But I can see why the situation worries you. I understand that many native plants have medicinal uses."

"That was our sole medicine for generations," Rose said. "These days, many of us still rely on it, though we do go to the doctor as well."

"I'd like to learn more about your medicinal plants. For example, that plant, *Dimorphocarpa wislizeni*," he said, choosing one at random. "Does it have a specific use?"

"I don't speak Latin. Point," Rose said. Knight indicated a plant with small white flowers and flattened fruit that looked like eyeglasses. "We use it as a medicine for itchy skin, insect bites, and other ailments. We call it 'gray kangaroo rat food.'"

"Very descriptive."

"Navajo plant names usually are. In many cases you can tell something about the plant by the name."

"Scientific names denote genus and species, and usually the genus name is descriptive. It's a way of identifying not only the plant, but its background—like a clan name." He regarded her thoughtfully, then added, "Considering you have no formal training, I'm surprised the tribe gave you the job you now hold."

"You have the education, but I'm the one who knows the uses for each plant." Bradford Knight was apparently trying to put himself in a position of superiority, but when it came to plants, she was too sure of herself to allow anyone to rattle her.

He nodded once and smiled. "Okay—it's a standoff between academic and field experience."

Rose gestured toward a spindly herb that stood about three feet tall. "Do you know that plant?"

"*Croton Texensis,* Texas croton."

"We call it 'spider food.' It's great for removing skunk smell from clothing."

Knight continued questioning her about the medicinal uses of the plants, and asking her to point out the ones that were endangered or of particular value.

Finally Rose pointed to a cluster of small daisylike flowers growing low to the ground. "Do you know those?"

"Chamomile, yes."

"I'm sure you know it's said to be a great cure-all for almost any stomach ailment."

He nodded. "So I've heard. Since there was no written Navajo language until recently, knowledge about plants must have been passed on from generation to generation by word of mouth. Remarkable. It's amazing how your people find a use for almost everything in your environment."

Maybe it was the way he said "your people" that made her suddenly feel like a rat in a laboratory cage. He was one of the most annoying, patronizing Anglos she'd met. For the first time, she wondered if it was a good idea telling him about the practical uses of local plants. Knight might just be seeking knowledge, but how he'd be putting that knowledge to use wasn't clear, and she didn't trust him because of where he worked. "We continue to keep our eyes and ears open. Some of the more recent findings about chamomile I learned from the Discovery Channel." She smiled at him. "You could say it's knowledge passed from word of General Electric."

She saw Herman, who'd approached from behind Knight, struggle not to laugh. Knight's expression was more of a scowl, however.

As Knight said good-bye and climbed into his Jeep, they began walking back to Herman's truck. Herman told her what he'd found. "I saw a few 'sweet cattail' plants in a dried-up marsh close to the river, but they'd been damaged as they were dug up, so I guess they were left to die. The same entrenching tool we saw before had been used, based on the marks left on the ground."

"I need to put the Plant Watchers on alert for this person. He or she is creating some real damage now, and has to be stopped."

"I agree."

"I'm meeting with Sadie Black Shawl later this morning so she and I can map out a strategy to locate as many of the missing Plant People as possible. I'll call this situation to her attention, and maybe we can find a way to include it in our report. If we make it *official*, then it'll be harder for the council to downplay the threat this plant thief poses."

By the time they arrived home, the young Sioux woman was there, sitting on Rose's porch, waiting. From what she could see, Boots had given her something cold to drink, and made her comfortable.

"Come in!" Rose greeted, noting Sadie seemed upset.

Rose led Herman and Sadie into the kitchen, the real heart of the house. Every important discussion, every major decision had been made here. It was the one place where guests felt like family, and family felt truly at home.

"I have bad news," Sadie said while Rose was pouring Herman and herself some iced tea. "Following the instructions I'd been given, after our first outing I made an official report. I gave it to my supervisor, and everyone seemed satisfied with it. But twenty minutes ago, just before I drove here, I got a phone call telling me I was being replaced with someone older and with more experience."

"Who did this to you?"

"John Begay, the same person who hired me. I'm being reassigned, at least that's what my records will show. The councilman said that the power company people felt you needed help from someone with more experience than me—a local person, apparently."

Rose wondered if Knight had made a quick phone call after they'd left him this morning. But it didn't seem likely. Something more than ego was at play here.

"What will you be doing on this new job?" Rose couldn't help but worry about Sadie. She'd deserved better.

The young woman shrugged. "Begay didn't know yet. But don't worry, I'll be fine."

Rose believed her. In a lot of ways, Sadie was tougher and more savvy than she'd been at her age. Choosing to leave her family and come so far south, here to the *Dinetah*, proved it. As a young woman, Rose's entire life had been wrapped up in her family. Her two children had been the center of her world. She'd wanted to nourish their dreams and give them an unshakable belief in themselves. Looking at both Clifford and Ella now, she knew she'd succeeded.

"But I still intend to help you all I can—on my own time. That is . . . if you allow me to," Sadie said.

"I'd welcome your help," Rose said. "We'll just make sure Begay doesn't hear about it."

Sadie finally smiled. Checking her watch, she stood up. "I have to go now or I'll miss my next class."

"Do you know who they picked to replace you?" Rose asked.

"John said it was someone connected to the new plant nursery. I was told you'd be notified today or tomorrow."

"All right, then, I'll wait for the news. I expect they'll tell me soon enough." Rose shrugged.

After Sadie left, Herman remained quiet for a long time as

Rose began washing and peeling potatoes at the sink in preparation for dinner.

"Are you sure you're enjoying these new challenges you've taken on?" Herman asked. "Your life would be a lot more peaceful without all the confusion and politics. And it's not like you don't have enough to do with your daughter and granddaughter here at home."

"I love my family, and I'm very proud of them, but I had other dreams once—things I was never given the opportunity to pursue. Now that my kids are grown, I have a responsibility to myself. For the first time in my life, I can do whatever I want, and helping the tribe in my own small way is what I choose."

As the phone began to ring, Herman went to answer it while Rose wiped off her hands with a small towel.

"It's your granddaughter's father." Herman handed her the receiver.

Rose greeted Kevin, but just as soon as he began speaking, she detected the concern in his voice.

"I wanted to fill you in before you got the official call so you'd be prepared," he said.

"I've already heard that my helper is being replaced."

He paused, then added with a laugh, "That shouldn't surprise me."

"But I would like to know about the person I'll be working with and I'd appreciate anything you can tell me."

"You're not going to be happy. His name is Curtis Largo, and I've heard that nobody likes to work with him."

"I know him. He works two jobs, one for the tribe, and the other serving special interests, like the mining and energy industries. They pay him consultant fees. It's more like bribes, if you ask me."

"He's the one. I heard that you two squared off at a chapter house meeting once."

"It wasn't the first time either. He and I disagree on virtually everything. Even on the rare occasions when he agrees with what I'm saying, his manner is so unpleasant that I'm always tempted to switch to the opposite side just on principle."

Kevin laughed. "I understand completely."

"Having the tribe assign him to help me will make my job a lot more difficult."

"Perhaps even more than you realize," Kevin said. "I've heard bits and pieces of conversations already, and I found out Largo has powerful friends on the tribal council. When he discovered what you'd been hired to do, he made several phone calls, trying to get your job. I suspect he'll be planning to advance his own agenda by holding you back and ruining your credibility. It's no secret that some in the council already think you have too much influence for a 'mere' citizen. So watch your back."

"I know I have enemies on the council. What I need is an ally."

"You have several of those you can count on. I'll be there for you, and so will the others who respect what you do. But that's not going to keep you out of trouble."

"I'm not worried. If they try to undermine me, they'll find out just how hard and effectively I can fight. I intend to complete the job I've started. It concerns an issue that's important to every single member of our tribe, whether or not they realize it now."

SIX

✖ ✖ ✖

The next two days were busy ones, and it was fortunate for Rose that her pickup was easily repaired. Having decided on a plan, she began surveying the better-known collection sites, going from place to place with one or more of the Plant Watcher volunteers. To save on travel time, she first selected areas accessed by large roads or the highway, going to the most distant ones first, then working her way back toward Shiprock.

As a group, they searched the foothills and canyons on the eastern slopes of the mountains along the dirt roads running north and south between Horse Mesa and Beclabito. Walking along in a line, side by side, they employed a technique Rose had heard her daughter mention when searching for evidence at crime scenes.

High on the slopes above Cottonwood Canyon, among the piñons and junipers, Rose finally spotted one of the plants on the list, then several more.

"Over here," she yelled to Herman, who was thirty feet away, keeping pace and searching his strip of ground.

"What is it?" Lena yelled to Rose from where she was working.

"Come and see, but remember where you are so we can

continue the search later," Rose reminded. While her two helpers converged, Rose noted other hardy-looking plants several feet ahead.

"That's 'sheep's food,' right?" Herman said as he came up beside her.

"Of course," Lena answered before Rose could. "This looks like a good collection site to record, and none of the plants here have been tampered with."

Rose nodded, smiling for the first time that morning. "It's good to find a place like this that's still undisturbed. I don't think I'll ever forget that place we found near the road where perfectly healthy 'children's food'—mariposa plants—were chopped into pieces. It's almost as if the person was a little crazy."

"He was probably angry," Herman said. "He broke off the bulbs while trying to dig them up, and lost his temper."

"Not exactly the attitude a person should have when collecting Life Way medicines," Rose said.

"The thief's lack of respect for our ways makes me wonder about something. Do you suppose this is the work of the evil ones?" Lena whispered the last few words.

Rose knew Lena was referring to skinwalkers, Navajo witches who practiced evil. To say the word out loud was the same as calling them. "I doubt it. The evil ones surround themselves with secrecy and collect only certain kinds of plants—frenzy medicines, not Life Way medicines."

Lena nodded slowly. "You're probably right. But whoever is doing this has no concern for the well-being of the *Dineh*, or our healers."

"I can think of a lot of Navajos who've been accused of that at one time or the other, including tribal council members, preachers, and lawyers. And there's a whole herd of non-Navajos in the Four Corners," Herman said with a shrug.

"Doesn't narrow down the suspect list much, as my daughter would say," Rose said with a sigh. "I just wish whoever it was showed more care in digging up the plants. The waste and the blatant disregard for our traditions is hard for me to deal with."

Soon they moved on to a new site and came upon a steep ridge too difficult to climb easily. Hours passed as they worked their way along the slopes slowly and carefully.

"Let's take a break," Lena finally said with a groan.

It had been a long, trying afternoon. They'd brought hats and drinking water, but the temperature had risen to the mid-nineties and working in the sun was becoming increasingly difficult for all of them. Yet, despite that, none of them wanted to leave until the area had been thoroughly searched.

"At least it's not July. It would be worse then," Rose said.

Herman, who'd come down to join them from his position farther uphill, took off his old straw hat and wiped his forehead with a red bandanna. Lastly, he took a long swallow of water from the old military-style canteen he'd clipped to his belt.

"Even without the help of the man assigned to work with me—who I've yet to speak with, by the way—the job is still getting done thanks to you two," Rose said. "This morning, before we left home, I was sent an instruction sheet the council wants me to follow when I record the data from the plant survey." She paused, then added, "My daughter's VCR directions are easier to understand."

"You need more help—the kind we can't give you. Why don't you talk to your daughter's professor friend? He may be willing to lend you a hand," Lena suggested.

They all knew Wilson Joe, who taught ecology and other life sciences in Shiprock at the college. "That's a good idea," Rose said.

"Let the two of us finish searching this area while you go

talk to him. I'll give her a ride home when we're done," Herman said, gesturing toward Lena.

Rose glanced at Lena, who nodded. "Then it's settled," Rose said.

As Herman walked uphill toward his search area, his eyes on the ground ahead of him, Rose glanced at Lena. "Have I ever told you how much I depend on you?"

Lena smiled. "It's mutual. I know that you'll be there for me always. It's good to have something in life that's as certain and sure as our friendship."

After saying good-bye, Rose walked to her truck and was under way a short time later, Lena's words still ringing in her mind. She'd said it well. Herman was a good companion, but Lena and she had shared the birth of their children and the death of their spouses. Through good times and bad, their friendship had been tested, but never found wanting. Because of this shared history and the comfort their friendship gave them, the bond between them had become unbreakable.

Rose arrived at Professor Wilson Joe's office an hour later. As she reached his open doorway, she saw him hunched up behind his desk, totally focused on the papers before him. Hating to interrupt, she waited at the door until he looked up.

"Hello! Come in," he said quickly, reaching up and adjusting his turquoise and silver bolo tie. "I hope you haven't been standing there very long. You should have said something!"

"You seemed so absorbed in what you were doing, I didn't want to interrupt," Rose said.

"I'm used to it," he said, inviting her to sit down. "What can I do for you?"

"I've come to ask you a favor," she said. "Have I come at a bad time? I can see how busy you are."

"I'm never too busy for you. Now tell me how I can help."

Wilson had a pleasant smile and such good manners.

He would have made the perfect son-in-law. But, for some reason, Ella had never considered him more than just a good friend.

Rose told him about the plant survey work she'd accepted. "But to complete the forms they want me to use every time I find one of the endangered plants, I'm going to need a field botanist to insert all the fancy scientific language and geographical terms. I wasn't able to keep the young student who was helping me because she didn't have any experience with local flora. At least that was the tribe's excuse. Can you suggest someone who can help me with that?"

"I'll be happy to lend you a hand whenever I can, but I'm teaching an additional course this semester for another professor who's on maternity leave. During the daytime, my hours are already set."

"Is there anyone else?"

"What you're asking is something that'll be very time-consuming, especially if it involves fieldwork, and I don't think any of the professors here have the time or the credentials you need. But I have a suggestion. There's a retired professor living in Farmington, and he's written several monographs on Southwest flora. I think I have his card. . . ." He opened the desk drawer and searched inside. "Yes, here it is."

Rose took it from him and read it silently: *Dr. William Hoff, Professor Emeritus, Botany, University of New Mexico.*

"I'll be glad to give him a call and tell him you'd like to speak with him. He's an expert on the flora of New Mexico and very highly respected. He's made himself available before as a consultant, just to keep active. But I should warn you, he's a bit eccentric."

"Eccentric means he doesn't fit the norm, which isn't necessarily a bad thing," Rose said with a smile. "I've been called that—and far worse," she added, laughing.

"Okay, then. I'll give him a call, and let you know if he's available. When should I tell him you'd like to meet?"

"How about this evening, or tomorrow morning? The sooner, the better."

"Okay. But if you don't mind a piece of advice?"

"Go ahead."

"I think you should complain to the tribe about the man they assigned you—in writing, if necessary. If he's not making himself available, and not doing the job, he shouldn't be paid for it."

"I agree. I intend to stop by the tribal offices next, and talk to a councilman face-to-face. Maybe I can get my so-called helper replaced."

Rose was in better spirits by the time she left Wilson's office. Now, no matter what happened, she had a chance to get someone with academic credentials to back up her findings. One way or another, the job would be completed, and done well.

Rose arrived at Councilman John Begay's office a short time later. She'd considered going to Kevin, but he'd already warned her that there'd be trouble. He'd done his part. Now the fight was hers.

Rose went to the receptionist and asked to see Councilman Begay. The young woman went to the adjacent office, then returned and sat down again. "Councilman Begay is in a meeting."

"I'll wait."

Rose walked over to one of the chairs, sat down, and folded her hands on her lap.

"It could be a very long time before he's finished."

"That's fine. I can wait as long as it takes."

Rose was willing to bet that John Begay wouldn't want her to sit in his outer office indefinitely. It wouldn't make him look good to anyone who passed by. After all, he'd hired her on behalf of the tribe.

Her instincts proved right, and within a half hour almost exactly, she was shown into Begay's office.

"This is still a very busy day for me, so let's try to make this quick. What do you need from me, Mrs. Destea?"

"I have a complaint to file, and if I don't get the situation resolved, I'll put it in writing and send a copy to every council member. My assistant was taken away from me after two days, and the Navajo man assigned to replace her hasn't been available. I've tried calling him, but he doesn't even return my phone calls. I see no reason for the tribe to pay him for a job he seems too busy to do. I think in these financially strapped times, the rest of the council would agree with me."

The councilman stared at his desk for several long moments, as if trying to gather his thoughts. At long last, he looked up. "I think it's time you heard a few hard facts," he said slowly. "Your knowledge of plants is well known, but your lack of formal education puts us at a disadvantage. To apply for grants, federal aid, and such—which we may have to do to remedy the situation we're facing—we need to attach people who have serious credentials to the paperwork we'll be submitting. Curtis Largo was hired to replace the young Oglala woman because he has two degrees—one in business management and one in agriculture. Curtis adds legitimacy—the kind the outside world understands. We need him on this, so you're going to have to work things out with him. I'm certain you'll find a way."

As his telephone rang, Begay picked it up and half turned away from her.

Rose stood up. For all intents and purposes, she had her answer. It hadn't been what she wanted, but she now knew what she had to do.

———

The next morning, Rose parked in front of a large pitched-roof house in northwest Farmington. It was a lovely home halfway up a small canyon, large and filled with fruit trees in the front and side of the house. It looked peaceful and very well tended.

Yesterday after she'd returned home, she'd called Wilson to see if he'd contacted the professor. He had, and the professor had been very agreeable, passing along his address and inviting her to stop by his home. Rose had called the professor herself immediately, and they'd set up an appointment for this morning. From everything Wilson had told her, the professor was already very interested in her project.

Rose knocked, then waited. No one answered, though she knew someone was home. There was a large SUV parked in the driveway, and she could hear radio music, jazz, coming from somewhere inside the house.

The doorbell had been taped over. She supposed that meant it wasn't working, so she knocked again, more firmly this time.

Rose heard slow, shuffling footsteps approaching, but then the sound stopped. She listened carefully and heard the sound of heavy breathing, but no one opened the door.

Worried, she knocked again. That's when she heard a set of fast footsteps approaching, and the door was quickly opened.

A tall, thin man with wire-rimmed glasses stood before her. He wore baggy jeans, leather sandals, and a red T-shirt that had the words FREE TIBET printed on them. A button pinned to the shirt in the vicinity of his heart read LEGALIZE MEDICAL MARIJUANA. Except for his age, which had to be in the sixties, the professor could have passed for one of many kids normally found on college campuses, at least in the last generation, or the one before. Rose tried to make up her mind about him, wondering how much of his attire was for shock value and how much reflected a genuine concern for the issues.

Suddenly the largest dog she'd ever seen pushed the

professor aside and came to stand before Rose. His jowls were droopy, giving him what appeared to be a thoughtful, soulful gaze.

"Oh, my," she managed. From his paws to the top of his head, the light brown animal was at least four feet tall. She guessed his weight at over two hundred pounds. The calf she and Herman had rescued was smaller.

"Don't mind Kenmore," he said. "He's a pussycat."

Hearing his name, the dog barked, but the deep resonance made Rose take a step back.

"Quiet." The professor glanced back at Rose. "I named him after my refrigerator because he's as big as one."

Rose gathered her wits and smiled back at Professor Hoff. "I'm Rose Destea," she said, realizing she'd have to use names around the Anglo. "I spoke to you yesterday afternoon."

"Yes, indeed! Come in, come in. I'm Professor William Hoff, but I prefer Willie."

Rose couldn't take her eyes off the dog, who was drooling copiously as he stared back at her. She wasn't totally convinced that he wasn't considering her a between-meals snack.

Following her gaze, he added, "Mastiffs drool by the bucketful, so don't mind him. But if he shakes, you might consider covering your face."

Rose started to cringe, but as she looked at the dog's benign expression, then at Willie's twinkling eyes, she laughed out loud. "Thanks for the warning."

As they sat down in the living room, the dog took possession of the easy chair across from the couch with an audible thud. He was truly formidable, and now that he had settled down, Rose breathed easier.

As she looked around, the first thing that struck her was the unusual decor. The couch she was sitting on was no couch at all. It appeared to be a full-sized bed with a decorative bookshelf on three sides. At the moment, one of the side shelves was littered with books that she could see were mostly about plants. Facing her on the opposite wall was a section of a totem six feet high and the diameter of a telephone pole, and to one side of it was a glass-fronted curio cabinet filled with objects from various cultures. Framed posters covered the walls, and all of them depicted nature scenes, most from the southwestern deserts or forests.

Rose shifted her gaze back to the professor and gave him a quick overview of the work she was doing for the tribe. "I need your help filling in the scientific names of the plants. I also need you to add all the appropriate terms to describe their immediate surroundings and general locale."

"I would love to help you," he said, genuinely interested. "I was told that you want me to fill in the scientific names for plants that you know mostly by their Navajo names. To do that, I'll need clear color photographs so I can identify them by the appropriate genus and species. I have a wonderful camera you can borrow that's easy to use," he said, and pulled it down from a high shelf. "It's very good for close-ups," he said, giving her instructions on how to use it. "You might practice with a few shots first, just to get yourself familiar with it. I've put a roll of twelve exposures in it now, so developing the film will be less costly."

"I really appreciate it," she said. "I'll take some right away."

"Are you going to do any plant survey work today? If you are, I'd like to go with you."

"I'm going to be doing some of my paperwork today, but I was planning to go in search of what we call 'plant with yellow root' early tomorrow morning while it's still cool. This plant used to be plentiful at one of my collection sites, and I'm hoping it'll still be there. Of course, I always check for other plants on my list as well."

"Can you describe this particular variety for me?" he asked. "I have something in the *Lilliaceae* family already in mind."

"It grows around three feet tall and has big leaves at the bottom and tiny ones at the top. The leaves are ruffled. It also has tiny berries that are pink to red in color."

"So it's not in the onion family. It sounds like *Rumex crispus*. The common, Anglo name is curly leaf dock."

"You're familiar with it?" Rose was surprised and happy to see that he was as knowledgeable as Wilson had said.

"It grows around riverbeds, right?"

She nodded. "And irrigation ditches or alongside irrigated fields. We use it in ceremonies and to revive someone who is unconscious. There are many plants I have to find, but curly leaf dock has an asterisk beside the name, so it means it's particularly scarce right now." She handed him a copy of the list.

Professor Hoff looked over the paper carefully. "I'll try to cross-reference my textbooks and speak to some ethnobotanists so I can find the Latin or common names for these. I could also come with you tomorrow and help you search. Two pairs of eyes are better than one."

She'd never shared her collection sites with a total stranger before, but if there ever was a time to make an exception, this was it. The Anglo man was providing her with some much-needed help. Since Wilson had recommended him, she was sure he could be trusted not to pass the knowledge on to others who might abuse the information. "I'll pick you up here at seven in the morning—unless that's too early," she added quickly.

"I'm usually up at dawn, so that's fine. Seven it is."

Rose was in a very good mood by the time she started the drive back. Deciding she should celebrate her victory, she stopped at the first gas station west of the city and called Lena to give her the good news.

"So I finally have someone who'll help me," Rose said. "I have a feeling Mr. Largo will be very surprised at what I can accomplish without his so-called expertise."

"That's wonderful news and something we should celebrate. I can meet you at the mall out on West Main in a half hour or so for an early lunch. It'll give me a chance to get my granddaughter some of those chocolates she likes so much too—the ones with coffee in them. Then you and I can treat ourselves to an ice cream at that special shop."

"Wonderful. I'll see you then."

Several minutes later, after gassing up the pickup, Rose was on her way to the mall. Lena knew her well. Ice cream was Rose's favorite indulgence. Although the locale of the shop had changed, the shop itself hadn't, and their ice cream couldn't be beat. Lena and she had met at the ice cream parlor over the years to talk about whatever was troubling them as well as to celebrate every day victories. It had become their special haunt.

They met at the south end of the mall outside the new superstore that carried everything from groceries and clothing to books. Lena picked up the chocolates she'd wanted to get for Jennifer, then they headed for the ice cream parlor at the other end of the center. As they wandered past a small shopping kiosk offering cell phone service, they nearly ran into Maria Poyer, who was coming from the opposite direction.

"Excuse me, Maria. I wasn't watching where I was going." Rose apologized, though it had been the young woman who'd been looking in the wrong direction.

Maria froze, an angry spark in her eyes as she looked at Lena, then back at Rose. "I sure hope that you're happy now. You won—at the expense of everyone else."

"I won what?" Rose asked. "I didn't enter any contest."

"Yeah, right. My research would have helped the tribe far more than your amateurish inventory of native plants. But you were the one who got hired, and that took away the little grant money the tribe had planned to award me. I could have brought the future to the Navajo People. Instead, they're backing you—the one person sure to keep us grinding corn between two stones and hauling around our babies on cradleboards."

"You're wrong about what I'm trying to do for the *Dineh*, Maria. Remember that the Plant People are at the heart of our ceremonies and rituals—the events that make us Navajos. Everything in life is interconnected. If one plants disappears, that affects the balance of everything else." Rose paused and took a deep breath. "But I'm truly sorry that your grant money disappeared. Maybe there's another source?"

"No, there isn't. At least not now," Maria said. "The sad thing is that you don't realize you're holding the tribe back. I've heard arguments like yours lots of time before. We are the earth, the earth is us. But we're much more than metaphorical dirt. You have to keep reaching upwards, to try and make things better. If we work to improve our farming, we can end up with hardier, more productive plants that will be so much better than what we have now."

"I'm not against introducing new strains, especially with plants that can feed us and our animals. But to welcome new Plant People, will we have to sacrifice the old? New things don't always turn out to be the blessing everyone thought they might be. The plants that are on our land have never failed us, though *we* have failed them many times."

"Sometimes progress demands sacrifice and risk-taking." Maria sighed and shook her head. "I want to help the tribe, and apparently so do you—but our ways of doing it are as different as night and day. I just can't compromise my convictions and common sense."

As Maria walked away, Lena glanced at Rose. "That one's got a warrior's spirit. She'll never give up fighting."

"But she's still got a lot to learn. She thinks all the problems on the reservation can be solved if we just bring in more of the ways of the outside world. What she forgets is that they have problems, too. When she understands we're going to need a unique solution, not somebody else's, *then* we'll be able to talk."

SEVEN
✖ ✖ ✖

As they entered the cool, clean, and sparkling white ice cream parlor, the worries of the day gave way to the excitement of her small victory in finding Professor Willie Hoff.

"I consider us both very lucky," Lena said after they began eating their favorite desserts. "We have very full lives. So many others our age can't say the same thing."

"That's true."

"I had such a wonderful time visiting my son in Albuquerque last month," Lena continued. "His wife and I went to the three biggest malls, visited that pueblo center and the museums around the zoo, and I got to see a class play my grandson was in. I would have liked to stay an extra day or two, but I just don't like to be away from our sacred mountains for too long. All that time away from home is hard on me these days. I feel . . . unprotected," she said at last.

Rose nodded. "Leaving the *Dinetah* invites imbalance, and that opens the door to trouble and illness. Navajos are always safest in the land the Holy People gave us."

"I wish my son would come home to stay, but I don't think that's ever going to happen, so I'll just have to go see him whenever I can."

"Well, you made it back last time with no ill effects," Rose said. "And you were away for nearly three weeks!"

"I'm happy and I'm here with you now. That's more than enough."

Rose noticed that Lena had deliberately avoided saying anything specifically about her health, and that seemed odd. An uneasiness Rose couldn't quite define began in the back of her mind, but she knew that pressing Lena for an answer she wasn't ready to give was a waste of time. She'd change the conversation, or simply refuse to discuss it.

"We better head back to the reservation. I've got to fill out reports on areas we've already searched," Rose said, then, as she looked at Lena, noticed how pale she looked all of sudden. Blaming it on the lighting inside the ice cream shop, she didn't comment on it.

Moments later, as they started to cross the parking lot, Lena slowed down, took, half a step, and swayed.

Rose reached out immediately to steady her. "What's wrong? Are you dizzy?"

"I—"

Lena's legs bucked, and Rose barely managed to lower her to the ground safely. Seeing an Anglo woman hurrying toward them, Rose called out, "Do you have a cell phone? My friend needs help."

As the woman dialed 911, Rose crouched next to Lena, holding her hand and resting her head in her lap.

"Don't worry," Lena managed wearily. "I'll be fine in a few minutes. I get these dizzy spells every once in a while, but they go away. . . ."

"How long has this been happening?"

Lena sighed. "Just a little while. I had the first one while I was still at my son's house. But it went away, and then I was fine. Just help me stand up. I'll be all right once I get to my car." Lena tried to lift her head, but fell back weakly.

"Just stay still," Rose said quietly. "Let's just wait until help comes."

"I don't want their help. They'll take me to the *Azee Al'i Hotsaai'*."

Rose smiled. When older Navajos were afraid, speaking their native language always comforted them. In this case Lena was referring to the hospital—what translated in literal terms as "the big place where medicine is given."

"I don't want to go there," Lena said in a whisper, "You have to help me get to my car."

"Absolutely not! You can't drive if you can't even sit up. Lie still."

Lena didn't argue, which was a good indication of how ill she really was. Rose was afraid Lena was having either a heart attack or a stroke, and the possibility of losing her best friend terrified her, though she was careful not to let it show. Lena was as much a part of her life as breathing.

When the paramedics came, Rose remained close enough for Lena to see her. When the emergency team checked her vital signs and concluded that Lena wasn't having a heart attack, Rose breathed a sigh of relief.

"You can't leave me alone with them," Lena said to Rose as they started to take her away.

"I'll follow the ambulance to the emergency room, and I'll drive your car so you won't have to send someone for it later." Rose could see the fear in Lena's eyes. "Don't worry. It'll be all right. I'll be there."

Rose followed the ambulance, and though she didn't try to keep up, she knew where they were headed, and managed to arrive only a few minutes after they did. While Lena was taken behind the doors of the ER area, Rose paced in the lobby of the emergency room. She asked to be allowed to stay with her friend, but they refused her repeated requests, maintaining that she'd just be in the way.

It seemed forever before an Anglo doctor finally came out to talk to her. "Your friend is very ill, and we're running tests in order to get a diagnosis. But she insists on being transferred to the medical center in Shiprock. She has no insurance, so we understand her concerns. We'll make sure she's stable, then an ambulance will transport her to the reservation."

"May I see her?"

"Yes, in a few minutes."

Rose went to one of the pay phones and called her daughter. Ella, who was at her office in the police station, picked up the phone right away and Rose told her everything. "She looked so afraid and so sick. But I don't think the Anglo doctors are going to be able to help her. She may have a Navajo sickness they can't treat."

"I don't understand, Mother. I don't know of any genetically linked Navajo diseases."

"It's not that simple, daughter." Rose explained that Lena had left the reservation, and that her absence had apparently caused an imbalance in her. "It happens," she said.

"Mom, I'm coming to meet you."

"You don't have to do that, daughter. I've got my truck, if you can take me back to where it's parked across town."

"My partner can drive it back for you. We'll ride back together, you and I. What do you say?"

Rose wanted to turn her daughter's offer down, but right now she didn't feel much like driving. Her hands were shaking. "All right."

It took another half hour before the doctor, a weary-looking red-haired young man with pale green eyes, came back out, but by then Ella had arrived and Rose no longer felt so alone.

"Your friend is stable and is going to be transported soon. But first she insists on talking to you."

"I'll go see her right now," Rose said quickly.

"One word of caution. We have verified that she's not having a heart attack, nor does it seem likely she'd experienced a stroke. Her blood pressure is on the low end of normal. But we need to keep her from getting overly excited. Until her doctors know exactly what's behind all this, it's best for her to remain calm and quiet."

"All right. But I better go in now. If she wants to talk to me, she won't calm down until she's allowed to do so." Rose glanced back at Ella.

"I'll be right here when you get back, Mom," Ella responded.

Relieved, Rose nodded.

The doctor led the way, then opened the curtain that surrounded Lena's bed so Rose could approach her friend. "You can only stay for a few minutes," he said, then walked away, closing the curtain behind him.

Lena looked at Rose, fear vivid in her eyes. "They won't find out what's wrong with me. But you and I know that I was away from our land for too long. I need a *hataalii*, not an Anglo doctor or some pills."

"For now, you may need both," Rose said resolutely.

"No. They won't understand," Lena repeated. "To them, everything that can't be measured or weighed is superstition or mental illness."

"There's a lot of truth to what you're saying, but they'll still do right by you. You're going to be moved to the hospital in Shiprock, back on Navajo soil again."

"After I'm there, bring your son to me. If he performs a Song of Blessing for me, I'll get better again and be able to go home. To stay in a hospital . . . a place where the *chindi* resides . . ." She shook her head. "We're taught to avoid places contaminated by death and this building is filled with it," she whispered. "I'm sure you can feel it too."

Rose nodded, then reached into the medicine bundle she always carried with her and took out two small pieces of flint. "Keep these with you," she said. "Flint has power and the *chindi* fear flint. In our Flint Chant, they stand for strength renewed, so they may help you get well too. As long as you have these with you, you won't have to worry."

Lena nodded. "I remember my mother teaching me that flint created a circle of protection around the person carrying it because of the light that flashed off it and the sound it made when it's carried."

"It's our greatest defense against that form of evil."

Lena regarded the pieces thoughtfully. "So I'll be safe until I leave. But it's not just the *chindi* that worries me. What about my garden? Someone has to water it and pull out the weeds, and it needs to be guarded, particularly at night. I didn't mention this to you earlier, but late last night someone dug up two of my plants. The thief took some 'falling on rock' that I was using to make tea."

"I'll go check on your garden, then get someone trustworthy to stay at your house. Don't concern yourself with anything except getting well."

The doctor came in and smiled at Rose. "It's time for you to let your friend rest."

Rose patted Lena's hand. "I'll be back to see you soon," she said.

Rose met Ella outside in the waiting area. "I have to go find your brother. Once my friend is back in Shiprock, she's going to need a Song of Blessing done for her, then maybe a Blessing Way later, once she goes home."

"I'll take you—" Ella began, when her cell phone rang. Ella took a few steps away from Rose and spoke hurriedly in low tones.

Rose watched her. She could tell from her daughter's expression that something else was going to require her presence.

As Ella placed the phone back in the case at her belt, Rose exhaled softly. "Has your second cousin driven my truck back to the reservation yet?"

"No, she's waiting for me right now. She's in the main lobby."

"Good. You can give me a ride back to where I left it parked. It's obvious from your expression and the hurried phone call that we both have duties to attend to."

Ella hesitated, then sighed. "I'm sorry that I have leave now. A witness has come forward in a case I've been working on for days."

"Then take me back to my truck. It's on the way to the Rez anyway. Then you can go about your business."

"All right. But, Mom, remember to take care of yourself," Ella added softly.

Rose knew what was on her daughter's mind. "What happened to my friend won't happen to me. Part of what led to this was that her loyalties were divided because the closest members of her family are living away from the Navajo Nation. But my life is not torn in half, and neither is my heart. I'm happy serving the tribe, and living where our ancestors lived."

"I envy you. I've always been pulled in different directions." Ella smiled at her mother. "You're together, Mom. It's always been that way with you."

Rose smiled, but said nothing. Her daughter had an idealized image of her, one she wouldn't try to change, but the truth was a lot more complicated than Ella thought. Back in the days when her husband had followed the religion of the white man, her heart had been broken many times. Her spirit had been constantly torn between her love for her husband and the course in life she had to follow to remain true to herself.

Ella dropped Rose off a short time later outside the mall, and Rose got into her pickup and drove home, her thoughts still on Lena. Clifford had many patients, but today she'd have to make sure Lena went to the top of his list. It was the most important thing she could do for her friend now.

Hours later. Rose sat in her kitchen drinking a glass of cold herbal tea. She was frustrated and exhausted. She'd stopped by her son's hogan earlier, but he hadn't been home, and neither had his wife and son. Rather than wait there and hope he'd return, she'd driven home and worked on the preliminary plant survey reports. She'd be recording the scientific information later with Willie's help.

Right now the house was quiet. Jennifer and Dawn were off with the pony again. As soon as Dawn came home from day school these days, her first stop was always the corral.

Rose called Sadie Black Shawl using the phone in the kitchen, hoping she could take care of Lena's home and garden for a few days. Sadie was young and experienced with plants, and was probably still looking for a job.

Sadie didn't disappoint her. "That's a terrific idea. I'm glad you thought of me," Sadie said. "It'll be great to be someplace quiet for a few days where I can get some studying done. I live with three other students in a small apartment just off the reservation and there's always something going on. Tell your friend not to worry," Sadie added. "I'll take great care of everything until she gets back."

"Wonderful. Can you go to her house tonight? Someone's been stealing her plants," Rose said, and explained. "If you leave the back porch light on, you shouldn't have any problems. Her house is close to the police station too, so if you need help, you'll have it."

"If I catch anyone, except for rabbits raiding her plants, I'll spray them with water from the garden hose. Just tell me how to get there," Sadie said, undaunted.

Rose gave her the address and directions, mentioning where Lena hid a spare house key so she could get inside, then hung up. Moments later. Rose was on her way back to her son's home, which was only a few miles away. Lena needed the best care, but she didn't have much money. Maybe once Rose spoke to Clifford, he'd agree to waive his fee or barter for something he needed. Eventually, Lena could trade him for some of the rare plants in her garden.

As she drove down the narrow dirt road that led to her son's hogan, a flash of light in her rearview mirror caused her to glance back. Rose's heart began to race as she saw a truck coming up from behind. It looked like the same vehicle that had followed her once before—the tan pickup. But this time the driver wasn't keeping his distance.

Rose saw the cloud of dust trailing the truck as the driver raced toward her at high speed. Suddenly realizing that he'd never be able to pass her on this narrow rut of a road, she slowed, gripped the wheel tightly, and started to pull to her right. Her pickup lurched as the left wheel entered the rut where the right wheel had been. With one wheel in the track and the other outside, she had to hold on tightly to maintain control.

Rose glanced in the rearview mirror, and her heart jumped to her throat. The truck was closing in from behind, but his path indicated he didn't intend to pass—he was on a collision course.

With the truck almost upon her, Rose decided she had to act fast or get struck from behind. Gritting her teeth, she gripped the steering wheel even more tightly, then veered sharply to the right, taking her foot off the gas. The truck shot past her as she left the road and careened down a hillside. Rose hung to the wheel, struggling to keep traveling in a straight line, afraid that if she hit the brakes she would flip over. For one breathless moment, she was certain that her old truck would hit a patch of sand halfway down the hill and overturn.

Somehow, the pickup remained upright, and she slowed enough to finally risk using the brakes. Rose brought the pickup to a stop, reached down, and turned off the engine.

She brushed a tear from her face. Perhaps the driver hadn't meant to hit her. She'd probably just overreacted because of his high speed. Memories of her nearly fatal accident several years ago, when a drunk had swerved into her lane and struck her nearly head-on, were still too fresh in her memory. She was still shaking so badly she was afraid to touch the wheel.

Rose took deep breaths, hoping to slow her pounding heart as she tried to make sense out of what had just happened. One of the first things that occurred to her was that there had been purpose and intent behind the driver's actions. Unlike her accident at the hands of a drunk driver, this incident had been a deliberate attempt to frighten her.

Anger swelled inside her as she started up the truck again and circled back onto the road, then parked to take a look around. Only the settling dust revealed the direction the other truck had taken. Remembering some of the things her daughter looked for at crime scenes, she reached for the camera Willie had loaned her, got out of her pickup, and photographed the tire imprints at close range. As a backup, she also made a quick sketch.

Doing something positive helped her feel more in control of the situation, and soon she was back on the road. A short time later, she arrived at Clifford's hogan, but there was still no sign of her son or his family.

Although the driver who had frightened her was nowhere in sight now, she still had to report what had happened. Rose walked to the front door of the main house. Clifford never locked it unless he was going to be away more than a day.

As she reached for the knob, she saw a piece of paper on the concrete step that had apparently been thumbtacked to the door at one point. It was from her son, telling anyone who dropped by that he was away visiting a patient and would be back later this evening. There was probably another tacked to the front of the medicine hogan.

Rose sighed softly. That explained where her daughter-in-law and grandson were. Her son had started taking his family with him whenever he had to drive long distances to see a patient and it was after school hours. Loretta and Julian would usually remain nearby playing while Clifford went in to take care of business. They were able to spend more time together as a family and that had eased some of the tension between him and his wife, who'd complained that he was always away with a patient.

Picking up the phone in the living room, Rose called Ella and recounted what had taken place with the truck. "I'm fine, so you don't have to worry. I also took photos of the tire tracks."

"What else do you remember? Did you see the driver?"

"No, I didn't," Rose answered. "I had to concentrate on my driving."

"Mom, unfortunately, there are a lot of tan pickups around. I need something more. Was it new or old?"

"I'm not sure. It was just a regular pickup—not new, not shiny . . . so, yes, maybe old."

"Was there anything distinctive about it?"

"Yes. It distinctly tried to run me off the road."

"No, I mean—Never mind. Do you think it might have been a drunk driver?"

"No, there was purpose to this. It wasn't random. Your brother's home is the only one down that particular road."

"The teens around here are always in a hurry, going nowhere fast, I'll look into it, and tell you if I find out anything. But Mom, you really should start carrying a cell phone. If you did, you could call for help immediately if you're ever in trouble."

"I don't want a cell phone. I have no wish to be within everyone's reach every moment of the day. I've done fine without a portable phone all my life, and I'll continue to be perfectly all right without it in the future."

"Will you at least think about it?"

"All right, but I still don't think I'll change my mind."

"Are you going home now?"

"No, I've still got some things to do. Before I get in touch with the other Plant Watchers and tell everyone what's happened to Lena, I have to give the news to Clara Henderson in person. Somehow, I have to soften the shock for her. Then I'll go by my friend's house and help her housesitter get settled. I'll see you later tonight, but don't wait up for me."

Rose hung up, left a note for Clifford asking him to go see Lena as soon as possible, then got ready to leave. Despite everything, she had to admit she'd never felt more alive. She was a woman on a mission and that gave her an incredible sense of purpose. Now, after all these years, she was finally beginning to understand why Ella was a cop and what drove her. They weren't that different after all.

EIGHT

✖ ✖ ✖

Rose drove to Professor Hoff's house the following morning and arrived around six-thirty. She loved the early morning hours. It was a time of peace and signaled a new beginning. All things were fresh, and possibilities seemed more like youthful promises.

Although she was early, she saw Willie watering his front yard with a handheld sprinkler attached to the garden hose. He waved as she pulled up and parked. Hoff's dog was lying on the porch, resting his massive head between his paws.

Willie went over and turned off the water, then coiled the hose neatly by the water faucet as she approached carrying the borrowed camera, notepads, and a map of the area they'd be visiting.

"I'm glad you're early. I've been looking forward to this so much, I got up early too. Kenmore would love to go as well," he said, glancing down at the dog, who'd stood up, stretched, then walked casually over to where they were standing. "Do you mind if I take him with us? We could go in my SUV. Kenmore's very good on outings like this, and he really loves being out in the field."

Rose glanced at the dog, whose tail was now wagging

furiously, and didn't have the heart to say no. "If you don't mind, it's fine with me."

"Great." Willie lowered the back tailgate, let out a short whistle, and the dog, exhibiting an agility Rose wouldn't have dreamed he possessed, leaped into the seatless back of the SUV. The section was completely covered with a thick carpet. "I removed the back seats a long time ago. Now he has plenty of room to stretch out, and I have floor space for supplies, like plenty of drinking water, whenever we go camping."

They first drove to an area close to Four Corners, west of the San Juan and just south of where it and the tiny Mancos River merged. It was higher in elevation here than at Shiprock, and Ute Mountain, said to resemble a reclining warrior, loomed just to the north.

While Kenmore lumbered on ahead, Rose pointed to the river just below the hill where they were standing. "I remember bringing my children here a long, long time ago. Just across from where that big sandbar is now, 'beeweed' used to grow. Some of our people, in times of hunger, have been saved from starvation by eating the greens from that plant. The brittle branches can also be used to start a fire. My mother taught me how to spin the twigs into a larger branch, adding a little sand as you go. A dry powder is formed that catches fire very easily. My son and daughter both learned the technique within a few minutes. Are you familiar with 'beeweed'?"

"Ah, that's an easy identification, because Anglos like me call it Rocky Mountain beeplant. Botanists have named it *Cleome serrulata*."

As Willie whistled, Kenmore returned quickly, then they walked down to the shore of the river and walked alongside the rapidly flowing water for nearly a mile, searching carefully. But they found none of the plants they were searching for, not even "beeweed." In one area where a small backwater had created a moist, fertile area, they found signs that the person with the entrenching tool had been active here too. Kenmore sniffed at the ground curiously, and it seemed obvious that some of the scent of the person remained, though the elements had washed or blown away all of the distinctiveness of any footprints.

"I can't tell you how this worries me," Rose said as they climbed up away from the river and hiked back to the SUV.

Willie took a deep breath. "I did some research last night. Would you let me guide you to another site? It's not far from here, maybe six or so miles farther downstream."

"That's fine."

Willie took them to an area where the river had meandered like a lazy bull snake, creating a wider lowland beside the river. Several farms were visible, and fields extended almost to the riverbed in a few places where the main irrigation canal fed smaller feeder ditches. Rose nodded as they reached a stretch of land that was familiar to her. "I'd forgotten about this place." Here the sandbar was so large it split the river into two channels and created an island with trees growing nearly fifty feet high. "I know some of the others have mentioned this place in passing. I believe it's probably a collection site for some of the older Plant Watchers."

He led her to a nearby irrigation ditch that ran parallel to a cornfield. "Do you have any idea who the person with the entrenching tool is?" he said, pointing again to some telltale holes by the bank. "Is it a Navajo, Anglo, medicine man, herbalist, or just someone stealing plants to sell off the reservation at some native plant nursery?"

"Whoever it is steals mostly our medicinal and ceremonial plants, so they have some knowledge not only of plants, but of our culture." Rose crouched by a damaged plant, then snapped two photos of it and of the holes left by the entrenching tool. "He found some 'plant with yellow root' growing here, but he's damaged this one, and since I can't see any other plants I can only assume he took whatever else was here."

"Some of these wild plants are almost impossible to transplant," he commented. "Curly leaf dock is a perennial and is pretty hardy, but still, unless the person gets all the roots and keeps them from drying out in transport, there are bound to be a lot of losses."

"That's probably why he takes so many. But none of the Plant Watchers would ever take the last plant, particularly this year when the Plant People are so scarce because of several years of very harsh weather."

"Is it possible that someone is purposely trying to harvest certain plants to extinction?" he asked.

"I don't know, but he's certainly making the rare ones even more scarce, at least at the usual sites." She thought of Maria Poyer, but even if certain ceremonial and medicinal plants disappeared, it didn't mean that the tribe would fund her experimental program. Rose took a deep breath. "There's another site, It's more remote, and only a few people know the way down from the bluff. That's where we should go next."

Rose led him to a high cliff on the west side of the river farther south back in the direction of the town of Shiprock. They parked away from the edge, then went to look over the bluff. The channel below was swift, and anyone approaching from the opposite bank would have to swim across or take a shallow draft boat or raft, a risky operation. A marshy backwater lay at the bottom, and a higher, wide strip of isolated ground was well populated with plants.

"How do we get down there?" Willie asked, looking in both directions. "The cliff extends at least a mile in each direction before there's a way down, and that green spot down there is surrounded by water and vertical cliffs."

"We'll have to leave the dog here, because the first part is too steep. But there is a way." Rose smiled. "My son, the medicine man, showed me."

With Kenmore lying in the shade of the SUV and tethered with a nylon rope to the trailer hitch, Rose led Willie away from the cliff to a clump of sagebrush. There was a hole to one side of the brush. "We go down there, squeezing past the brush. That is, unless the path has crumbled away since I was here last."

"Are you sure?" Willie stood closer and looked down. "Wait, I see light below. Let me lead the way, just in case."

Rose smiled at his protective gesture. Herman would have done the same. Willie lowered himself down to a dirt platform five feet below the surface. "Cool! All you have to do is duck under a ledge, and there's a narrow trail leading down the side of the cliff. You can't even see this from the other side, I bet. There's a ridge blocking the view of the trail. This place is excellent."

Rose laughed at his youthful enthusiasm, then slipped down onto the path. Five minutes later, after a steep but manageable descent, they were on a moist shelf that was covered with vegetation. The isolated area was only about fifty feet long and twenty feet wide, but contained many species of herbs and grasses, some waist high. Here, near two mature junipers, they found some "plant with yellow root" close to the cliff side.

"Curly leaf dock," he said with a nod. "It's often found at higher elevations, so the river must have brought the seeds down from Colorado or, more likely, Utah."

Rose took photos of the plants, then wrote a few notes on their location and condition. Showing them to Willie, she added, "Will this be enough for you to specify where we found them and the condition? I'm not going to report the route needed to get down here. That's a secret."

"Your notes are perfect. I'll add the scientific information today on the computer, and keep a running list. As soon as you have the photos developed, just let me know and we'll give the photo a numerical designation that will match up with this site."

Rose collected several leaves and a small cutting, placing them in a moistened paper towel, then in a plastic bag. Once she knew the plant cutting couldn't dry out, she placed the bag into a leather pouch she'd fastened to her belt where it wouldn't get crushed. "I'm sorry your dog couldn't come with us," Rose commented. "He seems very gentle for such a large animal."

"He is, but he can be riled. Once someone tried to break into my home. Kenmore didn't like it, and went after him. According to a neighbor, the burglar took off running, Kenmore at his heels. I was told the man set a new land speed record," he added with a chuckle.

Rose laughed. It was too bad Lena didn't have an animal this size guarding her herb garden every night. But then again, if an animal that size walked through the plants, or decided to start marking them . . .

A few hours later, after a productive morning, Rose returned to Shiprock in her own pickup. Her first stop was the hospital. After getting directions to Lena's room, Rose went down the long corridor, reading the room numbers as she passed. She hated hospitals. She'd been in this one herself for far too long after her accident, and the only good memory she had of that time was when she'd finally heard she could go home. Now the smells and the sounds combined to fill her with a strong sense of dread she couldn't quite shake no matter how hard she tried.

Rose finally found the right room, peeked inside to confirm Lena was there, and then, stepped through the doorway.

The ashen color of her friend's face was startling. From what she could see, Lena had gone downhill from yesterday.

Rose looked around and took a deep breath, trying to calm her nerves. Lena's lunch tray was still on the adjustable-shelf wheeled cart by her bed, and she obviously hadn't touched her food.

As Rose came up beside the bed, Lena's eyes opened. Rose smiled. "I see they brought you lunch. Do you need some help eating?" Without waiting for an answer, Rose cut up a small piece of turkey and fed it to Lena.

She took two mouthfuls, but then shook her head as Rose was cutting another piece. "No more," she said softly.

"You have to eat," Rose pleaded. "How else can you get well enough to leave?"

"Later. Just sit down and visit awhile."

"Has my son come by yet?" Rose asked, taking a chair and moving it over by the bed.

"Yes, and we spoke for a bit. He said a prayer over me, but we both know that more is needed. He promised to be back with an herbal tea, but the doctors have to approve before I can drink it."

"He'll see to it that they will," Rose said confidently. Here, on the reservation, the hospital tried to cooperate with tribal *hataaliis*, having seen the positive results Navajo rituals often brought. "I've got some good news," Rose said, determined to cheer Lena up. "The professor and I found some 'plant with yellow root,' and *all* the plants were in great condition."

Lena smiled for the first time. "That is good news."

Rose spent close to two hours with Lena. Trying to lift her spirits, she spoke of the past and of happier times.

"The old days just don't seem that long ago to me. You and I used to get into so much trouble at school. Do you remember Mrs. Franklin?"

"Our high school English teacher, the one with the blue hair and square glasses who always smelled like bath powder. She was *always* after us. How could I ever forget?" Lena smiled slowly. "I was so angry with her that day for accusing us of stealing melons from the cafeteria!"

"She saw us eating a slice between classes, and didn't even bother asking where we got it," Lena said. "I can just hear her now: There are no excuses for your irresponsible behavior.' Everything that happened in that school, according to her, was *our* fault. But we balanced things out real good. We found harmony," Lena said with a twinkle in her eye.

Lena's soft chuckle turned into a weak cough, but it was worth it to Rose to see her smiling again. "We came up with the perfect plan to get even with her."

"What's this 'we'? *You* thought of it. Of course, I was the one who knew how to pop open the trunk on her old car because my uncle drove the same model."

"I remember carrying that box of rotten cantaloupes from the cafeteria to the trunk of her car. And you found the frozen shrimp in the same garbage can. What a stroke of genius! Once the ice melted, the smell just kept getting worse and worse. She thought it was something she'd run over, or that had crawled into the engine compartment and died. The car stunk up the entire faculty parking lot by the second day, and she didn't find out what the problem was until the weekend. By then she was furious, but she couldn't prove we'd done it, so there wasn't anything she could say."

"But everyone knew. The entire senior class practically worshiped us after that," Lena said with a smile.

Rose laughed. "You and I sure got into a lot of trouble together, but we always stuck together and got each other through it. Remember that."

It was then that *Gishii*, Reva Benally, arrived.

After Rose and *Gishii* arranged to meet at Reva's home later that day to discuss the plant situation, Rose finally left. Lena seemed in better spirits now, so, commending herself for a job well done, Rose went down the hall.

She had just passed the gift shop and was close to the side exit doors when she heard rapid footsteps coming up behind her. Turning her head, she saw her old friend Charlie Dodge. Charlie was several years older than she was, and one of the tribe's most respected authorities on native plants. He seldom came into Shiprock, however, preferring to live on the Arizona side of the reservation near Teec Nos Pos.

"I'm surprised to see you!" Rose greeted warmly. "And *here* of all places."

"I was in the area, heard about our Plant Watcher friend, and came to visit her." Charlie was small in stature, but he had an undeniable presence about him. His weathered face and bright eyes commanded both respect and authority.

"I'm glad you came. Our friend needs people around her now who'll remind her that she's loved."

They walked out to the waiting area in the lobby and sat down together for a brief visit. "What have you been doing lately?" Rose asked.

"Mostly working on a new strain of plant that can provide us with a reliable, natural blue dye."

She nodded. "That particular color's always been a problem. Sumac and pulverized blue clay are sometimes used, but it isn't very good. And indigo dye just isn't native to the *Dinetah*."

"I've developed a new strain of 'blue pollen,' more as a result of luck than anything else. I used the old, reliable, but slow method of selecting seeds only from the plants with the darkest blue flowers, and cultivating for color. This spring I was surprised to discover one of my new plants was a mutation that has bright incandescent blue flowers. It's still not as dark a color as I would have liked for the blue dye I'm trying to develop, but I'm getting there."

"It sounds very promising."

"It is. I was even contacted by a pharmaceutical company that was interested in herbs that could be added to food as color enhancers. Apparently many people are allergic to the synthetic food colorings used now, and the trend is toward organics because they tend to be healthier."

"I'm glad good things are happening for you."

"They are, but you sound sad. Are you worried about our friend and her illness?"

"Yes, but I'm also worried about the Plant People," she said, and explained what had been happening.

He expelled his breath in a hiss. "That explains what happened to me recently. Someone got into my own plant garden a few weeks ago. They took some 'tenacious,' digging the plants right out of the ground, roots and all. Even in the best years that plant is never easy to find, so I was pretty angry about it for a while."

Rose pulled out the list of endangered plants the council had given her. "That's one of the plants I'm supposed to check on."

"When I went in search of seeds or seedlings to replant what had been taken, I saw someone had been digging up a lot more plants, not only 'tenacious,' but other medicinal plants as well. He devastated two of my collecting sites. I'm keeping my eyes open for this person. Maybe I can catch him and put a stop to this."

"Be careful. But if you do see the plant thief, send word to me. I'm very interested in finding out who he is."

"Sure. I'd be happy to do that," he said.

"Will you be going back home today?"

"No, I'm camping out tonight down by the river just south

of Hogback. Later, I'm meeting with one of the professors at the community college so we can discuss my new plant. Those petals are a blue you'll never forget and the flowers smell almost like lavender."

"I'd love to see your plants sometime."

"Whenever I'm home, you're welcome to stop by. I have them growing under special lights for now."

After saying good-bye to Charlie, Rose went to buy more film for the camera at a local grocery store, then drove to *Gishii*'s house. Her pickup was there, so Rose knew she'd already returned from the hospital. She hadn't even finished parking when her friend came out and invited her with a wave to come inside.

Rose handed her the cutting of curly leaf dock, still moist and in the sealed plastic bag, and *Gishii* accepted it gratefully. "I still can't believe someone dug plants up right out of my garden. He's lucky I didn't catch him!"

Rose told her about the raids on Charlie's and Lena's garden. "You're not the only one who has had this kind of trouble lately."

"I've also heard that some of our medicine men have had to buy herbs from each other, or trade, because they also can't find the plants they need."

Rose nodded slowly. "I think it's time we pooled our resources. We need a list of every plant growing in the gardens kept by the Plant Watchers. As a group, we may be able to provide much of what they need."

"That's a good idea, but since our group of friends all live in this area, there'll be plants none of us can grow because they require the coolness of the mountains, or other soil conditions not present here. Of course, even if we have other Plant Watchers across the entire reservation cultivating the plants that are scarce and can't be grown locally, the main problem will still exist."

"I don't know what else we can do."

"Tomorrow, five of our better-known *hataaliis*, including your son, are meeting on the west side of Beautiful Mountain at Water From the Rocks at noon. They're discussing what to do." Rose nodded. "Our mountains are said to be the forked hogans of the gods. It's a good place to talk about what's threatening us now. I'll go to Beautiful Mountain and see the *hataaliis* myself. I'll present my plan to them and see if they think it will be useful."

"Maybe you should think about this plan some more. Our gardens are to provide for the needs of our own families and clans," *Gishii* said. "Not all of us would share easily."

"We can't allow ourselves to think selfishly. We are all Navajo, and in a time of crisis, we have to pull together."

By the time Rose headed back home, the sun was setting and the sky was a vivid orange-red color, a beautiful side benefit, she knew, from the dust in the air. It had been a long, tiring day, but she'd accomplished a lot of good. Now, she was looking forward to spending time with her family.

Rose reached home within a half hour. As she came in the front door, scratching Two, her mutt, behind the ears, Dawn rushed up, her sneakers thumping across the thin carpet, and gave her a hug. But before Rose could even ask her about her day, Dawn wriggled away and ran back to the floor in front of the television. A nature show was showing on her favorite channel.

Rose smiled. Sometimes her granddaughter amazed her. She was just like Ella at that age, with the same streak of independence that was rare in children that young. Ella had loved her friends and her family, but like Dawn, Ella had been perfectly happy playing alone.

To her surprise. Rose found Ella in the kitchen and, as she came in, smelled the mutton stew warming on the stove. Rose looked at her daughter quickly and tried not to cringe. If Ella had fixed the stew, experience told her it would be inedible. Ella had never taken any interest in cooking, and invariably got distracted in the middle of what she was doing. That often resulted in a forgotten ingredient, or a potful of food that set off the smoke alarm. Last time Ella had fixed supper, even Two had refused to go near it.

"Did you . . ." Rose's voice trailed off as she tried to figure out a way to gently phrase the question.

"Relax, Mom. Boots fixed dinner. I'm just heating it up for you."

Rose smiled, but inwardly she was relieved. Boots was an exceptional cook. "Have you eaten already, daughter?"

Ella nodded. "My daughter and I finished our meal about a half hour ago. I would have waited for you, but she was hungry and I took the opportunity to have dinner with her. I rarely get to do that with my random hours."

"That's all right." Going to the stove, Rose served herself a steaming bowl of stew, took three pieces of fry bread from a paper-towel-lined dish on the counter, and returned to the table. As she ate, she told Ella about her day.

"The distinctive shovel marks and missing plants are pretty obvious, all right," Ella commented. "Why do you think someone's stealing our plants? What possible motive could they have?"

"I've been thinking a lot about that. At first I saw it as malicious, but that may not be the case. It's too much work for a troublemaker. The professor mentioned some good possibilities and it started me thinking. What if this person is actually trying to preserve our plants? Everyone knows that the Plant People are scarce because we've had several years of drought. Maybe someone is trying to save what's left by digging them up and replanting them in a special garden someplace where they can make sure they survive." Rose took several more bites. "But he or she's obviously in a hurry, perhaps worried about being seen, and several plants have been so damaged they were just left to die. And then there was one chopped to pieces, like the person lost their temper."

"Do you have any suspects?" Ella asked.

"Well, there's the new traditionalist *hataalii*. If he's setting up a business . . . that might explain the rare varieties that have been stolen from the gardens several of our Plant Watchers keep."

"You do realize that if your theory is right, *all* the Plant Watchers could be considered suspects?"

Rose nodded slowly. "And that, daughter, breaks my heart."

NINE

✖ ✖ ✖

The next morning after Dawn left for day school, Rose went for a walk outside. Her own garden was arranged in the form of a giant wheel, with different plants sectioned in the wedges between the "spokes."

She looked closely, searching for any sign that the plant thief had also visited her, but the only marks on the ground were ones she had made herself, and the plants were all in good condition. Two, despite putting on years, had excellent hearing, and if an intruder came around, Rose was sure he would bark loudly, and possibly even attack a stranger.

Rose walked around, lost in thought. Somehow she had to come up with a plan to take a look at John Joe's garden so she'd at least have a chance of ruling him out as the possible thief. But unless he was away seeing a patient, it would be a risky proposition. His medicine hogan was beside his home, she recalled.

Hearing footsteps, she jumped and turned her head. Herman was walking around the side of the house. "I saw you out here as I pulled up. I hope you don't mind that I came over. I don't think you ever heard my truck. You seemed a million miles away."

"You're always welcome," she said, calming down again, and updated him on what had happened and what she wanted to do next. "I've got to come up with a way to get into the *hataalii*'s garden and look for myself."

Herman stared at her like she'd suddenly grown a second head. "Have you lost your mind? He could have you arrested if he catches you, and you'd be facing no end of trouble, especially now that someone's been running around stealing plants. Do you want your daughter to have her first heart attack?"

Rose chuckled. "She'll have a very bad reaction if I get caught, all right, but I still have to do this."

Herman took a deep breath, then let it out slowly. "If you're bound and determined to go ahead, you'll need help. I could try and keep him distracted inside his hogan."

"You mean hire him to give you his professional advice on something while I take a look around? That could work!"

"It could also backfire," he warned. "He probably won't trust me, knowing you and I are such good friends. He's sure to wonder why I didn't go to your son."

"I think he'll be blinded by his own ego. He'll probably think you've shown uncommonly good sense."

Herman laughed. "I have to admit, from what I've heard about him, that sounds more in character."

Together they came up with a simple plan. "We'll drive up the road leading to his hogan slowly because you say it's really bumpy," Herman said. "Then I'll drop you off where he can't see you unless he happens to be watching out a back window. After that, I can drive to the front of his medicine hogan and try to keep him from going around back to where his garden is probably located. If he's not home at all when I arrive, I'll come back and help you look around."

"It won't take me but a minute or two, if I can get close enough. I know where it is already, more or less, so I just want a quick look around. I need to know if some of the plants that have been harvested ended up in his garden. I'll be able to tell at a glance how many of his plants are new arrivals, or if his garden is established with plants that have been growing there for a long time."

"If we get arrested for trespassing, your daughter will make sure someone lynches me."

Rose smiled. "Your nephews are cops. They'll protect you."

"Are you kidding? She's a real scrapper. She could take both of them at once—at least two out of three times. And if that isn't enough, she outranks them."

"Then you'll just have to charm her."

"I'm doomed."

Feeling a little tense, her heart beating faster as if she were looking for a rattlesnake she *knew* was out there somewhere. Rose walked toward the medicine man's home. She was trying to use juniper and piñon trees and any other cover she could find to screen herself from view. A familiar sound put her more at ease. Herman was coming back in his truck along the narrow track that served as a road, according to plan. He pulled to a stop beside her and pushed open the passenger's-side door.

"He's not there. There's no one around that I could see." He paused as she got in and fastened her seat belt. "Are you *sure* you want to go back there and look around?"

"Yes, but let's work quickly, because we have no idea when he's going to return."

"My point exactly. I wish you would reconsider."

"Not a chance, but if it helps, try to think of this as a golden opportunity," she said. "Park behind that cluster of junipers. Then, if he comes back before we're done, he won't see your truck right away."

"This is really risky," he muttered, then parked where she'd suggested.

Her hands shaking again, Rose walked toward the back of

John Joe's home. The fenced-in garden had been easy to spot, even on her first visit with Lena. The rest of the yard was naturally landscaped except for a lane where the man obviously parked his vehicle.

As they reached the garden, protected from rabbits and rodents by a three-foot-high fence of chicken wire and metal fence posts, Rose looked around and listened. "It's quiet. We're okay." She raised her skirt enough to step over the fence.

The plants weren't in rows. They were growing in nine or ten small rectangular beds defined by boards half buried, held in place by wooden stakes. She studied the various beds from the access paths made of strewn straw and alfalfa, which helped retain moisture and hold the loose soil in place, and served as a weed-reducing mulch. "This garden is well designed. He's got several common varieties here. There's some 'blue pollen,' and a few 'wondering about medicine.' One of those plants looks like it could have been replanted recently, but it's hard to say. He may have been digging out weeds, or just moved it to a better location."

"All right. You've seen enough. Now let's go."

"Let me make sure I brush out our tracks." Stepping back over the fence, she picked up a handful of dirt, scattering it over their footprints as she retraced their steps. She was nearly done, when she suddenly froze. Her heart rate shot up immediately.

"What? What's wrong?" Herman asked quickly.

"He's coming back."

Herman listened and looked around. "I don't hear or see a truck."

"He's coming back, and he's close," she repeated, hurrying toward Herman's vehicle and praying that she wouldn't panic and break into a run.

They were nearly to the trees where the truck was hidden

when John Joe's new truck came into view. He pulled up and stopped beside the garden.

"Hey!" he called out.

"Keep going!" Rose whispered harshly, more confident than before now that she knew they would make it. "Don't hurry and don't look back. Just pretend you didn't hear him." Anything else would have been like admitting guilt.

Herman's truck was less than twenty feet away, but by the time they reached it and jumped inside, Rose's mouth was dry and her confidence nearly gone. Herman drove off away from the house, slowly at first, then accelerating once they were out of sight. It was several minutes before he spoke.

"Do you realize what a disaster that could have been?" he managed through clenched teeth. "He probably recognized us."

"Maybe, but we're all right. Even if he knows it was us, he certainly can't prove anything. Nothing was harmed or is missing, and we didn't even leave any footprints near the garden." She was finally able to relax a bit.

"Was it worth it?"

She nodded. "Unless he's got another garden hidden elsewhere, I don't think he's our thief."

"But you still don't know anything for sure."

"True, but we've made headway. We've learned that he's probably *not* the one who's been removing the plants. That's something, at least."

They were silent for a long time as he drove back toward Shiprock. Finally, as they turned off the highway onto the gravel road that eventually led to her place, he glanced over at her. "My hearing is better than yours, and I never heard his pickup until it came around the side of the house. How did you know he was on his way back?"

"I can sense things sometimes. It's a gift. But others might prefer to say that, somehow, I heard the truck—that Wind, who always acts as a messenger, carried the sound. You can choose your own explanation."

Herman nodded. "Fair enough."

Grateful to be spared any more attempts at explaining what couldn't be explained, she leaned back in her seat and enjoyed the remaining ride.

By the time Herman left, it was ten forty-five, and Rose knew she had to set out soon if she wanted to catch the *hataaliis* while they were still at Beautiful Mountain.

Rose purposely hadn't told Herman about her plans. She had a feeling he'd had more than enough of her detective work for one day. She smiled, thinking of how nervous he'd been. Yet the truth was she couldn't remember the last time she'd had that much fun.

The trip took nearly an hour over mostly dirt or gravel roads, but she felt relaxed and filled with a determined sense of purpose by the time she reached the western side of Beautiful Mountain, which stood nearly a mile higher than the surrounding desert.

As she drove up a narrow canyon that led to the spot where most Navajos were forced to abandon their vehicles and walk, Rose glanced out the passenger's window. The road had curved from westbound back to a northerly direction a mile or two earlier, and she could see the path she'd already traveled, winding up from the gentle rise into the foothills. To her surprise, she saw a tan pickup back in the distance following her route. She tried to dismiss the uneasiness she suddenly felt, reasoning that she'd only noticed the truck after she'd turned off the main highway and the driver had made no attempt to close the gap between them. But, despite all that, seeing it there still disturbed her.

Rose clung to logic. There was no need for her to feel threatened. She was going to be with her son and others she trusted very soon and she couldn't panic every time she saw a tan truck on the reservation. They were as common as sand in the desert.

As she parked her truck and started the gentle climb to the spot where the *hataaliis* were meeting, her thoughts shifted to the Navajo healers. She couldn't help but wonder how they'd view her plans.

Rose walked slowly because her leg was aching now after her hasty escape earlier in the day. Ever since her car accident, she's always had problems with it. Determined not to give in to the discomfort, or admit she could have really used her discarded cane right now, she tried to keep her pace steady.

As she passed the circle of pines and entered the clearing atop a small hillock where the men were meeting, Clifford saw her and immediately stood.

"Mother, what are you doing here?" He came toward her quickly. "You shouldn't be hiking this far from home by yourself. Actually, you shouldn't be mountain climbing at all."

Refusing his offer to take his arm for support, and sitting down without help on one of the rocks, she faced Clifford and the five other medicine men. "I came here today to share information, and present you all with a plan I've come up with."

She looked at the men, all dressed in faded western-cut jeans and wearing long-sleeved cotton or flannel shirts. John Joe was there too, something that made her uncomfortable, although she tried not to show it. She studied the healers silently before speaking again.

John Joe was the only one of the five wearing shiny cowboy boots instead of moccasins or sneakers. All had leather medicine pouches at their belts and headbands in various shades of blue or white—the customary colors for a *hataalii*.

Rose had thought to change clothes before coming, but she now couldn't help but wonder if John Joe knew it had been her at his garden earlier, and if he'd show any sign of recognition or say anything. At the moment, all she could see on his face was a bored expression.

Rose glanced at Ben Tso, the oldest, who'd been a Singer in these parts before Clifford was born. His lined face spoke of power kept in check and of a lifetime of experience. Arturo Taugleche was younger than Clifford by a few years. His hair was long, warrior-style, and his face was filled with the fierceness the gods gave only to the young. He lived on the Arizona side of the reservation, south of Window Rock somewhere. Jimmie Nalcoce was a friend of her son's, a young man of slight build, with a slender, hawkish-looking face and an unimposing style. Yet, despite outward appearances, he was a highly respected *hataalii* in southern Utah.

She explained her plan to have information pooled and resources shared, with the Plant Watchers' cooperation, then added, "That will get us through this emergency situation, but with your permission, I'd like to take this plan a step further. You all have collection sites you favor. If you would share those locations with me, I'll personally visit each of those sites and see how many of the rare plants are still growing there, then add those to the master list."

"You don't really expect us to tell you where our collection sites are, particularly now that the Plant People are making themselves scarce, do you?" John Joe said.

"Watch your tone. She works hard to follow The Way and protect our people. She deserves your respect," Clifford said in a voice that cracked through the air like a whip.

John shrugged, then looked at the others. "Her idea sounds dangerous to me. We know someone is digging up the plants we need, and we already suspect this person has followed some of us. There's no other way the plant thief could have known about so many different locations. By giving away our best locations, we're just inviting more trouble."

"I agree," Arturo Taugleche said. "We have to protect the Plant People."

"I suspect we're dealing with a person who's digging up our plants so he can sell them to outsiders who want what they call 'Southwest gardens,'" Ben Tso said. "With a drought hanging over all of New Mexico, many people are turning to plants they don't have to water very much. My guess is that the plant thief has no idea of the harm he's causing by digging up the tribe's plants and selling them. Let's face it. Too many of our young ones wouldn't know 'white flowered medicine' from 'sheep's food.'"

Rose shook her head. "I think what we're dealing with goes beyond that," she said quietly. "Specific plants are being targeted, not just the more common shrubs or flowers. This thief has focused on plants like 'sheep's food,' 'beeweed,' and 'tenacious,' to name a few. These are plants we use both medicinally and for our rituals, not ornamental ones like yellow sunflowers or young piñon trees, which are so popular for landscaping."

A silence fell between them that no one interrupted for a long time.

Finally, Rose spoke again. "If we help each other out during this time of crisis, we can at least make sure we all have the supplies we need. This will give each of us something to fall back on. These plants belong to the *Dineh*, all the people."

"The risk to our native plant populations remains. We need to protect our sources if we're to continue treating our patients and performing our traditional ceremonies," John Joe said firmly. "I won't share my collection sites."

"Although he and I don't usually agree on much," Ben said, "in this I feel he's right. Sharing our collections sites will not solve the real problem."

"I will side with them," Arturo added.

Jimmie Nalcoce shook his head. "I don't know yet. I'm going to have to give this some more thought. Years ago my father showed me where I could find the Plant People and told me never to reveal those places. I've honored that request."

"But these aren't normal times," Rose said.

"Exactly," John Joe said. "But our traditions teach us that knowledge has to be guarded. To share all is to leave yourself bare. By revealing this, we're risking the welfare of our patients."

Rose had considered giving these medicine men the list of plants she knew to be endangered, but decided not to now that she'd received so little cooperation. If she shared, it might even encourage hoarding or profiteering, especially with John Joe. Finally she stood. "I understand the way you all feel, but please don't close your minds to other possibilities. In the meantime, should you need an herb or native plant you can't find, come to me. I'll do my best to help you."

Rose turned and walked toward the path leading back to her pickup. She could hear Clifford following.

"I'll walk back with you," he said, catching up.

"Thank you, but no," she said firmly. "We each have our own duties now." She saw frustration flash in her son's eyes, but she also knew that he'd respect her wishes.

As he turned around reluctantly and walked back to his meeting, she continued slowly down the path. As soon as she was sure he could no longer see her, she began favoring her leg. Concentrating on simply getting back, she moved carefully, making steady progress. The mountainside here was filled with rocks and the terrain was rough and difficult, but as soon as she reached the foot of the next slope, it would level out for a while.

She had only about twenty yards left to go when she suddenly heard a twig snapping behind her. Thinking her son had followed, she turned around and looked through the underbrush. No one was about. She waited for several more moments, wondering if it had been an animal, but, unable to spot anything, began walking again.

A few minutes later, on easy ground now, she heard the unmistakable sound of footsteps close behind her. The person was clumsy, obviously no hunter. If he was trying to remain undiscovered, he had all the finesse of an elephant.

"Who's there?" she called out firmly, turning around slowly in a complete circle.

There was no answer. The only thing she knew for sure now was that it wasn't her son following her. He would have spoke up, not wanting to frighten her like this. Besides, when Clifford wanted to move through the underbrush silently, even the animals didn't hear him. She reached down and picked up a stout piñon branch to use as a cane or a club.

After a moment she continued on. Rose took advantage of the easier ground and increased her pace now. By the time she reached her truck, she was badly winded, but as soon as she started the engine and got under way, she felt substantially better, and discarded her temporary weapon out the window.

Rose decided to head home—not out of fear, though admittedly this incident had unnerved her, but to regroup and try to plan out her next move.

By the time Rose arrived at the house, Herman was sitting on her porch waiting. Surprised, she hurried over to him. "How long have you been out here in this heat?"

"About an hour. Your granddaughter and her sitter offered me some tea. It was very good. Then they had to leave for a children's birthday party. Boots invited me to stay inside until you got home, but I thought I'd rather stay on the porch."

Rose smiled. Herman was very old-fashioned, and probably thought it would be overstepping the bounds of their friendship if she returned and found him inside her house.

"Come in with me," she said, inviting him inside.

Herman followed her to the kitchen and accepted another

glass of tea, "I went home, then realized that you probably had something else up your sleeve, so I came back and waited. I was sure you'd find some new way to get yourself into trouble." He studied her expression. "Something's happened, hasn't it?"

Rose told him about the truck following her, and later the person on foot up by Beautiful Mountain. Then she made him promise not to tell her daughter. "She'll worry because she's my daughter—and what's worse, she'll make me crazy because she's also a police officer. And the truth is that there's nothing she can do. This person is trying to frighten me— nothing more. They haven't actually committed a crime."

"But you can't tell if that's all they're prepared to do. There are stalking laws now in this state."

"I'll just have to wait and see what happens. If it continues, I'll file a report with the police. But no matter what, I won't let anyone prevent me from doing my job."

Herman wanted her to do more to protect herself, of course. They discussed her options for a full forty minutes, but were far from an agreement when Clifford stopped by.

He greeted Herman warmly, then poured himself a glass of Rose's herbal tea from the jug in the refrigerator.

"Son, after I left, did the other medicine men think some more about what I'd proposed?" Rose asked him.

"Yes, but they've decided to follow the advice of the new traditionalist," he said, referring to John Joe. "That's the first time that's happened. None of us have ever taken him very seriously before. Let's face it, he's barely learned the Sings. It's little wonder he gets uncertain results when he does one of his ceremonies."

Clifford shook his head despairingly. "Did you know that he also fancies himself an herbalist? Unfortunately, he's made some major mistakes, but his incredible luck always bails him out. Some of his patients have spoken about it—in private, of course, because nobody likes to make an enemy of a medicine man. In one case, he mistakenly gave out the wrong herb. Then, when his patient got sicker, he told the man that someone had put a curse on him, and charged him for an extra ceremony. When the effects of the herb wore off, the man got better, of course." Clifford expelled his breath loudly. "He's an embarrassment to all of us."

"Yet, today, they followed his lead," Rose commented, looking over at Herman, who was listening unobtrusively, sipping some tea.

"In this, yes. Tradition has a lot to do with it, and he brought that up at just the right moment to sway the others. And then there's the matter of your work for the tribe. They trust you, but they also know that you're required to make reports to the tribal council on what you find. They're afraid that any information they give you will eventually fall into the wrong hands, and they'll end up compromising the collection sites they're trying to protect. We've all heard that you travel with a camera, so even if you weren't specific about the location of the collection sites in your reports to the tribe, someone familiar with our reservation might be able to find their way there."

"I don't have to record what I find with the camera, son, and I don't photograph the plants at an angle that reveals the background very specifically. The camera is only used to help in categorizing *what* I find, not where I found it. I can write the information in a way that doesn't reveal precise locations."

"It's still risky, Mother. We're nearly certain that the thief has been following some of the medicine men. I haven't seen anyone trailing me, but two other *hataaliis* have reported to us that their collection sites have been ravaged. And the new traditionalist warned us to watch our plants. He said there were some Navajos wandering around one of his gardens just this morning, but they drove off when he yelled at them. He couldn't tell who it was."

One of his gardens, Rose thought, glancing over at Herman, whose eyebrows had risen slightly. She didn't know for sure if John Joe had actually recognized her when she'd taken a look at his plants. Did he really have a second garden, or was he just trying to mislead her?

"I understand their concerns—and yours," Rose said, putting speculation aside for the moment. "But I can be especially careful and simply not drive to any collection sites if there's any chance I'm being followed."

"You taught me that knowledge is a living thing that's meant to be shared. And I must admit that I've heard some of the healers discussing the collection sites others use, usu-ally with good intentions in mind. But you also told me that it's a sign of wisdom to know what to withhold. The new traditionalist was correct to remind us of our teachings. Can you understand that this isn't simply a matter of trust? It's about survival and about protecting the Plant People."

"If you prefer, I can give you a list of the plants that are said to be endangered. You can then tell me if they're still at the locations you normally search."

"I can do that." He leaned forward on the table and stared at his hands.

"There's something more on your mind," Rose observed, her voice soft. "Tell me why you came." She suspected he had bad news.

Herman started to stand and excuse himself, but Clifford motioned for him to remain seated. Herman looked at Rose, who nodded.

Clifford took a deep breath, then let it out slowly. "I spoke to your friend's Anglo doctor earlier today." He paused. "What he told me isn't good."

Rose tried to brace herself. She had to remain strong now—for herself and for Lena. "The Anglo doctors don't always know everything."

Clifford nodded. "They know she's very ill, but they can't figure out what's wrong with her. So far they've only been treating the symptoms, not the cause behind them."

"Then *you* have to be the one to help her," Rose said firmly. Herman nodded in agreement.

"To select the ceremony that will help her most, I need to bring in a hand trembler to help with the diagnosis. But this case is a difficult one and I need to get the best. I'm going to try and contact the woman who lives close to where the old trading post at Hogback used to be. She's the only one I'm certain will be able to accurately diagnose the trouble quickly and let me know which rite to perform."

Rose knew the woman, Sara Manus. She was a gifted diagnostician. "Have you ever worked with her before?"

Clifford shook his head. "I've asked for her help in the past, but her schedule is always full. It probably still is, but I'm going to try."

"When you go to her this time, tell her you're my son." Rose went to the drawer in the living room and brought out a small leather drawstring pouch. Inside was a small bear fetish. "Give her the fetish, and tell her I need her now. She won't refuse you."

Clifford looked at his mother in surprise. "You two know each other?"

Rose nodded. "When we were both girls, we were very close. A few days before our *kin-nahl-dah,* womanhood ceremony, we made a friendship pact. I gave her an eagle feather that my father had given me, and that his father had given him. She gave me this hunting fetish that had been in her family for generations and had recently been passed on to her."

"Do you think she'll remember?" Clifford asked.

"Although we haven't seen each other in decades, she'll remember. Women don't forget things like this," she added with a smile.

"Then I'll go today."

"While you do that, I'll go to our family's shrine and leave prayersticks. Afterwards, I'll carry on with the work I've been given by the tribe. It's what my friend would want."

After Clifford left, Herman remained seated at the kitchen table, and they both ate cold roast beef sandwiches and sipped iced tea. "I would like to go with you to the shrine."

"I don't want you to come only because you're worried about me. I *can* take care of myself."

"I don't doubt that," Herman said. "The reason I'd like to go with you is because I've already made a bundle of pollen and white shell, but my family's shrine is a day's drive from here. Yours is closer and, with your permission, I'd like to leave my offering there."

"Okay, but give me a few moments to gather up some things. I want to make sure my offerings are ones the gods can't turn down." Unlike in her husband's Anglo religion, when a Navajo prayed he never humbled himself. To plead or grovel showed the gods you were coming to them out of weakness, and they wouldn't respect or honor such a request. Offerings followed age-old rules that were meant to compel the deities to help.

She continued, "I have some blue pollen and I've collected bits of turquoise, hard coal, and abalone shell that I can leave, along with the prayersticks. And I know a *Hozonji*, a Song of Blessing, that's the property of my family. It calls for blessings for our family—but my friend is like family to me."

He nodded. "I also know a Song. We'll work together."

"Wait. There's one more thing I need." She walked to a drawer in the living room and pulled out a prayerstick wrapped in muslin. "This is a very special prayerstick. It's covered in whiteshell, turquoise, and abalone, and wrapped in buckskin. It was made for my protection by an old *hataalii* when I was just a teenager. Like a chanter's prayerstick, it will make what you pray for a reality if it's held while you make your request to the gods. So when I ask that my friend's health be restored, it will happen, if the gods accept my offering."

"These days, you should carry that prayerstick with you always no matter where you go," Herman said. "Protection would be a very good thing for you to have."

"We could all use some protection right now," she said softly, thinking of her friend and her beloved *Dinetah*.

TEN

✹ ✹ ✹

Rose and Herman walked up the rocky path that led to her family's shrine in the piñon-juniper foothills near Beclabito. Many of her clan came here to this spot where the small cairn of rocks stood inside a crevice between two sandstone boulders, under a low cliff face. Once, long ago, when her clan had first come from Arizona, they'd run completely out of water by the time they'd reached this spot. Both animals and humans were close to dying. Afraid and out of options, they'd done a Song of Blessing and left an offering for Changing Woman. The very next day they'd found a nearby spring.

To their clan this was now a place of good luck. Rose placed an offering of turquoise, abalone, and a piece of rare cannel coal on the cairn, then sprinkled blue pollen on it. Finished, she sang her Song. It was a powerful chant but a simple one. She called to the mountains, and Mother Earth and Father Sky. Her song rose upward, reverberating with power and the strength of the ones who had come before her. As the last note faded away and silence prevailed, she stepped back.

Herman came forward and placed his offering down on the rock cairn. Even the birds grew quiet as his chant rose upward, filling the air with the richness and strength of spirit that had held the *Dineh* together since the beginning of time.

His Song appealed to Sun and the Hero Twins, calling for peace and harmony.

When they at last stood in silence, they felt the comfort that came from having united in beliefs that were as old as the desert itself.

"I'm glad you came with me," Rose said simply.

As they walked away from the sacred place, Herman took the path that led to where he'd parked his pickup, but Rose stopped him before they'd gone more than a few yards. "I'd like to search the low areas around here for the missing Plant People. Can you stay a little longer?"

"Sure. As long as we have enough daylight to work, that's no problem."

"Darkness doesn't set in until eight or so right now. We'll have at least two hours." Rose reached into her purse and automatically brought out her camera. Then, realizing what she'd done, she stared at it for a moment. "My son is right. There are times when knowledge has to be withheld. I'll have to take close-ups of the plants so the professor can identify them, but also be very careful not to give away where they are. The council will have to get by without knowing the Plant People's exact locations. There's no telling where that information will end up unless I protect it."

"I agree completely. It could do more harm than good," Herman said, nodding. "Who is this professor you mentioned?"

"He's an Anglo man my daughter's professor friend recommended. He seems to know a great deal about plants in New Mexico," Rose said. "I think he'll be a very good work partner for me. I provide him with the photos, and he'll fill in the scientific names the council wants included in the report. They're determined to make sure that the report is written in a way that will command respect in the Anglo world in case they have to present it to a federal agency to get special funding.

Of course, the professor's credentials are ones the Anglo world will accept easily."

"What about the Navajo man assigned to work with you, the one connected to the nursery?"

"I think he was put there because of his political influence. He wants to make himself look better and make me seem incompetent, and maybe even sabotage the project in the meantime. He's been no help. That's why I've found a way to work around him."

"I'm glad that everything is working out." He took a deep breath as the breeze rustled the evergreens, filling the air with the familiar scent of pine and juniper, and the subtle sharp but dry aroma of gray-green sagebrush. "Tell me which of the Plant People you're looking for. If I know them, I can help you look."

"This is an area where 'oak under a tree' was once found. The leaves and twigs are wonderful rheumatism medicine, but are usually very close to the ground, like a creeping vine. It's an evergreen. Bits of the plant can also be used to remove bad luck."

"I know it. The plant has a habit of growing where nothing else does, like in the shade and around the base of ponderosa pines. It has small yellow flowers."

"That's the one," she said. "Also keep an eye out for 'hummingbird food.' My friend likes to make a drink by boiling the scarlet flower. It's sweet to the taste and very good," Rose said. "I'd like to bring her some, if I can find it."

As they went farther into the narrow canyon searching for these particular plants, Rose heard laughter and, through a break in the underbrush and trees, saw some youngsters crouched beside some plants.

She placed a finger to her lips and crept forward. Herman tried to hold her back, but Rose pulled away and continued ahead. She was determined to find out if the teens were the ones responsible for digging up the native plants.

Rose crept up carefully, Herman right behind her. Well hidden behind mature sagebrush, she crouched down and watched.

There were three young teens, two girls and a boy. The oldest couldn't have been more than maybe sixteen. Rose didn't recognize any of them.

"Yeah, that's the plant we're looking for," the boy said, checking the small notebook he carried. He was wearing jeans and a sweatshirt that said CHIEFTAINS, Shiprock's public high school team. "I heard my mom say that everyone wants this plant and nobody can find it. That's why I borrowed her book. Now that we've found it, we can sell the plant and pick up some cash for ourselves."

"What's it called?" the smallest of the two girls said, trying to look over his shoulder. She was wearing jeans and a sleeveless T-shirt. Her long hair was pulled back in a ponytail.

"It's called 'hidden one.' No, wait, that's just what they call the root. But that's the part we need. It's supposed to be good for treating sore gums, and also for making dye to color yarn and stuff."

"I burned my gums the other day on a microwaved burrito and have a sore spot. I want to keep a piece for myself, okay?"

The boy nodded. "Yeah, you won't even have to pay if you're nice to me."

"You wish. Just hurry and dig it up, will you? I thought we were going to that movie in Farmington tonight," the other girl said. She was wearing heavy makeup and a cranberry-red tank top that was obviously a few sizes too small.

"Take a pill. I'm having trouble with my mom's shovel. The handle is all loose."

"So why didn't you take a better one?" the one in the ponytail said, scowling. "You'd probably do better digging with your hands."

When they stepped back, Rose saw that the boy was using an old long-handled garden spade instead of an entrenching tool. She wasn't sure whether to feel relief or disappointment. To her, they were hardly more than children.

As the boy stepped around to the side, she realized what he was trying to dig up. What they had wasn't 'hidden one.' They'd found 'bad talk,' a highly poisonous plant. If the girl with the sore gums tried chewing the root, she could die.

"Stop!" Rose came through the brush and marched right up to the kids. "You *cannot* take that plant. Don't even touch it."

"Old woman, this isn't just *your* Rez. We can take whatever we want," the boy said, standing up and nearly matching her five-foot-nine height.

"That's not the plant called 'hidden one.' What you have there can *kill* you. It's what we call 'bad talk.' It's used in witchcraft."

The boy gave her a suspicious look. "Or you could be lying 'cause you want it for yourself."

Herman came up beside Rose, facing them, arms crossed. "As far as I'm concerned, you deserve what you get. Why don't you boil it in water when you get home, then drink it? If you really think we're lying, that's one sure way to find out for yourself."

Rose looked at Herman, horrified. "No, don't even think of doing that. It *will* kill you then."

The boy's expression was one of defiance and skepticism. "We were taught about poisonous plants in biology class. I never heard of 'bad talk.' "

"But you should have heard about jimsonweed," Rose said. "That's the name the Anglos give it."

The boy took another look at the plant, his eyes wide. "Forget it! Let's go to town instead!"

The trio left, ignoring Rose's efforts to find out who they

were, and drove away quickly in an old Volkswagen that they'd driven down the arroyo. After they were gone, Rose sat on a rock and took a deep breath. "If the kids have taken it upon themselves to dig up things they neither know nor understand, we could have some fatal poisonings, or a least several really sick kids."

"Boys that age trying to impress girls will do almost anything. They don't think—they just act."

"You really took a chance goading that boy," Rose said. "I couldn't believe you did that."

"Sometimes my sons would challenge me like that boy did you. More often than not, the only way for me to get their attention was to stand up to them and give them something to worry about."

"I'm glad *my* son was never like that," she said, a touch of pride in her voice.

Herman rolled his eyes. "Remember my melon patch?"

Rose smiled, recalling the summer Clifford had swiped a few of Herman's best melons. "Okay, he wasn't perfect." She paused, then added, "Actually, he experimented with some of the plants in my garden once—seeing what they'd do to him, you know? But he got really sick and it scared him. After that, he began listening to my lessons about the Plant People."

By the time Rose got home, Dawn was already asleep, and Ella was sitting alone on the living room couch with a mixing bowl heaped full of chocolate ice cream.

"Daughter, how can you eat so much ice cream at once? Doesn't it give you a headache?"

"Mom, the least of my worries is a little brain freeze. I had an extremely bad day—close to a world record. So I stopped at the gourmet ice cream parlor—your favorite place in Farmington— and loaded up on quality ice cream. Now I'm going to sit here

and indulge myself." She held out her bowl. "There are two fla-
vors of chocolate and even some raspberry vanilla about
halfway down. Join me?"

Rose looked at her daughter, then went to the kitchen for a
spoon. She'd save sensible for another day.

The following morning Rose called the hospital and checked
on Lena's condition. There was no change. She'd hoped that
the gods would work more quickly, but it apparently wasn't
meant to be.

Fear over Lena's condition filled her, but she forced it back,
focusing on the work before her. Rose called Sadie Black
Shawl, who was housesitting at Lena's. I need your help," she
said, and told Sadie about the kids she'd seen digging up the
poisonous plant.

"It's a good thing you were there. Jimsonweed is extremely
toxic."

"Summer school is in session right now, so I'm going to
stop by the high school today and try to find out who those
kids were," Rose said. "Then I'm going to ask the principal to
warn the students in school now, and the rest of them this fall,
about the dangers of acting without knowledge of the Plant
People. If we can make the kids understand, we might be able
to keep this from happening again."

"And you want me to go with you?"

"Yes. You have book knowledge. Mine comes from experience. Together, we have something useful and valuable to offer
them."

"Agreed."

"Wonderful! I'll meet you at my friend's house a bit after
nine."

Rose glanced through the open curtains of the kitchen. She

knew just by looking that it was still early, and she had some time left. Everyone relied on watches and clocks these days, but she still operated on Indian time as often as she could.

Rose greeted Dawn as she ran into the kitchen with Two already at her side. "Good morning," she said, giving her granddaughter a hug. "Are you ready for breakfast yet?"

She nodded. "Juice, please."

"Apple or orange juice?"

"Orange juice, please."

Rose brought Dawn her cup. As she turned to make her granddaughter some oatmeal, Jennifer came in.

Jennifer went to the stove and took over preparations for Dawn's breakfast. "Please, may I? I like doing this, and it'll help me keep my mind off things with my grandmother."

"I know you must be worried about her, Boots. But she'll get well," Rose said softly. She has to, she added to herself.

Jennifer sighed, but said nothing more.

Respecting her housekeeper's wish not to discuss it, Rose headed out of the kitchen. "I'll leave you with Dawn, then. I have to get ready to go."

Rose went to her room to brush her hair and finish getting dressed. As she stood by the mirror and pulled her hair back into a bun, Ella walked into the room.

"After I get off work today, I'm going to take my daughter to Albuquerque with me for the weekend," Ella announced.

"Albuquerque? Why?"

"I'd like to take her shopping, to the zoo, that new children's museum near Old Town, and things like that."

Rose turned around to talk to her daughter. "I wish you wouldn't. It makes me nervous to see her leave the reservation."

"She'll be with me, Mom. You *know* she'll be safe."

"Yes, I suppose so," Rose said quietly. "But it's hard when she's not here. I miss her."

"Then come with us," Ella said. "It'll be fun, and it would do you a world of good to get away for a few days."

"I can't. Not now," Rose said. "There's too much happening here that requires my attention." She took a deep breath and let it out. "But go ahead and take her. You two don't get the chance to do things like this very often."

"We'll be back Sunday afternoon," Ella said, giving Rose a hug. "And if you change your mind about coming, we'd love to have you."

"I won't change my mind," Rose said firmly.

Rose returned to the kitchen, where Dawn was eating breakfast. "You're going to have such a wonderful time with your mother this weekend! Remember everything you do, so you can come home and tell me all about it on Sunday."

"You come too!" Dawn said.

"I can't, *sawe*," she said, using the Navajo work for my darling. "But think of the fun you'll have with your mother and all the interesting things you'll see."

Dawn smiled. "It's a big-girl trip."

Rose hugged her tightly. "Take care of your mother for me."

"Okay."

Rose headed out the door quickly, hoping no one would notice the moisture in her eyes. She loved her granddaughter more than she'd ever thought possible. In Dawn she could see the future—of their family and of the *Dineh*.

ELEVEN

—— ✖ ✖ ✖ ——

Once she was under way in her pickup heading toward the main highway, Rose's thoughts drifted to Sadie, and she found herself wondering if the young Sioux woman would find staying at Lena's home by herself too lonely.

When she arrived at the small wood-frame house, Rose saw Sadie outside watering the garden, one plant at a time.

She joined Sadie. "Are you ready to go to the high school?"

"Give me a minute to change. I guess time got away from me."

"No, I'm really a bit early," Rose assured her.

Sadie went inside, and emerged a few minutes later changed out of a T-shirt and cutoff jeans into full-length slacks and a cotton blouse. "I'm glad you invited me to go with you today. It's really quiet in the house with only the cat for company, particularly because he only understands Navajo. When I first came, I thought the quiet would be great for studying, but it can get a little spooky. I guess that I've become used to a certain amount of chaos around me."

"I understand perfectly, believe me," Rose said as they got under way. "I always thought I'd love having the house to myself after my kids were grown, but when my husband died I discovered that there is such a thing as too much quiet. I didn't like it at all." She recalled that dark time. She'd lie in bed some mornings desperately trying to find a reason to get up and get dressed—and some days she hadn't found one.

"But now with your daughter and granddaughter both there, aren't things totally crazy?"

Rose laughed. "At times."

Once they arrived at the high school, not far from Lena's home, a student escorted her to the main office. Before long, they were shown into Principal Duran's office. Rose introduced herself and Sadie, then recounted what she'd seen and described the teens and the Volkswagen beetle as closely as possible.

"I should have expected something like this. We have a few real enterprising kids that are always angling for a way to make some quick money regardless of the risks."

"Some of the Plant People are so scarce they shouldn't be picked at all—but to pick without knowing . . . that can be extremely hazardous."

"I'll go through our student vehicle files first, then ask around if it proves necessary, until I find out who they were. Then I'll speak to their parents." He paused, then added, "You're a member of the Plant Watchers, aren't you?"

Rose nodded. "I am. I've been part of that group almost all my adult life." She looked at Sadie, then back at Principal Duran as she detailed her own credentials.

"I wonder if I can impose on you and the others to hold an informal meeting here for our summer-session teachers. You can teach them all you can about the dangerous native plants and what they can do to people. We, in turn, will see that the kids get that information through their classes. When the new school year starts this fall, perhaps we can do it again."

"I was going to suggest something like that myself," Rose

said, explaining how Sadie's expertise complemented her own. "Then we have a deal?"

"Absolutely." Rose turned to Sadie, who nodded.

"Do you think you could persuade some of our *hataaliis* to join you? Maybe they can tell us about the ritual uses for the plants. I think most of us modernists and our Anglo teachers would find that fascinating."

Rose hesitated. One Navajo never spoke for another. "I'll ask and see what they say."

"Good. Call me whenever you have a chance, and let me know when you'd like to schedule the first information session. We still have a month of school to go." Principal Duran handed her his card, and gave one to Sadie as well.

Thanking him, Rose and Sadie left his office and walked down the outside stairs to the north parking lot where her pickup was parked.

"That seemed to go pretty well," Sadie said as they climbed into Rose's pickup.

"Yes. Now I'd like you to come with me so I can introduce you to the other Plant Watchers."

"I'd be honored."

They arrived at *Gishii*'s place east of Shiprock a short time later. The group of women were gathered underneath the shade of an old cottonwood tree, some seated on folding chairs and others on an old log that had been fashioned into a crude bench. As she looked at her other friends, Rose found herself missing Lena more than ever.

Although theirs was normally a lively, animated group, today Rose could see sorrow and concern reflected on their faces. Those that were talking were speaking much more softly than usual, and it was easy to guess what was on their minds.

"We heard that she's not getting any better," Clara Henderson said in her ancient voice.

"She will. She just needs time," Rose said firmly. Words had power, and talk of this kind was dangerous.

Rose quickly introduced Sadie to the group, giving them some of her background and telling them about her contribution to the plant survey work until she'd been replaced for political reasons. "And now she's taking care of our dear friend's garden while she's in the hospital, and helping me organize talks at the high school."

"We can help you gather material as well for your talks at the school, like maybe collecting some plant cuttings for you to show the teachers. But I wish they'd allow our new friend to speak directly to the kids," Clara said, gesturing toward Sadie. "I'm not sure that teenagers will listen to their teachers. They'd be far more likely to pay attention to someone who's young."

"I suspect they'll listen to their teachers on this matter," Sadie said. "Even the most stubborn and rebellious don't want to die."

As the meeting progressed and they began to discuss the plant survey work, Rose took extensive notes based upon the recent observations of the others. "Oak under a tree" had been found in several places, for example, and Rose documented the location in her notes, making sure not to be too specific.

After two hours of reports and observations, the meeting's focus turned to refreshments.

As they ate small fried pies made from canned peaches and dried apples from last year's scant harvest, *Gishii* stood and looked at the others, getting everyone's attention again. "I hope all of you who live in our area are planning to go to the chapter house meeting tonight. We need to present a united front."

"What meeting? And a united front against what?" Rose asked.

Gishii looked at her, surprised. "I assumed you, of all people, would know. The man who was assigned to work with you," she said, referring to Curtis Largo, "will be there. He'll be talking about the reclamation efforts that have been made by the power and mining companies."

"I wasn't told a thing, but that shouldn't surprise me," Rose said, shaking her head. "He has done everything in his power to avoid working or meeting with me. Believe me when I tell all of you, he is *not* our ally."

"Then that's all the more reason for us to be there," Jane Jim said firmly.

"Absolutely," Clara said. "If nothing else, we have to make sure he doesn't misrepresent anything and mislead others."

After everyone had finished their refreshments and the meeting ended, Rose and Sadie left to continue working on the plant survey. With Sadie's help, Rose knew that she'd be able to catalog each species under the proper genus name, and, at least today, there would be no need to take photos for Willie or even make sketches. So that she wouldn't even be tempted, Rose had left the camera at home. To ease the concerns of the *hataalis* she'd decided to rely on sketches from now on anyway. She'd be returning the camera to Willie as soon as she could. Although she was sure that a real close-up wouldn't have revealed much of anything except the condition of the plant, she was hoping that this would persuade some of the *hataaliis* to cooperate with her. Getting the opportunity to visit their various collection sites would have really helped her determine the extent of the problem the Plant People were facing.

As they arrived on a dirt road near Monument Rocks, a tall formation northeast of Shiprock, Rose glanced at Sadie. "I'm searching for a plant called 'salt thin.' Mixed with mutton fat, we use it as an ointment on burns. Although the first time the ointment is applied the pain is said to be excruciating, it soon soothes, and I'm told it works even better than any of the Anglo medicines."

"It doesn't sound familiar. Can you describe the plant for me?"

"It has very thin leaves and a salty taste," Rose said, "and is seldom over two feet tall. It's a very compact shrub."

Sadie shook her head. "All I can think of is spiny saltbrush. Does it have thorns?"

"No, though it looks a bit like saltbrush. It could be related, I suppose. It has tiny flowers, like saltbrush, but not this time of year."

"Sorry. It doesn't ring any bells. Try to find it, and if I still don't know what it is, I'll research it."

Rose spent most of the day trying to find the plant, searching along Salt Creek and south toward Chimney Rock. In one area near the dry creek bed Rose found the familiar marks left on the earth by the entrenching tool. "These digging marks are fresh, and if you look close you can see where the person wiped out his tracks. That shows that whoever is doing this knows very well he shouldn't be taking the plants. He's harvesting everything," she said, picking up several dead plants left around the holes and then setting them back down. "He'll decimate the Plant People if he continues."

They worked until late afternoon, but then Sadie, who had evening classes, had to return to Shiprock. Rose's spirits were low when they reached Lena's home and she pulled to a stop to drop Sadie off.

"Don't give up hope," Sadie said, aware that Rose was very discouraged. "I'll research this plant tonight on campus. Maybe once I find out its scientific name, I can come up with some other places it's likely to grow. At the very least, we can try locations that have similar altitudes and soil conditions."

Rose arrived home a half hour later. She was hungry and tired, but she had no intention of missing the chapter house meeting tonight.

Two met her at the door as soon as she went inside, his tail wagging, and she was glad for his company. The house was silent. The note on the table with the name and telephone number of the motel where Ella would be staying told her that her daughter and granddaughter had left early.

Rose had nearly two hours before the meeting, so there was no need to rush. She'd always hated an empty house, but Two seemed determined to make it up to her. The scruffy-looking mutt followed her everywhere, even after she'd fed him his dinner. Normally he would have gone to sleep, but today he seemed interested only in keeping her company.

When Rose went into the bathroom to take a shower, he insisted on coming in, and laid down by the door. "Just like me, you're lonely. Is that it, Two?"

He looked up at her, sighed, then rested his chin on his front paws. Rose allowed him to stay and, after a quick shower, put on her favorite terrycloth bathrobe. She'd only just finished tying the belt when Two suddenly stood. The hair on his hackles was standing straight up, and he gave a low, deep growl that made Rose's skin crawl.

She stayed where she was and listened, trying to hear whatever he did, but the house seemed quiet. When she looked down at the mutt, she saw that he was frozen to the spot, listening as she was.

Then she heard the squeak of the rocking chair. Her first thought was that Jennifer had returned, but one look at Two told her that wasn't it.

The dog's growl intensified, but although normally he would have shot after whatever was creating what he perceived as a problem, today he held his ground, remaining with her.

Rose crept into the bedroom, her back to the wall, while Two stood at the end of the hallway like a sentinel. Rose created a quick plan in her head. She'd use her bedroom phone and call the police, then, if necessary, lock herself in the room and keep the dog with her.

As soon as she reached for the telephone, Two took off down the hall. His bark was filled with a menace she would have never thought the gentle mutt capable of mustering. Suddenly she heard the kitchen door slam, but from the sound of his barking, she knew Two was still in the house.

The next moment she heard a vehicle racing away, and sensing the danger had passed, she rushed to the window in Ella's room, which faced the front of the house. All she could see was the vague outline of a vehicle in the cloud of dust. Returning to the bedroom, she finished her call to the police station, giving them her name and address. She then walked into the kitchen, where Two was still sniffing at the closed door. As she looked around, her gaze fell on a note left on the table. The intruder had apparently helped himself to the pad beside the kitchen phone.

She started to pick it up, then, remembering her daughter's comments about police work, pulled her hand back. The message, in pencil, was written in crude block letters:

STOP MAKING TROUBLE OR PAY!

Rose dropped down onto the chair. When she'd first tackled the problem facing the land, she'd known she was in for a fight. As it was at the moment, the power companies didn't like her one bit. She'd threatened their profit margin and public image. Unfortunately, she had enemies elsewhere as well, even within the tribal council, because of her public stand against gambling and her questions about the move to build a nuclear power plant.

Figuring out who'd left the note would be tough unless the intruder had left fingerprints. There were just too many possibilities.

Justine Goodluck, her daughter's partner at work and second cousin, arrived less than ten minutes later, having driven at high speed from the station. By then, Rose had gotten dressed.

Rose told her what happened and pointed out the note. "I didn't touch it. It's still there, waiting for you."

"Good."

"But there's something you should know. This was my fault. I didn't lock the back door," Rose admitted, exhaling softly. "There was a time when none of us locked our doors. It just wasn't needed."

"You can't do that these days," Justine said, "not since you've become such a public spokesperson for tribal rights. You've ruffled too many feathers."

"Two earned his keep today," she said, and explained how the dog had stayed with her.

"He's always been a good watchdog," Justine answered, looking outside, where Two was still sniffing the ground along the driveway. "Have you noticed if anything was taken?"

Rose shook her head. "I don't think so. I looked around after I got dressed, and couldn't find anything missing."

Justine retrieved a fingerprinting kit from her vehicle, then began dusting for prints around the kitchen door. "Any ideas who it might have been?"

"I've been asking myself that ever since I heard the door slam and someone driving away. I think it's probably the same person who has been trying to scare me off the job I'm doing for the tribe," she said, and told her about the tan truck that had been following her.

"Does Ella know about that?" Justine lifted several prints, then worked the top of the kitchen table where the notepad had been resting.

"Yes." Rose watched Justine work, then added, "Whoever it is is just wasting his time trying to scare me. I've spent most of my adult life as a Plant Watcher. What kind of guardian would I be if I turned my back on our living heritage at the first sign of trouble?"

"A wise one. There are a lot more plants than Rose Desteas. Remember that you're more important than the plants—which can be replaced one way or another."

"Someone who faces danger every single day advises me to turn tail and run?" Rose asked, eyebrows raised.

"I'm prepared for trouble. That's why I carry a gun—a *big* gun," Justine added, then began putting away her equipment. "I've got several prints, but they may all belong to you and your family. I recognize Ella's already, and Dawn's, based upon size. We'll have to wait and see which ones belong to friends and your housekeeper, Boots. Meanwhile, you be very careful."

"I'm careful—well, most of the time. I just never thought of locking the back door during the day."

"I'm going to need a complete list of everyone you think might want you to stop working on the plant survey, including tribal council members. And add the names of any other people you consider enemies too." Justine sat down at the kitchen table and invited Rose to join her.

"Ella has a list like the one you want."

"I'd rather not wait until Sunday, and I don't know if she kept a copy in her office. Let's work on another one right now."

"Yes, of course."

Justine took a notepad out of her shirt pocket. "Just give me any names that come to mind."

"There's Curtis Largo, the man who's supposed to be helping me with the plant survey. He doesn't do his job, and I've already complained about him. He works for the Navajo Forestry Department." She paused and considered others. "Maria Poyer doesn't like me very much," Rose said, and explained the circumstances. "But deep down, I think she's a good girl. Then there are the ones connected to the power company, like Bradford Knight and his bosses. I think they would be very happy if a house fell on me," she added with a tiny smile.

"Do you make enemies everywhere you go?" Justine commented with a chuckle.

"I have to stick up for what's right. If that means I make some people angry, then that's the way it'll have to be."

Justine nodded slowly. "I can understand that, but from now on, lock your doors, even during the day. And if you have any more problems, call me right away. You have my direct number, don't you?"

"Of course. I memorized it and my daughter's a long time ago."

After Justine left, Rose checked the time. The chapter house meeting wouldn't start until eight, but if she got there early, she'd be able to gauge the mood of the people. After giving Two a big soup bone as a reward, she started toward the door. She was reaching for the knob when the phone rang.

"Mrs. Destea, this is Bradford Knight," the speaker said. "I was wondering if I could stop by and take a look at your notes and data on the native plants situation. I'm going to recommend that certain plants be used to reclaim some of the problem areas, but I want to make sure I'm not suggesting the use of rare or endangered plants."

"My report is still being drafted, but even if that weren't the case, it's for the council's use, so it's not mine to share."

"They were planning to send us a copy of the finished report anyway. I was just trying to make sure we weren't working against each other."

She took a deep breath, then let it out again. "I understand, but my report is nothing more than handwritten notes and sketches at the moment," she admitted.

"That's fine, I don't mind. May I come over and take a look, then?"

His insistence made her uneasy. "No, I'm sorry, Mr. Knight. My work just isn't ready for anyone else to see right now. I'd have to sit down and explain some of my shorthand and symbols before it would even come close to making sense to you."

"We could work on it together. I have time tonight," he pressed.

"I don't, I'm sorry. Right now I'm going to attend a local chapter house meeting."

"Tomorrow morning, then?"

"No, that won't work for me either. I need to make a special trip to see a friend of mine. He's an expert on native plants— even more so than I am in some respects."

"Maybe he can help me. Could you give me his name?"

She hated the use of names, but when dealing with the Anglo world, it was often unavoidable. "Charlie Dodge," she said.

"I know Charlie. Maybe we can all meet at his home over by Teec Nos Pos."

"Mr. Knight, I'm going to be late. Have a nice evening," she said, hating the way he didn't take no for an answer.

"Very well. Good night, Mrs. Destea," he said coldly.

Rose picked up her keys and went out the door, locking it securely. Two was on the front porch now, lying in the shade beside one of his water dishes. He knew he wasn't going with her, and she hated to lock him in the house this time of year. It could feel stifling in the late afternoon even with evaporative cooling.

As Rose drove off, she mentally prepared herself for the chapter house meeting. Tonight, she intended to make her presence known. She'd tell everyone about the land and the Plant People, and make sure that they knew the truth. No one would pull the wool over the *Dineh*'s eyes while she was around.

TWELVE

✖ ✖ ✖

When Rose arrived at the chapter house, the colorful Navajo flag was flying high from the single flagpole in front of the building. As she parked, she could see several of the Plant Watchers gathered near the front doors. Sadie was with them.

Rose stepped down from her pickup and glanced around as she walked toward the small crowd gathered in front of the building. This time of year it was always hotter inside the building than out, and as usual most smart Navajos were waiting until the last moment to enter.

Curtis Largo was leaning against the side of a Forestry Department pickup talking to a group of modernists, judging from the way they were dressed. Seeing Largo wave at someone across the parking lot, she curiously turned to see who it was and was surprised to see Professor Willie just exiting his SUV. He waved back at Largo, then, seeing her, walked over.

"I hope you don't mind my being here, Mrs. Destea. I heard of the meeting, and I accepted an invitation to attend from one of the nursery employees."

"Which one?" she asked, unable to repress her curiosity despite realizing it might be considered rude.

"Curtis Largo. We met someplace or the other several years ago," he answered. "Mr. Largo called me earlier and said that my scientific expertise might come in handy tonight. Of course, he doesn't know I'm already working with you."

"Do you plan to tell him?" Rose noted out of the corner of her eye that Largo was watching them.

"I'm going to surprise him with the news tonight," he said with a smile.

Rose laughed. "Good luck."

As Willie walked off to talk to an obviously curious Largo, Rose went over to where Jane Jim was standing. Jane was wearing a long indigo skirt and a white satin top. The blouse, which wasn't tucked in, was held close at the waist by a shiny concha belt. Her other jewelry, a large silver and turquoise squash blossom necklace with matching earrings, was traditional as well. "You look very nice tonight," Rose said.

"I'm going out after the meeting," Jane said, a touch of pride in her voice. "My daughter and I are having dinner in Farmington. I seldom get to see her these days. You're lucky to have your daughter and granddaughter living at home."

"I am," Rose agreed with a nod. "They're away for the weekend right now, and the house sure feels empty without them."

"My daughter lives in Santa Fe, and rarely comes down except on holidays. I asked if she wanted to attend the chapter meeting so you could all see her, but she's getting together with old friends instead. At least we can visit later on tonight."

Rose nodded. "That'll be something you can look forward to, and a lot more fun than what lies ahead for us here," she said, gesturing to the groups already forming—factions, some would have said.

"I wish our Plant Watcher friend wasn't in the hospital. She would have loved to have been here," Jane said.

"I'm going to go see her tonight after this meeting ends," Rose said. "I think she needs the company—and to know we all miss her."

Jane nodded. "I agree. I was there earlier today, and I got the same feeling. She wanted to know everything that was going on. I took that as a good sign."

"Have the doctors come up with any medical reason for her illness?"

"She said they'd found her to be anemic, but that they didn't think that alone was bad enough to cause her sudden weakness and dizziness."

"Our friend needs a *hataalii* more than she does a medical doctor," Rose said with a sigh.

Jane nodded. "She said that your son had stopped by, and that a hand trembler has been called and would be coming very soon."

Rose felt a wave of relief wash over her. Lena would get the help she needed now. Sara had come through for her, just as Rose had known she would.

As everyone began to go inside, Rose followed the crowd. Glancing around the room, she noticed that the modernists preferred the front-row seats, while the traditionalists gravitated toward the back. That sign of division troubled her, so she took a seat as close to the middle as possible.

As everyone took their seats, the committee president opened the meeting, standing in front of a microphone to speak. Old business was taken care of first, then arguments between families about rights within the grazing districts had to be settled. Speakers were recognized in turn by the presiding official, and they were given the choice to use the microphone or stand and speak from their chairs. Finally, Curtis Largo was introduced and took the floor, fidgeting with his bolo tie as he began speaking.

"Most of us are here tonight because we're worried about what will become of our land. I won't attempt to argue on behalf of the power companies, because we can all see that most of their reclamation efforts have fallen short of the agreed-upon goals or failed completely. But it's not too late. They're working with us now—with the *Dineh*." He cleared his throat and continued, his hands now crossed over his chest. "Most of you know that I work for the tribe's Forestry Department. But to give our best to this new reclamation effort, I've also enlisted the help of those we call the Plant Watchers. I've been working closely with that group and, with their expert advice, we *will* find ways to successfully reclaim those areas that have been stripped of everything except Russian thistle and snakeweed."

Rose stood, and was recognized by the man conducting the meeting. She began by introducing herself, though most knew exactly who she was from previous meetings. "I am called Rose Destea, of the Red Yaibitchai People, born for the Water's Edge Clan. You've heard the last speaker tell everyone that he and the Plant Watchers are working together. But that's not so."

A murmur went around the room, and she waited a few seconds before continuing.

"It's true that he was hired by the tribe, but he's yet to actually work with me or the others on anything. The Plant Watchers have met twice in the past week to discuss the problems and the man who just spoke was absent both times. Several of the Plant Watchers have walked miles across tribal land, taking stock of the condition the Plant People are in. The man who just spoke has never come with us to help. And tonight he's tried to reassure you with empty promises of success. But those of us who have actually gone out and looked know just how much danger our land is facing. Some of our native plants are disappearing."

There was a rumble of voices now. Rose knew that people

were angry now—some at Largo and others at her, but the truth had to be told. "I'm not the only one who sees that we're in a crisis situation. The other Plant Watchers know, and even the Anglo ecologist from the power company said as much to me once in an unguarded moment."

Curtis, who had remained standing beside the microphone, waited until she sat down, then he spoke again, anger flashing in his eyes. "Brad Knight, the Anglo ecologist, is working hard to correct the problems facing us, just as we all are in our separate ways. Mr. Knight has studied the problem and come up with several proposals that are scientifically sound and make good sense. Unfortunately, Mrs. Destea and a few others want all the reclamation work to be done using only native plants. That's not practical in terms of time or expense."

Rose took her turn. "We've never said that only native plants had to be used. But it would be wise to protect our resources by encouraging the growth and reintroduction of plants that are native to our area. Those who failed in their attempt to reclaim certain areas need to learn from their mistakes. It's even more expensive and time-consuming to use the *wrong* plants, and have them die when they're no longer cared for and watered regularly."

"The power plants have tried to use native plants, but as most of us know, they do not replant well," Curtis countered without waiting to be recognized. "Most die once disturbed."

"This is where special knowledge is necessary," Rose added. "We have varieties within varieties. It's a matter of knowing what plant to choose for the new conditions. Lamb's-quarter, for example, is a kind of goosefoot. It grows tall and needs lots of water. Galleta grass, on the other hand, is tough. It can survive no matter how dry it gets."

An elderly Navajo at the back of the room stood up and waited to be called upon. "The Anglo companies made us a promise when they began to strip-mine. They said they'd put things back the way they were when they were through mining. Now the only things that grow in the land they supposedly reclaimed is snakeweed that poisons livestock, or cheatgrass that hurts them when they eat. Something has to be done."

"So why can't more suitable native plants, like the ones the Plant Watcher suggested, be introduced to the areas that need to be replanted?" a young Navajo woman sitting in one of the front seats suggested.

"The plants aren't always available, for one," Largo said.

"That's true," Rose replied. "It may take time to find the right plants. But if we cultivate these areas carefully by choosing native plants that will feed our animals, and, in turn, ourselves, we would be doing the tribe a great service as well as repairing the damage that has been done."

As Rose sat down, she saw the cold look Largo gave her. She wanted to be angry with him in return, but she couldn't quite manage it. Life was hard for those like Largo who had lost contact with their heritage and roots. The color of their skin and their features marked them as Navajo, but their minds told them they were Anglo. Theirs was the hardest road to follow. They wanted to be part of a culture that would never fully accept them.

The discussion went on for another hour, but when the meeting finally ended, Rose felt satisfied that she'd made her point clear. After saying good-bye to her friends, she walked slowly to her truck and slipped behind the driver's wheel. Tired and ready to go home, she reached up to adjust the rearview mirror, and caught a glimpse of Willie—Professor Hoff—speaking to Maria Poyer.

Because he was neither a Navajo nor a member of that chapter, he could not actively participate in chapter house business unless invited to do so.

Intrigued, she watched them for a moment. Their conversation seemed very intent. Then Maria turned and walked to a tan truck, much like the one that had followed her twice before.

As Maria got under way, Rose climbed back out of the truck, and unable to suppress the instinct that urged her to investigate, she studied the tire tracks left by Maria's truck.

She pulled out the sketch that she carried in her purse. The impressions appeared similar to the one in her drawing, down to the little diamond shapes on the treads and the pairs of diagonal marks in alternating rows. Of course, that alone didn't really prove anything. The truth was that there were at least three other tan pickups in the parking area. She checked the tires of the closest one and found similar tread marks. Rose wrote down the brand name and number codes which would identify a specific tire type. But the coincidence of finding the right combination of color and tread mark on the truck Maria drove made her wonder. Rose made a mental note to watch Maria, and maybe even Professor Hoff, more closely from now on.

Suddenly realizing what time it was, Rose hurried back to her truck and drove quickly to the hospital. It was late and undoubtedly past visiting hours, but with luck, they'd let her come in for a short visit—if Lena wasn't already asleep.

At the hospital, Rose walked purposefully down the hallway. The staff didn't generally stop anyone who appeared to belong there. Moments later, she reached Lena's room and went inside.

Lena was awake, and the television set was on, but she was staring absently across the room. Hearing Rose approach, Lena turned her head and gave her a weak smile. "I'm glad you came. I've been wanting to talk to you."

"I'm here," Rose said quietly, sitting next to Lena's bed. "I can't tell you how much I miss you." Rose told her about the meeting she'd just attended. "I just couldn't believe that man, actually telling people that we were working close together when he hadn't even seen me since he got the job."

"Now he's going to be angry, and you can be certain that he'll do his best to discredit you."

"Perhaps, but he'll have to regain some credibility after tonight, and I'll fight him every step of the way." Rose looked at Lena and, in her heart, knew that her friend was growing worse instead of better. Fear crept into her heart, but she tried her best to push it back and not let it show. "And you have to get well, old friend. I miss you and I need you to help me fight for the Plant People."

Lena nodded wearily. "I'm just so tired lately."

"Then maybe you should rest," Rose said, standing up. "I'll come back tomorrow."

"Before you go . . . have you seen *Cháala?*" she asked using the Navajo name for Charlie.

Rose knew she was talking about Charlie Dodge. Lena and he were good friends. "Not today. Why?"

"The other day when he visited, he promised to come back today with a some 'gray knotted medicine.' The doctors said I could have some. They call it horehound and they seemed to think it was okay if I made a tea from it."

"Maybe he's had problems finding it."

"Maybe so," Lena said slowly. "But that old horse always keeps his word. If he said he'd come by, he would have, even empty-handed."

Rose nodded. Lena was right.

"He said he was going to his favorite collection site—the one over by Teec Nos Pos."

"I'll see what I can find out. If I remember correctly, his old truck is not in very good condition. He may be stuck some-place," she said with a sigh, "or have run out of gas and had to hike back."

Lena nodded, then closed her eyes. "I'm glad you came."

Rose turned the television set off and slipped out of the room. Now she had two friends to worry about. They both knew Charlie, and he would have come if he'd been physically able to make it at all. That was just the way he was, and it was unfortunate that this had happened now, because Lena didn't need one more thing to worry about.

By the time Rose arrived home, it was nearly ten. Two met her at the back door, and she was glad for his company.

"Come on, old dog. It's just you and me tonight," she said, letting him inside first. This time, before she'd taken more than a step into the kitchen, she turned and locked the door.

Still very worried about Lena and Charlie, Rose didn't sleep very well at all that night. She tossed and turned so much, throwing off the covers, then gathering them up again, that Two finally jumped off her bed, choosing to lie on the floor instead.

At sunrise, she went outside and said her prayers to the dawn. Then she came back inside and fixed herself some breakfast. This was her favorite meal of the day, and with no one else to cook for, she decided to indulge herself. While a fresh pot of tea was brewing, she fixed scrambled eggs with sausage, wrapped it in a homemade tortilla, then smothered it all with salsa and cheese.

This morning, she'd eat a good meal without rushing, then she'd go out and find Charlie. She figured she'd catch him beside the road somewhere between Shiprock and Teec Nos Pos, just across the state line in Arizona, trying to fix his truck—which he usually did quite well. As he'd told her on more than one occasion, he knew his truck better than some men knew their wives.

It wasn't even seven-thirty when she heard someone pull

up the driveway. She glanced outside through the kitchen window and saw the outline of a man she didn't recognize sitting in a truck. She tried to catch a clear glimpse of the man's face, but she wasn't able to see him clearly until he stepped down from the cab and leaned against the door, waiting.

It was Ben Tso. Rose hurried to the porch and invited him inside. She had nothing but respect for the elderly *hataalii*. Through the years he had learned many Sings, and he was one of the most trusted medicine men in the Southwest.

"Come in, old friend. What brings you here this morning?"

"I needed to talk to you in private."

"Then come into the kitchen. Would you like some breakfast?"

He smelled the fresh herbal tea, glanced at the food on her plate, and nodded. "I really would, thank you very much. I haven't eaten since early yesterday. I've had to travel to see several patients."

Rose smiled. She loved cooking for people, and the truth was she'd missed it this morning. She fixed him a breakfast burrito, then brought out some fry bread she'd warmed in the oven, placing it beside a dish of butter.

"This is a feast! I didn't mean to put you to so much trouble," Ben said.

"It's no trouble at all." She waited until he had eaten the burrito and was on his second cup of tea before speaking again. "Now tell me what's brought you here today."

"Yesterday I went to a collection site that has always been lucky for me. I needed to find 'frog tobacco' to make a tea for a patient who was saved from drowning. But I wasn't able to find the plant anywhere. After checking another site where I'd found it before and still coming up empty-handed, I spoke to several other *hataaliis*. No one has been able to find it anywhere, except for a few immature plants too small to use.

Not even the new traditionalist singer had any to sell."

"Let me check my reports." Rose went into the next room and brought out her notes. They were mostly scribbled on notebook paper, but after a moment she looked up. "I'm sorry, I haven't come across any collection sites for it, and neither have any of the Plant Watchers."

He nodded, then exhaled softly. "There used to be some plants over by Twin Lakes, but when I went to search this time I could see that someone had beaten me to it. Several plants were dead—dug up and left to rot in the sun—but there were twice as many holes as plants, so whoever dug them up took an equal number with him." He paused. "I haven't seen anyone use a GI shovel like that since I was a Marine on Okinawa during the war—but that's exactly what was used to dig up the plants."

"I know what you're talking about. I've found identical marks at other collection sites all over the Four Corners."

Ben paused for a long time. Finally, he looked up. "You suggested that we share the information about our collection sites with you. Well, those of us who met on Beautiful Mountain gathered together again last night at your son's hogan and we decided on a plan. We want you to act as a primary storehouse of information—keeping the exact locations of the collection sites a secret. Then, when one of us needs something, we could come to you and you could get it for us. That way the locations would never be compromised, and we would all still share the blessing the Plant People bring."

"And all have agreed?"

"Not all. The new traditionalist didn't, but the rest of us in this area are ready to give you the location of the sites, if you'll agree."

Rose nodded. "I will report the availability of the plants—or their scarcity—to the council, but I will withhold the location of the collection sites all of you give me."

"Good." He reached into his pocket and gave her four lists. "These are the sites. I have all of them, but I didn't look at any of the lists except for my own. Only you will have all the knowledge."

Rose understood the faith they'd placed in her and was determined not to let them down. "I will make it a point to search for 'frog tobacco.' If I find any, I will let you know."

Ben finished his tea and, thanking her, stood. "Your son wanted me to tell you that the hand trembler will go to the hospital today."

"Thank you for telling me," Rose said.

"I better get started. I have a lot of patients to see today." Ben headed to the door, then stopped. "Have you seen any 'salt thin'?"

She shook her head. "But it's one of the Plant People I've been trying hard to find. Do you need it right away for a patient?"

"No, but I was told that it's getting quite scarce. I like to have some on hand for people who get burns, so if you find it, just send word to me."

After Ben left, Rose walked outside, locking the door behind her, and went to her truck. Maybe Charlie, once she found him, would be able to tell her about "frog tobacco" and "salt thin." He knew each of the Plant People far better than she did.

After patting the dog on the head, she climbed into the truck. Rose had just started the engine when she saw Herman Cloud pulling into the driveway. She sighed, frustrated by what would undoubtedly be another delay. Although she was always glad to see Herman, tracking down Charlie wouldn't be easy, and she'd have to get going soon.

Herman climbed out of his own pickup and came over, leaning into her passenger's side window. "Where are you off to now? Can you use company?"

Rose considered it, then nodded. "Actually, I would like some companionship. I'm going over to check some sites between Beclabito and Teec Nos Pos this morning," she said, and explained.

"That's a lot of ground to cover."

Rose exhaled softly. "That may be a good thing. I have to search for 'salt thin' and 'frog tobacco.' Some of our *hataaliis* are looking for it."

"I know both of those plants. I can help and save you some time."

"Good. Hop in my truck and we'll get going."

As Rose drove them east toward the highway, she enjoyed the cool desert morning air that came through her open window. She loved early morning drives in June. Later, the day could get spectacularly hot, but the morning temperatures were always pleasant and invariably brightened her mood.

"I spoke to the nurses at the hospital this morning. They said that there's no change in our friend's condition," Herman said after they'd traveled a few miles.

Rose nodded. "I saw her last night, and I'm very worried. Once we find *Cháala,* I want to bring him by quickly. I think seeing him again will make her feel better. She's always had special feelings for him."

Herman smiled and nodded. "I know, and I think he does for her too, but he's not the kind to get married. Never was. He likes his lifestyle too much—no attachments, comes and goes as he pleases. I heard he has a new, larger trailer now too."

"It sounds like you envy him just a little bit," Rose said, eyebrows up.

He laughed. "Most men do," he answered, then grew serious. "But I love the family I still have. I'm glad every day of my life that I have those boys . . . men, now." He reached for the radio and turned it on, finding the Navajo music station.

Fifteen minutes later, cruising down the highway, Rose tensed, an odd feeling she couldn't shake creeping slowly over her. Alert and uneasy, she turned off the radio, not wanting any distractions.

Herman sat up. "Is something wrong?"

"I thought I heard a funny noise. Hush and listen."

For several minutes all they heard was the hum of tires on the road. Then it came again, a soft rattling sound. She recognized it in an instant. "Don't move, it's close. I can feel it in my bones. I just don't know where it is."

"Where *what* is?" He listened, and they heard the sound again. "Never mind," he whispered. "I recognize it."

"Only one thing makes a dry rattling sound like that—a rattlesnake." She pulled slowly over onto the shoulder of the road. "And if it's rattling, it feels threatened and is telling us to watch out because it's ready to strike."

THIRTEEN
✖ ✖ ✖

Rose switched off the ignition and then sat very still. They had just lifted their feet up onto the seat and were all hunched up. "Try to pinpoint its location without moving."

"I'm not even breathing," Herman whispered back.

Rose listened, but now there was no sound except the ticking of cooling metal from the engine. Then, as she shifted in her seat, she heard it moving again. "I think it's behind my seat in that storage area somewhere."

"Then stay still. Let me see if I can find out exactly where it is." Moving slowly, he unbuckled his seat belt and swung around, getting onto his knees with a creaky groan. "I'm getting way too old for this." Then he peered over the back of the bench seat. "It's coiled at the moment, directly behind you, but it can't strike at anything, not from where it is now. Open the door and jump out quickly."

Rose didn't hesitate. Opening the door quickly, she scrambled out and stepped away from the cab, turning around to watch for the snake. Herman had gone out his door at the same time, and now hurried around to join her.

"How on earth did that thing get inside my truck?" she managed.

"There's no way it could have crawled into the cab by itself," Herman said. "Not unless you left the door open all night and put in a ramp for it to use. I know you didn't park against a hill or under a large tree branch."

Rose's eyes widened in horror. "Someone put that thing in there on purpose!"

"Yes," Herman said quietly. "You don't do that by accident."

"I thought they were only trying to scare me . . . but now they mean me harm. We both could have been bitten, or been in an accident. What if my granddaughter had been with me?"

"Maybe the person knew she and your daughter the police officer weren't at home," Herman said, taking a closer look at where the reptile was still hiding.

"From what I can see," he said, "the snake was in an open gunny sack when it was placed behind your seat. Our voices and the motion of the truck, along with its bad mood after being trapped in the sack, must have triggered its rattling," he said, then added, "You know it's rare for a rattlesnake to actually kill an adult, but it could have made you very sick."

"Maybe the person was hoping I'd have a car accident."

Herman pursed his lips, lost in thought for a moment. "Whoever did this was not just trying to scare you. He's obviously prepared to go a lot further than that."

"I can see that now." Rose took a deep breath, determination pounding through her with every beat of her heart. "And that does scare me. But if they think they can make me back off, they're in for a surprise. My daughter and I are alike in that way. We don't let anyone frighten us away from doing what's right."

"I know that," Herman said slowly, "and so do all your friends. Whoever did this not only doesn't know you very well, he has underestimated you badly."

Rose looked into the cab through the open doorway.

"It hasn't even tried to slither out. I think we're going to have to help it escape."

"I'll go find a long, sturdy branch," Herman said. "Then I'll try to pick it up by the middle and lift it down to the ground."

Herman moved away and started searching. There weren't many branches of any length around them, most of the vegetation in that spot being shrubs and grasses.

"Wait," Rose called out to him. "There should be a spare shovel in the bed of the truck. My daughter always makes me take one along in case I get stuck, and I remember putting it back after I got my truck from the shop."

Herman nodded, and walked around to the tailgate. "It's here." He climbed up and unfastened the shovel from a small bracket that held it down to the bed with a wing nut.

"It's too bad my son isn't here. He was picking up snakes by their tails when he was ten. He's never gotten bit either," Herman said with a laugh, jumping down from the bed with the shovel.

Working carefully, Herman kept the business end of the shovel poised while Rose moved the lever that allowed the seat to move forward or back. As the seat shifted, the snake, once again feeling threatened, started to coil and rattle furiously.

"Here you go." Herman slipped the blade of the shovel under the snake, which immediately coiled into a tight spiral on the metal surface. Stepping back, Herman swung the blade around, and moved quickly away from the vehicle across the highway, which was clear of traffic at the moment. When the snake started to move up the handle, Herman lowered the shovel blade to the ground, dropping the handle and stepping back.

The shovel bounced slightly, and the snake slipped off onto the ground. Instead of coiling again, it quickly slithered away under a clump of brush.

"Good work!" Rose called from beside the truck as Herman picked up the shovel and came back across the road.

"It'll go on with its life now, as long as it stays off the highway," he said.

"Good. Since snakes are related to Thunder and are the earthly form of the Lightning People, harming it in any way would have worsened the drought we're having."

"All things are connected. To kill anything without cause is dangerous," Herman agreed.

"Snakes have to crawl through hot sand and rocks because they can't walk, and they will never have possessions of their own. We should be kind to them, otherwise the gods will think we don't appreciate who we are and all the things we have."

They were on their way down the highway once again after Herman stowed the shovel in the back. "You know, if there was one thing I wish I could make everyone understand, it's that I'm fighting for more than the lives of a few of the Plant People," Rose said. "Everything is part of the whole. If even one of the Plant People moves on, it starts a chain of events. Plant People, like us, depend on each other." She shook her head and lapsed into a long silence.

Herman never interrupted her thoughts. He was always at ease with her. Rose leaned back in her seat and enjoyed the silence. When two minds thought alike, there was no need for endless chatter.

Once they reached the roughly hewn canyons between Beclabito and Teec Nos Pos, not having seen Charlie along the entire route from Shiprock, Rose slowed the truck down. They both began watching for his vehicle or tire tracks at places where Charlie might have turned off the highway. After several more minutes had gone by, Herman spotted a fresh-looking trail leading toward a known collection site. Rose turned the truck around and followed the tracks, trying to catch a glimpse of Charlie or his truck.

She wasn't surprised he'd come here. This was a large area with varied terrain, moisture supplies, and soil types—a region favored by Charlie and others because so many varieties of Plant People grew undisturbed here.

Getting out of the truck when the risk of getting stuck became too great, they searched on foot, looking not only for Charlie and his pickup, but also for important plants. Here, at least, there were no signs of the small pointed shovel that she'd seen at so many other sites closer to Shiprock.

"The Plant People like it here. Smell the fresh blossoms and the scent of sage, pine, and juniper? Even the plants that we haven't found anywhere else are thriving in this location," Rose said softly. "There's even 'frog tobacco' and 'salt thin.'"

"I can understand why they live in this place. Things are peaceful and undisturbed here. But something else is troubling you. I can hear it in your voice," Herman said as he continued along the parallel search he was making about twenty feet to her left.

She shook her head. Words had power, and she was afraid to speak too soon, but something was wrong here. She could feel it as plainly as she could feel the ground beneath the soles of her feet.

"Look, there's a pickup over there on the bluff," Herman said, pointing. "Isn't that his?"

"It sure looks like it." She looked completely around in a circle before moving again. "But I don't see him anywhere."

"He could be out of sight, farther away from the edge," Herman suggested.

"That sounds like him. He hates to climb, so he's either somewhere along the top looking for an easy way to drive down, or he's gone off in the other direction," Rose said, trying to remember all she could about Charlie's work habits.

They walked along the base of the cliff, trying to spot where Charlie might have found an easy way down. Finally, Rose stopped and listened for a moment. "I don't like this. The birds should be flying away from the area our friend is disturbing as he walks, and he loves to whistle little tunes as he works, but there's only silence out here. Even the birds are quiet."

"Are you sure that's his truck up there? If it is, maybe it broke down and he walked back out to the highway to hitch a ride."

"It's possible, but I haven't seen any of his tracks, have you?" Rose asked.

Herman shook his head. "I haven't seen any human tracks, except ours."

"He favors thick-soled work boots that give good snake protection. Those leave clear impressions."

"We'll just keep searching. He may be beneath that old truck, trying to breathe some life into it. That thing is nearly as old as I am," Herman joked. "If he starts it up, we'll hear it all the way across the valley."

Rose took a deep, steadying breath. "I'm worried. The other day at the hospital I asked him to check on the plant thefts, you see . . ."

Herman nodded, obviously remembering their recent experience with the rattler, and didn't press her to say more.

They continued along the bottom of the cliff, but couldn't see where anyone might have climbed down. When they got to the spot right below where Charlie's truck was parked, Rose looked up, then pointed overhead. Two vultures were circling. "I'd have spotted them sooner if I'd been looking up instead of down. They're after something," she said, her voice taut.

"Probably a sheep or a cow that wandered off," Herman said.

"Nobody has grazed their animals here in a long time. We would have seen their tracks." Rose shuddered. Like most Navajos, she made it a point to avoid contact with anything that was dead. For courage, she reached into her pocket and grasped her medicine bundle, but still her uneasiness grew.

As they continued along the foot of the cliff, Rose's uneasiness intensified. Suddenly they both stopped at the same moment. Twenty feet ahead, lying on the rocks directly below the drop-off, was the broken body of Charlie Dodge.

Rose held her breath and stared in horror. There was no doubt that her friend was dead. His limbs were bent at odd, unnatural angles and his head was turned sharply to one side—his neck no doubt broken. Blood stained the rocks and earth around his body. His eyes were staring at nothing, but they seemed to cut right through her. Rose turned her face away.

Herman found his voice after a moment. "We have to go find a telephone now. We need the police . . . or someone," he managed.

Rose wanted to speak, but the words were all lodged in her throat.

"He obviously got too close to the edge," Herman said, looking up.

Rose shook her head, but still couldn't speak. That wasn't the explanation for whatever had happened here. Charlie had had vertigo for as long as she'd known him. There was no way he would have been anywhere near the edge of the cliff.

They'd called the police from a pay phone in Teec Nos Pos outside a gas station, then returned to the area to wait for the officer to arrive. They'd also left a white handkerchief on a stick beside the highway to let the police know where to turn off the main road.

It was shortly past noon now and the temperature was

climbing steadily, though thunderclouds were starting to appear to the southeast. Uncomfortable sitting in the truck, Rose got out and found a boulder to rest on beneath the shade of the cliff well away from where the body was located. "I'll want to go up there after the police come," she said, gesturing to the top of the cliff.

"You mean you want to climb that rock face?"

"We don't have to climb. We can drive along until we find an easy way up."

"But why? What do you expect to find up on the cliff or in his truck? Down here is where he . . . the body . . . ended up."

Herman stopped talking. He knew, like her, that references to the dead were dangerous, especially in a place where the *chindi,* the evil part of a person, remained after death.

"I have to find out what happened. He was my friend, and part of the reason he was here was because of me. I'd asked him to help me search for the Plant People."

"You aren't taking responsibility for this accident, are you?" he asked, surprised. "Surely you realize that whatever happened here had nothing to do with you."

"I don't think we know what really happened here," she said simply. "Not yet."

"So let the police find out," Herman said.

"I will, but I also need to take a look around myself."

"Your daughter's bullheaded stubbornness when she's working a case has given her an almost legendary reputation. Now I know who she gets that from."

"Who says my daughter is bullheaded and stubborn?" Rose demanded.

"My nephews," he said, then stopped. "They say that with respect, not as criticism," he added slowly. "Do me a favor? Don't tell her, or I'll have a lot of explaining to do."

"I won't. But my daughter isn't stubborn. She knows her

duty as a police officer, and that's why she never gives up."

"And you?"

"I'm not an officer, but I have a duty to my friend."

It took nearly an hour before a dusty white tribal unit arrived. Rose suddenly wished she'd been on the New Mexico side of the Rez. At least there she knew practically all the patrolmen, and more importantly, they knew her daughter, who was the senior investigator. Ella would have been kept up on every phase of the investigation and Rose couldn't think of anyone she would have rather seen handling the case.

"I'm Officer Vernon Dearman," the young Navajo man told them, having to duck down to climb out of the vehicle without bumping his head. He was tall, even taller than Ella, wearing the khaki uniform of the tribal police. "I'm here in response to your call. I understand you knew the victim. Is this his name?" Officer Dearman held up a small notebook with *Charlie Dodge* printed on the page.

Rose and Herman nodded at the same time. "The body is over beneath the cliff," Rose said, pointing to where what used to be Charlie was lying. "Do you want us to show you?"

"If you don't mind," he said, looking them both over carefully, and apparently deciding they presented no danger to him.

Rose nodded. Although she was aware of Herman, neither looked at the other as they carried out their duty. As they neared the spot where Charlie's body lay, she slowed down, then gestured ahead.

Forcing herself not to look at the body, Rose studied the surroundings instead while the officer did whatever police do when examining a dead man. On the ground there appeared to be the faint impression of prints—but someone had tossed sand over them, obscuring the basic pattern. She couldn't even estimate the size of the shoe, but she knew someone had been there.

"Do you see the footprints?" she asked the officer, who had

his portable radio in hand now, calling for someone to come and pick up the body.

The officer finished his call and looked around casually. "Where?"

She pointed. "They lead away from the body."

He crouched down, studied the ground for a while, then shook his head. "These don't look like fresh tracks, and the victim hasn't been dead for more than a day, I'd guess. Maybe they're old tracks the victim left from a previous trip. Too much sand's blown over them."

"Or maybe someone sprinkled sand over their own tracks."

The officer shook his head. "You'd think he'd have done a better job of hiding them had it been done on purpose. Besides, it looks like the victim fell from above. He wouldn't have left tracks unless he tried to stand and failed, but from what I can see, that didn't happen. Your friend probably died on impact." He looked up at her, wariness on his face. "Do you read a lot of mystery novels?"

Rose knew what he was thinking. "I just observe, that's all."

She saw Dearman studying the cliffside. "There's a section up there that caved off very recently." He then glanced down and pointed to the chunk of fresh earth below the body. "As you can see, it's beneath the victim, which suggests what may have happened. Have you been up there?"

"No," she said in a choked voice. "But I'd like to take a look. Is that all right with you, providing I don't disturb the crime scene?"

"Crime scene? This still looks like an accident to me." As he studied her face, the light of understanding dawned on his features. "Your name sounded familiar. *Now* I know who you are. I saw you on TV speaking out on the gaming issue. Your daughter is with the homicide team working out of the Shiprock station."

Rose nodded. "Yes. She's in charge of the Special Investigations Unit."

The officer looked around, noting the darkening skies overhead. "All right. Before it starts to rain, if it's going to, let's go take a quick look at what's up there. Just in case you're right, I want you two to ride with me. That way we'll only leave one additional set of tire tracks."

After the officer covered the body with a heavy canvas drop cloth, they climbed into the tribal police unit. Once seated, Rose saw there were no handles on the rear doors, and unlike Ella's Jeep, there was a screen separating the back from the front. It made her feel like she was in a cage.

Officer Dearman blazed his own trail up to the top of the high mesa, circling around until he found a suitable route. Rose could hear the sound of underbrush caving beneath the wheels. It was a rough climb, but they made it despite a few difficult sections.

The officer opened her door from the outside, and Rose got out and looked around. Herman slid across the seat and came out the same way. Immediately, she spotted the small holes that had been dug not far from Charlie's truck.

Dearman stopped and looked at both of them. "Stay here. I need to take a look around before any other footprints contaminate any potential evidence. And under no circumstances should you go anywhere near the edge of the cliff. It's caving off."

Rose remained where she was, but her gaze went everywhere. Charlie's ancient truck was there, the door closed, and everything appeared normal. But there were two distinctly different sets of tire tracks.

"There was another vehicle here," she said, "and it wasn't our pickup either."

The patrolman nodded. "You're correct. And it looks like someone was digging up plants over there. But that's hardly a surprise. The victim is a well-known Plant Watcher who lived not far from here. I met him by the highway one time when he had a flat."

Rose obeyed the officer's instructions not to move about, but she wanted to study the area where the plants had been dug up. "I can't tell from here, but will you look for me and tell me if the shovel marks are unusual?"

"What's unusual about a shovel?" Dearman asked.

"I want to know if the marks were made by one of those small GI folding shovels, what's known in the military as an entrenching tool. Do you know what I mean?"

"Sure, My dad had one that he took on fishing trips. What's significant about that type of shovel? The victim was one of those Code Talkers too, a Marine. Perhaps he used one."

"He didn't. But *someone* using one of those tools has been digging up native plants, the types that have special uses in our culture, at various collection sites throughout the Four Corners. The tribe asked me to check into the condition and availability of certain ceremonial and healing plants, and that's how I found out what was happening."

The officer studied the ground carefully. "The holes do look as if they were made by an entrenching tool. See these scrapes on the dry ground? But it also appears that whoever was here with the plant expert didn't even get out of his vehicle. I see only one set of footprints."

"He must have, or he couldn't have made the shovel marks. The footprints have been obliterated, covered up, like the ones below. Up here, it was done even more skillfully. He used a branch to smooth them out, then sand. He had a clear view of the area from up here, so he didn't have to worry about someone sneaking up on him while covering up the tracks. He could take his time."

The officer studied the ground for a long time without

speaking. "The marks are too indistinct for me to confirm that. But even if you're right, that doesn't meant it was murder. The person who was here at the time of the accident may not have wanted to get involved with an investigation after his friend fell."

The patrolman spotted a hand trowel on the ground and went over to where it was lying. Beside it was a large plastic trash bag that held several plants that had been dug up with the soil packed around the roots. "It looks like the victim came here to collect some herbs, ventured too close to the side, and fell over when the ground gave way beneath him."

Rose shook her head. "That's not likely. My friend used cloth bags to collect plants he intended on replanting, wrapping the roots in damp cloth. My friend was also very afraid of heights. He wouldn't have collected anything close to the edge— not even gold."

"But we don't know how close to the edge he was," Dearman countered. "A good two feet of the edge may have broken away, from the looks of it," he said, pointing below.

"Will the medical investigator examine the body?"

"That'll be up to my supervisor and the medical investigator. Autopsies are only done when the cause of death isn't obvious, or when it appears to be connected to a crime."

"The victim was a man who dedicated his life to our tribe," Rose answered. "He deserves to have the questions surrounding his death settled. If I'm right, his *chindi* will demand justice." She knew that modernists didn't really believe in the *chindi*, labeling what they didn't personally believe in as superstition, like most Anglos did. But a part of them would always still believe. Some cultural teachings were too ingrained to completely dismiss. She was counting on that now as she waited for the officer's reaction. Seeing him squirm, she knew she'd gotten to him.

Dearman cleared his throat. "I'll pass your statement on to my superiors, along with my report. They'll have to make the decision."

As they were talking it began to drizzle, and in less than a minute it turned into a downpour.

As the officer placed the plants and the hand trowel into the trunk of his car, Rose found herself wishing that she'd had the camera with her. Now there was no way to record the tire prints and digging marks. At least the body below was covered by the canvas cover Officer Dearman had used.

As she walked back to the patrolman's car, the falling rain hid her tears. Her friend was gone, but the good he'd done for the tribe would live after him. There was no greater epitaph.

FOURTEEN

✖ ✖ ✖

Rose got up early the following morning. She'd worried about Lena, and how the news of Charlie Dodge's death would affect her, all night long. Close to dawn Rose finally made the decision not to tell her, at least not right away. The news of Charlie's death would just make things worse for Lena.

After feeding Two and making sure she let Ben Tso know where "salt thin" and "frog tobacco" could be found, Rose picked some huge yellow sunflowers from the back yard, Lena's favorites, and placed them in a large blue vase containing her special cut-flowers water mix. That would keep the blossoms fresh for days.

Reaching high up in the cupboard, she took down a small box of cactus pear candy she'd made herself last month. The recipe was one Lena had given her many years ago. As she went into the living room in search of her purse, she heard the sound of someone driving up the gravel driveway.

Two ran to the door and stood there, but didn't bark. He seldom did unless he sensed trouble.

Rose walked to the window and saw a new pickup with tinted glass stop beneath the shade of the tall elm. A moment later, the driver got out, and she saw it was Curtis Largo.

Rose sighed. He was the last human being she wanted to see today. Without waiting for her to invite him inside, he strode toward her front door.

Annoyed by his lack of manners, she went out to the porch and stood there waiting.

"Good morning, Mrs. Destea," he said, climbing up the steps.

"I was just on my way out. How can I help you?" she asked coldly.

"I came to see the work you've done so far on the plant survey report. As you pointed out the other day, we *are* supposed to be working together, and I'm going to share responsibility for the report you'll be turning in."

"I haven't formalized my notes yet."

"Then let me look at what you do have, and we can talk about your plans for the presentation," he said, undaunted.

"I've tried to get your help before—several times, in fact—but you were too busy to even return my calls."

"But I'm here now."

Although she'd refused to let Bradford Knight look at her work, Largo was part of the tribe, and the council had specifically asked her to work with him.

She reluctantly invited him inside and showed him her notes. At least she'd stayed up last night typing them up on her daughter's computer. She'd intended to give Willie the printout along with her black ink sketches. "It's not finished, of course, but the maps I've drawn identify a general area and my sketches detail the condition of the plants, as do some of the photos I took."

"But you haven't been specific enough with the locations, and that reduces the credibility of the report. You're asking them to take your word for it—not reporting your findings in a scientific manner that can be verified by others."

"I can't reveal the collection sites. This report will go to outsiders as well, and could fall into many hands. The Singers who cooperated with me did so on the condition that I not disclose the exact locations." She paused, then took a deep breath. "And I agree with their decision. Those sites have to be protected."

"The tribe hired you to look into reports that some of our native plants are becoming endangered. You were supposed to investigate the matter thoroughly and report all the pertinent data. You haven't complied with that, and from what you've just said, you have no intention of doing so. When I pass this news along to the council members, I have a feeling they'll want to talk to you themselves. You may even be replaced by someone more qualified."

"They're welcome to do so," Rose said, ignoring that Largo was obviously after her job himself. "As a matter of fact, I invite them to bring up the issue."

Largo tried to pressure her for more information on the exact locations of her survey, but Rose refused to give him any details. Once he realized that he was wasting his time, Largo finally left.

Rose watched as the man sped off in his truck, leaving a huge cloud of dust behind him, then sat down again. As much as she disliked Largo, she had to admit he'd made a good point. The council was paying her to do more than deliver a report that basically said "trust me."

Yet, she couldn't give them precise information that would serve as a map to locating plants. The sites were under attack, and they needed to be protected. She considered what she knew. If the *hataaliis* were right and someone was following them, the thief would soon have an impressive body of knowledge concerning their sources, and be able to do untold harm. The thought filled her with disgust. It was bad enough that this thief was taking the Plant People—but turning all of them into accomplices made the deed even worse.

Rose took the box of candy and the vase with the flowers she'd cut for Lena, and drove directly to the hospital. She needed to see her friend today even more than ever. Rose was very worried about her. Although she'd make it a point not to tell Lena about Charlie, she was prepared to do whatever she could in order to quiet her fears. Lena had to be protected until she could find harmony and recover.

Rose arrived at the hospital a half hour later and went directly to Lena's room. Daylight streamed through the opened curtains, and in the bright light, Rose could see her friend's features were sunken, and her face was the color of ashes. Lena's eyes were dull and lacked focus. Frightened, but not daring to show it, Rose picked up a small visitor's chair and moved it over beside the bed, sitting down.

Lena looked at the vase of sunflowers Rose placed on the nightstand beside her and smiled weakly. "Thank you. These must be from your garden."

"They are. I also brought you some candy. Would you like a piece?" Seeing Lena shake her head, Rose placed the box beside the flowers. "I'll leave the box next to your bed so you can have some whenever you want."

"Did you find our friend?" she whispered, referring to Charlie.

Rose had never lied to Lena, but this time she had no choice. "He's found some of the plants that our medicine men needed so badly, and is trying to find a way to make sure everyone gets a fair share. He couldn't come back as he'd planned." That last part was certainly true.

"He knows the Plant People better than anyone. He'll do what's right." Mercifully, Lena didn't notice that Rose couldn't look her in the face.

Rose fought the tears that had begun to form in her eyes. Afraid that Lena would notice, she stood up and, pretending to search for a paper towel to clean up a few drops of water she'd spilled from the vase, stepped out of the room.

She was leaning against the wall, a few paper towels in hand, when Herman came up. "What's wrong? Is it our friend? Is she worse than before?"

Rose shook her head, then explained what had happened. "She just can't know what happened to *Cháala* yet. She won't be able to handle the news. But I've never lied to her before."

"You can't let her see you this upset, she'll know something is going on. Go on home. I'll tell her that you realized you were late for a meeting. Meanwhile, I'll take the paper towels and wipe up the water you spilled." He paused, then added, "Make sure you tell the others who might visit that we're keeping the news from her. We don't want her to hear the news accidentally. But wait, what about the television? Does she listen to the news?"

"Not usually. She's always called the TV news a 'litany of doom.' I hope she doesn't get so bored she picks up the habit while here," Rose said. "But you're right. We have to do something more."

"I'll tell her granddaughter, the rest of her family, and *Gishii* by phone right away. I'll also be going to a special meeting of the Plant Watchers this afternoon, so I'll tell all the ones I see there as well, but I'm sure *Gishii* will spread the news long before that."

"I'll go in now and see if I can distract her from her illness. She needs to take her thoughts away from it."

"Remind her how much I miss her," Rose added, her voice trembling.

Herman reached for her hand, but Rose shook her head. If he sympathized now she'd break down and cry. And once she started, she wasn't sure she'd be able to stop. Rose moved back, and looked at Herman for a moment, asking him silently to understand. His gaze filled with sympathy and compassion, and he nodded. Satisfied, she walked away.

After calling all of Lena's family members she could reach from home, Rose met the Plant Watchers at their scheduled gathering place southeast of the San Juan bridges in Shiprock. This spot was part of Clara Henderson's land—the allotment that her family had been given decades ago by the tribe. Here, upon a former sandbar that once stood in midriver, the Plant Watchers would learn about successful methods of enriching even the poorest of soils.

They were all seated on folding chairs in the shade of an old grove of cottonwood trees, and the Navajo nursery representative had not yet arrived. Rose took advantage of the moment and told the group about Charlie Dodge's death, cautioning them not to pass the news to Lena until she was better able to handle it.

The news had already reached most of them, but as they grieved together for their lost friend, Rose felt closer to them than ever. They were all grandmothers, with the exception of Sadie, the young Oglala Sioux woman, and they'd all seen death visit many times over the years. Somehow, they would survive the loss of Charlie's friendship as they had the other passings that had touched them, and go on. As Navajos they knew about survival, and as women, they'd learned how to endure the pain life often brought.

Yet, Rose bore an additional burden—that of guilt. She couldn't forget that she'd been the one who'd asked Charlie to look into the theft situation, and now he was dead. That was why she'd never give up until she had answers. If his death wasn't linked to her request, it would loosen the weight of guilt. If it was, she'd see justice done.

Another hour went by, and they discussed everything

they'd learned about building up the soil, increasing water holding capacity, and adding valuable nutrients and organic matter, but the Navajo nursery representative still failed to show up. "This may be partially my fault," Rose announced, aware that Curtis Largo worked for the nursery. "I'm having a very difficult time getting along with the man I was assigned to work with—a bureaucrat from the Navajo Forestry Department. He may have told the others not to work with us as a way to get back at me." Everyone sympathized with Rose as she told them what had happened.

"He may be an obstacle in your way, but the Anglo professor sounds like the perfect person for the job. He cares about his work, and sounds knowledgeable," Jane said.

Rose looked toward the road. "Maybe he can come and teach us better ways to restore our land and improve the soil."

"What's happening with the search for the Plant People? Have you made any progress in determining what's going on?" Fannie Woodis asked.

"The medicine men believe they're being followed to the collection sites, but they haven't actually seen anyone. Someone's watched me too, but he's always kept his distance. Of course, I've made sure I'm alone before I actually go to any site."

"Could this person who's following some of us to the collection sites be responsible for our friend's death in Arizona?"

Rose considered it. "I really don't know for sure, but it's a possibility."

"Then we all have to be extra careful that no one follows us when we go gather the Plant People," Fannie said firmly.

"My son usually takes me to gather the Plant People I need because I don't drive anymore. He'll watch out for him," Clara said.

"Just remember. Don't try to catch him," Rose said quickly,

recalling the rattler that had been placed in her pickup. "It's too dangerous. Just get a good look at him, then go. Once we have a description, we can turn everything over to the tribal police."

"I suppose you know that there's another chapter house meeting tonight—an emergency one—called to address the problem of the vanishing Plant People? After the last meeting, word got around and now the whole community knows that someone is stealing our special plants, and that some of the rare ones are disappearing or dying out. Enough people got worried, so it justified calling for a special meeting to discuss the problem. I got a phone call early this morning," Jane Jim said.

Rose remembered Curtis Largo's unexpected visit. Now she understood what had motivated that. He'd come to her home to get ammunition—anything he could use against her. He'd hoped to be able to tell everyone how little she'd done herself, and how she'd been wrong to blame him—after all, he'd even come to see her. Tonight, she suspected that Curtis would bend the truth any way he could to come out in a favorable light, especially after the last time. She bit back her anger as she told the others.

"We'll call everyone else we know and make sure they go tonight," *Gishii* said. "You'll have all the support you need."

Rose knew that *Gishii* was a bit of a gossip and spoke to practically everyone in the area. She had no doubt that once her friend put the word out, people would come.

After Rose said good-bye to the Plant Watchers, she drove directly to her son's home. She'd just parked her truck when Julian, her grandson, came running out the front door of the house.

The six-year-old ran over to her pickup, waiting impatiently as she climbed out of the cab. "*Shimasání!* Come and see!" Considering himself too old to take her hand any more, he ran over to a brand new bicycle leaning against the side of the house and stood proudly beside it. "I can go anywhere now! I even rode to your house today!"

"Do your parents know how far you're going all by yourself?" Rose said, suddenly worried. Julian had wanted a bike for a year now, but she'd advised Clifford not to buy it for him. She'd worried that Julian was too young to have the freedom it would pose.

"I won't get hurt. I know how to ride now! I went all the way up to the mesa behind your house, and from there I could see *everything*!"

Rose's chest tightened as she studied the mountain bike. It had tires meant to be driven over uneven terrain and soft, sandy ground. With this he could go practically anywhere. But, on a reservation where secrets were becoming all too common, there was no telling what a child could accidentally stumble across.

Before she could say anything to him, Clifford came out of the hogan, an elderly Navajo man right behind him. Recognizing Ben Tso, Rose nodded.

Seeing them motion for her to come join them, Rose left Julian and walked over to talk to the men. "I'm glad you're both here," she said. "May we go inside the hogan to speak?"

The *hataaliis* sat on the west side, the place of honor, and she sat in the north, as was customary for women. "I know the *hataaliis* have been on their guard, so I wanted to know if any of you have seen someone following you," Rose said.

Ben shook his head. "We were just discussing that particular problem. We've all seen the marks left by that little Army shovel, some very fresh, but no one suspicious is ever around by the time we get there. Sure we've seen neighbors in the area, and once or twice we've seen one of those white gas or oil company trucks, or a power plant service pickup, but they're common sights these days."

"Although our patients are our first priority, we've all decided to take a more active role in trying to stop or prevent these thefts," Clifford said. "We're asking people we know and trust to keep an eye out for anyone who grows native medicinal plants in their garden and to call us if it appears that the garden has grown significantly in the past several weeks. If the thief is one of our own, we'll find him."

"That's a good idea," Rose said. "I'm glad you thought of it."

Ben Tso stood up. "I have to travel to see a patient, so I have to be on my way. But please don't get up. It was good seeing both of you again."

He walked out, and several moments later they heard his vehicle driving off. Rose remained where she was.

"What's on your mind, Mother?"

"I'm worried about your son and his new bicycle. If you'd bought him a horse instead of that thing, he could still have had fun, but at the same time he would have learned about responsibility. There would have been balance in his life. With a bicycle . . ." Rose shook her head. "Do you realize how far he's going and the trouble a young boy can get into by himself?"

Clifford nodded and exhaled softly. "A bicycle costs a lot less than feeding and caring for a horse. That's why I chose it. But I require him to wear a safety helmet, and have forbidden him to go anywhere that's not within sight of the hogan. Yesterday he apparently rode up onto the mesa between your home and here and saw someone wandering around the canyon searching for something. I've been uneasy about it ever since. For all I know, it could have been the plant thief, and if the man saw my son . . ."

"Did your son recognize the person, or remember what he looked like?"

"He said he only saw him from far away. He was about to go up and talk to him when he saw a coyote, got scared, and came back home."

"A coyote?"

He nodded slowly. "That's what he said, but I have a feeling that what he saw was a dog. I've searched the area looking for coyotes, and I've found no indication of any." He pursed his lips and remained silent for a few moments. "I've asked my wife to go visit her mother for a few weeks and take him with her. They're leaving in a few hours. It's the safest course of action."

"You're right," Rose said. "I know it's hard for you to send them away, but I don't think you had another choice."

Clifford looked up at her. "And how have you been doing without my sister and her daughter around? Is it too quiet at home now?"

"I've missed them, but I've managed, even though I've had a few problems."

"Like what?"

His eyes grew wide as she explained about the break-in, then added the news of the death of Charlie Dodge, and her fears that the plant thief might have caused it.

"You should have told me right away, Mother. I would have come over and stayed with you."

"I'm not a child, son. Don't treat me like one. I deserve to be shown more respect than that. I can take care of myself—and I have."

"I meant no disrespect. But I don't want anything to happen to you."

"Nothing will," Rose said confidently. "Two is there with me, and I have a telephone. Tomorrow your sister will return as well. I'll have police watching me hang out the laundry if she has anything to say about it."

Clifford nodded. "She doesn't mean to interfere as much as she wants to protect you. It's her nature."

Rose nodded. "And it's mine to follow my own path."

Hearing the sound a vehicle, Clifford went to the door of the hogan. "It's my patient."

Rose stood and walked to the door of the hogan. "I'll leave you to your work, then."

As Rose climbed into her truck, she saw Clifford greet the middle-aged Navajo woman who'd just arrived. Rose was proud of her son. He was using his healing gifts to care for the tribe. She was proud of her daughter too, but dealing with Ella had always been much more difficult. Her daughter had always taken pride in going her own way. Danger, to her, was simply an interesting part of life, and certainly not something that would ever deter her from doing what she felt was right.

Suddenly Rose realized that she'd described herself as well, and the thought irritated her. "Ella, you're a difficult daughter even when you're not here," she whispered to no one at all.

Rose arrived alone at the chapter house meeting, which was scheduled to start after sundown. Men were outside talking and smoking, and kids were playing, running up and down the field behind the building, shouting back and forth.

As she walked from her parked truck toward the double doors of the building, Herman appeared from behind a row of vehicles and came over to join her. "The Anglo professor came up to me a few minutes ago. He said that you'd invited him?"

"Yes, I thought his presence as an authority would help me if any of the council members who are against my work decide to come tonight and challenge what I've done. I can ask the committee chairman to allow him to speak if it becomes necessary."

Among the crowd that had gathered there Rose caught glimpses of the Plant Watchers, and waved whenever she caught the attention of someone she recognized. "I wonder how all these people are going to fit inside the meeting room," Rose commented. "I haven't seen a crowd this large since the gambling issue came to a vote."

As Herman and she entered the crowded hall, Jane Jim came up. "We've saved a seat for you on the fifth row. It's the only one left. News that the traditionalists would descend here today must have reached a lot of ears, and now the modernists and new traditionalists are streaming in just to keep things even. I'm sorry there isn't another chair," Jane said to Herman.

"I'll stand in the back with the overflow. I just hope they don't have to send some of us outside because of the fire code problem." Herman shrugged. "See you after the meeting?"

Rose smiled and nodded. Hearing someone tap the speaker's microphone, Jane led her to their chairs among the group of Plant Watchers and sat down.

There was a brief introduction, a Navajo prayer, then the business at hand was brought to the forefront, leading with the situation with the Plant People. The new director of the nursery, who was chairing the meeting, presented an overview addressing the rumors, then opened the floor to questions or comments. Rose stood, and the committee chairman invited her to come up to the microphone at the front of the room.

She reported briefly on her observations, then added, "We're going to have to be careful with the plants that are scarce. Digging them up indiscriminately will have disastrous results."

There was a lengthy silence in the room as she returned to her seat. Then, just about the time she sat down, rumbles began to grow.

One elderly woman she recognized as Lena Clani's closest neighbor stood. "We've been taught from our childhood how to pick the plants we need. We ask the Plant People's permission, and leave an offering, then we take only what is necessary. That has always been our way. But now we go in with shovels. I don't blame the Plant People for not wanting to be around us anymore."

Another woman Rose recognized as one of the nurses at the hospital stood up as soon as Lena's neighbor sat down. "Plants are plants. They come, they go, as we've seen during the cold winters and recent drought. We're no longer living in the sixteenth century, so we can't afford to hold on to outdated thinking. Why are we blaming people for natural events? Some plants eventually die off. That's the way it is. If certain plants are really necessary for our spiritual and healing needs, then let's grow them at the Navajo Forestry Department nursery. We can maintain them there, and make them available to those who feel they need them."

The woman was deliberately ignoring the work of the plant thief, and she lacked some basic plant knowledge as well, such as the fact that some plants needed special conditions not present at the nursery. But Rose had to admit that some of what she said had merit, at least in concept.

She was about to support the basic concept when Maria Poyer stood up and took the floor. As Rose glanced in her direction, she noticed that Willie was sitting next to her. Before she could guess at the reason, Maria began speaking.

"If some of the Plant People want to move away, wave them good-bye. We'll develop more suitable plants, varieties that are more drought-resistant, better able to take the heat, with more nutritional value for us and our livestock, and with higher yields. We've always been poor because we refuse to take the knowledge that off-reservation schools teach and make it work for us. Clinging to the old ways simply because that's what we've always done will only lead us in circles."

As she took her seat, Ellen Mihecoby stood up. Rose knew her. She was of the Lone Tree Clan, traditional enemies of her people. Rose would have sooner trusted a rabbit to deliver carrots than believe Ellen would do anything but work mischief here today.

"We've heard Rose Destea tell us all that part of the problem is that plants are being overharvested. Now the traditionalists will look at the modernists, and vice versa, and everyone will blame everyone else. But the simple truth is this—only certain traditionalist groups are harvesting our native plants and using them for ceremonies or healing. If anyone's overharvesting, that's where we have to look. They know the best sites, and by their own admission, they've been all over the Rez searching for these plants. I can't think of better suspects."

Rose stared at her, aghast. The woman had publicly accused her and the Plant Watchers. Seething, but determined not to let it get the best of her, Rose stood. "As traditionalists, we follow the ways that have been taught to us for generations. We learn as children to never take more than we need, nor would we ever harvest the best. Using an entrenching tool to gather up the plants root and all, often destroying two plants before a third is successfully removed, is *not* the traditionalist method. We are not inept, and if we wanted to take a plant, it would be done in such a skillful way that no one could ever detect it was gone. Anyone who understood our teachings would know *that*."

She looked over at Professor Hoff and saw him waving at her, obviously wanting the chance to speak. Rose also noticed Maria was looking at him and her expression indicated she was annoyed.

Rose immediately asked the chairman's permission to allow Hoff to make a comment, pointing out his extensive credentials relevant to the issue. There were a few groans from some in the gathering, but Willie was allowed to speak.

In just a few sentences, Hoff mentioned his recent work with her, verifying her conclusions concerning the problems with local plants and expressing shock that anyone would believe Rose or the Plant Watchers would harm the tribe's plant legacy.

When Hoff sat back down, Rose was pleased to see Maria wouldn't even look at him, she was so angry.

Then, as several other people stood and spoke, the battle lines became fixed. It didn't take long before the meeting became more of a shouting match than a discussion. Finally the committee president took the floor again.

"Our prayer at the beginning of this meeting said that we'd come together to make things beautiful for each other. But look at what we're doing. We're dishonoring the land and the Plant People by arguing about them in this way." The stern admonition brought an uneasy peace. "I vote that we close this meeting for tonight. Nothing good can come when everyone is angry."

The meeting adjourned promptly thereafter, and as everyone left the building, Rose saw Professor Hoff and Maria leaving together through the side door. Their body language suggested Maria was still upset with him; still, their obvious friendship made her uneasy.

Deciding that the time to speak with them together had come, Rose headed for the same exit, but the moment she stepped outside, Ellen came up to her.

"For what it's worth, I really do think you should take a close look at your own people. Even if you're innocent, the Plant Watchers and the *hataaliis* are the obvious suspects. I heard recently that two girls—granddaughters of two Plant Watchers—were caught trying to dig up jimsonweed. There was a boy with them too, and I understand that he comes from a traditionalist family. My daughter goes to Shiprock High School, and everyone's talking about the incident. I believe you were the one who called it to the principal's attention."

Rose's heart sank. She'd suspected as much after hearing

the boy say that he'd gotten the drawings from a book his mother kept at home. But she hadn't wanted to believe it, and had shut the offending thought from her mind. Now, as Ellen confronted her with it, she knew it was the truth.

"Children make their own choices," Rose said sadly. "As parents, all we can do is our best. Traditionalist families face the same challenges as everyone else."

"When the kids from traditionalist families get caught between what they're taught at home and the real world, trouble is bound to follow. Look at the mess created by something as simple as a plant book one of the parents kept," Ellen replied.

"Modernist families face problems with their children too, such as drinking and drugs," Rose reminded.

Ellen shook her head. "You're just too stubborn about the old ways. You won't even come to the church your own husband founded. You should, you know, if only out of respect for him. I go each Sunday and people still ask about you."

"Do you go to the Catholic church as well?" Rose asked.

"Why? I'm not Catholic," Ellen replied.

"Nor do I belong to *your* church. So why can't you understand that I chose a different path than my late husband?"

Ellen was about to reply when she glanced to the far end of the parking lot and suddenly scowled. "I have to get going. My cousin parked next to me and I *know* how she drives. I don't have insurance either. . . . " Ellen stormed away.

With a sigh, Rose looked around, trying to remember where she'd parked her truck, when elderly Linda Bidtah came up to her. Rose greeted her in Navajo.

"Do you really believe that someone is deliberately stealing our Plant People?" Linda asked.

"Yes, I do, and in fact one of the areas that has been disturbed is not far from where you live. Have you seen any strangers hanging around or walking about?"

Linda thought about it, then shook her head. "No, I'm sorry."

As Linda walked away, joining her family, Rose saw another traditionalist woman she knew and walked over to greet her. Arlene Allison lived in the area around Crystal, another of the ravaged sites.

"You held your own very well inside," Arlene praised as Rose came up.

"Thank you," Rose said. "I'm glad to see you and I'd like to ask you a question. Have you seen anyone hanging around out by where you live? There are several collection sites near you."

"I haven't seen any strangers, and only a few of my neighbors," she said, then lapsed into a thoughtful silence. Moments later, she spoke again. "Come to think of it, something a little unusual happened about a week ago. I saw a gas company truck parked in the middle of a field near the area where I graze my sheep. I figured he was either lost or had run out of gas, but when I decided to walk over and ask him if he needed help, he drove off."

"Did you see the driver's face?"

"No, not clearly, I never got close, but he had one arm outside the driver's-side window, and from the skin tone, I'm pretty sure he was Anglo."

As someone called out to Arlene, and the woman walked away, Rose looked around for Herman, but he was nowhere to be seen. Lost in thought, she began walking to her pickup. The appearance of a gas truck around Arlene's house bothered her. She was almost certain that there were no gas lines around there. Everyone in that area used bottled gas or wood stoves. The gas truck shouldn't have been there—unless the gas company was planning on putting in new lines, or a new gas well had been drilled nearby. Or maybe the tribe was planning some kind of new development. She made a mental note to check into it.

Rose was about to get into her truck when Herman came over. "My nephews came to the meeting and have asked me to join them for some pie at the Totah Café. Why don't you come with us?"

Rose shook her head. "Thanks, but no. My daughter and granddaughter should be home soon and I want to see them both. I've missed them."

After saying good-bye to Herman, she got into her truck, glanced into the rearview mirror ready to back out, and saw Maria Poyer getting into Willie's fancy SUV. On impulse, she decided to make another attempt to talk to them and maybe learn exactly what their relationship was.

Rose waved, trying to get Professor Hoff's attention, but he was focused on maneuvering past another vehicle and apparently didn't see her. They sped off. Making up her mind to find out more about them, Rose started the truck and drove out of the parking lot.

Maybe, after she got a chance to visit with her granddaughter, Ella would be able to give her some pointers on what to do next.

FIFTEEN

—— ✖ ✖ ✖ ——

When Rose stepped inside the living room, Dawn leaped off the sofa and launched herself into her arms. Rose held her tightly, smelling the baby powder from Dawn's recent bath and suddenly remembering how she'd done the same for Ella at that age. "I'm so glad to see you back home!"

"*Shimasáni*, come with us next time!"

Ella looked at her daughter. "Hey, we did all right by ourselves, didn't we?"

Dawn nodded but said nothing.

Ella smiled at her mother. "She really did miss you."

"I missed her, and even you, daughter." Rose smiled at Ella, and gave her a hug as well.

Dawn had to tell her all about the trip, and chattered on almost nonstop until it was time for her to go to bed. Tonight, Rose insisted on reading her bedtime story. Truth was, she'd really missed her granddaughter, and she wanted to spend just a little more time with her.

Rose heard the phone ring as Dawn finally started getting sleepy. Rose was thankful that Ella picked it up quickly. Dawn fell asleep halfway through the story, and Rose tiptoed out. As she stepped into the kitchen, Ella was waiting there for her, leaning against the counter, arms crossed.

"Mother, how could you *not* call me?"

"I'm capable of reading her a bedtime story by myself, daughter."

"Don't play innocent. I know you heard the phone. I just spoke to Justine and you know darned well what I'm talking about."

Rose exhaled loudly. "It was my fault, I forgot to lock the back door, and someone got inside. But Two ran him off. That's all there was to it. You know, there was a time when locks weren't needed here."

"Mother, quit avoiding the real issue. Just about anything could have happened to you. Don't you see that?"

"But it didn't, and that's what we have to focus on."

"When did our roles switch?" Ella asked, exasperated. "You used to worry about *me*. Now here I am, worrying about *you*."

"Balance. That's something that will help us both walk in beauty."

Ella shook her head. "Mom, all I wanted was for you to live a nice settled life. Is that too much to ask?"

Hearing Ella saying the same thing she'd told her daughter countless times, Rose glanced up quickly and, seeing the twinkle in Ella's eyes, burst out laughing.

The following morning, after Dawn had gone off to day school and Ella had left for work, Rose sat outside in the porch with Two. She needed time to think, so she was going to spend a quiet morning at home.

She'd only been sitting there for five minutes when she saw a vehicle coming up the road. A moment later a young woman pulled up in a green pickup. Rose invited her in, recognizing Ben Tso's granddaughter, Mae.

"Granddad asked me to stop by today and give you a message," Mae said. "He spoke to a patient of his about the Plant Watcher who used to live over past Teec Nos Pos."

Rose knew she meant Charlie Dodge, and her heart began to beat faster.

"Apparently he was seen with a tall man, maybe an Anglo. That's not much of a description, but that's all he was able to get from his patient. The woman lives out by Beclabito, and had spoken to the Watcher on the same day his body was found at the bottom of Rabbit Bluff. She told granddad that, as she was leaving, she glanced back and saw a truck drive up. Then a tall light-skinned man got out and joined the Plant Watcher."

"Did the Watcher and the Anglo stay there, or did they leave?" Rose asked quickly.

"They each got into their own pickup and drove up a dirt trail toward Rabbit Bluff."

"Your grandfather's patient has to tell the police. It's very important."

"Grandfather knows that, and tried to convince her, but she refused. She doesn't like to talk to people she doesn't know, especially about dead people."

"Can you tell me who she is? I may be able to talk to her and make her understand."

"No. Granddad said to tell you that he'll talk to her again, but he can't say anything more unless his patient allows it. He also asked that you not try to find out who it is because this has to be her decision."

Rose bit back her frustration. It shouldn't have surprised her. This was the way things usually worked on the reservation. Traditionalists, particularly the older ones, seldom trusted the police department, an institution they saw as an invention created to uphold *bilagáana* laws.

"Ask him to insist, if he can. It's possible that Anglo man was the last person to see our friend alive. It's also possible he's the one who's been taking our plants." As Mae nodded, she continued. "By any chance did his patient happen to mention seeing a gas company truck?"

Her eyes grew wide. "No. Don't tell me that they're going to put up housing in that beautiful spot!"

"I don't know if they are. I've just heard reports of a gas company truck appearing at some very unlikely places."

"She didn't mention it as far as I know. But traditionalists who choose to live way out there between Beclabito and the state line don't like the way the towns are encroaching on old reservation communities. If Granddad's patient had seen a gas service truck, I'm sure it would have bothered her enough to tell him about it." She glanced at her watch. "I've got to go now."

"Thank you for stopping by."

Rose went inside the house and called a friend of hers at the gas company. "Susan, I've been hearing about a gas service truck driving around in places where there aren't any utilities," She said, giving her the general locations. "Do you have any idea what it might have been doing there?"

"We have no new developments we're working on, so that's not it. My guess is someone was taking a lunch break."

"Thanks. I appreciate it."

"Anytime. That ointment you made when my daughter had that terrible rash really took care of things for her. I'm glad I was finally able to do something for you in return."

As Rose hung up, frustration rippled through her. She still wasn't sure what part—if any—the gas company truck played. For all she knew, the employee was trying to scout out a secluded spot to be with a girlfriend or boyfriend.

Rose went out to work in her garden. Sometimes it was the only thing that cleared her mind. She was busy pulling newly sprouted weeds in one section while the hose soaked another when she heard the phone ring.

Rose went back into the kitchen, promising herself that the next time Ella offered to buy a cordless, she'd say yes.

Before she even picked up the receiver, her stomach tightened. The news the caller would bring would upset her.

Rose forced herself to pick up the receiver anyway.

"It's Kevin," he said.

"Good morning."

"I have some news for you. You know that I still serve as a tribal attorney?"

"Yes."

"In that capacity, I'm now taking care of some business associated with your friend—the Plant Watcher who passed away."

Rose scarcely breathed. She wondered if he was about to tell her that Charlie's killer had been found—or, at the very least, that the police had accepted the fact that he had been murdered.

"The deceased left a letter asking that when he died, his body should be buried in a particular spot just north of the old Hogback trading post, at least where it used to be, but we haven't been able to find any surviving family members who can carry this out. The tribe buries all unclaimed bodies in a tribal cemetery." He paused, then added, "I thought you'd want to know."

Burials . . . the dead . . . She wasn't sure she could handle any of this. "Isn't there any way for the tribe to honor his request? He was a military veteran, and did so much for the tribe by working with the Plant People."

"We'll never be able to go through the paperwork necessary in time to get it done. Later on, though, his body could be moved, I suppose. I wouldn't have said anything to you, but you were mentioned in his letter, and his modest savings account is now yours."

The news surprised her, and made her miss Charlie even more. "Give me a while to think about how to take care of this. Is his body in Arizona? I thought that they might do a medical workup just to make sure it wasn't murder."

"The official making the final decision has read the patrolman's report and concluded that it was an accident."

"They're wrong, you know," she said quietly.

"It *was* their call," he said firmly.

"All right. Give me a few hours to figure out a few things, then I'll be in touch with you," Rose said.

As she placed the phone down, her hand began to tremble, then her body. Charlie Dodge's final request *had* to be honored, and if there was no one else, it fell onto her to see that it was done.

Rose took a deep breath, and then looked up Dr. Carolyn Roanhorse-Lavery's office number. If anyone could help her now, it would be the tribe's medical examiner.

Rose dialed the number and Carolyn answered after the second ring.

Rose explained why she was calling, though she couldn't bring herself to mention Charlie's name out loud, even knowing Carolyn wouldn't have been concerned. "I follow traditional ways. Can you help me find anyone who would be willing to dig the grave and bring the coffin?"

"There's an Anglo man who often works for me. I think he'd be happy to help you."

"I have another favor to ask," Rose said in a heavy voice. "I believe my friend was murdered—probably pushed off that cliff, a place called Rabbit Bluff, over by Teec Nos Pos and just on the Arizona side of the reservation. My friend wouldn't have jumped or gone so close to the edge willingly because he was so afraid of heights, so you might be able to tell if he put up a fight. I asked the police to look into it, but the investigating officer apparently just looked at the position of the body and wrote it down as an accident. I'm sure that if *you* examine the body, you'll be able to find some evidence that will make them investigate a little further."

Carolyn remained silent for several moments. "All right. I'm not busy right now, which is a good thing, I suppose, so I'll do it for you. But, just so you know, I would have said no to anyone else who'd asked me the same thing. The paperwork on this is going to be tricky."

"You'll be doing the tribe a great service," Rose said.

"But if you're wrong, all this is going to cost the tribe some money." She took a deep breath. "No, never mind. I'll cover the expense in my budget somehow."

"You won't have to do that once you find something. I'm right about this," Rose said firmly.

Carolyn said nothing for what seemed an eternity. "I believe you," she said at last. "Over the years, I've learned that the intuitions the women in your family have are as reliable as the next sunrise. I know the numbers to call, so I'd better get to it. I'll be in touch with you later."

Rose placed the phone down, tension gripping her body. She wasn't wrong—and, now, everyone would know—including the killer, who'd thought his crime wouldn't be discovered.

The following afternoon, Rose got the call she'd been waiting for.

"I've finished the autopsy," Carolyn said. "Tissue and fluid samples will have to be analyzed, but I have preliminary results. Your friend didn't die from the fall."

"I knew it," Rose said quietly.

"But it wasn't murder. Not exactly, anyway. He died of a heart attack. He may have fallen as a result—or it's possible the heart attack was caused when someone threatened to push him off the cliff. But your instincts were right. There's more to this case than meets the eye. I've sent the results to the homicide investigator at the Chinle Police Station, and after he checked with his superiors, he called back and told me that the case will be reopened."

Rose exhaled softly. "It's a beginning."

"I've also found someone who will take the body from our morgue to where he wanted to be buried, behind that old trading post. It's the Anglo man I told you about. The burial will take place in about two hours."

"I've got to visit my son first for a special medicine bundle, then I'll go straight there. But I won't come all the way to the grave site. My friend knew me too well to have expected that."

As Rose hung up, she thought about Charlie. She'd said good-bye to too many people she'd loved throughout her life, and it never got any easier. Time passed, and the memories robbed pain of its sting somewhat, but there was never any way to recover what was lost.

As she grieved alone, she remembered the story her mother had told her once to help her understand the things that defied explanation. It was part of the teachings of the Navajo Way, and the story was one she'd committed to heart.

Rose closed her eyes and thought back to those days. She could almost see her mother's gentle face and hear her soft voice as she told the story: *In the beginning, the hero twins, Monster Slayer and Child-of-the-Water, the sons of Sun, were sent to conquer the monsters that preyed upon man. Just when they'd thought that they'd freed the earth of all the evils there, they met four strangers—Cold, Hunger, Poverty, and Death. Cold told the heroes that they could kill her, but if they did, there would be no snow and no water to give the crops in the spring. Realizing that she was needed, the hero twins let Cold live.*

Then the brothers met Hunger. The monster explained that if they killed him, the people would lose their appetites and there would be no more pleasure in feasting and eating. So the heroes let him live as well.

Poverty was an old man dressed in dirty rags. He urged them to kill him and put him out of his misery. But he also warned that if he died, old clothes would never wear out and people would never make new ones. Everyone would be dirty and ragged like he was. The heroes knew that they had to let him live.

Finally they met Death. She was old and bent and frightening to behold, so the heroes were certain that they should kill her. But she warned them to think hard before they did because if she ceased to be, the old people would not die and give up their places to the young. She told them that as long as she existed, the young men could marry and have children. She assured them that she was their friend, though they didn't know it yet. The hero twins allowed her to live, and that is why we still have death.

As Rose opened her eyes, her mother's voice and face faded once again to the back of her memory. The story comforted her now. Even in dying there was balance and harmony.

After she arrived in front of her son's stacked eight-sided log medicine hogan, Rose parked and then remained seated, waiting for her son to appear. Before long, Clifford came to the entrance of the hogan and invited her in by cocking his head.

Rose walked over to meet him. "Good afternoon, son. My old friend from Teec Nos Pos is being buried today. I wanted to know if you had a special medicine bundle I could use."

"You're going to the grave site?" he asked, surprised.

"No, but I'll be close by. I need to see this through. It's a duty. . . ."

"There's no relative?"

She shook her head. "None that can be found. I've accepted the responsibility."

Clifford gathered substances from several pottery bowls,

then placed several pieces of flint into the small medicine pouch. "Take this. It will give you protection," he said. "Let me know if you need to talk or if there's anything else I can do to help you."

"Thank you, son."

As she walked back to her truck, she couldn't help but notice that it was a beautiful day—the kind that Charlie had loved. He'd lived a full life, and done his service to his country, and to the *Dineh,* the Navajo people.

Remembering Charlie's letter and instructions, she once again began to wonder about his unusual request. That location hadn't been one of his plant collection sites, nor was there anything particularly noteworthy about the area except that it was once a gathering place for Navajos who'd come to trade and purchase off-reservation goods.

The Hogback trading post was located just at the eastern edge of the Navajo Nation, and wasn't close to where Charlie had lived most of his life. Most puzzling of all, Charlie never been the kind to do things without purpose. Sadly, his reasons would probably remain a mystery to her forever now.

An hour later, she arrived at the old, dilapidated half-adobe building, which butted up against the nearly vertical sedimentary rock walls of the Hogback. Though the painted signs still remained advertising Navajo rugs, the store had been abandoned for some time. Fifty yards to the north, at a spot halfway between two large boulders and not far from the base of the tall Hogback ridge, the man with the Laverys—Carolyn and her husband Michael, was digging the grave. The ground was soft, and it wasn't long before he was waist-deep into the earth.

Suddenly the man yelled and jumped back out to the surface where the Laverys stood. Rose saw him gesturing down, agitated. Carolyn and Michael stepped forward and peered into the hole.

Rose had a feeling that they'd just discovered the reason

why Charlie had been so adamant about being buried at this spot exactly halfway between the boulders. Tightly grasping the *jish* that her son had made for her, she approached slowly, torn between curiosity and the need to stay away.

Rose came within ten feet of the grave site, then stopped and peered down into the hole. Holding her breath and saying a prayer, she took another step forward. Even at this distance, she could see what had disturbed them. There appeared to be an old wooden box, the length of a coffin, already there. It was falling apart, with large gaps between the boards. Fortunately, she couldn't see inside.

"Did your friend ever tell you why he'd chosen this exact spot?" Carolyn asked.

Rose shook her head. "Who among the Navajo talks about graves and burials?"

Carolyn took a deep breath. "That box looks like two packing crates nailed together. I want to make sure that it holds a body, not something else. It might just be something that came from the old trading post."

Carolyn looked at the Anglo man who'd dug the grave. He had remained beside the hole, still looking at the large box. "The thing is falling apart, Jerry," Carolyn told him. "Pry back one of the boards so we can see inside."

As she heard Carolyn's instructions, Rose's legs nearly buckled. When the workman pried back a loose board with the shovel and she heard the creak of the wood, she shut her eyes tightly. A heartbeat later, the board broke loose with a thud—it was too rotten to really snap—then nothing.

No one said a word. Unable to stand the sudden, total silence, she opened her eyes and saw Carolyn and Michael crouched down beside the pine box. Rose stepped back, horrified, as Carolyn reached for something inside the container and pulled it out.

"This person was buried in what I think is a World War II Marine uniform," Carolyn said thoughtfully. "And this dog tag," she said, glancing down at what she was holding, "identifies the body as that of your Plant Watcher friend—the man we came here to bury today."

Stunned, Rose stared at Carolyn as she handed the metal tag to her husband. "But that's impossible." She looked back at the inexpensive pine casket that contained Charlie's body. "What in the world is going on here?" Rose looked at Carolyn, then Michael, and finally the Anglo man who'd uncovered the old grave, but no one had any answers.

SIXTEEN
—— ✖ ✖ ✖ ——

Michael Lavery stood by his wife, still looking at the dog tag, a small rectangular piece of aluminum, which had a slender piece of frayed cord attached. "Soldiers usually wear two dog tags. Where the other one?"

Carolyn glanced inside the box again. "There's only that one tag."

"I know that in the military, at least the way it used to be, one tag was taken off by the burial detail for recordkeeping and the other was left on the body. Since this was no military burial, I would have expected both to still be there. One thing's for sure, another Navajo would have never kept one of the dog tags as a memento."

"I've known my friend for thirty years or more. How did the man buried in this grave get *his* dog tag?"

"I don't know, but I'm going to have to call the police," Carolyn said. "By several feet at least, we're still on tribal land, so that means Shiprock and tribal jurisdiction."

Rose sat on a sandstone rock in the shade of Hogback, well away from the grave, as they waited. Charlie had wanted them to dig here. Finding the body had not been an accident. But she still had no idea what it all meant.

Carolyn cleared her throat and walked over to Rose. "There's a patrolman being dispatched and he'll be here shortly. Because I would have been called to this scene anyway, my husband and I are going to save time and take a closer look at the skeleton. We want to try to figure out if there's any evidence concerning how he died. You might want to go for a small walk."

"Yes, thank you." Rose stood and walked away. Behind her, she could hear the men shoveling away the remaining dirt from around the box. With a shudder, she headed farther south toward the old trading post to wait.

Sometime later Carolyn came to meet her with the police officer who'd responded to the call, a man Rose recognized as Sergeant Joseph Neskahi. Rose stood up as they approached and braced herself.

"My husband and I checked the skeleton, but there's no physical evidence to indicate he was murdered. The police chief has decided not to move the body from the grave it obviously has been in for decades, and a local judge concurred after a quick phone call. The general consensus is that we've found an unmarked grave dating back to the forties, and we should leave it alone."

Rose nodded. "Put my friend's coffin beside that one, then. This is where he asked to be buried, and I think we should respect that."

Carolyn glanced at the man she'd hired for the burial and gave him a nod.

"But will you do one thing for me first?" Rose asked Carolyn. Without waiting, she added, "Fingerprint the man we came to bury, and send his prints to the FBI in Washington so they can compare them to his military records. I'd like to confirm who he really was, now that there is apparently some doubt."

"I agree, otherwise we may have to dig the body up later

anyway," Neskahi said. Then, looking at Carolyn, he added, "Doctor, what do you say?"

Carolyn nodded. "Consider it done."

Rose stood way back as Carolyn opened Charlie's coffin, with the help of her husband, and completed the task. When the coffin was finally interred, alongside the decomposed body already there, Rose felt an undeniable sense of relief. It was now time to leave.

Thanking everyone for their help, Rose returned to her pickup and drove away. She would never return here again.

Rose decided to stop by her son's hogan before she went home, though she had to pass by her house on the way. Even with the *jish,* she felt she needed something more to protect her now.

When Rose explained the circumstances to him, Clifford winced. "You were right to come back here first."

Clifford sang a Song of Blessing over her, and as he did her worries lifted. She felt clean again. Had she been near the body of an enemy, Rose would have had a proper Sing, one that would have lasted over a week. But this and the *jish* would be enough for now.

Once she got home, Rose showered and changed. After having a light snack, she sat out on the porch to watch her granddaughter playing under the shade of an arbor made of tree branches.

The heat soon became uncomfortable, and Rose went back into the house. She'd just poured herself some iced tea when the phone rang.

It was the councilman who'd hired her. "This is John Begay. We've received a complaint concerning your survey work that we need to look into. We need to see what you've done so far."

She knew that Curtis Largo had done as he'd said, telling

Begay and other officials that her report wouldn't meet their requirements. "I'll have a preliminary draft ready for you tomorrow by ten in the morning."

"That'll will be fine. We'll see you then."

Rose immediately called Willie, first thanking him for speaking on her behalf at the chapter house meeting, then getting to the point. "I really need your help, Professor," she explained. "If I could give them grids or coordinates that will specify a general area in the scientific terms they so love, I believe that would still satisfy them. Also, I'm going to need to indicate the scientific names for the plants, and more details, in scientific terms, about the soil conditions and terrain."

"Come on over to my house right now. Bring everything, including any computer files you may have saved on floppy disks. We'll get that report in tip-top shape in no time."

She detected his confidence and enthusiasm, and knew that he would enjoy the challenge. "I really appreciate this, Willie."

"Don't mention it."

Rose gathered the few photos, her many sketches, notes, and the maps she'd drawn, and a copy on diskette of her text files from Ella's computer, then set out for Farmington.

When she arrived, the front door to his home was open, and hearing her truck, Kenmore pushed the screen door open and ran toward her, tail wagging. The mastiff's powerful body looked too big to make a quick stop and Rose braced herself, her back against the truck. But Kenmore came to a dead stop just inches before her, and sat down, his tail wagging furiously. She didn't have to lean down to pat his head, something that never failed to impress her. It was a very good thing that Kenmore was an agreeable dog.

Willie came out the door a moment later and laughed at the sight of her and the dog. "Don't just stand there, come on in!" he greeted.

Willie led her into his den, and together at a large desk, they began to compile her notes and sketches into a formal presentation. Willie scanned her sketches onto his computer, then printed them out.

The final draft looked very professional, and Willie added a final touch by binding the approximately eighty pages in a special folder.

"I don't know how to thank you for this, Professor. It looks wonderful, and gives them what they asked for without forcing me to violate any confidential information."

"It should impress them—and shut them up, at least for a while," Willie said with a smile. "Now we should celebrate. Why don't you stay and have dinner with me? I have some steaks we can put on the grill, and some fresh corn on the cob."

She couldn't say no, not after he'd spent most of his afternoon helping her. "Let me call home and tell them not to expect me, then I'll be happy to join you." Rose asked to use his phone, and was shown back into his den.

"I'll be outside getting the grill started," Willie yelled as he walked back into the kitchen.

Rose sat down at his desk, and as she spoke to Jennifer, the phone cord brushed against a paperback novel Willie was reading and knocked the book to the floor. As she discussed Dawn's dinner, Rose picked it up, but a photo that had been tucked inside the book fell out. Rose reached for it next and saw that it was a Polaroid taken of Willie and Maria at a party.

She'd hung up and was studying the photo when Willie came in.

Seeing the photo in her hand, he asked, "Did that photo drop out of the book? I've been using it as a bookmark to remind myself to get a frame for it. It was taken at a birthday party a friend of mine threw for me a few months ago."

"I know the woman," Rose said.

"Ah, and you saw her with me at the chapter house meeting. Your tone suggests you don't like her. Is that it?" he asked.

"It's not a matter of liking or disliking, but there is tension between us because of our different philosophies."

He nodded slowly. "Maria is a very bright young woman, though a bit too idealistic—a common ailment a lot of young people share. In time I think she'll be a great asset to your tribe. Don't underestimate her ability, or her intentions. All she needs is a few more years of experience and maturity."

He placed the photo back in the inside flap of the book. "I came to ask you if you'd like your corn broiled over the coals or boiled."

"Whichever way you prefer is fine," Rose answered. There had been a strong undercurrent of emotion laced through his words when he'd spoken of Maria. Despite his clear, logical answer, she had a feeling that there was more going on between them than he was saying.

Rose joined Willie in the kitchen, and proceeded to make herself useful husking the corn while he marinated the steaks. Once the coals were ready in the barbecue, they went outside to the patio in the back. As they prepared dinner, Willie was uncharacteristically quiet. It was clear that something serious was weighing on him.

Twenty minutes later, when they sat down to eat, Rose realized that he'd cooked a small steak for Kenmore as well, a reward for the monstrous dog, who had rested on the grass the entire time, watching but not nosing the food. The dog seemed very happy.

"Kenmore's reward isn't entirely altruistic," Willie explained, seeing her watching him as he placed the steak down inside a dog dish the size of a Dutch oven. "When he watches us eat, he'll start to drool. Soon afterwards, he'll shake—and after that, I guarantee, our appetites will be ruined. On the other hand, if he gets a steak now, he'll eat and then lie down for a nap."

"You certainly know your animal," Rose said with a laugh.

Willie smiled. "I spoil him, but he's my family, and he's great company. I lived alone for many years after my wife died. Then I got Kenmore. These days I can't imagine not having him around. A man couldn't have a better buddy."

"A pet can make a lot of difference. After my husband died, there was a period of time when I lived completely alone. My daughter came home several months later after she resigned from the FBI, but the days before she arrived were long ones for me. I'd never lived completely alone until then—not ever. Dog showed up at my door one dark night, and after that was my constant companion. Of course, Dog was a lot smaller than your Kenmore."

They chatted amicably through dinner. Then, as they gathered up their plates and took them back inside, Willie's mood grew somber.

"Recently I learned that the Plant Watcher who died just inside Arizona was a friend of yours," he said.

She looked at Willie in surprise, wondering how he'd known and if he'd been a friend of Charlie's. She nodded. "He was a dear friend."

"At first I was told that the police had ruled what happened to him as an accidental death. Later, a friend of mine who does contract work for the tribe transporting bodies told me that an autopsy had been done. Do you know why?"

"It was necessary."

"Why?" he pressed.

"Because I knew he'd been murdered," she said, deciding to be completely honest. He deserved that from her after all the help he'd given her. "Now, thanks to the autopsy, we all know that the fall didn't kill him—it was a heart attack, which may have been caused by the fall itself, or by being forced to the edge of the cliff where the ground was unstable." She paused, then slowly added, "I've also managed to learn that an Anglo man was seen with him the day he died."

Willie took a deep breath. "That Anglo could have been me. I went to see him to learn more about Navajo herbal medicine. I wanted to include the information in a book I'm writing. But I wasn't the only one who came to see him that day. After I left, just as I got onto the main road, I saw a gas company truck heading out to his camp."

"When you talked to him, did our friend mention that he was expecting company?"

"No, it was just the opposite, in fact. At one point I asked him what he planned to do that day and he said that he was going to stay out a bit longer and see if he could find some herbs he was looking for. He said that whenever he went out into the desert by himself, he was always at peace because he could almost feel the interconnectedness of everything. I remember him saying that in particular, because I mentioned the Global Consciousness Project being conducted by Princeton University and we got sidetracked discussing that for nearly another hour."

"The what?"

He smiled. "It's an experiment that's found a way of measuring the concept that one mind interacts and combines with another and then another until there's what they've called a global consciousness." Willie paused and smiled. "It's a fancy way of saying that all things are interconnected. Isn't it funny how we're all just beginning to discover what the Navajos have known since the beginning?"

Rose smiled. "We've gone from being labeled primitive and superstitious to being called insightful. Isn't that always the case when people suddenly find that they agree with you? That must have amused him."

"Yes, it did."

Her thoughts back on Charlie, Rose continued. "Did you happen to get a good look at the driver of the gas company truck?"

"No, I didn't. I just remembering catching a glimpse of it on my rearview mirror as it turned off where I'd just been."

"So you can't really say that the driver met with our friend—just that was heading in his direction when you last saw him?"

"Yes, precisely."

"When you two were speaking, were you at the top of the bluff?"

"No, we were in the valley below." He watched her for a long moment. "You know that a heart attack could have simply been caused by his age, maybe exertion from climbing onto the bluff, and the fall was subsequent to it," he said gently. "It doesn't have to be murder."

"But it is," she said simply. "And I will prove it."

The following morning, as Rose was getting dressed for her meeting with John Begay and the other tribal officials, Ella came into the bedroom and greeted her mother with a Cheshire-cat smile.

"Hey, Mom, what's this I hear? You've got another boyfriend? And a professor, no less! I need to start learning your tactics. I've yet to find one guy to go out with regularly, and now you've got two."

"You're being impertinent," she said with a tiny smile.

"Fess up, Mom."

"You may get more of an answer than you wish," she said, deliberately teasing her daughter's imagination.

Ella stared at her, surprised. "You can't stop there!"

Rose laughed. "There's nothing between Professor Hoff—Willie—and me. I stayed for dinner because he said he had something to discuss." Rose told Ella what she'd learned and watched her frown.

"Mom, I don't like this. If what you suspect is true, you're going to stir up a hornets' nest."

"Maybe so, but I have no other choice."

"Let *me* look into it."

"Other officers are already involved. You don't need to take on more responsibilities—you've got enough to do already."

"Yes, but I can find the time to—"

Rose shook her head. "Whatever extra time you can find, you need to spend with your daughter." She met Ella's gaze and held it. "If I need your help, I'll let you know. Until then, we'll do what we are each called upon to do for the tribe."

"But Mom, I—"

Rose held up one hand. "You seem to think of me as someone you have to take care of, but I'm not. I've been taking care of myself for a very long time. Why is it that you trust me to take care of your daughter, but not to take care of myself? That, daughter, doesn't make a lot of sense."

"Mom, I know you're a fighter and that you have a bright mind, but you're going into territory you're not familiar with. When you pursue a criminal, or start digging up secrets others want to keep covered, trouble comes at you from every corner."

"Daughter," Rose finished putting up her grayish black hair into a bun. "I intend to be careful. But if someone caused my friend's heart attack, I *will* find out about it."

"Do you realize that, even if you do, you may never be able to prove it in a way that will lead to a prosecution? You might get sued, that's all."

Rose smiled. "I'm not as concerned with the Anglo system of justice as you are. To expose a killer in our midst will restore balance in a way that goes beyond Anglo justice. And if he's a member of our tribe, it will be even more so."

Rose saw understanding flash in her daughter's eyes. She knew what happened when the tribe shut someone out. They simply ceased to exist as far as the tribe was concerned. No one spoke to them, no one acknowledged their presence.

"You rely on your weapons and backup," Rose continued. "I rely on my wits and common sense. Your weapon can misfire or jam, and backup may never arrive." She paused and looked directly at Ella. "Now tell me who has the better deal."

"Mom, you should have been a lawyer," Ella said, following her into the kitchen, then grabbing her pistol and ammunition from the top shelf. "I'll see you later tonight. In the meantime, be careful."

After Ella left, Rose gathered her reports and notes and placed them inside a large purse which normally remained stored on a closet shelf. The beautifully decorated, hand-tooled leather purse, more like a portfolio with handles, had been given to her by her late husband many years ago, and was still in fine condition.

Today, she was going in prepared with a report that would be even better than the council had expected, and the knowledge gave her confidence. Ready to do battle, she grabbed the keys to the truck and left home.

SEVENTEEN

✖ ✖ ✖

It was a few minutes past ten when Rose met with four tribal council members in a committee meeting room with a long, shiny wooden table and soft, comfortable chairs with padded armrests. Franklin Lee and Bernice Pioche were both were in their early sixties and wore modernist clothing. Their expressions were somber, as were those of John Begay and Kevin Tolino.

Bradford Knight and Curtis Largo joined the gathering as well, having come in just after her. The two men sat to the right of Rose and, like her, across the table from the four council members.

When Councilman Begay asked to see the report, Rose presented him with the two copies Willie had printed off, then remained quiet as they circulated around the table.

It seemed an eternity to Rose as the council members murmured among themselves and turned the pages. Out of the corner of her eye, she could see Curtis and Bradford stealing furtive glances at each other as they leafed through the copy a councilman had passed to them.

"I think these are wonderfully done," Bernice said at last, putting her reading glasses away.

"But they're not what she was hired to do. They are *not* location-specific," Largo argued.

Bernice gave him a stony look. "She's protecting the sites. That's reasonable, particularly since copies of these reports will go to people we hardly know, let alone trust."

"It wouldn't make sense to trust strangers with important tribal secrets," Kevin added. "Besides, one can't identify a specific plant on a map unless it's an enormous tree. Living things are subject to constant forces, and next season such a map may be obsolete."

"I still can't sanction a report I've yet to see before today except as disorganized notes. I was hired to work with her, but we've yet to do so," said Largo.

Rose cleared her throat. Having anticipated this issue, she brought out a piece of paper listing by date and time every contact she'd attempted to make with Curtis, and the outcome— usually leaving a message asking for a return call. She set it down so the council members could read it. "This is a record of the many times I have tried to contact our tribal expert to solicit his help, but apparently his other duties have prevented him from responding. Out of respect for his scheduling conflicts and conflicting priorities, I've found another authority with very impressive credentials the Anglo world respects."

Largo dismissed her list with a gesture. "This woman is using the temporary assignment the tribe generously granted her as an excuse to stir up trouble on every front. Recently, I understand that she actually unearthed the resting place of a Navajo buried in an unmarked grave. In addition to disturbing the remains of our ancestors, she's apparently taken it upon herself to prove that the plants are endangered as the result of a conspiracy perpetrated against the tribe."

Although she was furious, Rose concentrated on remaining

calm. "I have seen evidence—which can be corroborated by several other well-respected members of our tribe—that some of our rare plants are being harvested almost to extinction by one or more malicious individuals," she said, deliberately not telling them about the entrenching tool. "That's a fact. As far as digging up a grave—those circumstances have nothing to do with my job for the tribe," Rose said firmly. "That can be verified by tribal police officers in Arizona and New Mexico, two highly qualified medical examiners, and a tribal council member currently at this meeting."

"What she says is accurate and true," Kevin said. "The burial situation was a separate matter involving a tribal member. I asked her to get involved."

"Mr. Knight," Bernice said, "we haven't heard from you yet. What is your interest in this?"

Knight looked pale, but as he spoke, his face became red immediately. "I was asked by my tribal contacts to use native plants whenever appropriate to reclaim and restore the areas where mining has taken place. I personally requested a list of endangered plants from Mrs. Destea to make sure I stayed clear of those, but she refused to show me the report. Having given the matter a lot of thought, I'm now asking that the council rescind their request altogether, and allow my company's experts to choose the plants that are to be used."

"Why? You'll eventually get a copy of the report," Bernice said. "Expecting to get one before the tribe does is very presumptuous of you, I believe."

"Perhaps. But as I said, I've given this a great deal of thought. The truth is that native plants are problematic. Although the many varieties we've chosen in the past have all been very difficult to keep alive once they're transplanted, I support the suggestion made by some members of the tribe who advocate using genetically engineered or hybrid plants designed to survive and flourish in local environments. I think those plants would have a much better chance of surviving the shock of transplant, and be far more useful in the long run." He went on to formally detail some of the plants Maria Poyer was working with, and explained their uses as forage for livestock.

Bernice looked at Rose. "What do you say to this?"

"Transplanting plants isn't always easy," Rose admitted. "The Plant Watchers have advised the power company to be very selective and use only the strongest native plants—the ones that know how to survive. The Plant People like to choose homes they can be comfortable in. The scientist world calls it "succession," I was told, but it all amounts to the same thing. One plant will prepare the land for another, if you choose right. Tumbleweeds protect the soil from the wind, then snakeweed comes and, because of their long roots, pull nutrition up from the soil. Other plants follow, and in time the land is restored."

Knight exhaled loudly. "We *have* tried to use native plants, but the failure rate is still unacceptably high. Mining *has* changed the soil structure. I strongly advise the council to consider letting Maria Poyer work with us to reclaim the land. We'd all come out ahead then."

Curtis Largo nodded. "I agree. Plants come and go and that's the way it is with everything. If we have the means to develop and introduce better, heartier plants, they'll provide for the tribe, and the project will pay for itself in the long run."

"Everything *is* connected," Rose replied, "so we have to be very careful which plants we consider, because that will affect other living things, like the wild animals. When you upset the balance, bad things tend to follow. If we introduce something new, we also have to safeguard the old because that's what provides for us now."

"But the old plants *are* dying off," Largo said. "You said so yourself."

"We've had problems with drought and bad weather, but I *never* said that the plants were dying off. What we're concerned about isn't a natural shift in populations due to the environment. What we have is a problem due to the theft of the Plant People. That should be addressed and handled before we tackle anything else," she said, looking at each of the council members. "What we're dealing with is far more than normal attrition."

"What do you propose? We can't put the police on this, or the Forestry Department either. Both agencies are understaffed as it is," John Begay said.

"We have many eyes of our own working on this right now," Rose said. "The Plant Watchers will help me observe and gather evidence against this thief. Once we learn who's responsible and why, I'll present that information to this council."

"Do you have any idea who this person is?" Kevin asked.

"I have nothing I can discuss yet. But sooner or later, he'll make a mistake that will lead us directly to him."

The council members asked them to leave the room so they could discuss the matter, and Rose joined Largo and Knight out in the hall.

She sat down in one of the empty chairs against the wall to wait.

Largo sat beside her, leaned over, and spoke in a soft voice. "You made me look like a fool."

"I just confirmed the obvious," she said casually.

He glared at her, then got up and strode across the hall.

Rose saw Knight looking at her. "Well, have you got something to say too?" she said.

He hesitated, then cleared his throat and spoke. "Joining a gardening club isn't that unusual for a woman your age, but these Plant Watchers sound like activists on a mission."

"We adapt to the situation," she answered with a shrug, "and we do what has to be done."

Almost forty-five minutes passed before they were called in again.

Bernice spoke first. "Mr. Knight, we understand the problems you're facing, but we can't approve genetically engineered plants in reclamation areas until we know much more about them and their long-term effect on the environment. If you feel strongly about this, please prepare a report that will help address our concerns."

"I'll ask Maria Poyer to work with me. You'll get your report."

"That's fine," Bernice said. She then looked at Curtis Largo. "You obviously have a communications issue with Mrs. Destea that needs to be resolved. Make it a point to be available to her whenever she calls. We're passing this recommendation on to your supervisor today."

He nodded curtly.

Last of all, she looked at Rose. "My fellow council members and I believe that everything you've turned in today shows well-conducted research, thought, and a great deal of work."

Rose felt a wave of relief sweeping over her.

"But the plant theft situation worries us all very deeply. Many of our people rely on the Plant People for medicine and for rituals that are vital to our beliefs, and we can't allow these plants to be harvested to the point of extinction. This council needs to know exactly how critical the situation is, and for that reason we are asking that you deliver your complete report two weeks from today."

"Two weeks? But that's nearly impossible. There's so much to do yet—"

Bernice held up one hand. "Come up with a random survey, if necessary, that gives us a statistically reliable estimate we can take to the entire council. If the situation is that critical, we can't afford to wait much longer."

By the time the meeting ended, Rose was exhausted. She'd fought well, but there was an even heavier mantle of responsibility on her shoulders now.

She thought of Lena and how they'd supported each other through the years whenever one of them faced a crisis. Now they were both engaged in battles, and neither one of them could help the other. Needing to see her friend, Rose drove directly to the hospital from the tribal offices.

Rose went in through the side door and walked down the hall leading to Lena's room. As she approached the open door, she heard a familiar voice. Sara Manus was inside, and a ritual was in progress.

Rose stood silently in the doorway as the hand trembler asked Gila Monster, who was all-knowing and could see the future, for his help. Rose knew that Gila Monster, whose front legs shook whenever he moved forward, would now cause the trembler's hand to shake and guide her to the truth.

Sara's hand began to tremble and her hand was drawn to the area over Lena's heart, then to her head. The cycle repeated itself many times.

The ceremony took about twenty minutes. Finally, as Sara's eyes became clear and focused again, she looked down at Lena, who lay very still. "Your heart is sad and you're troubled."

Lena nodded.

"I will speak to your *hataalii*. You need to have a Blessing Way to bring you peace. But while you're here, you will need Life Way medicines and a Good Medicine Song to be sung for you to Beautiful Flowers, the Chief of all Medicines."

Afterward, when Sara left, Rose met her in the hall and gave her friend a big hug. "I'm so happy that you came."

Sara reached into her pocket for the small turquoise bear fetish. "I brought it back for you," she said, handing the fetish to Rose. "Keep it with you always, and if you need me, I'll be there. No friendships run as deep as the ones we make when we're young—before life teaches us not to trust or give our hearts. As adults we learn to protect ourselves by holding back so we have something we can cling to when things go wrong. But once we start doing that, we sacrifice the closeness that came with innocence." She smiled. "And that's a long-winded way of telling you I miss you and think of you often."

"Can you come back into the room and visit for a while just as a friend?"

Sara shook her head. "I'm sorry, I've got patients waiting for my return." She paused thoughtfully, then added, "I met with our friend from Teec Nos Pos the day before he died. He told me about the problem with the Plant People. Are you any closer to finding out who's responsible for all this?"

"No, but I won't give up until I have answers," Rose said.

"I'll keep my eyes open as well," Sara answered, hugging Rose again. "Good-bye for now, but my thoughts will be with you."

"One more thing," Rose said, stopping Sara before she could leave. "Did our friend from Teec Nos Pos mention having seen anyone hanging around where they didn't belong?"

"Only in general terms. He hated seeing outside companies working here on our land. It saddened him to see new television or phone company cell towers right in the middle of our wilderness areas."

"I feel the same," Rose said quietly.

As Sara hurried off, Rose finally went inside Lena's room. She looked thinner and paler, but Lena's eyes sparkled with alertness today. Sara's visit had already done some good.

"The hand trembler came. Did you see her?" Lena asked.

Rose nodded. "I waited outside. You look better already."

"I miss my home and my life," Lena said. "But my friends come to visit, and that helps."

Lena began coughing, then, worn out, lay still again. Rose swallowed back her fear. "You keep fighting this thing, I need you around. It gets lonely without my best friend to talk to at night after the day is done."

"You'll still have company. Your family is always there. I've always envied you for that. With my son so far away . . ."

Rose patted her hand. "Your daughter and granddaughter are always here. Think about them."

Rose knew that Lena had always favored her son and it broke her heart daily to know he'd chosen to leave the *Dinetah*. She looked down at their hands, aware of how old they seemed. Did people really age naturally, or was it the weight of too many shattered dreams that wore them down and ultimately broke them?

Rose stayed with Lena until she fell asleep. Later, as she walked to her truck, Rose thought of her daughter and granddaughter, and how much she loved both of them. Tonight, she'd spend time with them—time devoted only to family.

Rose spent the following afternoon alone, driving and hiking around to new locations, trying to find some of the herbs and plants that had all but disappeared from the area. After a long, exhausting, fruitless day, she finally headed home.

As she drove slowly up the gravel road leading to her house, it was so quiet all she could hear was a dog barking in the distance. Suddenly realizing that the only dog in the immediate area was Two, she pressed down harder on the accelerator.

She was almost home when she spotted a figure running away from the house toward the arroyo beyond the horse corral, Two at his heels. Dawn's pony, Wind, was running around in circles, whinnying and kicking up dust.

Fear swept through Rose in waves, but she managed to keep

her wits. Pulling to a stop quickly, she ran toward the house, knowing she had to call Ella immediately. As she reached the front porch, she heard the sound of an engine roaring away, and spotted a cloud of dust from just over the hill beyond the arroyo.

With her heart pounding at her throat, she stepped inside the front door. It was unlocked now, though she knew she'd locked it when she left earlier. As she stepped inside and looked around, nothing in the living room was disturbed, but the broom was lying there on the rug. As she walked into the kitchen, she saw that the intruder had kicked the locked back door open, and that was probably when he'd run into Two, who'd been inside. This morning, knowing how long she'd be gone today, she'd left a kitchen window open just far enough so Two could get inside by climbing onto the woodpile, then through the window. A chair was positioned just right so he could climb back out again.

When she discovered a large, raw beefsteak on the floor, she knew what had happened. The intruder had hoped to bribe the dog, throwing the meat through the window, but shredded strips of a nylon jacket on the kitchen floor told her it hadn't worked. Two had waited for the person to come inside, then done his job anyway.

Turning around, she looked back at her broom on the living room floor. There was a tuft of Two's hair in the bristles. The intruder had used the broom to fend off Two long enough to get into the living room and close the door to the kitchen, then had the rest of the house to himself or herself. But the minute the intruder had left the house through the front, Two had given chase by climbing back out the kitchen window.

As Rose picked up the phone and dialed Ella, she realized that the camera that had been sitting on top of the corner desk was gone, and so were the handful of photos she'd kept there. She told her daughter what she'd discovered.

"Mom, don't touch anything. I'm on the way."

"I'm going outside to search for Two."

"No, don't. Wait until I get there. I'll be home shortly."

"He's my dog and I'm going to look for him. I'll probably be outside when you get here." Before her daughter could argue, Rose hung up, then hurried out the back door. At least the pony had settled down again from the excitement.

She whistled for Two, then walked through the corral in the direction of the arroyo and tried again. Ten seconds later she saw the dog coming back, head up and tail wagging, obviously proud of himself.

Rose laughed and crouched down to pet him. "You did just fine, Two. Thank you for protecting the house. Let's go get you a treat. You certainly deserve one."

Rose went inside with him, threw the steak into the garbage in case it was contaminated with something meant to harm the dog, then found a large soup bone in the refrigerator.

"Here you go," she said, placing it on his rug in the kitchen. "Enjoy."

As she washed her hands, Rose heard the wail of a siren.

Her daughter was on her way home.

Rose waited as Justine and Ella dusted the back door and the broomstick for prints.

"Mom, which photos are missing? Are they ones to a particular location?"

"No, not at all. They were photos that I included in my survey report, so now they're a matter of record." She paused, then added, "Well, except for the roll I hadn't quite finished that was still in the camera."

"Who do you think would have wanted the photos badly enough to break in?"

"A lot of people have a stake in what I find or don't find. You already have a list."

"Those people all had alibis for the time of the last break-in, Mom. Can you think of anyone new?"

"I'll give it some thought, but offhand, no."

As Justine began to take prints around the desk, Officer Ralph Tache, the third person on the Special Investigations Unit, came in. Ella snapped at him for being slow to respond.

Ella then focused on Justine, directing her in the tone of a Marine drill instructor, if not the language.

Justine and Tache exchanged a quick look, but neither said anything.

Rose knew exactly what was going on. Whenever her daughter acted like this, it was simply because she was scared. Having an intruder here twice constituted an open and recurring threat to Ella's family, and something like that would shake Ella to the core. The more frightened Ella was, the more aggressive and demanding she became.

Just then Dawn and Jennifer came in. Jennifer gasped, but Dawn glanced around calmly, then looked up at Jennifer. "It's okay. It's just messy. Did we get a burglar?" Dawn asked Ella.

Ella, who'd been all set to comfort her daughter, looked at Dawn in surprise. "What makes you say that?"

"It's like TV," Dawn said, and shrugged, looking over at Justine and Tache, who, like Ella, had pistols at their hips and were checking for physical evidence. "Can I go to my room?"

"Sure," Ella said.

Rose watched the little girl leave. "You're not as alike as I thought, daughter. At her age you would have stayed and been in the middle of everything, asking questions and trying to figure it all out."

Ella looked down the hall at her daughter, who was in her bedroom, and smiled. "She's checking her favorite toys. It's not lack of curiosity. She's prioritizing."

Justine burst out laughing. "Oh, I think you've got a future cop in the making there, but one who's destined for administration."

Ella grimaced. "A desk jockey? Ugh!"

Justine and Tache finished their tasks shortly after dark, then left in their vehicles. Ella announced she was returning to the station and, reminding Rose to lock the doors even when she was at home, left.

Five minutes later, Rose heard a vehicle, and went to the curtained window for a look. The moon was out, and it was bright enough for her to see that it was her son Clifford's truck. She unlocked the front door and waved for him to come in.

Rose poured him some herbal tea, then they both sat down at the table. "What brings you here, son?"

"I need a few special plants for the ritual I have to perform for your friend, but there's one I haven't been able to find," he answered.

"If I don't have the plant you want in my garden, I'll ask the other Plant Watchers. Either way I can make sure you get whatever you need."

"I'm searching for 'white at night,' what the Anglo world calls white-stemmed evening primrose. I've asked some of the other *hataaliis*, even that new traditionalist medicine man that annoys you so much, but none of them have any to share or sell, and don't remember seeing it at any of their regular collection sites either."

"I don't have that particular plant in my garden. It doesn't do well at lower altitudes, but I'll check my notes. I didn't include it in the initial report I turned in, but since it is one of the endangered Plant People, it will be part of the finished survey. Give me a moment to check my notes. I'm sure I've got something in there about it." Rose went to her desk and suddenly realized that along with her camera and photos, the small notebook she'd been using was now gone.

EIGHTEEN

——— ✖ ✖ ✖ ———

The next morning *Bizaadii* came over. He'd heard what had happened from his nephews, who were police officers. "I've got a very solid door in the back of my truck. Once I'm finished, not even Arnold Schwarzenegger will be able to break into this kitchen."

Rose tried to assure him that it wasn't necessary and that she'd hire someone, but Herman wouldn't take no for an answer, or even payment for the materials he'd already purchased. Rose fixed him a hearty breakfast in exchange and Herman ate a Navajo taco—which combined pinto beans, chile sauce, fresh lettuce, tomatoes, and cheese, all over a large fluffy piece of warm fry bread. After washing it down with a mug of coffee, he began to work.

An hour later he had the solid-core door installed and a brand-new lock on it. He showed her his handiwork proudly, gave her the keys to the deadbolt, then began packing up. "You were lucky that the doorframe wasn't damaged. But I've got to be going now. My nephews are taking a few days of vacation off and we're all meeting up at my cabin so we can fix the place up."

"I'm glad that you're getting a chance to spend time with them."

"So am I. Neither my son in California nor my police officer nephews ever ask for my help these days," Herman said candidly. "And, to be honest, I've missed that."

"My daughter is the same way. She never asks for anything unless it concerns my granddaughter. And even those instances are rare. Though we live under the same roof, my daughter's life is very separate from mine."

"Children grow up and redefine themselves. That's the way it should be. But I'm going to enjoy this time with the boys."

After saying good-bye to Herman, Rose went through the house and made sure everything was locked up except for the small gap in the kitchen window. Two was still working on his bone in the kitchen, but if anyone tried to come in, their arms or legs would be next on his menu. Giving the sturdy dog a pat on the head, she went out to her truck. Soon she was on her way to the tribal offices to get a copy of her own plant survey report.

She'd been unable to find the computer floppy disk with the copy Willie had made for her after printing it out, and he'd erased the file on his computer voluntarily that same day, insisting she should maintain control of all the material herself. Rose believed that whoever took the camera and photos must have taken the disk as well, because she'd left it all on the desk.

As she drove into Shiprock, she tried to recall what she'd written about 'white at night' in her notes, but she just couldn't remember. Maybe something in the report she'd turned in would jog her memory.

An hour later, Rose left the tribal offices with a copy of her report in hand. Unfortunately, this preliminary survey only verified the absence of 'white at night' on sites that had been surveyed. But there was one collection site that was so remote few knew about it. There were several small sand dunes along the south end of the Chaco River, an intermittent stream, that often supported some of these plants. It was possible that site could provide her son with what he needed.

Rose arrived forty minutes later. Even in this extremely dry, barren stretch of desert beyond the southern end of the Hogback, she could see evidence of the trenching tool around the perimeter of the low dunes. As many plants had been left to die as were taken, based upon the holes, which had obviously been hastily dug.

She searched long and hard, walking along the dried-up streambed and investigating every old sandbar that she could find, but two hours later, she returned to her truck empty-handed. Trying not to let her own frustration undermine her, she focused on what she could do next. She'd go home and contact every one of the Plant Watchers, if she had to. One of them was bound to be able to help. Together, their gardens contained a huge array of plants that could be made instantly available to Lena. Clifford only needed to locate one plant, but it might turn out to be like trying to find a needle in a haystack, unless someone could help Rose out.

When she arrived home, the phone was ringing. She hurried to answer it.

"It's Carolyn," the familiar voice said. "I ran the fingerprints I collected from the body of your deceased friend through FBI and military databases and I've got some unexpected news. The fingerprints I took from the man you knew don't match those in Charlie Dodge's military records."

"If those in the military are correct, then *who* was my friend?"

"All I can tell you for sure is that he's not the man who joined the Code Talkers and served in the military during World War II."

"But my friend *did* serve during the war. The few stories he told me were too vivid to have been made up. And I'm sure I can find others who've known him since the war who can verify that."

"I don't know what to tell you. All I'm sure about is that your friend was Navajo, had a driver's license and other records that say he was Charlie Dodge, but he wasn't the Charlie Dodge the military fingerprinted in 1943." She paused for a moment, then added, "I did get something faxed to me which I thought you might want to have. It's the service record for the Charlie Dodge the military knew. It includes a photo, so I thought you might want to see that."

"Does the photo belong to the man I knew?" Rose asked, still trying to make sense of things.

"Maybe, but it was taken so long ago, I'm just not sure. It's a portrait shot of a young Navajo man," she said. "But I have no way of knowing what your friend looked like in the fifties or sixties, since I never knew him. The photo might be more help to you." Carolyn paused for a moment. "I'll leave a copy of the file at the main reception desk in the hospital lobby. You can sign it out whenever it's convenient."

"Thank you. I appreciate everything you've done."

After Rose hung up, she sat down and tried to sort things out in her mind. How could one Navajo have taken the identity and place of another without anyone finding out? Perhaps this was the reason the man she'd known as Charlie Dodge had always lived such an isolated life. But even so, someone must have known what happened. And now she wondered who the man in the Marine uniform had been. Charlie had to have known about him. She was sure that had been why he'd had them dig in that spot.

Her next call was to Willie. "I need to find 'white at night.' It's extremely important. I've been to the places where I've seen it grow, but there are no plants there now. I've heard my son call it by a name that is undoubtedly familiar to you, white-stemmed evening primrose. Can you help me find it? I need it for a healing ritual a friend of mine needs to have."

"I know the plant. I used to see it along the edge of roads, growing beside white-flowered wild mustard."

"Yes, that's the one."

"Does it have to come from Navajo Nation land?" Willie asked.

"No, but it must come from somewhere between the sacred mountains to be effective," Rose replied.

"Let's go search for it together. We can cover twice as much ground if we work as a team," he said. "Why don't you meet me here at my home in, say, an hour and a half? That'll give me enough time to do some research."

"All right. I'll see you then."

Rose called Jane Jim and then Clara Henderson, and although neither had the plant in their gardens, they each divulged a collection site they'd used successfully in the past for "white at night."

Excited by the promise the new leads held, Rose hurried to her pickup truck. She'd stop by the hospital first since it was on her way, pick up the photo that Carolyn had left for her at the desk, visit Lena for a short while, then go meet Willie. Today, things would begin to get better for Lena, she was certain of it.

By the time Rose arrived at the hospital she couldn't wait to see the photo. Even if it dated back to a lifetime ago, she was hopeful she'd be able to identify the man.

Rose picked up the envelope and, on the way to Lena's room, opened it up and looked at the papers. The young man in the 1942 black-and-white photo certainly resembled Charlie, but she just couldn't be certain beyond any doubt that it was him. Disappointment and frustration twisted her insides, but she took a deep breath and forced herself to calm down. She'd find the answers she needed, no matter how long it took her.

When she reached Lena's room, her friend was lying on

her back, her eyes shut and her body still. For a moment Rose froze in the doorway fearing the worst, but then she saw Lena draw in a breath. Rose walked quietly to the chair placed by the bed and sat down. If Lena was asleep, she wouldn't wake her up. She'd just sit with her for a while.

A moment later, Lena opened her eyes and looked over at her. "I knew it was you," she said softly. "I recognized your footsteps."

Rose glanced at the vase filled with daisies on the table beside the bed. "Those are beautiful," she said.

"They're from my daughter. My family came to see me earlier. My son came too, and he really wanted me to go to one of the big hospitals in Albuquerque and have the doctors there examine me. I said no, and now he's angry."

"You know what's best for you," Rose said firmly.

"My daughter values the old ways and so does my granddaughter, but unfortunately my son does not."

"All he has to understand is that *you* do," Rose said staunchly.

"It's never easy, is it?" Lena exhaled softly. "After the hand trembler was here I felt better, but now I'm back to where I was. I understand your son needs to find one of the Plant People that has moved away."

"I know the plant, and I'm searching for it now. I'll find it for him, don't worry."

"Work fast, dear friend," she said in a whisper-thin voice.

"You know I will."

Rose said good-bye, and had just stepped out into the hall when one of the Anglo doctors approached her.

"Are you Rose Destea?" he asked.

"Yes," Rose answered.

"Her family spoke to me about you. They advised me to ask you for your help when you came in to see Mrs. Clani."

"I'd be happy to help any way I can. What is it that you need?"

"Your friend has some heart irregularities that we can deal with, but her state of mind isn't good at all. If there's anything you can do to help keep her spirits up, you'd be doing her a great service."

"I'll do my best."

With a nod, he went inside Lena's room to check on what he referred to as her vital signs.

Rose hurried down the hall, eager to leave the hospital as soon as possible. She hated every second she had to spend in the building, especially after seeing the sign with an arrow pointing down that said MORGUE. It only meant that it was in the basement, but it still made her cringe.

Rose hurried to her truck, wanting to get under way quickly. Today, as she searched the Rez for the herb Clifford needed for Lena's Sing, she would also stop and visit one of the men she knew had been a Code Talker during the war. One of the sites she intended to check out was near his home. She'd show him Charlie's photo and see if he could identify him.

She'd met Jeremiah Brownhat many years ago during a Fourth of July celebration. He'd had some fascinating stories to tell about his days in the Code Talkers. Charlie had been there at the time, and they'd spoken about sending messages to each other while serving in different units.

Rose joined Willie forty minutes later in Farmington. Kenmore the mastiff came with them, jumping in the back of the professor's SUV immediately.

They went to Jane Jim's collection site first. It was barely off the reservation near a place the local people had named the Dunes, for obvious reasons. They searched the perimeter of the area for over an hour, but 'white at night' was nowhere to be found. Much of the area around the sand deposits had been dug up and disturbed by the countless motorcycles that climbed up and down the sand at nearly all hours of the day.

"I just thought of something that might help," Willie said as they headed back to the SUV. "Maria Poyer has an area on her family's land she uses to grow some of her experimental plants. She might have an engineered plant that is similar in composition to 'white at night.' Do you want to give her a visit and see if she does?"

Rose shook her head. "We need to use the Plant People the Holy People gave us, not some altered form, if the ceremony is to be effective," Rose said. "Can you understand?"

"Sure, but you might consider paying her a visit anyway. I think you'd find her a knowledgeable ally, and she may just happen to have one of these primroses."

"Do you know Maria well?" Rose asked, forcing herself to keep her tone casual.

"She and I have worked together in the past. She was my student at one time too. Of course, that was a long time ago."

"What do you think of her position on the plant issue?" Rose asked. Willie had worked with her, and become an ally she could depend on, but she was beginning to understand that people—and allies—were changeable.

"I see no reason not to introduce new strains of plants to the reservation—ones that would give extra nutrients to both cattle and people—but I also see your point about making sure it doesn't force out the plants that are already important to the tribe." He paused, then added, "But, truth be told, this is the tribe's business, not mine, and I only advise when I'm asked."

After checking another site along the way that Willie suggested, they headed for the one Clara Henderson had recommended. About halfway there, Rose asked Willie to make a small detour. "I need to talk to a friend who lives just up that rise," she said, pointing with her lips, Navajo style. "It involves the death of the Plant Watcher we both knew."

"Do you think the person you're going to see is involved?"

"No, not at all, it's just . . ." But she hesitated to say more. Curtis Largo had accused her of neglecting her business. If Willie really wasn't her ally . . .

"If it makes you uncomfortable to explain, you don't have to say anything else. I'll be happy to take you wherever you need to go."

She wanted to trust Professor Hoff, but his association with Maria had already raised too many questions in her mind. On the other hand, if he'd wanted to make trouble for her, he already had more than enough ammunition.

"It's complicated," Rose said at last. She then told Willie about the second body and the matter of Charlie's identity being in question. "No matter what his real name was, he was a friend of mine, and since he obviously wanted us to find the remains of this other man, I intend to follow it up until I learn the truth behind it all."

Willie nodded. "I suppose you also need to understand why a man you considered a good friend kept a secret like this from you," he said, glancing over at her. "Right?"

He'd managed to hit on the one thing that bothered her most about the situation. "Yes. I've always thought of myself as a good judge of character, and I need to know if I was wrong to trust him all these years."

"I understand." Willie glanced at her and nodded. "I really do, you know." He paused for a long moment before continuing. "I know firsthand how secrets can undermine everything—even the way we see ourselves."

She gave him a questioning look, but didn't press him. Soon, he continued.

"When I was fresh out of college," he said in a faraway

voice, "I fell in love with a Navajo woman while working on what became my first published handbook on southwestern plants. I was very ambitious back then, and knew I'd have to travel a great deal and do all I could to get my name known in order to get ahead. I asked her to marry me, and she said she wanted to, but she wouldn't leave the reservation."

"So you left but never forgot her?" she asked, accurately reading his tone of voice and expression.

He nodded. "But I returned to the area on business a few years later, and decided to look her up. When we saw each other again, it was as if our years apart had never existed. We spent the night together, but the following morning, all the problems that had kept us apart were still there. I couldn't stay and she wouldn't leave, so we parted for good."

Willie's gaze was fixed in the distance. "A month or two later, I passed through again on my way to accept a teaching assistant's position in Denver and heard she'd married someone from the tribe. Eight months after the night we spent together, a mutual friend of ours wrote to tell me that the woman I'd loved had died giving birth to a baby girl."

"You think it was your child she was carrying?" Rose asked quietly.

"I never knew for sure, and to try and find out would have caused more harm than good, so I let the matter rest."

Rose nodded, understanding. He hadn't given her any names, but she had a feeling that he believed that Maria was his lost child. If that was the case, then he was, at best, a dubious ally.

They arrived at an old stone house at the edge of a small meadow southwest of Sanostee near a place called Old Pine Spring, partway up the Chuska Mountain Range. The Arizona state line was only three or four miles west of there, Rose knew.

As they waited in Willie's SUV for someone to invite them

in, the professor leaned back in his seat. "Kenmore and I will wait in the car. If it gets too hot, I'll walk with him over to the shade of those ponderosa pines," he said.

"I won't take long," Rose promised, "if I'm invited to visit."

A moment later, Rose saw an elderly man in faded jeans, a long-sleeved flannel shirt, and a headband come outside to greet them. Jeremiah hadn't changed much, except for more gray in his long hair, and a bit less energy in his stride. He'd used a cane for many years, and now more than before. Rose left the truck and went to join him.

Once inside and seated in a worn brown-and-yellow-striped couch, Rose explained to Jeremiah why she'd come. "I'm trying to find out who my friend really was," she said after filling him in.

"This story surprises me. I knew the same man you did. We fought the same campaigns and we went through Code Talker school together. I have no doubt he was who he said he was. Maybe the government made a mistake when they finger-printed him. They processed a bunch of us Navajos back then."

Rose handed him the photo from the military papers. "Is this the man you knew?"

"Sure looks like him. I remember those days clearly—sometimes better than things that happened a few days ago."

Rose laughed. "Yes, me too, sometimes." She looked at the photo again and then placed it back in her purse. "Did you ever wonder why he never settled down anywhere?"

"Some of us carried memories of the war we never could put behind us," he said slowly. "I always thought that the war had scarred him somehow. His unit went through some tough times, I know. Half his battalion were casualties at Iwo Jima, though he escaped untouched, at least on his body."

Rose thanked Jeremiah, then went back outside to join Willie. She didn't doubt that the horrors of war could follow a man until the day he died, but somehow she had a feeling there was more to Charlie's story. The skeleton in the Marine Corps uniform with a Charlie Dodge dog tag was still unexplained.

As Willie and she continued to search for "white at night," Rose had to struggle against the fear that swelled up inside her as the hours passed and they failed to find any specimens of the plant. By the end of the afternoon, though the dog seemed to have had a great time, they still had nothing to show for their efforts.

As they walked back up the hillside toward the road where the SUV was parked, Kenmore, who was sniffing the ground ahead of them, stopped and barked once. Rose spotted a man through a break in the treeline, about twenty yards ahead, digging up something. He turned and glanced in their direction, but Rose only managed to get a fleeting glimpse of his face.

She quickened her pace, wondering if they'd gotten lucky enough to catch the thief at work. Kenmore, at Willie's command, stayed with them without running ahead. As they drew near, Rose realized it was John Joe. He was digging up a small "wondering about medicine" plant.

Glancing at the mastiff often, he continued working, picking up the plant and placing it carefully in a small pot made of fiber and peat. "This is for my garden, or should I say gardens," he said, and his expression confirmed for the first time that he knew she'd been the one checking out the garden at his home. "I know there are only a few of these plants around the Rez these days, but if I leave it here, it could soon become nothing more than forage for a wild animal. As you yourself said, we have to protect the endangered Plant People."

"Not by taking the best," she answered, scowling.

"There are other plants here, and I have left an offering for its neighbors," he said, indicating several other examples of the herb, and a small piece of turquoise placed on a flat stone.

"But we shouldn't argue now. This is a holy time." With that, he picked up the potted plant and, using a plastic water bottle, soaked the container thoroughly. Nodding to them, he walked to his blue truck, which they could now see was parked about fifty feet behind Willie's SUV. He'd arrived after them, obviously, and she wondered if John had somehow followed them.

Rose checked his footprints after he'd gone. His feet were larger than the ones left by the person who'd been with Charlie the day he'd died. John also wore cowboy boots, not the hiking kind with ripples that she'd seen in the area near Charlie's body.

"What are you doing?"

Rose smiled. "Acting like my daughter, the policewoman," she answered. "I'm no expert, but I'm searching for little details that might help me explain what happened to my friend." She then realized that Willie's shoe size was closer, but the wrong pattern. Of course, he could always change shoes, but then again, he'd already admitted to having been with Charlie that day.

"The Singer didn't have an entrenching tool," he said.

"I know, but someone with one of those GI shovels came here," she said pointing to an area about twenty feet ahead where the ground was disturbed.

Willie walked over and crouched by one of the holes, studying the remaining dried-out leaves and plant debris curiously. "Whoever is taking the plants is sure targeting the rarest ones."

"You were speaking of Maria Poyer before," Rose said thoughtfully. "Do you think it could be her?"

His eyes were sharp and alert as they focused on her. "What makes you say that?"

"She may be trying to prove to everyone that we don't need the Plant People as much as we think we do. One of the best ways to do that is to make sure no one can find any."

"I don't think she'd do that," he said firmly. "I could see her carefully collecting some of the plants and trying to graft or hybridize them into stronger versions of the original. But taking them so recklessly, and destroying so many others in the process like this?" He waved his hand over the desiccated plants that had been uprooted and shook his head. "No way. Whoever is doing this is in an awful hurry, or some kind of mad panic. Look how carelessly some of these have been dug up."

"Or that's what he wants us to think. The thief has to be someone who either knows precisely what the plants mean to The People and wants to effect change—or someone who's got some kind of secret agenda we still haven't been able to uncover."

"You'll probably come across this person someday when you least expect it," he warned. "And if that happens, you could be in a great deal of danger."

He hadn't said it, but she knew precisely what he meant. Whoever had killed Charlie wouldn't hesitate to commit murder again. If she wasn't careful, she might end up sharing Charlie Dodge's fate.

NINETEEN

✖ ✖ ✖

Hours later, Rose glanced around the kitchen, having just finished tidying up. Ella was in the living room with Dawn, and it was time for her to join her family.

"Are you okay?" Ella asked as Rose entered the room. "You've been awfully quiet tonight."

Rose looked over at Dawn, who was engrossed in a cartoon video. "There was a letter in the mail for me when I got home. It was written by your child's father, acting in his capacity as a tribal attorney. It informed me that my friend's savings account, which he bequeathed to me, is now legally mine. So are all his possessions, except for his new trailer house, which will be taken back by the finance company. I'll donate most of his things to the church your father founded, but I have to figure out what to do with the money he left me. That represents a lifetime of savings and I want to use it in a way he would have approved."

"You could invest it in a program to reintroduce some of the native plants that are so scarce."

Rose nodded thoughtfully. "That's a very good idea. He would have liked that," she said, then sighed loudly. "I said that with such certainty, but since he wasn't the man I thought he was, I obviously didn't know him as well as I'd like to think. The simple truth is that I don't even know what his real name was." She told Ella about the photo and her visit with Jeremiah. "He believes my friend was who he said he was, but until I learn the identity of the person who was already in the ground, I can't know for certain."

"Maybe I can help. But first I'll have to take a look at the military service record that was faxed to the ME's office. I'll call my friend. I bet she's still in her office. She can fax me a copy here at home, then I can help you look it over for clues that might give you a lead."

It didn't take long to get Carolyn to fax a copy over to Ella's combination fax/copy machine/printer in her small home office. Once all the pages had come through, Ella brought them into the living room and placed the papers on the coffee table, where they could both examine them.

"They monitored all his passes off base carefully," Ella said, "and from what I can see here, he only came home once on furlough—after basic training and before he went to the classified Code Talker school. That training was listed in code, of course, but there was an insert in his file added much later when the program was declassified."

"What about his family? Does it say anything about them?"

"He had a younger brother by the name of Gilbert who was only sixteen in 1943. Both their parents were listed as deceased by the time Cha . . . he enlisted." Ella barely avoided mentioning Charlie's name, something that wasn't normally done around a traditionalist until several days after the deceased had passed away.

"But the brothers must have had other relatives. Who raised the boys if their parents were dead? And whatever became of the younger brother?"

"It doesn't say here." Ella paused. "You could try and check the boarding school records—if they go back that far and if the boys went to school at all. But be aware that old records may be hard to find, or they may refuse to let you look even if they are available."

"In that case, I'll ask *Gishii's* oldest daughter. She used to work in administration at one of the boarding schools before they closed all of them down. She won't refuse me."

Ella smiled. "If there's anyone who knows how to cut corners, it's you, Mom."

Ella turned around and saw that Dawn had turned off the television and was listening to her talking story book.

Rose smiled. "At her age, you were never interested in stories or storytelling. You wanted to be outside running or playing. The hardest thing for you to do was sit still."

Ella nodded. "She's her own person in a different time. Do you ever wish you could peer into the future and see who she'll be in fifteen years?"

Rose laughed. "No, thank you. I'll take things one day at a time. That's about all I can handle."

Rose watched her daughter tending to Dawn. How quickly time passed these days! She was proud of her family. Raymond and she had done well raising Clifford and Ella. The two were as different as could be, but both were strong and loving people in their own ways. And now there was Dawn, a part of her too. In her granddaughter, Rose saw a future that was yet to be determined, but one filled with infinite possibilities.

"Mom? You have such a peculiar expression on your face."

Rose chuckled. "I'm thinking that someday she'll grow up and have children, and you'll be where I am right now."

"Is that a curse or a blessing?" Ella asked.

"Both," Rose said with a smile.

The following morning, after a much-welcomed rainy night, Rose set out early while there were still gray clouds overhead and actual humidity could be felt in the air. She'd received a call from Sadie Black Shawl and something in Sadie's tone had worried her. The young woman had seemed too subdued.

When Rose arrived at Lena's home, she saw Sadie outside, kneeling by some plants in the garden. Seeing Rose, she waved.

"I don't know what made you stop by, but I'm glad you did," Sadie said, brushing the dirt from her jeans as she stood.

"I had a feeling something wasn't right."

"Let's go inside and I'll tell you about it."

In the kitchen, Sadie poured them both a cup of coffee from the pot on the counter, then suddenly looked at Rose. "I'm sorry. I didn't even think. Do you drink coffee?"

"Sometimes, but I prefer it with cream and sugar, lots and lots of both."

Sadie brought over the sugar bowl and the container of coffee creamer. "My mom and I always discussed whatever was bothering us over coffee, and I got used to the ritual," she said with a sheepish smile.

Rose waited patiently for her to begin, noticing how ill at ease Sadie appeared to be.

"Last night after I went to bed I heard a strange noise outside. The porch light was on, so I turned it off so I could see through the window. That's when I spotted someone outside running back to his truck. It roared off before I could get a good look at the license plate."

"What was he after, do you know?"

"I went out with a flashlight after he was gone and took a good look around, but I couldn't see what he'd taken." She hesitated, then added, "But I found footprints that prove he was by the garden. That's why I wasn't going to tell anyone. I knew that if the news got back to your friend that someone had been messing around in her garden again, it would really upset her."

"You're right about that, so let's keep it between us for now. Do you remember what the man looked like?"

"I was still half asleep, and I only saw him from the back. All I can tell you is that he was tall, had wide shoulders, and ran like he had a bear chasing him," she said. "Later, after I calmed down, I remembered that everyone's looking for 'white at night' for your friend. That's when I began to wonder if the man I saw was one of your tribe's medicine men who'd come to check her garden."

"If the person had been here on legitimate business, he wouldn't have run," Rose said, "or come at that hour. Traditionalists don't like to be outside roaming around late at night."

"I also found out something else. . . ." Sadie took a deep breath. "I've been trying to help by seeing if I could find any patches of 'white at night' up in the canyons north of here. That's pretty rough terrain that the older Plant Watchers usually don't visit. I didn't find any of the plants, but I ran into Sara Henderson, Clara's daughter. She was up there working on one of her paintings. Sara told me that two of the Plant Watchers have had plants taken from their gardens late at night. But the thief didn't take any endangered plants, just a few varieties that are hard to locate."

"Like what?"

"Joe-pye weed, for one."

"That's used to heal deep cuts, particularly puncture wounds," Rose said thoughtfully.

"I know. It was one of the varieties I listed in a medicinal plant report for one of my botany classes."

"You did a report on herbal medicine?" Rose asked. "I'd love to see it sometime."

"Sure. It's in my computer. Let me print out a copy for you."

Ten minutes later, Rose sat in the living room reading the term paper. As she glanced at the footnotes on the first page, she noticed that Bradford Knight was one of the experts cited. "I didn't know Mr. Knight was an authority on herbal medicine," she said.

"I found that out during my initial research. He's written several papers on the subject recently too. Although they're not specific to plants found on the Navajo Reservation, I found them useful. He also has several articles on the Internet. Would you like to see them?"

"Yes, I would." She was curious to learn the Anglo man's viewpoint on herbal medicine. She had a feeling it wasn't something he practiced or really endorsed. For many educated Anglos, herbal medicine was simply a primitive substitute for someone who mistrusted or couldn't afford conventional medicines.

Sadie went to a specific site she'd bookmarked on the computer. On the table of contents listing the writers that had contributed to the literature on the site, Rose saw Professor William Hoff's name as well.

"So he also writes about herbal medicine?" she asked, pointing.

"He's one of the best. His articles are really wonderful. I think he believes in herbal medicines—and he uses them himself. I don't know that for a fact, mind you," Sadie added quickly. "But that's what he said in one of his articles."

"Do you remember which article it was?" The news had come as a surprise and now Rose intended to learn more.

Rose sat at Sadie's computer for quite some time reading the articles both men had written. In one, Willie claimed to have successfully used *Penstemon barbatus,* also known as beardtongue, as a cough suppressant.

From the photo Rose recognized the plant. Navajo called it

"hummingbird food," and it was one of the endangered plants. "He used 'hummingbird food' as cough medicine," Rose told Sadie. "We use it in the same way. Does it say anywhere in here when this article was written?"

Sadie reached for the arrow key and scrolled down. "It was published in 1980, so it would be sometime before that."

Back then, "hummingbird food" had grown almost everywhere. Rose remembered the story Willie had told her about falling in love with a Navajo woman. It was entirely possible that she'd taught him about their native plants.

Bradford Knight's articles were written in a completely different tone. He treated the subject exactly the way she'd suspected he would, stating that none of the health claims had been proved, and that reliance on dubious medicinal plants could result in harm to the user, not only from ingesting folk herbs that could have hazardous side effects, but by delaying the ill person's visit to a physician.

"I really appreciate your help with this," Rose said as she finished the second article.

"No problem. It was my pleasure," she said. "Are you going plant hunting today?"

Rose nodded. "Yes, but I have to make another stop first."

"Do you mind if I tag along with you? I'm going a little stir crazy. I thought I wanted to be alone so I could study, but there's such a thing as being too alone—and studying too much," she added with a smile.

"I'd love to have your company, but I should warn you that I have to go to my friend's trailer, and that's bound to be difficult, and very sad," she said, and explained about Charlie's final requests.

"From the sounds of it, you'll definitely need a friend along, so it'll work out for both of us," Sadie answered. "I'll drive so you won't have to worry about anything."

They said little to each other during the forty-five-minute drive to Charlie's trailer home near Teec Nos Pos. The tension and discomfort she felt about entering the home of a recently deceased Navajo built inside her with every breath she took.

Soon they arrived near the base of a low cliff and parked in front of a shiny new single-wide aluminum structure, topped with an evaporative cooler. Rose stepped out of the SUV and glanced around. Charlie's truck wasn't around, and she guessed it was still at the place where he'd died or, more likely, had been towed to the impound yard at Chinle. The vehicle would have to be sold to someone off the reservation. Charlie had loved that relic more than anything else, and possessions that dear to a person called to their *chindi*. She wouldn't go near it now, and neither would any other Navajo following The Way—a traditional Navajo's path.

Rose noted that except for a small garden delineated with wooden stakes and white twine, the ground around Charlie's home had not been disturbed from its natural state. She walked to Charlie's trailer, climbed up two steps to a metal porch with decorative railing, and opened the door. It hadn't been locked.

As she went in, instead of the stale odor associated with closed-in rooms, she became instantly aware of the pleasant aroma that seemed to fill the entire living area. It was a wonderful scent reminiscent of flowers and fruit. She looked around and found only one flowering plant inside. Somehow the pot had crashed to the floor beside the long planting bench below a large western-facing window and underneath four long fluorescent light tubes.

As she crouched by the shattered pot, she noted the vivid blue-violet flowers and remembered Charlie telling her about his search for a blue dye. But he'd mentioned having ten plants, and there was only one damaged specimen here.

"I'm going to take this little plant back with me. But there should be some others in here as well. Help me look," Rose said, finding an empty pot on a shelf and carefully transferring the damaged plant into it.

They searched both ends of the trailer, including the bedroom, but there were no more blue flowering plants. Stepping outside, she looked at the native plants Charlie had growing in his garden, but there were none of the endangered ones on her list. "Those plants will continue to flourish here, tended or untended," Rose said, then went back inside Charlie's home.

While Sadie finished repotting the damaged plant with additional soil taken from outside and added water to it from the tap in the sink, Rose went to Charlie's desk. It was actually a large shelf that was attached to the wall by a piano hinge and held level by two small chains. Rose searched through the few papers there and found some bills, including one for the trailer, but nothing of a more personal nature.

As Rose moved from one end to the other, she searched the drawers throughout the mobile home. The one thing that struck her was the absence of photos or anything that might reveal a bit about him. It was almost as if Charlie had never had a past. But then again, maybe he hadn't—at least not his own.

Then, at the back of a drawer in the kitchen containing eating utensils, she found a single dog tag. It was old and scratched up, but it looked identical to the one found on the makeshift casket unearthed at Hogback. Its presence here confirmed the link between Charlie and that long-dead Marine. It seemed too important to leave behind, but it was such a personal item that it didn't seem wise to take it either.

Sadie came up behind her. "What do you have there?"

Rose showed the tag to her. "One identical to this was on

the body found when my friend was about to be buried. I think it may be evidence of something, but I don't know if it is too dangerous to carry around. It was very personal to my friend at one time, and now he's dead."

Sadie nodded. "My tribe has different beliefs about the dead and their property. I don't mind keeping it for you, just in case it's needed later on by the police or lawyers. If we leave it here, it's only going to get thrown away and lost," Sadie said.

"Thank you. It sounds like a good idea." Rose handed her the dog tag, and Sadie placed it in her pocket.

Two hours later, after a fruitless search for anything that might reveal more about Charlie's true identity, Rose walked to the door. Except for the Charlie Dodge dog tag, the only things of significance were the pink slip on his truck and the loan papers for the trailer, which he'd purchased less than a year ago after making a down payment of five thousand dollars. She stood there for a moment, taking one last look at her friend's home, then continued to Sadie's SUV. She would never return to this site.

As they drove back to Shiprock, Rose glanced at Sadie. "I have to go to the high school next and attend to some business, but I should go in alone, and it may take a while. Would you prefer it if we went back and I got my truck?"

"The high school is on the way, so it makes sense to stop there next. I'll be happy to wait for you outside. I have a book in my purse. I never get to read books for pleasure anymore and I've got a great romance I've been wanting to read."

"You read *those?*" Rose asked, grimacing. She'd never approved of the white world's emphasis on romance. She understood the necessity of pairing, but in her mind the right pairing had very little to do with romance.

"Believe it or not, it's got a Navajo hero, so it sounded interesting," she said, and smiled when Rose grimaced.

"Well, since you don't mind, let's stop there when we get into town," Rose said.

When they arrived at Shiprock, they turned and drove into the parking lot of the high school, just south of the road they were on, Highway 64.

Rose opened the door, then glanced back at Sadie. "If it gets too hot, just come into the front lobby and sit on one of the benches," she said, "or wait in the principal's office."

"I've always tried to stay away from places like that," Sadie said with a smile. "Don't worry about me at all. I'll be fine."

Rose hurried up the front steps and went inside quickly, headed straight for the main office. Asking the first adult she saw for assistance, she was guided to Sheila Jim's desk. Sheila, after the last government boarding school on the mesa had closed down for good years ago, had started as a records secretary here, a position similar to her old job.

Sheila looked up and, seeing Rose, smiled. "Well, hello. This is a surprise. Sit down."

Rose took the seat she offered. "I've come to ask you a favor," she said, and explained that she was looking for anything to do with Charlie's past. Although forced to use his name here, she didn't feel threatened by the *chindi* because she doubted Charlie had ever been here.

"I'm not sure I can help you. The records you want date back to the Great Depression. Back then, things weren't as organized as they are now, and there were only a few staff members at the boarding school, which was in the valley then. I worked at the last one here, up on the mesa across town, of course, and those records ended up at tribal headquarters in Window Rock. But the real old records—I have no idea where they might be."

"Who might know about his or his brother's childhood? Can you think of anyone?"

Sheila considered it for a while. "There is one person that might, but I'm not even sure he's still alive. My mother would visit him at least once a month when I was in high school, and he'd always take time to talk to me about plants and the old ways. He lived out by Rattlesnake."

"Can you tell me anything more about him?"

"His name was Ha ... Ha something." She shook her head. "He was a traditionalist, so he never used his real name. He wanted to protect his Navajo name, and he'd never had an Anglo name because he never went to school."

"Could it have been *Ha'asídí?*"

"Yes, that was it! I remember now."

Rose knew the man, but she too wasn't sure if he was still alive. He had to be over eighty if he was, but some of their people were strong and lived long lives.

"Thanks. I appreciate the help you gave me."

"I'm sorry I couldn't do more," Sheila said.

Rose walked outside to where Sadie's SUV was parked. She was still sitting behind the wheel, engrossed in the paperback novel. As Rose slipped into the seat, Sadie dogeared the page she was reading, set the book down beside her, and started the engine.

"Where to?"

"Let's stop at my house to put this plant in a safe place then I want to track someone down. He used to live in a hogan out by Rattlesnake. I remember him walking all the way into Shiprock once a week, then sometimes carrying back a load of groceries if he couldn't find a ride home."

Sadie looked at her thoughtfully as they were heading south of Shiprock. "I met an old man wandering around in that area not long ago over by Shiprock Wash. In spite of this four-wheel drive monster, which should be capable of going almost anywhere, I managed to get myself stuck in the soft sand of an arroyo, and he came out of nowhere. Scared me half silly, but he knew that area like the back of his hand. He was very old, but he had more energy than I did, and his thinking was as clear as springwater. He helped me dig out and showed me how to stuff brush in front and around the tires to get enough traction to pull free. If it's the same person, he was very much alive just a few months ago."

"He sounds like the man I'm looking for."

"You might ask him about 'white at night' if we find him," Sadie added after a moment. "I remember that he was out collecting plants when he found me stuck in that sandy arroyo."

"You're right. There was a time when 'white at night' could be collected around the sides of the arroyos flowing away from Ship Rock all the way to Rattlesnake. Of course, that was a long time ago."

After leaving the plant in Rose's kitchen to recover under the light, they traveled north again, then west. At long last, after wandering around for nearly a half hour looking for the right dirt road, they arrived at a hogan near a small oil field. Rose asked Sadie to stop fifty feet away within view of the east-side entrance, which had a door in place of the traditional blanket-covered entry.

"If he's inside, he'll come out," Rose said.

"That's assuming he knows we're here. What if he's hard-of-hearing?"

"We can wait outside by the vehicle, but we shouldn't approach because he's a traditionalist. It would be considered rude." Seeing the empty sheep pen constructed of cottonwood branches, Rose studied the area, noting the globe willow tree that shaded the pine-log hogan. *Ha'asídí* had made another concession or two to modern times. His hogan had a tarpaper roof and a metal chimney, which meant a woodstove had taken the place of a fire pit, and the joints between the logs had been sealed with some kind of stucco or plaster instead of mud.

"The tracks over there by the sheep pen look fresh. My guess is that during the day he probably takes his livestock along the arroyos where it's cooler, and they feed on the grass that grows in damper soil."

"I got stuck in one of those arroyos near here. Do you want me to try and take you to that same spot—emphasis on *try?* I'm not sure I can find it again."

Rose smiled. "I lose track of distances around here sometimes too, and end up going down the wrong road. But as long as I can see the mountains to the west, or Ute Mountain over there to the northwest, I can always reorient myself at least on directions."

"I'll try to remember that," Sadie said, "but if you get down into the arroyos, you sometimes get turned around and have to get to higher ground to see landmarks."

Sadie continued west, with the pinnacle of Ship Rock on her left. A low, wide, and currently dry arroyo with the equivalent of sandbars in the center appeared before them, running in a southerly direction. They reached a hard spot down on the arroyo where the seasonal flow of rainwater had created a gravel deposit near the center of the channel, and Sadie stopped the vehicle. As they climbed out, they could hear someone whistling farther down the arroyo, but they couldn't see anyone.

"I think it's coming from around the next bend," Sadie said. "But it's hard to say for sure because of the way the wind carries sounds out here."

"Wind is said to hide or uncover secrets at will," Rose whispered. Then she stood perfectly still for several moments. "Over there," she said at last, gesturing.

As they walked around a curve in the arroyo, they saw an old Navajo man bent over, picking some plants growing near the edge of a smaller channel. Several sheep were grazing on the grasses atop a high spot in the wash where the sun shone most of the day. A few goats were farther downstream, and she could hear a bell as one of the animals moved.

"*Yáat'ééh*," *Ha'asídí* greeted in Navajo, standing up as Rose and Sadie approached.

"*Aqalani*," Rose answered, using the word for greetings.

"I remember you, young lady," he said, chuckling as he glanced at Sadie. "Are you lost again?"

Sadie laughed. "No, this time I came on purpose."

He shifted his gaze to Rose. "I know you, of course, and your children. Are you in search of plants?"

"Yes, I am. And information too."

"Maybe I can help with both."

She told him about Charlie Dodge, not mentioning his name specifically, but she knew from his expression that he'd already heard.

"My daughter told me about his passing. I was sad to hear the news. I saw him just a few days before his death when he came here to the New Mexico side searching for plants. He said that he was working with you to locate some of the Plant People who had moved away."

"That is so," Rose answered. His English was surprisingly good. The elderly didn't always speak the language of the Anglos.

"But there's no 'salt thin' or 'frog tobacco' here," he told her. "Is that what you're looking for?"

"Right now I need to find 'white at night.' I believe it used to grow in these parts."

He nodded. "It does still—or it did until someone came and dug up most of the plants I knew about."

"Did you happen to find strange shovel marks on the ground?"

He nodded. "You mean the holes made by a little pointed

digging tool?" Seeing her nod, he continued. "I recognized the pattern it made on the ground because I used a GI shovel back during my days in the Marines. It seemed like all we did was dig foxholes and trenches," he recalled.

"Did he take all the 'white at night' plants?"

"No, there are still some young plants left, and a few old, weak ones."

As they walked up the canyon together, looking at the few plants along the inside curve of the dry channels, Rose glanced over at him. "I've been trying to find someone who knew our Plant Watcher friend when he was young, way back before the war. Did you, by any chance?"

"He always said that I was one of the few people who'd known both him and his brother, but if I ever did meet his brother, I don't remember it."

"Did he ever speak to you about his brother?" Rose asked. This was the first time anyone had even referred to Gilbert Dodge.

"Only rarely. His brother died in an accident and it was painful for our friend to talk about him because they'd been very close."

"Did he ever speak of his parents?"

"All he ever said to me was that his mother and father died while he and his brother were still young and the years that followed were hard for both of them. They went hungry a lot of time until he joined the Marines. His pay kept both of them going."

Rose looked at him thoughtfully, a new picture emerging in her head. Maybe the body in the grave was Charlie's brother. But if that were the case, why had Charlie put one of his dog tags and his Marine uniform on him when he was buried? Had it been a way of honoring his little brother's wishes? Charlie had said that his brother had died in an accident. If he'd felt responsible somehow . . . Or maybe it had been an attempt at a deception of some kind.

Rose sighed. Yet none of it explained why someone had killed the man she'd known as Charlie, or told her if his death had been connected to the plant thief.

As they reached an area where another arroyo joined the main channel, *Ha'asídí* stopped. " 'White at night' grew here," he said sadly. "But whoever dug up the other plants must have come back to take what was left."

Rose saw all the pointed shovel marks on the ground. "The thief must have learned the hard way that 'white at night' doesn't transplant well. And now there are none." Rose thought of Lena and felt anger swell inside her. She would find the plant her son needed for the ritual if she had to walk every inch of land between the Sacred Mountains.

TWENTY

— ✖ ✖ ✖ —

Hours later, alone again, Rose drove to Willie's home. The situation was critical, and she still had no idea where to find "white at night." Maybe if they combined their knowledge of the plants and the area, they'd be able to figure something out.

Rose parked in front of the professor's house and saw Maria Poyer coming out the door. Uncertain, Rose hesitated to get out of the pickup, but Willie, who was standing in the doorway, saw her and waved at her to come in.

"I'm sorry if I've interrupted something, Willie," she said, joining them, "but I have a serious situation and I could use some help." Rose turned to Maria. "Yours too, if you're willing to give it."

"You want *my* help?" Maria asked, surprised.

"Come in, then, both of you. Let's talk," Willie said.

He led them back into the living room and Rose waited until everyone was seated, included Kenmore, who'd come out of the kitchen, his mouth still dripping from the water he'd been drinking.

"I have a problem and I'm really not sure what to do next," Rose said, and explained about Lena's illness for Maria's sake, and the need for the specific plant in a healing ceremony.

Maria nodded gravely. "I knew that some of our people believe strongly in the power of the Plant People to cure, but I never realized their reliance on them could produce a situation like this."

"The Holy People gave us the Plant People and taught us how to use them when we become sick. They have to be collected in a certain way, special prayers have to be said over them, and specific methods are used to prepare them. They're *our* medicine. You may choose to believe in another way, but it doesn't make our way less effective or worthwhile."

"Mrs. Destea is making a very important point here, Maria. You already know that a lot of medicinal compounds are derived from plants, such as quinine, codine, digitoxin—used to make digitalis—and salicin."

Maria nodded. "Salicin comes from the bark of certain willows, and inspired the development of aspirin. I'm not dismissing the value of certain plants, or denying that there are probably others around we don't know about yet."

"But it's more than that. Maybe it's because you're not looking at it from the same perspective as the patient," Willie said. "In recent years, medical science has come to accept the fact that a patient's mental attitude can affect the course and effectiveness of treatment, sometimes critically so. This has led to other studies which seem to demonstrate that when a patient is prayed for, their recovery rate improves and at times there's a complete reversal of the condition. Medicine men function as the tribe's healers and clerics. Theological arguments aside, there's little difference between what the traditionalists believe and what the Anglo world is just starting to accept."

Maria nodded slowly, then met Rose's gaze. "I may never end up going to a medicine man myself, but I've never been against herbal remedies or what might be called psychological help, especially when someone's health is at stake. If you want my help finding this plant, you've got it, but I don't even know where to start looking."

"Once we decide what conditions are needed for the growth of this plant, we can select locations to search," Willie said, leading the way to the den. "We can rule out those places already surveyed, and divide up the remaining potential sites. We can't expect to cover them all, because it's only the three of us, but by deciding on a plan, we can guarantee no effort will be wasted."

By the time they finished, Rose felt more positive than she had in a long time.

"If we find a healthy plant, do you want us to dig it up?" Willie asked her.

"Yes, but be careful that you don't damage the roots. This plant has to be preserved, pollen sprinkled on its roots, and then replanted."

As they got ready to leave, Rose noticed that Maria seemed much more reasonable now that she understood that something immediate and crucial was at stake for a real person, not just a concept. Her positive response to a crisis was comforting to Rose. Maybe someday they'd work together for the land and The People.

"I'm glad she's helping us," Rose said as Maria drove off in her truck.

"She's a bright young woman, but Maria sometimes has difficulties listening and accepting ideas other than her own because her ego gets in the way. You've helped her open her mind to compromise and cooperation between cultures that are a hundred years apart, and that's going to make her an even better scientist. But she still has a ways to go and she can be quite stubborn."

Rose nodded. "Has Maria been able to continue any of her work? If she maintains certain safeguards, I think her work could be a benefit to the tribe. But I know she needs funding.

All that research and development won't pay off until she has something to sell or market."

"She's had to put her work on hold for now. I have a few contacts, and have managed to get matching funds for her out of a special state program, but to make it work, she still needed to have the tribe put up half the money. That was a roadblock I couldn't surmount, and neither could she."

"You've helped me, so I'll see what I can do. I know Maria's important to you. She has your smile, and your cheekbones too."

Willie met her gaze. "You've already figured things out, I see." Seeing her nod, he continued. "Maria doesn't know, and I'd like to keep it that way."

Rose nodded. "I understand."

"I know that it would be possible to find out for sure if she's my daughter through DNA testing. I just don't think it's fair to turn her world upside down that way. But in my heart, I believe she's my daughter, so I'll do whatever I can for her."

Rose returned to her truck, lost in thought. She would go by Kevin Tolino's office first. It was on her way anyway. If anyone could help Maria get matching funds, it would be him.

Rose arrived at Kevin's office a little more than a half hour later. He was alone, working on his computer.

Seeing her, Kevin smiled, stood, and invited her to take a seat. "What can I do for you?"

Rose told him about her problem finding the right plant for Lena and how Maria Poyer was now working with her in the search. "But it's not fair that the money the tribe is paying me to do the survey is taking away her chance to continue her research. The state has promised to match whatever funds the tribe puts up. Surely there's some money somewhere that the tribe can offer her. She can have the money my friend left me too, though it's not much."

"I'll see what I can do," Kevin said with a tiny smile. "But I doubt it would amount to any substantial funding."

"Do your best. The way things are going, someday we may have to rely on her plants," Rose said, standing up.

"Is the situation that bad?"

Rose nodded slowly. "Yes, at least for a few species. And now a life is at stake."

Rose made plans to spend the afternoon searching the area that Willie had mapped off specifically for her. Although she'd wanted to take someone along, Sadie was in class, and no one else was readily available.

She was traveling down the highway when she saw the flashing lights of a police unit behind her. Curious, Rose pulled over, and a moment later Ella jogged up to her.

"Hey, Mom! Where are you off to? I got off work early today, but it turns out Dawn's at a birthday party. If you're working on something interesting, can I tag along?"

Rose knew that despite Ella's casual tone, her daughter was worried about her. "You'll be bored. I'm off to search for 'white at night.'"

"Great. I'll help. I know I've disappointed you by not being able to take part in Plant Watcher work like I intended to a few years ago, but I'd still like to learn when I have time," Ella said. "Since we're not far from home, let's stop by so I can leave my patrol unit there, then I can ride with you."

Twenty minutes later they were under way in Rose's truck. Ella had come armed, something that Rose found disturbing, though she knew her daughter was always on call and was required to carry a weapon. But collecting plants was prayerful work and the presence of a gun was jarring. "Do you really think you'll need your pistol? Maybe you should leave it in the truck."

"I can't do that," Ella said simply. "It wouldn't be a good idea for a variety of reasons, including department policy." Ella paused, then switched the subject abruptly, a sure sign that she considered the matter closed. "So tell me what you've learned about the death of your friend the Code Talker. Have you found out anything new?"

Rose filled her in, and told her about the dog tag for Charlie Dodge she'd found in his home. "There's one thought that bothers me a great deal. I can't help but wonder if my friend killed his brother somehow—accidentally, of course—and buried him there. The uniform might have been a way of pleasing a little brother who'd always wanted to be just like his big brother."

"Maybe, but if that's what really happened back then, I can understand why he would have wanted to keep it a secret. He would have been ostracized by everyone, even if it had been proven to be an accident. Killing a close relative is one of the ways a skin . . . an evil one," she said correcting herself quickly, "gets his power. No one would have trusted him."

"You do well not to use the word and risk calling them to you," Rose said. Speaking of skinwalkers was always dangerous.

Ella nodded, then continued. "The brother that took on the identity of the other may have been forced to do so in order to survive," Ella said. "Of course, if it was a murder, one committed during an argument, let's say, then that puts the matter in a completely different light."

Rose shuddered. "I have to know the truth. And I also need to learn how and why my friend was killed."

"Mom, you don't know that he was. He fell off a cliff after having a heart attack, remember?"

Rose gave her a steady look.

"Okay—you're sure he was murdered—but that's not

enough in a court of law. How are you going to prove anything?"

"First, I have to uncover the truth. After I do that, we'll see what needs to be done to put the one responsible in jail."

Ella took a deep breath and let it out slowly. "Mom, when you investigate something like this, the answers you find aren't always what you expected or wanted."

Rose nodded, knowing exactly what Ella meant. "My friend might have been guilty of a crime that resulted in his burying his own brother in a secret grave. That's true. But I have to know."

"I wish I could help you officially, but even if he killed his brother, the police still have no reason to investigate, because the killer and his victim are both dead."

"That's all right. I'll handle it my own way, but I'm seeing this through to the end. I have no other choice. If my friend was killed because of his knowledge of the Plant People—or, more to the point, because I asked him to help me locate certain plant communities—then I have a debt to repay, and this is the only way I can do that."

"Mom, think this through carefully. If your friend was forced off a cliff, then the killer got away with murder. But now you come along and become a threat to him."

"I know where you're heading. You don't have to spell it out for me. But it doesn't change anything. If you want to help me, then find out who broke into our home."

Ella's face grew hard. "I've tried. I checked everyone on the list you gave me. Without prints, I've got nothing, but I questioned all the suspects. None of them had really solid alibis for the second break-in, so I couldn't rule anyone out." Ella paused for a moment, then added, "Do think that ties in to the death of the Code Talker?"

"I'm not ruling out the possibility."

Ella nodded. "Spoken like a cop."

"My daughter's a great detective," Rose said. "I've learned from her over the years."

Rose and Ella spent the next several hours searching for "white at night" along the arroyos and intermittent streams in her designated area, but it was all to no avail.

"We *have* to find it," Rose said, stopping to rest atop an old sun-bleached, half-buried cottonwood limb that had been washed away after breaking off the tree. "I can't stand the thought of Lena . . ."

"I know, Mom. We'll find the plant."

Yet, after three more hours of fruitless searching had passed, they still had nothing. Ella convinced Rose that it was time for them to head home. "Maybe the others found a place where some are growing. You never can tell," Ella said as they returned to the truck.

Rose shook her head. "No. They haven't found anything. I can feel it here," she said, pointing to her heart.

Ella gazed thoughtfully off into the distance. "We've looked where it's supposed to be," she said. "How about if we start looking in places where it's not supposed to be?"

Rose smiled sadly. "That works well with police work, but not so much with the Plant People. They come from seeds, or roots from the parent plants, and require certain specific conditions."

As they reached the main highway, Ella glanced toward Pastora Peak, way over in Arizona. "Mom, do you remember the old grocery store and gas station that used to be just this side of the Arizona state line when I was a kid? Off the highway near Beclabito?"

Rose nodded. "It was a trading post before that. Everyone used to stop there to talk and catch up on the news while they bought sodas, snacks, or gasoline. But it closed down after they built the new place on the highway . . . at least I think it did." She paused, then added, "I haven't been there in years—since your father stopped having those church revivals all over the reservation."

"Let's go check it out. If anyone is still around there, they might be able to give you a clue that will help you figure out who your Plant Watcher friend really was. He lived in that area all his life."

It took them a while to find the turnoff because of highway construction. "I don't think anyone's come up this way in ages," Rose said.

As they drove up the winding road, which led through red sandstone canyons dotted with piñons and junipers, Rose searched her memory. "I remember that Jerry and Cammy Hatcher ran the place. Jerry was an Anglo, and Cammy a Navajo from Many Farms. I think they both passed away several years back, but I remember that they had a daughter a few years older than I was. They named her Merline."

As they pulled up to the crumbling adobe building, it appeared to be completely deserted. Windows were broken and the door swung back and forth on one hinge in the breeze.

"Well, that's that. No one's here," Ella said. "Sorry, Mom. My idea was a bust."

"Not so," Rose said. Just over the next rise, she could see a curl of smoke. Rose opened the car door, and as a breeze rose, the scent of burning leaves became pronounced. "Someone's working in their yard. Can you smell it?"

"Yes, I can."

"The road up ahead doesn't look good enough to risk driving across in my old truck. Why don't we walk from here?"

"I'm up to it if you are, Mom."

The old wood-frame house was less than a half mile away.

Rose kept her eyes on the ground, always searching for "white at night" and the other plants on her list.

They'd traveled halfway when Rose felt Ella's mood change. They hadn't spoken and she hadn't looked at her daughter, but she *knew*. There had always been a special connection between them that couldn't be easily explained.

"What's wrong, daughter?" she asked softly.

"I'm not sure, but there might be someone up on the hill just west of us. Don't look and keep walking at the same pace. If I'm right and someone's there, I don't want to tip him off."

Rose resisted the impulse to sneak a quick glance. "It could be someone tending their animals, looking for firewood, or just walking around."

"True." Ella reached up and felt the badger fetish hanging from her neck. "I just don't think we're in any immediate danger, but I don't like the idea of someone up there watching us."

"We've always suspected that the reason the plant thief knows the best sites is because he's been following some of us. Maybe he decided to follow me this time."

"Just stay close to cover, Mom, beside the rocks if possible, and go through that stand of pines ahead."

"Do you still see him?"

"I never saw anyone—just a flash that could have come from anything that has glass or metal."

When they reached the pines, they stopped and looked around, listening. "Well, daughter?" Rose shrugged after a few minutes.

"Okay, let's move on." Moments after they reached the next clearing, they both saw a woman coming down the hill.

"It's a traditionalist," Rose said, noting her long skirt and velvet blouse.

"But not the person who's been watching us," Ella pointed out. "She's coming from a different direction."

The Navajo woman, who was around Rose's age, came up to join them. "I didn't want to be nosy, but we don't see a lot of strangers around here. Are you lost?" she asked.

"No, we're looking for information about the people who used to run the old store and gas station back there. It was a trading post before that," Ella said.

The woman looked at Rose and suddenly smiled. "You're the last person I expected to run into out here."

Rose, recognizing her, greeted her warmly. Mae Brownhat had been a classmate of hers in high school. Over the years, they'd continued to meet sporadically in class reunions, but it had been a good fifteen years since they'd both attended one. In that time, Mae had put on some weight and there were a few more lines around her face, but otherwise she'd changed very little. Rose wondered if she looked as good to Mae. She would have liked to think that she'd aged as gracefully as her friend.

"You used to live in Teec Nos Pos. You've moved?" Rose asked.

She nodded. "When my family moved away to Kayenta, I chose to remain in the Four Corners, but I needed something to do. Then I heard that Merline Hatcher needed live-in help, so I came here."

"What happened to her?" Rose asked.

"She has rheumatoid arthritis and has a very difficult time getting around these days. She should move to the city, but this was the home she shared with her parents and the place where she was happiest. She doesn't want to leave."

"We have to go now," Ella said, taking her mother's arm and urging her along.

"Daughter, what on earth—"

"Someone's up there watching us, and I don't want to stand out in the open until I know who it is. Let's get moving."

"Who is it?" Mae asked.

"I don't know," Ella said, hurrying them.

"We'll be safe up at the house and it's not far," Mae said quickly.

"Take my mother with you. I'm going to find out what's going on," Ella said.

"No, daughter, don't—" Before she could even finish the sentence, Ella was already moving into the trees. "Forgive her," Rose told Mae. "She's a police officer, and it's hard for her to stop being one even when she's not on duty."

Mae hurried toward the house, with Rose beside her. "I can't imagine any danger out here except during the winter, when you might freeze to death."

They walked a little farther, and Rose, not one to miss an opportunity, asked, "I've been looking for 'white at night.' Have you see any around here?"

"No, I haven't. We keep a small garden with medicinal plants, but the things we grow are common all across the reservation."

"Have you had any of your plants dug up and stolen recently?"

Mae stopped in midstride and stared at her. "How on earth did you know that?"

"It's a long story," Rose said, following her toward the house just ahead.

A full twenty minutes had passed, but Ella still hadn't returned. Rose tried to push back the faint stirrings of fear that crept through her. Her daughter was all right. She would have sensed it if Ella had been in trouble.

Merline positioned her wheelchair across from where Rose sat on the old sofa. "My mother loved this land. Everything here reminds me of her, and I've kept the house the same as it was then. She always told me that as long as I lived within the

Sacred Mountains, I'd be protected. That's why I've stayed."

Aware of the way Merline held her misshapen hands protectively against her, Rose gave her a sympathetic smile. "Are you all right? Your hands must give you a lot of pain."

"They do. But there's a special tea Mae makes for me that helps."

Mae smiled. "It's a mixture of 'falling on rock' and 'big yellow on top.' That's why I started the garden—to make sure we always had our own supply handy."

"Earlier you mentioned that someone dug up some of your plants. I'm very interested in learning more about that. We've been having some trouble with a plant thief lately," Rose said, and explained briefly about her survey for the tribe, and the instances of theft she'd discovered. "What did he take?"

" 'Wondering about medicine.' I only had one of those plants here too. They're very hard to grow."

"Did he take it roots and all?"

"Yes," Mae answered. "But I'll keep an eye out for this thief from now on. If we see anyone digging up plants, I'll get word to you immediately."

"Don't confront him, he could be dangerous. Just try to get a good look at his face or his vehicle so you can describe or identify him," Rose said, going to the window and looking outside. "My daughter will be back soon," she said, unable to explain, even to herself, how she knew.

A minute later, Ella came out from behind a cluster of junipers and walked to the house.

Rose opened the front door and greeted her. "Did you find who you were looking for?"

"There was no one up there by the time I got up the hill," Ella said, frustration coloring her tone. "You came from the other direction," she said, looking at Mae. "Did you see anyone up on the ridge?"

"No, I sure didn't."

"I'd like to see the hole the thief left behind when he dug up your 'wondering about medicine' plant," Rose said.

Mae took Rose and Ella outside, along with Merline in her wheelchair, and pointed to the ground at a spot near a pile of ashes where some leaves had been burned only recently. Rose wasn't surprised to see the arrowhead type of shovel point that was distinctive of the GI shovel.

"Who knows that you have a garden with medicinal plants?" Rose said.

"Almost everyone," Mae said, "and not just around here. We went to lunch at the Totah Café yesterday and ran into *Gishii*. We spoke about plants, and especially our gardens."

"And she loves to gossip," Rose finished with a tiny smile. "Did you notice anyone else interested in what you were all talking about?"

Mae considered it and shook her head. "There were plenty of other people around, but I never really looked. We were having too much fun to worry about anything else."

Rose glanced at Merline, who shook her head. "If you happen to see any 'white-at-night' growing around here, will you send word to me immediately?" she asked, telling them about Lena.

"You can count on it. Is that why you came, to find the plant?" Merline asked as they all returned to the living room.

"Partly, but I had another purpose as well," Rose said. "I know your father ran the trading post from the thirties to the fifties, and I wondered if you remember him ever talking about the Plant Watcher from Arizona who died recently. Do you know who I mean?" Seeing Merline nod, Rose continued. "Or maybe you know someone else who might be able to give me some information about him."

"I don't remember my dad ever talking about him. I wish I

could help you, but—" She stopped speaking and suddenly smiled. "Wait a minute. My Dad kept scrapbooks with photos all the years he ran the trading post. He had wanted to write his memoirs someday. There are lots of pictures and news-paper clippings in those books. Do you think they might help you?"

"They might. May I see them?"

"Give me a hand, Mae?" she asked, as she turned the wheelchair around and went down the hall. Moments later, both women returned holding several thick scrapbooks.

"The pages are very old and will tear easily, so please be very careful when you handle these," Merline said.

"I will." Rose took them and went back to sit on the couch. The scrapbooks contained everything from newspaper head-lines pertinent to the times, to photos and mementos. Rose concentrated on the photos, most of which were black-and-white snapshots held in place by those old glued-on corners. She didn't recognize most of the faces, but some, like her hus-band's, were forever etched in her mind.

"I never knew my husband and your father were friends," Rose said.

"They may not have been. Dad loved to take photos of peo-ple he thought were interesting for one reason or another, and those prayer meetings and revivals of your husband's always attracted a lot of attention."

Rose could certainly understand why he'd thought her husband Raymond was interesting. Although Raymond had been a walking mass of contradictions, he'd possessed an undeniable charisma that had drawn people to him wherever he went. The large servings of food he always provided at his church crusades didn't hurt either.

Near the middle of the fourth scrapbook, filled during the war years, Rose spotted what she'd been looking for among several pages showing soldiers in uniform. She found one labeled *Charlie and Gilbert Dodge and Bruce Gunn*. A young Charlie Dodge in uniform stood beside a younger Navajo man she assumed was Gilbert, his brother. The resemblance between the two was striking. Behind both stood a tall, muscular Anglo young man she took to be Bruce Gunn.

Ella looked over Rose's shoulder. "Who's the Anglo man?"

"It says here that his name is Bruce Gunn, but I don't remember any family around here by that name. Do you?" Seeing Ella shake her head, she glanced at the other two women. Merline shrugged, but Mae remained thoughtful.

"The name sounds familiar," Mae said, "but I can't quite place it. You know what? Clara Henderson might be able to help you. She's met almost everyone who has ever lived in these parts."

"That's a great idea," Rose said. "May I borrow the photo?" she asked, looking at Merline. "I promise to take good care of it and bring it back undamaged."

"All right."

After saying good-bye, Ella and Rose walked back to the truck. "Daughter, what did you find up there when you went to look around? Something disturbed you. I could see it on your face when you returned."

"Someone had been there, but the really curious thing is that he went to the trouble of wiping out his tracks."

"With a branch?"

"No, he used the old Indian way—sprinkling sand over the footprints so it all blends together."

Rose remembered the tracks that had been obliterated around the cliff where Charlie Dodge had died. The same method had been used there.

It took a moment for the realization to hit her. Then, as understanding dawned on her, a shiver ran up her spine. This could mean only one thing. Charlie's killer now had his eye on her.

Although it wasn't easy, Rose kept the observation to herself. She knew that there was nothing her daughter could do, since there was no hard evidence to substantiate any of it. The police didn't believe a murder had taken place.

This would have to remain her fight—one she'd have to see through alone—at least for now.

TWENTY-ONE

✖ ✖ ✖

Later that evening during visiting hours, Rose headed out to the hospital. Unfortunately, no one had found the plant needed for Lena's ritual. Now Rose had to do whatever was necessary to try and keep Lena from losing hope.

When Rose walked down the hospital corridor twenty-five minutes later, she was surprised to see Herman leading Lena down the hall. Lena was dressed in her regular clothes and, from what Rose could see, was having a lot of difficulty walking. She was leaning heavily on Herman.

"What's going on?" Rose asked quickly, joining them.

"I'm going home. The doctors here can't help me." Lena's voice sounded hollow and weak.

"They're allowing you to leave?" Rose asked shocked.

"Allow? I'm an adult. I don't need their permission."

Rose looked at Herman, hoping to understand what had precipitated Lena's sudden decision, but he simply shrugged.

"She was heading out of her room, though she was barely able to stand, when I found her," Herman said.

"What are you thinking?" Rose glared at Lena. "This is crazy. You're not well enough to be walking around. Who'll take care of you at home?"

"What does it matter? I'm getting sicker here," Lena said

quietly. "They can't do anything about it. They test for this and for that, and nothing comes of it. I just want to go home."

Rose tried to think of a way to stop her, but knew that when Lena made up her mind, that was that. Not that she blamed her. She knew Lena would never find peace here at the hospital. People walked the halls at all hours. Machines beeped or whirred constantly, and everything squeaked. Most of all, death shadowed these halls. She'd hated every second she'd spent here after her collision with the drunk driver.

"You were here long enough to know how difficult this place is," Lena said almost as if reading her mind. "This isn't for you and me. When we try to follow rules that make no sense to us, everything gets worse, not better."

"Have you told your doctor what you're doing?" Rose asked.

"Yes. He said he'll sign the release papers—under protest." Lena gestured toward the nurses' desk. "There he is now. You might suggest he hurry up, because I'm leaving," she said, creeping along slowly toward the door, Herman supporting her.

"I'll take her home. Don't worry," Herman assured Rose. "Sadie and Boots will be there waiting for us. I've already called them. You can meet us there."

With a sigh, Rose went up to the Anglo doctor. Many young doctors like him came to the reservation to pay off their college loans, or as a substitute for military service, but few stayed after they'd met their obligations.

"Before you ask, I would have preferred Mrs. Clani stay," the doctor said. "But she may be right. This isn't the best place for her. We've compensated for her blood pressure problems and have given her pills to take care of her tachycardia, but she's been getting steadily worse. She's depressed, unhappy, certainly not eating, and her red blood cell count is not good. I have no experience with tribal customs, but I do know how important a positive outlook can be to a patient. I'm really beginning to think that unless she gets traditional Navajo treatment she'll continue to deteriorate. The only time she showed any improvement was after the . . . what do you call her . . . the hand trembler came."

Rose nodded. "You've given up, then?"

"No, not at all. I'm still going to send by a nurse practitioner to monitor her vital signs daily on an outpatient basis. I'll work with the practitioner and treat Mrs. Clani's symptoms, but for the most part, I'm going to let her handle things her own way and see what happens. But she and I have made a deal. If she gets worse at home instead of better, then she comes right back. You and her other friends need to make sure she keeps her part of the bargain."

Rose hurried outside and found Lena already inside Herman's truck. Rose helped her strap her seat belt on, then nodded to Herman. "I'll follow you."

Twenty minutes later, they arrived at Lena's home and were greeted by Jennifer and Sadie. Herman led Lena inside and Rose stopped to talk to Jennifer.

"Will you need to stay here, Boots, now that she's home?" Rose asked. "If you do, that's fine, but let me know, because I have to find someone to help with my granddaughter."

"I'll be here at night, and my mother will stay during the day," Jennifer answered. "Mom isn't a traditionalist like my grandmother and me, and they don't always get along, but they do love each other. If Mom should need a break, Sadie has agreed to remain here as well."

"I'm glad you've worked it all out," Rose said with a nod.

Rose helped Lena to bed, and as Lena sank into her own familiar mattress, she sighed contentedly. Rose could feel her relax. Her friend had been right to come back to the home she loved.

As Lena closed her eyes and her breathing became rhythmic, Rose reached into her purse and brought out the new *jish* her son had made for her before she'd been to that grave site. Right now she wanted Lena to have whatever power and protection it could give her.

Leaving the medicine bundle by her bedside, Rose tiptoed out of the room.

The following morning after taking care of her own garden and tending Charlie's plant, which had perked up, Rose checked and learned that Lena had slept peacefully through the night. Relieved, she drove to Clara Henderson's home.

Clara lived just off the reservation near Waterflow with her daughter Lori, who worked in Farmington during the day. Clara loved her old farm near the river, and had told all the Plant Watchers on more than one occasion that she enjoyed being alone during the day. She could move at her own pace, not have a television or radio blaring at her, and could come and go as she pleased.

Rose pulled up in front of Clara's home, a low, wood-framed, pitched-roof building, and waited in the truck. After five minutes, when no one came out to greet her, Rose climbed out of her pickup and looked around. Closer to the river where an old orchard gave way to the bosque and a high levee protecting the farmland from floods, she could see a hunched-over figure moving along the sandy soil. The entire area was dappled with sunlight and shadows from the tall canopy of old cottonwood trees. Clara's white wool shawl gleamed in the sun like a beacon.

Rose walked down to meet her. Clara had slowed over the years, but she still said her prayers to the dawn and went for long walks every day.

As Rose drew near, Clara spotted her and waved. "You're

just in time," she said. "I just took a long walk, said a prayer and scattered some corn pollen in the river, then picked some 'big yellow on top' to add to our stew tonight."

"At least there's still plenty of that around," Rose said.

"How is our friend?" Clara asked, knowing exactly what had been on Rose's mind. "I heard she insisted on going home last night."

"She seems a lot happier in her own house, but a ceremony will have to be performed soon and there's still no 'white at night' to be found anywhere."

"I know. I've searched too, without any luck," Clara said. "I did find some 'gray sunflower.'" Clara brought a small cutting from the hand-sewn leather pouch she carried. "Will you take it to our friend and tell her to remember the legend? When Horned Toad was in mortal danger, he ran under 'gray sunflower.' Lightning and chaos rained from the heavens, but he remained safe," Clara said. "It can do the same for her."

Rose nodded and smiled. "She'll appreciate it."

They walked back up to the farmhouse, and once inside the kitchen, Clara slowly ambled to the stove, filled a kettle with water, then placed it on the gas burner.

"Tell me what brings you here," Clara said.

"I'm trying to find someone—a person I'm hoping you know or remember." She told her about Charlie and everything that she'd learned. "I found a photo of his brother—who looks almost like his twin—and they were standing with an Anglo man by the name of Bruce Gunn. Do you happen to know him or his family?" Rose handed her the photo.

"I knew a family by that name years ago, but I have no idea where any of them are now." Before Clara could say any more, they were interrupted by the sound of a car driving up.

Rose went to the window so Clara wouldn't have to get up. "It's *Gishii*," she said.

"Invite her in," Clara said.

Minutes later the three women were sitting around the small kitchen table. *Gishii* had brought her special corn–sunflower-seed bread that she made by grinding her own corn into meal, kneading it into a dough, then adding the seeds for flavor. They each took a piece and ate as Rose told *Gishii* who she needed to find.

"I don't know if it's the same man you're looking for, but I do know someone with that last name. I teach gardening classes at the Farmington Retirement Village north of Thirtieth Street. One of the seniors there goes by the name of Bruce Gunn, but, of course, it doesn't necessarily mean that it's the same man you're looking for. But he is in his late seventies, which is the right age."

"I'd like to meet him. Can you arrange it?"

"I can try, but I don't know his telephone number, nor do I know which of the cottages at the village is his home. I can talk to him next week during class, or we can go over there now and see if we can find him around the recreation building. That's where many of the residents spend a lot of their time."

"Sooner is better," Rose said.

"Okay," *Gishii* said, then looked at Clara, their host. "After I finish in Farmington, will you help me come up with the right proportions for gold dye? I have several pounds of cliffrose twigs and leaves, and I've found some alum at the base of the rock cliffs to add to it, but I haven't had much success getting everything mixed together right."

"Come back anytime and I'll be glad to help you," Clara said. "I'll be around all day."

After saying good-bye to Clara, Rose walked out with *Gishii*. "My truck or yours?"

"Let's go in mine. I have a sticker on the bumper that will get us past the security guard easily. Clara won't mind if you leave your pickup parked here."

They were on their way five minutes later. *Gishii* was unusually quiet for a long time, but Rose allowed the silence to stretch. Finally *Gishii* spoke.

"I don't know why knowing our old friend's real name makes such a difference to you. He was who he was—regardless of the name he chose to use."

"I need to do this for myself," Rose admitted, then took a deep breath and let it out slowly. "But it's for his sake too. He was the one who made sure that we would find the other body— probably that of his brother. He wanted the truth to be known."

"It's a lot to take on, after so many decades have passed."

"Yes, it is, but I won't give up." Everything was connected, and a pattern would emerge sooner or later. As it was now, it was possible that Charlie had been killed because of who he'd been instead of what he'd been doing for her. It was a shred of hope Rose clung to desperately out of her own selfishness or guilt.

Thirty minutes later, *Gishii* drove through the entrance to the retirement community, a pleasant, well-landscaped collection of small houses arranged in five dwelling arcs connected by sidewalks. There were no roads inside the complex itself, just large landscaped areas with stone walkways that cut through them.

"All the cottages here are numbered, and the residents can be as independent as they choose to be. There's nursing care provided for all of them, and recreational activities are part of the package as well. That's where I come in. I teach gardening, and help with the pottery classes," *Gishii* explained.

"There are a lot of cottages here," Rose observed, noting at least five of the curved rows radiating outward from the center. Each individual unit had a small garden area in the front and, she supposed, in the back. All were well tended.

"We provide gardeners for those who can't or choose not to garden. The people here seem very happy."

They wandered around the main building, the recreation center, but it appeared all but deserted at the moment. "There must be another activity going on now, maybe even a field trip. Usually we'd see at least four or five people in the indoor pool and twice that number in the outdoor one." *Gishii* paused, lost in thought. "Let's circle around the complex and see what we can learn."

As they walked around the complex, Rose felt uncomfortably hot. The facility appeared to be relatively new, and there were no tall trees to provide shade. Unfortunately, it was over ninety degrees today.

"Will anyone go outside their homes in this heat?" Rose asked.

"Keep an eye out for anyone heading to one of the pools. That's our best hope."

Halfway around the circle of cottages, Rose saw a well-dressed woman in her late sixties carrying a cheese tray. She was hurrying toward them along the circular walkway.

"We're in luck," *Gishii* said. "That's Lydia Gonzales coming. She's in my gardening class." *Gishii* waved at her, then glanced at Rose. "Remember, here I'm just Reva."

After introducing Rose, *Gishii* added, "I'm glad I ran into you. We're looking for Mr. Gunn. Do you know where we can find him?"

"At the welcome party, probably. We have a new resident, and nearly everyone is there," Lydia said, glancing down at the cheese platter. "Just follow me. I'm on my way there now."

They walked down to the patio door of a nearby cottage, a white stucco unit with a newly mowed lawn, and went inside. Lydia led the way through the mass of perfumed, silver-haired women, and Rose was introduced to everyone, including Bruce Gunn, who insisted on firmly shaking her hand. The touch, from a stranger, made her uncomfortable, but she tried not to let it show, focusing instead on why she was there.

Although his first and last name matched the man she was searching for, she couldn't tell if he was the same person pictured in the photo or not. Too many years had passed. The man before her had dark hair, dyed, obviously, to hide most of his gray, and he wore thick-framed glasses, but the age seemed right.

Coming up with a strategy to get the information she needed, Rose went over to the buffet table. She had a feeling that if she stayed where she was and didn't press it, he'd come to her. In a room filled with older women, older men often had a tendency to seek food and refuge. The obvious place was by the buffet table. The round dining table was filled with every kind of party snack available, all in heirloom serving dishes that looked like some she'd seen in antique stores. She took a small paper plate, filled it up, then waited.

It happened slowly. Gunn worked his way through the gathering and eventually, with a nod of greeting, joined her and began to fill his plate with everything the buffet offered.

"The deviled eggs are particularly tasty," Rose suggested.

"That's good to know. I skipped breakfast, so I have to stock up now. I'm still a growing boy—though the growth generally takes place laterally."

Gunn placed several carrot sticks on his plate, then looked at her and smiled. "I'm not fond of raw vegetables, but as long as they're on my plate, I can pretend I'm eating healthy."

He sat down next to Rose in one of the unoccupied folding chairs against the wall. "What brings you here to our community, Rose?" he asked as he ate.

"I came to speak to you, actually. We have a mutual friend who passed away recently."

He nodded. "I heard. Bad news always travels fast, especially that kind of news in this kind of community." He shrugged, then added, "Charlie always mentioned your name to me whenever we met, though admittedly that hasn't been very often lately—not since I moved here."

Rose waited, but when Gunn offered no more information, she pressed him. "I came to find out who he really was."

Understanding and a trace of sadness shone in his eyes. "He told me a long time ago that this day would come." He paused, picking at his food. "You must have found his brother's body," Gunn added, his voice whisper-thin.

"Yes, but only because he told us exactly where to dig."

He nodded. "That secret was one that always ate at him, you know. The past followed him every day of his life." He stood. "Let's go for a walk and you can tell me how you tracked me down and why you want to know. I've kept this secret my entire life, and talking about it goes against the grain even now."

"I understand." As they left the party, going back out through the patio door, Rose saw some of the women watching her curiously. She had no doubt that *Gishii* would be grilled for information about her. From what she could see, Mr. Gunn was one of the few bachelors present.

"Now tell me what led you to me and why you need to know," he said as they walked toward a covered picnic table beside the recreation center.

"My involvement in this started when my Plant Watcher friend—the person I always knew as Charlie—died," Rose said. She left out her belief that he'd been murdered, but when she mentioned that he'd been working at the top of a cliff and fallen to his death, she saw the flash of surprise in Gunn's eyes.

He led her to the bench, then remained standing, leaning against the massive support of the canopy which provided the overhead cover. "I have a feeling you're trying to find out why a man with vertigo was up on a cliff," he said. "Do you believe someone pushed him over the edge?"

"Yes, I do." The candor in his gaze and his voice called for nothing less from her.

"Now you need to know why he kept this secret from you, and who he was before he assumed Charlie Dodge's identity. You need to see the whole picture to find answers." Seeing her nod, he exhaled softly. "All right, I'll tell you what I know. The man you knew as Charlie was really his younger brother, Gilbert."

"I began to suspect that when I first learned that Charlie had a brother, but I need to know the rest of the details." She paused, then in a soft voice added, "It's very important to me."

Gunn took a deep breath. "I'm not particularly proud of my part in what I'm about to tell you, though heaven knows we didn't have many other options at the time."

He lapsed into a long silence before he finally continued. "Times were hard back then for nearly everyone in New Mexico, but life was especially cruel to boys like Gilbert and Charlie Dodge, who had nothing but each other. Their father had died shortly after Gilbert was born, and their mother worked hard to provide for her two sons. Six months after Charlie enlisted, she died of tuberculosis. Gilbert, who'd quit school a year before to help his mother, had a job chopping and hauling wood for Jerry Hatcher at the trading post, making less than a dollar a day. Most of their clan had been wiped out during the influenza epidemic following World War I, so he wouldn't have been able to get by at all if it hadn't been for Charlie, who always sent half his Marine paycheck home."

"Were you also too young to enlist?"

He shook his head. "I was Charlie's age, but the Army had already rejected me because I have flat feet. Gilbert and I were both stuck wanting to enlist and not being able to do it, so that gave us common ground and we became really good friends. He and I spent most of our free time together back then."

"What happened to Charlie?" she asked softly, getting him back on track.

"I'm getting to that," he said, then continued in a strained voice. "Charlie came home on leave after basic training. He was a lot tougher-looking and more confident in his new Marine uniform, but, deep down, he was the same old Charlie. He'd always had a reckless streak in him, and now it seemed even worse with all that gung-ho Marine attitude.

One afternoon, he got hold of one of Jerry Hatcher's pistols, a big Colt .45, and insisted on showing us what a good shot he'd become. You see, Gilbert had always been the better shot, so Charlie had something to prove. He started twirling the loaded pistol on his finger like a Hollywood cowboy."

Rose felt her breath catch in her throat. She knew in her heart what was coming next.

"He lost control, the pistol started to fall, and he made a grab for it. The gun went off and the bullet struck him right in the heart. Even if it had happened in the finest hospital in the world, they'd have never been able to save him. By the time I checked for his pulse, he was dead."

"But it was an accident. Why didn't you both just report it?"

"I started to, but Gilbert stopped me. He said that his brother was dead and nothing would bring him back, but if I kept my mouth shut, he might be able to do some good for our country and make both their lives count for something. He told me that he was going to try and take Charlie's place in the Marines." Gunn paused, took a deep breath, then continued. "I told him he was crazy. Charlie had gone through basic and Gil had no training at all. But Gil's mind was made up. He'd always been a better marksman than Charlie, and he was sure he could pick up whatever skills he needed along the way. Anything he didn't know, he'd learn from the other Marines."

"Boys that age often overestimate their capabilities," Rose said.

"Gilbert was a survivor, and I knew that if anyone could pull it off, it would be him. At that time, there was nothing on the Rez for him except poverty and hardship. By taking his brother's place he would at least have a chance to make something of himself."

"But without any training, you could have just as easily been condemning him to death."

"To me, back then, the issue was more black and white. He could take his chances and die honorably fighting for his country, or die slowly of starvation or maybe by freezing to death the following winter. Their woodstove was broken, and his chances of getting another without the money from Charlie's paycheck were slim to none."

"They looked a lot alike, certainly, but wasn't he afraid that someone would spot the switch?"

"Charlie had already been scheduled for additional training, which I found out years later was Code Talker school. It was a new program, nobody had seen his brother there, and Charlie's uniform fit Gilbert perfectly."

"So you buried one brother and gave the remaining one a chance to find his destiny," Rose said at last.

"That's exactly what we did," he answered. "We both felt Charlie deserved a coffin, so we made one for him out of scrap lumber and two packing boxes, then buried him that same night by the Hogback, not far from the trading post. From that day on, Gilbert ceased to be. Only Charlie existed." He rubbed his eyes. "After we buried his brother, I made Gilbert a promise that I'd never tell anyone what had happened as long as he was alive. Of course, we both knew that after his stint in the Marines was up, he'd have to stay away from Shiprock. Neither of us could afford to have someone recognize who he really was and start asking questions."

Rose nodded but didn't comment.

"He finally returned home fifteen years later. By then, no one recognized him—including me. He'd changed, physically and mentally, so it all worked out." Gunn fell silent for several long moments. "As you can see, his murder couldn't have had anything to do with who he was or became."

Rose knew now that Charlie had died because of his search for the endangered native plants—work that she'd brought to him.

"What do you plan to do with this information, Rose?"

"The police don't believe it was murder. So it's up to me to find the answers and restore harmony. And, somehow, that's exactly what I intend to do."

On the way back to the reservation an hour later, *Gishii* was uncharacteristically quiet. Rose stared out the window, lost in thought.

"Old friend, I can't stand the suspense. I know you've learned something that's upsetting you. What is it?" *Gishii* asked.

Rose told her what Bruce Gunn had said, knowing Gilbert had wanted the truth to come out. "So I inadvertently ended up causing his death by asking him to help me find the missing Plant People," Rose said finally in a shaky voice. Pausing, she pulled herself together. "What scares me the most is that I may end up losing two friends, not just one, if I don't manage to find one of the Plant People the *hataalii* needs for the ceremony. And I can't ask anyone else to help me look for the plant she needs—not until the killer is caught."

"You won't need to ask for help. We'll give it to you whether you want it or not."

Rose smiled. "Then warn the others for me. They need to know the risks."

Soon they pulled up in front of Clara Henderson's home. As *Gishii* parked, Clara hurried out, at the best speed the ancient woman could muster, to meet Rose.

"You have to go over to Lena's house right now. Her daughter just called and she needs your help. Lena is getting ready to leave."

"Leave? You mean return to the hospital?"

"No, no, to their family's hogan up in the mountains."

The words sank in slowly. She knew precisely what was going through her friend's mind. Lena was getting ready to die, and was worried that although her modernist daughter would never give the *chindi* a second thought, her granddaughter, a traditionalist, would never willingly step into a place where a death had occurred. Rather than have her home become a source of contention between them, Lena was going up to the hogan to die.

TWENTY-TWO

——— ✖ ✖ ✖ ———

As Rose drove up to Lena's home, she saw Lena's daughter, Ruthann, holding on to her mother's arm in the open doorway. "You're not going anywhere, Mother. I'm not taking you there, and you can't drive yourself. You're in no condition for anything like that."

"I have to go," Lena said, pulling to get loose.

Rose hurried over to the front porch, smiled at Ruthann, then touched Lena's arm. "Let's go back to your room, old friend. You and I can speak in private there."

Lena met her friend's gaze, then nodded. As Rose led her back across the living room, Ruthann dropped down heavily onto the couch, exhausted.

Lena half staggered down the hall, with Rose trying to steady her, then sat down heavily on her bed. "I can't stay here any longer. I had a dream last night where I was told that 'white at night' is gone from the reservation forever. That was a sign for me. I know now that I'm going to die soon, but I don't want it to happen in the hospital, where I'm a stranger, or here at home. I have good memories of the hogan. It's where I grew up, and that's where I choose to die. But I need to go now while I'm still strong enough to make the journey."

"You're not going to die. I won't let you. It's not your time.

I know that in my heart. I'll call my son so he can come and do a Sing that will keep the dream from coming true." Rose noted how the exertion had bathed her friend's forehead in perspiration, and Lena seemed ready to pass out. "You have to relax. Lay back on your pillow and think of all the things you've yet to do."

"Your son can't stop what has already happened, old friend," Lena said without emphasis, lying back as Rose had asked.

It was the flat, colorless tone of her voice that frightened Rose the most. She'd met others who had declared they were going to die, and those people usually did, even though they'd often seemed in perfect health.

"I'll find the plant that's needed. I know I will," Rose said.

"You can't, not this time." Lena smiled wearily. "I remember when my mother took to her bed—a woman who, like me, had never been sick a day in her life. The Anglo doctors couldn't tell us what was wrong. A *hataalii* was supposed to come and do a Sing for her, but his horse went lame, and he had no other way to get there in time. Mother asked my father to take her outside the hogan because she wanted to sleep under the stars, like she did when she was at the sheep camp during the summer. She was dead before morning."

"That was your mother—not you. You still have time."

"Yes, there's time, but not much. That's why I have to go up to the hogan *now*." Lena struggled to sit back up again, but sagged back onto her pillow with a groan.

Rose fought the panic that swelled inside her. One of them had to stay calm. "Why don't you and I make a deal? You're safe and comfortable here, so let's take advantage of that for now. If you let me know when the time draws near, I'll see to it myself that you die near the hogan, and under the stars, like your mother. Will you trust me to carry out that promise?" Rose reached over and placed her hand on Lena's and gave it a squeeze.

"All right."

Rose sighed with relief. Only one thing would cure Lena now—she needed the right Sing. "I have a present for you from our oldest Plant Watcher." Rose reached into her purse and brought out the sprigs of 'gray sunflower,' then hung them upside down near the window according to tradition. "She wanted me to remind you of the story about Horned Toad."

Lena smiled. "I know it well. Thank her for me," she said in a thin voice.

"I'm going over to see my son right now. He'll take care of things for you." Rose swallowed, making sure her voice remained steady when she continued. "You're my closest friend, Lena, and I can't lose you. Trust me to find the plant you need. I won't fail you," she said confidently.

Rose left the house feeling far less confident than she'd allowed anyone to see. The truth was she didn't know where else to search. But to tell Lena the truth would have robbed her of all hope and there was no way she could have done that. Lena needed her now, just like Rose had needed her countless of times in the past. They were there for each other—always. That was the bedrock of their friendship. She'd find "white at night" no matter what it took.

She arrived at her son's hogan a half hour later. She'd surprised herself by making the thirty-minute drive in less than twenty-five. Clifford came out of his hogan to greet her and Rose quickly climbed out of her pickup.

"Have you found the plant you need yet?" she asked.

"No. All the *hataaliis* have joined the search, but we've had no luck so far. One of the others needs 'baby newborn' for a Blessing Way, and none of us have found that plant either."

"It's a little early for it to be covered in blooms, and without the flowers, it's easy to overlook. It's never more than ten inches high."

"Our new traditionalist medicine man had one plant in his garden, and it wasn't in good shape, but it did have one small flower. He sold the pollen to the other *hataalii*."

"And now there's no more?" Seeing Clifford nod, she quickly added, "Won't you need some too?"

"I still have some I collected last year. If the *hataalii* had come to me first, I would have given him what he needed, of course."

Rose nodded. "I've been giving this a lot of thought, son, and I think we need to get a large group of people involved in our search. My friend is running out of time. Tell everyone who might be able to help that there'll be a meeting this evening after sundown in my home. We'll get maps, and coordinate areas, and send out parties of two or more working together to search in a wide pattern first thing tomorrow morning. Whoever is responsible for taking the plants and killing my friend will not attack a group of people, and he can't possibly follow more than one group."

"I'll get the word out."

After Rose got home, she called Willie. He, in turn, promised to phone Maria. "In the meantime," Rose said, "I know that you have your own database on plants. Will you see if any 'white at night' or 'baby newborn' is known to grow anywhere near our borders? We may have to take Plant People from outside the Sacred Mountains if there's absolutely no other choice."

"I see from the master list you gave me that they're what we call evening primrose and Parry bellflower. I'll be happy to check it out for you, but I don't think I've ever kept track of either variety," he said.

"But remember, the closer to our borders, the better."

"I'll see if any of my colleagues have kept track of them and bring whatever information I can find to you tonight."

Rose hung up and got hold of *Gishii* next, who then promised to call all the Plant Watchers and their friends.

"Will a few of the *hataaliis* come to the meeting at your house?" *Gishii* asked. "Their presence would boost the spirits of those of us who are losing hope."

"All I can tell you for sure is that my son will be there."

Rose called Sadie next. "I'd love to take part," Sadie said immediately. "I have some wonderfully detailed maps we can use too."

"Bring them, then."

"You might ask your daughter if her police officer friends will help. They are trained to observe and search."

"Good idea."

Rose checked all her notes and her plant survey reports for any comments she might have written in about the two plants, but she found nothing that could help her. Knowing that her plan was well under way, Rose went to the kitchen to fix snacks for the people who'd drop in tonight. She fixed chile fingers—little bits of chile and cheese and onions wrapped in bread dough, then fried in butter. She had enough for an army by the time she finished, but she knew people loved these snacks and they'd go quickly.

Around five, Ella came in, Dawn with her. "We've been shopping!" Dawn said, showing her some new blue jeans and a blouse that had wonderful cartoon animals painted all over it.

"She picked those herself," Ella said. "She didn't like anything I picked for her."

"You see? Life *is* fair. You drove me crazy just like that when you were a child," Rose said.

As Dawn left to go play with Two, Ella went to the refrigerator and brought out a can of cola. "I gave our babysitter the afternoon off to be with her family. I know the Clanis are devastated by all that's happened."

"They're very frightened," Rose said. "I am too," she added softly.

Ella gave her mother a hug. "Lena will be fine. She's as strong as you are."

"Yes, but even the strong can have their spirit broken. Her son doesn't live on our land and that breaks her heart every day. She's always loved to spend time gathering and collecting plants, and now the Plant People are moving away. Sometimes it's just the *ch'ééná* that kills us—that sadness for what can no longer be. Our heart breaks first, then the body follows."

"Can't my brother help?"

"Not without the Plant People the gods gave us. If the Sing is not exactly right, it will most certainly fail."

An hour later, people began to arrive, some bringing their friends as well. Those in the greatest numbers were the Plant Watchers and their families. Word had spread. By the time the meeting started, over one hundred people were crowded shoulder to shoulder in Rose's small living room.

Maria gave out copies of topographical maps that she'd sectioned off into quadrants. Although no one knew exactly where the two plants could be found, except in generalities, Willie had used what information he had to assign search areas. He explained the geographical sectors and divided them, assigning sections that made sense logically to the groups of people, who had divided themselves into more than twenty teams.

Everyone, it seemed, was eager to help in this emergency. Several people from the Christian church her husband had founded and even a group of young people from the high school's science club came to help. Rose was happy to see all them—from traditionalist to modernist—working together. The search would begin tomorrow, a Saturday.

By the end of the evening, Rose had reason to hope—both for her friend Lena, and for the reservation. If they could come together like this in a time of crisis, there was no doubt in her mind that they would remain strong as a tribe.

Once the people began to leave, Maria came up to Rose and took her aside. "I just wanted to tell you that the tribe has guaranteed me a small amount of money for my research. The state will match it and I'll now be able to continue my work. It's not much, but I'll get by."

"I'm glad to hear that."

"I know I wouldn't have gotten this without your help," she added.

"I'm not your enemy. I never was."

Maria nodded slowly. "I tried to make things difficult for you. I really thought that it was you or me, and I honestly felt my way was better for the tribe." She paused, hesitant to continue. "I did some things I regret . . ." she said slowly, and never looking directly at her.

It took Rose a moment to understand. "That explains why Two growled when you got out of your car this afternoon. Did you come into my house while I was in the shower and try to scare me?"

Maria averted her gaze. "That was me, but I wouldn't have harmed you. I just thought that if I could get you to give up the work you were doing, the tribe would have the money to pay me. I know it sounds selfish, but it wasn't, not really. I honestly felt that I could offer the tribe more." She took a deep breath. "I'm taking a chance telling you this now, but when I confided this to Willie, he felt I should, and I agreed with him. There are things happening now that demand all your attention. You don't need to be distracted or worried about who broke into your house. But I hope you will forgive me. The tribe needs both of us—what we have to offer is different, but necessary."

"What you've told me will remain between you and me," Rose said quietly and without recriminations. "But tell me this.

Did you come back a second time and take my photos?"

"Photos?" Maria shook her head. "No, and I never took anything, I swear it. Your dog scared me half to death. He looks like such a placid animal, but he's very protective."

Rose smiled. "Yes, he is."

"I may still disagree with you about some of the native plants, but I'll make up what I did to you somehow. Then there'll be balance and harmony between us," Maria said quietly. "At least more than before," she added.

Rose smiled. "Just help us find the plant my friend needs. That'll be enough."

Rose said good-bye to everyone, including her son and the other *hataaliis*. All had come except John Joe, who'd said that he had "other commitments." Herman, who'd been one of the first to arrive, stayed behind and helped her clean up. Ella made herself scarce, giving them a chance to talk privately by taking Dawn outside to tend the pony.

"I was surprised to see you here tonight," Rose said as she began to dry off the serving platters Herman had helped her wash. "I know you've been up in the mountains."

"I came down to a trading post for some flashlight batteries, heard about the meeting, and came back right away. You needed me—whether or not you realize it."

Rose nodded. "It's a difficult time for me." She told him about Lena wanting to go to her family's hogan in the mountains. "I said I'd do it, but when the time comes, I'm not sure I'll have the courage."

"You'll do what you have to do, woman, just as you've always done. You have more courage than anyone I've ever met—including your daughter."

"We have different kinds of strengths." Rose took a deep breath. "But I *will* keep my promise, somehow."

At sunrise, Rose said her prayers to the dawn, and then left home to begin her search. Everyone would be doing the same today, all day, as long as it took. Ella would join them later today, if she could take time off from the undermanned police force.

They'd set up a communications plan so that if anyone found either of the plants they were looking for, they'd contact Wilson Joe directly, who was standing by at the college switchboard. Also, each search team was responsible for calling Wilson at two designated times to check the status of the search.

It was around two in afternoon by the time she took a break. Willie, who was searching with her, reported in to Wilson and learned that there was still no positive news from anyone. Rose sat down on one of the boulders and drank the rest of the water she'd brought. As she looked across the field, she saw Willie talking to Bernadette Tso, a member of their group. Moments later, he walked across the canyon toward her. His downcast expression told her that nothing had changed.

"We've scoured every inch, but there's nothing here," he said. "Our helpers are heading back now. The heat is starting to get to many of us."

"It's got to be in the upper nineties. I'm going to head back too," Rose said in a whisper-thin voice. "We can resume later in another area, as planned, when the weather cools off."

"Last night I asked some of my former students to search the area right outside the reservation within the Sacred Mountains, but they haven't found what you needed," he said, readjusting the cell phone clipped to his belt. "Our best bet now is to talk to those whose routines require them to be traveling around the back country and ask them to keep an eye out for those plants."

One person came immediately to Rose's mind—Bradford Knight. The ecologist for Southwest Power Company had to spend a lot of time out in the field. Maybe he'd be able to help them in this time of crisis, if only to provide good publicity for the company.

As the other people who'd joined them at this particular search site walked back to their vehicles, Rose noticed how quiet they all were compared to their earlier, enthusiastic banter. Frustration and sadness were mirrored in all the faces she saw.

Rose, who had come in her pickup alone, now got under way. As she drove toward Shiprock, she tried to figure out the best way to approach Knight. They weren't exactly on good terms with each other.

Deciding to stop by the house and wash up first, she turned south on Highway 666 and headed home. She'd just reached the front door when Ella pulled up behind her in her police unit.

"Mom, I was hoping to catch up with you here. I haven't been able to take any time off. Did any of the groups have any luck?"

Rose shook her head. "No, and it's been a very difficult day." As Rose unlocked the door and went in, Two came up to greet her, but Dawn wasn't home. "Where's my granddaughter?" she asked Ella, who was right behind her.

"Boots needed to stay at home today to help out, so she recommended another traditionalist—Anna Woodis, your Plant Watcher friend's granddaughter. I called her, she said yes, so I took Dawn to her house."

Rose nodded. She'd met Fannie Woodis's family many times, and she approved of Jennifer's choice. "Why couldn't she come here?"

"She's licensed for day care and watches several girls at her home. I've dropped by twice today and the kids are very well supervised. My daughter is having a terrific time."

Rose sat down on the sofa. "I'm glad that's working out, at least."

"What's your next move, Mom?"

"I was hoping to get Bradford Knight's help. He tracks around the reservation a lot and it's possible he's seen the plants we need so badly now."

"That seems like a long shot. What makes you think he ever noticed those two plants in particular, or will remember where he saw them?"

"Desperation, probably," Rose said with a wry smile. "He's my last hope. The only other person I know will probably have the plants is the thief, but I haven't been able to figure out who he is."

"Then that leaves you with Knight for now." Ella was about to say more when she got a call. Unclipping the cell phone at her belt, she spoke quickly.

After a moment, she ended the call. "Mom, I've got to go. There's a disturbance at the high school. Some kids are squaring off in the parking lot and I'm needed for backup. Summer school brings its own problems, I suppose."

Rose watched as her daughter left, but her thought were on the plant crisis. The thief was the key. As a last-ditch idea formed in her mind, Rose called *Bizaadii,* then Sadie Black Shawl, *Gishii,* and Fannie Woodis. The search had been halted until it cooled off later in the day, so they'd all returned home.

An hour later they all met at *Gishii's* house east of Shiprock.

"Tell us your idea. No matter what it is, you can count on us. We all want to help our friend get better," *Gishii* said.

"There's only one person who's likely to have the plants we need—the thief," Rose began. "Although I don't know who the thief is yet, I have some ideas of who it might be—suspects, as my daughter would call them. To find out if any of my guesses are right, I'll need all of you to work with me. We need to follow each person on my list and see where they lead us. *Bizaadii,* Fannie, I'd like you to follow Curtis Largo. But it's very important that he doesn't spot you, because it could be dangerous if he knows what you're doing. Stay far away from him, but see where he goes and who he meets."

"Got it."

"*Gishii,* Sadie, I need you two to focus on our new traditionalist *hataalii.*" There was no need to mention him by name. That description was enough to identify him.

"Who will you be following?" Herman asked.

"I'm going to check out Bradford Knight. I need to ask him if he's seen 'white at night' or 'baby newborn' anyway. After that, I'll give him plenty of room, then see if he goes anywhere on the Rez."

"You're doing that alone?" Herman asked, his tone rising.

"There's no one else I can ask. I tried to call Jane, but I haven't been able to reach her at home. But don't worry. I'll be careful."

He shook his head. "It's too dangerous."

"I'll go with Rose," Sadie said. "*Gishii* can keep calling Jane until she reaches her, then make the arrangements with her."

"But that could take hours," Rose protested.

"It probably won't," *Gishii* said, "but, even if it does, it's safer if we all have someone with us who can go for help."

"We need cell phones," Sadie said. "I've got one, so Rose and I are covered."

"My nephews both have them. I can borrow one of theirs," Herman said.

Gishii considered it. "Jane's daughter has a cell phone, maybe Jane can borrow hers."

Taking the phone book, Rose looked up the addresses. All the suspects were listed except Knight, but she already knew where to find him.

"We're all set," Rose said. "We'll stay in touch."

As soon as the rest of them were on their way, Sadie and Rose climbed into Rose's truck.

"Why don't you call Knight on your cell phone and find out if he's still in his office?" Rose asked. "If he is, make an appointment for later this afternoon, and tell him it's urgent. In the meantime, we'll go to his house." Seeing the surprised look on Sadie's face, she added, "I'd like to take a quick look around his home, and I can't do that if he's there," Rose explained. "It would be a way to rule him out quickly, perhaps."

"You don't plan to break in, do you?"

"No, of course not. I just want to look around his yard and see what kind of herbs and plants he grows."

Sadie dialed and asked to speak to Knight. Moments later, she hung up. "Done. He said he was planning to work late tonight anyway, so he'll be glad to meet us at five."

A short time later, they arrived at a comfortable-looking ranch-style home on a large, fenced-in lot with an orchard of old apple trees. "We're in luck," Rose said. "The houses are far enough away from each other that his neighbors will have a difficult time seeing us poking around."

"I didn't see any cars parked in the driveways, so the people in this neighborhood probably all work."

Rose got out of the pickup and looked around. "See if you can find a way to take a look into his back yard. Just be careful in case he has a dog."

"Okay. What are you going to do?"

"I'm going to see if any doors or windows are open so I can poke my head inside. Then I'm going to check his mailbox."

"Be careful. Tampering with the mail is a federal offense," Sadie said.

"I'm not going to tamper—I'm just looking."

Rose found all the doors and windows shut or locked

partially open, as was the custom in a part of the country where swamp coolers were so common, so she went up to the mailbox at the end of the drive. Taking the envelopes from the box, she sorted through them. They were mostly bills, but one envelope at the bottom of the stack had come from the Research and Development Division of Herbal Promise, a pharmaceutical company.

Sadie came back as Rose was putting the mail back in place. Reading the expression on Rose's face accurately, she smiled. "What did you find?"

Rose hesitated. "It's probably nothing, but I'm going to check it out further," she said, telling her about the letter she'd found from Herbal Promise. "Without reading it, which is something I wouldn't do, I can't know for sure, but it's definitely worth looking into."

"You're thinking that he might be working in cahoots with a pharmaceutical firm, and taking the medicinal herbs from the reservation for testing?" Seeing Rose nod, she added, "We have an appointment with him in thirty minutes. Why don't you ask him straight out if he's affiliated with any of the pharmaceutical companies?"

Rose shook her head. "He'd probably deny it, and it would just tip our hand," she said. "The first thing we have to do is find out if he's seen 'white at night' or 'baby newborn' anywhere. Then, after that question is answered, let's try and see how long he's planning to be in the office tonight. With luck, we'll have time to go to your computer and gather up more information on both Herbal Promise and Mr. Knight. Then we can get back to his office and follow him once he leaves work. If he's already gone by then, we'll try to catch him at home, and see if he goes out later."

"That's a good plan, but we can keep an eye on him at the same time we do the research you want. I have a very good laptop computer, and we can connect it to my cell phone and go on the Internet right here in the pickup."

"All right. We don't have time to stop and get your computer now, otherwise I'd suggest going there first, but once we leave his office, we'll get your laptop and then go right back to keep an eye on him," Rose said, driving in the direction of the coal power plant where Knight had his office. "By the way, what did *you* see around the back of his house, besides the apple trees? Anything interesting?"

"There's quite a bit of land back there—maybe two acres or more. There's a huge outbuilding in the center of the orchard—maybe it's a barn. I couldn't really see much more than that because of the trees in the way. But if we drove up onto the mesa to the north, we might be able to see over the trees, providing we have a good set of binoculars."

They arrived at Bradford Knight's office, in an administrative building beside the massive power plant facility, right at five o'clock. The secretary ushered them in, and as they took a chair, Knight looked up from the computer. He looked tired, and his face was pale for a man who spent so much time outside.

"I understand that you had to speak to me on an urgent matter. What can I do for you?"

"You travel around the reservation, studying the land as part of your work, and must spend a lot of time looking at the vegetation," Rose said. "Do you ever notice the small shrubs and native plants, or do you just study the varieties that could be used in land reclamation?"

"My main concern has been reclamation. Restoring the ground cover effectively and economically is what my job's all about. Why do you ask?" Knight turned away and coughed into a handkerchief.

"We desperately need to find a plant the Navajos call 'white at night.' You would know it as the white-stemmed evening primrose. The plant has white flowers that turn reddish pink as they fade. The primrose grows about a foot high and has white stems with dull green leaves. The flowers only open from late afternoon to midmorning."

"I know the plant you're talking about. You can sometimes find them along the roadside . . . but, come to think of it, I can't recall having seen any recently. This damned drought may be responsible for its decline."

Her heart sank. She asked about "baby newborn" next, using the Anglo name, parry bellflower, but he wasn't able to help her with that one either. "If you see them—"

"I'll call you immediately," he said, finishing her thought. "But if you don't mind my asking, what's the urgency?"

"We need the primrose so an important lifesaving ritual can be done. Parry bellflower is also used in the same ritual, and the medicine men have very little on hand."

"I'll make sure to keep an eye out for both plants, then," he said. "Is there anything else?"

"No, that's all. Thank you for your time," Rose said, standing up. "I hope we haven't kept you from leaving."

"Oh, no, I still have a ton of work to do. I've missed a few days lately. Coming down with something, I think." Knight coughed again, then nodded to both women as they reached the door.

When they reached the parking lot, Sadie's phone rang and she answered it. A moment later, her face turned ashen and her eyes grew wide. "I don't know how to tell you this," Sadie said.

"It's about my friend, isn't it? She needs me to come to her?" Rose asked, correctly reading Sadie's expression. In her heart, she already knew what was happening, but she hoped that this time, her intuition would be wrong.

Sadie nodded. "Lena has asked that you go to her now and fulfill the promise you made her."

Rose felt the tears stinging her eyes. Lena was dying and there seemed to be no way for her to stop it. Swallowing back her tears, she climbed into the truck with Sadie. It was time to honor her word and carry out her duty.

As they rode toward Shiprock, she tried to think of a way to prevent this from happening. Finally she came up with a plan that might buy Lena, and the search, just a little more time.

TWENTY-THREE
——— ✖ ✖ ✖ ———

Rose sat by Lena's bedside. "Are you sure you want to do this?" Rose asked, her voice strained.

"It's our way," Lena replied.

"Will you consider another alternative?" Rose asked, hoping Lena wouldn't fight her on this. When Lena didn't immediately refuse, Rose quickly added, "Will you return to the hospital?"

"What good could that possibly do?"

"You'll be closer to all of us who want to visit, and you'll be giving the modernists in your family a final gift they'll never forget. By going there, you'll give them peace of mind." Rose really hoped Lena would accept. By doing so, it might make her a little more stubborn, and if there was anything Lena needed right now, it was a reason to keep fighting for her own recovery and not give up.

Lena sighed. "All right. Let it be the way you suggest. To be honest, I'd hate for them to be reluctant to visit that old hogan because of bad memories. It's a big part of our family history."

Rose walked out of the room and met Lena's daughter, Ruthann. "She's agreed to go to the hospital."

"I don't know how to thank you! I was going crazy thinking

of her over at the hogan lying on a dirt floor. That would certainly kill her."

"It was our way once," Rose answered.

"But not anymore," Ruthann answered staunchly. "If she has to die, then let her do it someplace clean and comfortable, in a soft bed with heating and cooling, fresh water, and with all of us beside her. And someplace where medical help is available, in case they can intervene."

Rose sighed. She still couldn't really believe that she, of all people, had suggested the hospital, but she was desperate. Maybe Lena's refusal to die in such a place, or perhaps even the Anglo medicine, could help keep Lena alive until the plant was found.

Ruthann made arrangements for an ambulance to transport her mother, and Rose waited until they came and carried Lena into the vehicle. With a heavy heart, Rose watched her friend being driven away. Slowly her fear and sadness gave way to resolve. "Do you have that computer of yours handy?" she asked Sadie.

"Of course, it's still here from before. Do you want me to bring it along when we go to keep an eye on Knight?"

"Yes." As Rose drove east toward the power plant turnoff, Sadie connected with the Internet. She found the public Web site the company had, but it was of little use to them because the information only listed the chief company officers, which didn't include Bradford Knight, of course.

"You need more than I can access on a public Web site," Sadie said. "You need the kind of information a police officer—perhaps your daughter—would be able to get."

By the time they reached the power plant, they saw all the day-shift offices were dark. Unfortunately, Knight's vehicle was no longer in the small parking lot set aside for administrators and their staff.

"Instead of going to his house to see if he's there, I'm going to drop you off and then go home," Rose said. "You're right about the information I need. I'm going to ask my daughter to help out."

Rose dropped Sadie off at the Clani house, where she'd remain to take care of Lena's garden and house-sit. While still at Lena's, Rose called home. No one answered, so Rose decided to stop by the police station and see if Ella was in her office.

Ella was behind her desk scowling at some reports when Rose walked in, escorted by the desk sergeant. "Mom! What brings you here?"

"I need your help." Rose thanked the desk sergeant, who left to return to his post. Once they were alone, Rose told her daughter what she'd done and learned, courtesy of Knight's mailbox.

Ella stood, walked to the door, and shut it. "Mom, have you gone completely crazy? You could have been arrested."

"I don't have time to argue about my methods now, daughter. I need more information on Bradford Knight. That's why I'm here."

"Let me see what I can do."

Ella logged on to her computer and searched out databases until she had a list of company officers for Herbal Promise, which was a subdivision of a larger, well-known pharmaceutical company. Knight's name did not appear. "Let's see what happens when I search under Knight's name and Herbal Promise together."

It took Ella about five minutes to track down the information. "Knight is listed as a scientific consultant to Herbal Promise," she said. Then, working on that information, she was able to go deeper into other databases. "And it's a well-paying job too."

"You have to investigate this man thoroughly, daughter."

"On what grounds, Mom? I can't go after anyone based only on gut feelings and information that was illegally obtained.

Get me something more and I'll see if I can help you. What I need is something that connects him to an illegal act."

"You'll have it!" Rose announced, then stood and thanked her daughter. She left the police station filled with purpose, and using the pay phone outside, called *Bizaadii* using the cell phone number he'd given her earlier.

"I need to borrow something from you. Where are you now?" she asked.

"I'm home. Curtis went home and settled down for the night watching TV, at least that's what it sounded like from outside, so we figured we'd go home too. What do you need?"

"You know those fancy binoculars that you use on those trips into the mountains? I'd like to borrow them for a few hours."

"Okay. Come on over."

Rose arrived twenty minutes later. Herman came out of the house, the binoculars around his neck. Before she could say anything, he opened the passenger door to the truck and slipped onto the seat. "Where are we going?"

Rose was speechless. She'd wanted to do this alone. Herman tended to be too cautious and she was prepared to take whatever chances were necessary to accomplish what she needed to do. She cleared her throat, then whispered, "You don't want to be involved in this."

Herman's reply was definitely not in a whisper. "I'm already involved, old woman. I spent the entire afternoon following Curtis Largo. He's such a disagreeable man, and he seems to spend far more time visiting friends than working. I wasted all that time, and got absolutely nothing except bored. He's supposed to be an expert on plants, but even his yard is a disaster. There's no garden there—just tumbleweeds and two brown, withered ponderosa pines that probably never received another drop of water from the time they were planted." He fastened his seat belt. "Let's go," he whispered.

Rose didn't argue. There was no time. She needed to make sure she had enough daylight to do what she had to do, and the sun was already low in the sky. It would be setting within the hour.

"What are we after?" he said.

"I need to find out if Knight has a greenhouse or a garden for native herbs in the back of his property." She filled him in on what Sadie had found. "If he's the thief, it's very possible he's doing research for a big corporation using plants stolen from the Navajo Nation. That would explain why he's been digging up so many of them. But he may also be innocent. The first step in finding out the truth is to see what's in his back yard in the middle of that apple orchard. If he's our man, that's where I think the plants will be."

"If he catches you, he'll charge you with trespassing, harassment, stalking, or worse."

Rose laughed. "*Stalking?* I can just see my daughter's face. Imagine me stalking anyone. That alone makes the risk more than worth it."

"Your loyalty to Lena may get you in a great deal of trouble, woman," he muttered, then added, "which won't help her, by the way."

"This isn't just about Lena. It's also about my other friend who died searching for the Plant People."

"Then we'll do it together."

"But even if Knight's guilty, we could both end up in jail unless we can prove it. Are you sure you want to help me?"

"Yes. This is something I have to do as well for the same reasons you mentioned. My nephews may not understand my decision, particularly if we end up in trouble, but we can't turn back now."

"All right, then," Rose said. The truth was that she was glad to have his company. She valued Herman's friendship, though it was very different from what she shared with Lena. As women who'd known each other for a lifetime, they'd talk about anything and everything whenever they got together, but talking to Herman wasn't as easy.

"What are you thinking?" he asked.

She decided not to answer his question, and subtly changed the subject instead. "I just can't believe how critically important it has become for us to find just one 'white at night' plant. This thief has to be stopped."

He nodded, deep in thought. "It'll happen."

A short time later they arrived at the top of a high levee that extended for miles along the south side of the San Juan River, which ran through Farmington. They drove along the dirt road until they found a spot where they could see Knight's home on the floodplain just below, less than a few hundred yards away. Rose walked over close to the edge, then asked Herman for his binoculars.

He handed them to her and Rose focused on Knight's property. But there were too many apple trees obscuring her view. All they could see was the roof of the house beyond the orchard, and the glow from the lights of the outbuilding.

"If it was winter, I could probably see pretty well, but there are just too many leaves and branches in the way. I'm going to go in closer," she said.

"Let me have a look first," he said, taking the binoculars back. After a few minutes, he lowered the binoculars. "You're right, but we can't get any closer without going onto his land. It's too risky. What if he's home? There are lights coming from the outbuilding, obviously."

"I'll be careful and stay hidden as much as possible."

"No, I'll do it," Herman said, and started down the levee on a narrow trail before she could argue.

Rose followed him, refusing to be deterred. Once they got

onto Knight's land, she knew she could sneak from tree to tree quieter than any man.

Herman slipped underneath the fence where a drainage ditch exited the property, then went to the closest apple tree and hid behind the trunk. Rose stayed a few feet behind him and, once she was in the orchard, caught a glimpse of a huge low building in the center of the rows of trees.

The roof was glowing, but suddenly darkened. Then she saw light as a door on the end of the building door opened and shut. She came up behind Herman, who was looking toward the building from his hiding place. "Stay back. We'll get caught," he whispered harshly.

"Shhh." Rose took his binoculars, then used the tree trunk to hold them steady as she looked. "It's a greenhouse," she whispered. "The building is low, with a clear plastic or glass roof. That glow we saw earlier was from the plant lights, I'll bet. I have to figure out a way to get in there."

"No way. It's almost dark now."

"Precisely."

"What are you going to do, pick the lock on the door, or break a window and climb in? He's home, or someone is. The door just opened and closed. We can't go in there."

"Sure we can. The greenhouse lights are out, which means he's gone elsewhere, probably to the house. We just need something that will distract him while I search the greenhouse."

"No. You'd be taking too great a risk for what you could get out of it. Even if you got in and were able to assure your daughter that there are plants there just like the ones that are missing from the reservation, that's still not proof of anything. He could easily claim that he'd gotten the plants while off Navajo land. Meanwhile, you trespassed and broke into his greenhouse."

"You're right," Rose said, crestfallen. "But if he has 'white at night,' I could take one of them and give the plant to my son."

He shook his head. "You won't be able to do anything at all, or be of any use to your friend, if you get caught and land in jail. And for all you know, he has alarms around that greenhouse, or even traps. People who have something to hide usually go to great lengths to protect themselves, and aren't worried about being legal or illegal."

Rose mulled things over. "What we really need is to catch him digging up plants on the Rez. I bet he goes out at dusk. He spots the plants during the day while conducting legal business, then comes back and digs them up at night when most of us are asleep. Working in the dark would explain why he damages so many plants trying to remove them."

"That makes sense, but what can be done?"

"We need a video camera that can operate on low light."

"A high school teacher friend of mine has one. I think he bought it while studying bat populations along the river for some state agency last summer. At least that's what one of my nephews told me. He'll lend it to us, I'm sure."

"How long will it take you?"

"I'll call him now on the cell phone, and if he says yes, then we can go pick it up." Herman dialed and spoke to his friend. After a minute, he hung up and glanced over at her. "We can pick it up anytime."

She considered it. "I'd really like to go check in on Lena before we set out. I want to make sure she holds on. How long will it take you to go get the camera and bring it back?"

"An hour."

"Then you can do that while I check in with my friend."

Rose drove to her home and dropped Herman off by his truck. As she pulled to a stop, her thoughts circled around the one piece of the puzzle that still didn't seem to fit. "There's one thing I sure wish I could figure out," she said. "People have reported seeing a gas company truck driving around in places where there isn't any gas service, and when they tried to approach, the truck drove away. That's got to be connected to the thefts, but how?"

Herman shrugged. "It might be totally unrelated."

"My feelings tell me different. But I guess that's not the most important thing to worry about now. My son needs that plant, and he needs it soon."

As soon as Herman drove off, Rose headed to the hospital. She intended to make sure Lena knew she was always first in her thoughts.

Upon her arrival Rose walked directly to Lena's room. The good-luck plant she'd given her was beside the bed, along with other flowers, candy, and gifts from relatives, judging from the cards. Seeing that Lena's eyes were closed, Rose decided to leave a note, but before she could reach for a pad and pen, Lena's eyes opened.

Seeing Rose, Lena smiled wearily.

"You look better," Rose said, noticing that the pallor on her skin didn't seem so pronounced tonight. Maybe her friend was regaining her health even without the ritual.

Lena opened her hand slowly, and nestled in her palm was Ella's badger fetish. "Your daughter stopped by and said I should keep it for now. She said it would help me fight."

"And it will," Rose said softly, thanking Ella in the silence of her thoughts. "Its power has saved my daughter more than once. You hold on to the strength it gives you."

As Lena closed her eyes again, Rose tiptoed out of the room.

Rose and Herman met earlier than planned. He had insisted on driving now that the last remnants of daylight had given way to the night, and they were now parked beneath the overhanging branches of a cottonwood tree just down the street from Knight's home. The streetlight outside the driveway leading onto his property made it easy for them to keep an eye on the place.

"So now we wait?" Herman asked.

She nodded. "If I'm right, he'll wait until well after dark, then set out to harvest the plants he's already decided to collect tonight."

An hour passed slowly. Reaching into her large purse, she pulled out two burritos. "One is made with chicken, the other with mutton. They've also got plenty of beans, cheese, and salsa. They're cold, but the green chile will warm you up."

"Great, I was starving. Thanks!" He gestured ahead. "His porch light just went out." Herman set down the binoculars. "From the looks of it, he's not getting ready to go anytime soon."

"Do you think it's possible he spotted us down here?"

"I'm sure he hasn't. He hasn't come to peer out his windows or anything like that."

While Herman ate first, Rose used the binoculars to keep her eyes on Knight's car, parked close to the house. Time passed slowly. After an eternity of waiting, Rose suddenly spotted movement. "He just came outside. Get ready."

Herman reached for the ignition, planning on starting his own truck after Knight had already put his vehicle in motion. But Knight, wearing some kind of uniform now, walked past his truck and headed toward a small, detached garage.

Rose's heart fell. Maybe she'd been wrong about him, unless he had another car they'd never seen before.

"Why doesn't he use his truck? It's perfect for reservation travel," Herman mumbled.

Rose, who had not taken her eyes off Knight, added, "I have a hunch what's in the garage."

"Ah, right. Another vehicle that doesn't say 'I'm Bradford Knight's truck,' perhaps?"

When Knight drove out of the garage in the white gas

company truck, a cold chill raced up her spine. Before she could comment, Knight pulled out of his driveway onto the street. The lights on his phony utility truck were still off.

Rose and Herman ducked down as he drove past them, then they both looked up. Halfway down the block, Knight finally turned on his headlights.

"You're too far behind. We're going to lose him," Rose said as Herman started his pickup's engine.

"Don't worry. I know what I'm doing. There's no other traffic right now on this stretch and that's why we have to hang back. He's going to see our headlights in his rearview mirror as it is."

They followed as Knight turned and headed west. Knight continued on for nearly ten minutes before crossing the San Juan River and traveling south down Highway 371. The state highway roughly paralleled the eastern edge of the Navajo Nation for miles.

Once they passed the popular recreation site known as the Dunes, Knight took a dirt road to the right, crossing a natural gas pipeline, then entering Navajo land near Amarillo Canyon. The gas company truck left a plume of dust in the air, eerily visible in the moonlight.

"Slow down, or he'll see the dust trail that we leave behind as clearly as we see his," Rose said.

Herman nodded. "I think the dust he's throwing up would hide our presence as long as he goes straight, but he might see us if he makes a sharp turn to either side. I'll stay back a bit farther, just in case."

They remained on his trail for another thirty minutes. The moon, full and bright, lit their way, and even without Knight's headlights and taillights, the white color of the truck was distinctive. Meanwhile, she knew from experience that Herman's green pickup only faded into the darkness, looking like a medium-gray shadow in the limited light. Finally the trail of dust settled, the head- and taillights they'd been watching disappeared, letting them know that he'd parked.

Herman got as close as he dared, then pulled off the road behind an eroded sandstone formation that, in the dark, looked like a scoop of half-melted ice cream.

"We'll have to go on foot from here. Otherwise he might hear the engine," Herman said.

"Grab the low-light camera and let's go," Rose answered.

"I've used this kind of camera before, so I'll climb up just below the crest of that hill and use the zoom lens once I spot where he's gone."

Rose nodded. "While you do that, I'll go alongside the road, staying behind cover. I want to see for myself what he's digging up this time."

"What if he has a night job for the natural gas company, maybe as a night watchman or something like that?" Herman whispered.

"Then he shouldn't be out here, should he?" Rose replied. "He's guilty. I have no doubt about that now. All that gas company stuff is just a disguise."

"Just be careful," Herman whispered.

Rose moved silently through the brush, stopping often to wait and listen. Once she located Knight, she'd find out what he was after, then back away. She didn't want to confront a man who was most likely a killer.

As Rose drew near, she heard a soft thump, and saw Knight chopping at the hard ground with what looked like a small pick. Moving closer, she recognized it as a GI entrenching tool, with the blade turned to a ninety-degree angle. Still needing to find out which plant was being uprooted, she went a few steps closer, hiding behind a juniper, and crouched low. Knight had found several "baby newborn" and, from the gunnysacks behind him, had already dug up at least half a dozen of the healthiest plants. A few had been cut by his careless strokes—he wasn't using a lantern to see—and they were scattered on the ground where he'd thrown them.

A sense of outrage filled her, but she crept back to the truck, following the plan. Moments later, Herman joined her.

"He's our man, down to the GI shovel," Herman said. "I've got it all on tape, but I'm not sure how clear his face will be. The magnification was good, so the image was large enough, but the angle wasn't right. The juniper on that rise above him cast shadows on his face. My guess is that the image will come out distorted."

"He may be going someplace else now," Rose said, pointing. "You'll have another chance."

Knight went back to the truck and loaded up the plants after sprinkling the gunnysacks with water from a big jug. Then he picked up three orange cones placed around the vehicle, and tossed them into the truck bed. Herman filmed the activity, and made sure he got the license number of the truck.

Rose glanced over at Herman. "We have a shot of him digging up the plants, and another of him loading the plants into his truck. His face may not be perfectly clear, but there are two of us to testify that it was him, and that he was on Navajo land at the time. If the truck is a phony, the natural gas company will probably have a criminal complaint of their own to make too. But that will come later. What we need to do now is take advantage of the fact he's not at home and go back there and take a look inside his greenhouse. Maybe we can find something that will connect him to our murdered friend."

"You'd have to break in, and that's against the law."

"Either way, I'm going."

TWENTY-FOUR

—— ✖ ✖ ✖ ——

By the time they returned to Knight's neighborhood and their parking spot beneath the cottonwood, all the lights inside the area residences were off except for a few porch lights. Rose headed along the fence line of Knight's home, working her way toward the back, with Herman right beside her. It took a few minutes, but they found the gap under the fence they'd used earlier, and slipped beneath it into the orchard.

Together, they walked quickly through the orchard and up to the large greenhouse. Discovering that the door had no lock, she opened it and went inside, Herman a step behind her. It was warm and not overly humid, what she'd expected from a greenhouse specializing in desert plants rather than, say, orchids. There were no overhead plant lights on now, only a few fluorescent bulbs placed near the floor that would enable Knight to move around without turning on the main lighting.

The first room, apparently, was where plants were being developed from cuttings or grafts. Most were so immature it was difficult to identify them, but she recognized a few as plants from her list of endangered species. Labels were placed on the pots, using code numbers and dates. Many pots were encased in plastic bags and had overhead light fixtures. None of the lights were turned on at the moment.

As they entered the second room through a large but open doorway, she saw it was crowded with four rows of waist-high planters lined up like school cafeteria tables. Like in the first room the lighting was dim, but it was easy to see now that her eyes had adjusted. There were hundreds of individually potted plants native to the reservation—some she recognized immediately as species that the *Dineh* were having a lot of trouble finding. On each pot was a computer-printed label with a code number, date, and location where they'd been found. Looking quickly, she saw that they all appeared to be sites on the Navajo Nation.

Rose turned to tell Herman to videotape everything, but saw that he was already doing so. As the camera whirred softly, Rose walked down the long rows, searching for "white at night." In a row of large plastic pots near one corner she found several of the elusive plants.

With her heart hammering in her throat, she picked up three of the smallest pots, placed them securely into an empty five-gallon plastic bucket with a wire bale, and handed them to Herman. "Take these to my son," she said. "They're emergency medicine, and Lena needs them right now. They were taken from our land, according to the note attached to the pots."

"Let's both go," Herman said, lowering the video camera, then taking the plants from her carefully. "We have all we need now."

"I can't leave yet. This is my one chance to search for something that will link Knight to the murder of our friend. I strongly suspect that he was the one who stole those special plants that our friend had been developing. If I find any growing here, that will connect him to those missing plants and the break-in of his trailer."

"But you can't afford to get caught on his property. Our word might not carry much weight if we're facing trespassing charges," Herman reminded. "The videotape might get thrown out as evidence."

"But it would still provide a reason for the authorities to search this place. Besides, I don't plan on getting caught. If I see him return, I'll just sneak out the other door before he spots me. As long as he doesn't know we've been here, he's not going to suspect anything," Rose replied.

"Just make sure he doesn't see you. I'd rather lose these plants than have you get hurt," Herman said.

"I'll be fine. Just go, find a phone, and tell the police you saw a trespasser here in the greenhouse. Then deliver those plants to my son. Once the police arrive I'll show myself and tell them I saw Knight digging up our plants earlier tonight on the reservation and followed him here. I'll explain that I stayed to make sure he didn't get the chance to destroy anything in the greenhouse when he saw the police arrive. Once they see the plants for themselves the evidence on the videotape will be all the corroboration they need."

"Promise to leave if he comes into the greenhouse before the police get here?" Herman said, turning toward the door.

"Of course. I don't want him to know we're on to him. That's the best way to protect the Plant People. If anything happens to all these plants, we might not have others to replace them, at least not for years, and some could be lost to us forever. As a Plant Watcher I owe this to the tribe and the Plant People. Now go."

Herman stood there. "I should be the one who stays. *You* take what you need to your son and bring the police."

"I can't do that. This is *my* duty, and since the tribe hired me, it's also my job. Also, as a Plant Watcher, I'll be able to recognize our friend's special plants easier than you can. Get the videotape away from here and protect it, then drive that hot-rod truck of yours as fast as you can and take the plants to my son."

As soon as Herman was gone, Rose fought a sudden surge of panic. She needed to focus. Herman would be back soon with help, but in the meantime she still had a job to do. Although Lena would finally get the medicinal plants she needed so badly, Charlie Dodge's death still cried out for justice.

Finding a flashlight on a workbench in the first room they'd entered, Rose returned to the big plant room and walked slowly down each row, using the increased lighting to help speed up her search. She found a planters filled with "frog tobacco" and "salt thin." Halfway down the final row, Rose became aware of a fragrant and familiar scent. Searching for the source, she saw several plants on a planter next to the greenhouse wall. The small violet-blue flowers had a scent that was as unique as the vivid hue of their petals. Only one man had ever managed to create a variety like that. Those plants were Charlie's special hybrids. Rose had wanted a link and now she had it. The only way Knight could have had these hybrids was if he'd taken them from Charlie.

The gas company truck, the presence of the native plants at his greenhouse, the video of Knight digging up the plants disguised as a gas company employee, and now these dark blue flowers, matching the one she'd rescued from Charlie's trailer, would all combine to make the case against Bradford Knight. She was trying to find other evidence to use against him, when she saw the beam of another flashlight through the greenhouse window. Rose ran to the far door and turned the handle, but the door wouldn't open. She tugged, looking for a lever or a key to turn, but the door refused to budge. Either it was locked from the outside or the door mechanism was damaged, but there was no time now.

———

Just a few seconds before the other door to the greenhouse opened, she turned off the flashlight, ducked down, and crawled underneath the closest planter. Crouching low, she made her way on her hands and knees to a hiding spot halfway between the rows.

A moment later, Knight flipped on a row of overhead lights, set the gunnysacks down on a potting bench, then gave in to a long coughing fit, his body shaking by the time it subsided. Rose recalled his coughing before, and his pale skin, but he seemed even worse now. She wondered if perhaps he was suffering from something far more serious than a summer cold or a virus.

Peering out of her hiding place, she saw Knight reach into his pocket, take out a medicine vial, and pop some pills into his mouth. He took out a hip flask from his back pocket and drank something to wash down the pills. After another short coughing spasm, he began to remove the varieties he'd dug up that night from the damp gunnysacks and started to pot them.

She recognized the "baby newborn" plants. They weren't in great shape, but she could see that he'd taken great care not to disturb the roots and had wrapped them carefully in the damp cloth. Remembering the plants he'd destroyed in the darkness, she realized now that he probably lost a fourth or more of everything he tried to dig up.

As Knight worked on the potting bench, his back to her, Rose decided to crawl down the row of planters toward the door. Her eyes on Knight, she only moved when he was active and making noise. She was one planter away from the end of the row, almost even with him, when Knight accidentally dropped the small trowel he was using. It bounced on the concrete floor, landing just underneath the edge of the planter between Knight and where she was hiding. Rose froze, trying to melt into the shadows.

Knight reached down for the trowel and looked right at her. "You!"

Rose scrambled out from beneath the planters on the opposite side, placing a row of plants and tables between them. Instead of ducking beneath to grab at her, Knight ran to the door and blocked her way, holding the trowel in his hand like a knife. "How dare you break in here!"

Rose stood straight and calmly brushed the dust off her clothes, trying to keep her heartbeat from going through the roof. She knew that she had only one chance now. She had to convince him that the game was up.

"A friend of mine and I followed you tonight. You went south past the Dunes in that gas company truck, the one you hide in your garage, then west onto the reservation. We know you've been digging up plants from Navajo land. You've been leaving marks all over with that military-style shovel of yours. A lot of those plants, the ones you didn't destroy when you dug them up, are growing here now. But you've taken the life of an old Navajo man too, pushing him off the cliff and trying to make it look like an accident, and it's no longer just simple theft. The police are on their way here now."

His eyes narrowed. "You're here alone. Who are you trying to fool?"

"You didn't see my car outside, did you?" Rose asked, appealing to his logic. "That's because I didn't come here alone. My friend went to take the evidence we have to the police, then bring them here to arrest you."

"You're on *my* property without my permission. If I get arrested, so will you."

"For what, trespassing inside the greenhouse of a criminal? It will be dismissed automatically once the evidence we've obtained reaches the district attorney. You're the thief, and you're the one who's committed murder. The hybrid plants back there, the sweet-smelling dark blue ones you took from my friend's trailer, are the link between you two. He would have never given you his special plants—something he'd spent years developing one step at a time. The gas company truck you've been driving—is it a phony or did you steal it—also links you to him. Witnesses who were in the area at the time he died saw that truck turn off the road and head straight toward where he was, below that mesa. It's over for you now. The evidence is all here for the police."

"You're misinterpreting the so-called evidence you have. I didn't murder anyone." He looked down at the trowel in his hand and lowered it. "Charlie and I were having an argument over business and he fell. It was an accident. That's all."

When he didn't say anything more, Rose pressed him. "You were arguing about the plants?"

"No, the company I work for funded his research, which is why I have the plants here. The hybrids he developed would have been a great natural, completely safe dye, especially for food coloring."

"You're telling me that you two worked together?" Her jaw dropped. It would explain some puzzling things about Charlie's income and his generally secretive personal life. Still, it was a bit hard to take.

"Yes, we worked for the same company, though technically Charlie Dodge was my employee. I paid him cash because he didn't believe in checks. How do you think he managed to buy that new mobile home? At first he and I worked together well. We both needed the work and the income it provided, so we shared our expertise. He told me about the medicinal plants your medicine men used so I could research them. I stood to make a great deal of money selling the results of my research to the pharmaceutical company. But then I was diagnosed with an advanced stage of lung cancer.

That's when I remembered the stories people all around the reservation had told me about a miracle plant that cured cancer patients. I knew I had to find it."

Rose had hated the thief who'd damaged or destroyed so many plants with his careless, hurried digging, but now all she could feel was pity. "There is no such plant. Rumors like that have been going around as long as I can remember, but the truth is our people die of cancer too."

"You're wrong. The plant's uses and preparation were described to me in detail by an old man who lives out by Mount Taylor. They called him *Hosteen* Natoni—Mr. Natoni."

Rose nodded. "I know him, and I have no doubt he heard that story from someone else. It's something that has been passed down for generations—like what people in the cities call an urban legend. But it's false hope. There is no such plant."

"Natoni told me that only a few could identify the plant because that knowledge had nearly been lost over time. One of them was Charlie Dodge. But Charlie wouldn't talk about it, so I stepped up my research with the plants I knew your medicine men used, trying to find the ones with known anti-tumor compounds. I worked day and night, but I haven't been able to find the right plant."

"You're searching for a mythical plant," she said softly. "I'm truly sorry."

He focused his gaze on her. "So it's all over for me, is that what you're saying?" Knight didn't wait for an answer. "If that's the case, then so be it. But I won't spend the last few months of my life in jail. This greenhouse, and you, have to go." He reached behind him and brought a can of spray lubricant down from a shelf, then sprayed the pungent liquid up and down a wooden structural beam which reached all the way to the roof.

Then he pulled out a silver lighter from his pocket. "They

328 * AIMÉE & DAVID THURLO

always said that being around someone who smoked was dangerous to your health." Knight flicked the wheel with his thumb, and a long blue flame appeared.

"No!" Rose grabbed the closest pot, which contained a small cactus, and threw it at him.

The blow caught Knight on the head and he dropped the lighter. But he steadied himself quickly and reached for the large shovel resting against the greenhouse wall to his right. "It'll be more merciful if I knock you out first. You'll never feel the fire, because the smoke will probably kill you before then."

Rose looked around for a weapon, but there was none. In desperation, she casually scooped up some potting soil and held it in her fist as she stepped back, giving ground. As he raised the shovel to swing at her, she threw the soil right into his eyes.

Knight staggered back coughing, and Rose ducked past him, bolting for the door. As she yanked it open, she ran right into Sheriff Taylor and Ella.

"Mom!" Ella yelled as she reached out to steady her. "Are you okay?"

Looking over Rose's shoulder, Ella suddenly saw Bradford Knight burst through the doorway, his shovel raised. Pushing Rose behind her, Ella and Sheriff Taylor both reached for their pistols.

As Knight lowered the shovel, Rose took an unsteady breath. "I don't think I've ever been happier to see you, daughter."

TWENTY-FIVE
———— ✖ ✖ ✖ ————

Rose was sitting in her daughter's office at the Shiprock Tribal Police Station when Big Ed Atcitty, the police chief, appeared at the doorway.

"I've seen the videotape," he said, "and when the crucial frames are viewed one at a time, it's easy to identify Knight as the person doing the digging."

"If he'd been able to complete his work, he might have been a rich man," Ella said. "From what we saw, he was creating quality samples of the herbs the tribe commonly uses for medicinal purposes. He intended on providing dried specimens for lab extraction, then selling those pure extracts to the pharmaceutical company he worked with along with the information on their health applications. Herbal remedies don't have to go through the same rigorous testing program that prescription drugs do, and he would have saved the company years of trial-and-error research. But then things went wrong."

Rose nodded, understanding. "Cancer shows no mercy," she said. "I just wish I knew how he managed to learn about so many of our collection sites."

"I can answer that," Ella said. "He admitted that he'd followed several medicine men when they were gathering their herb medicines, and though they may not readily admit it, according to Knight several medicine men talked freely about the collection sites their 'competition' used."

"I wonder if my friend, the man I knew as Charlie, found out he was being followed and that's why they'd argued that day."

Ella nodded. "Knight has been plea-bargaining in order to get better prison accommodations and medical care. He told us that Charlie spotted the phony utility truck, remembered having seen it several times before, and decided to sneak up on whoever was inside. When he saw it was Knight, Charlie confronted him. They got into a scuffle that escalated and your friend suddenly collapsed and died. Knight told you the truth, he didn't kill him, and the autopsy supports his story. Charlie *did* die of a heart attack. The most we'll be able to pin on Knight is the theft of reservation plants and tampering with evidence at the scene of a crime. Involuntary manslaughter is a possibility, but the prosecutor doesn't think it'll stick. Knight made it look like Charlie had fallen off the cliff because he didn't want to report it and get involved in an investigation." Ella paused, taking a breath. "He'll have to answer for a lot in court. I've heard that the natural gas company is thinking of suing Knight for pretending to be one of their employees too."

"At least Knight can't dig up any more plants," Rose said.

"But you will have to answer for a few things also, Mom. What you did was illegal. What'll make the evidence stand is that Sheriff Taylor and I went there to investigate a disturbance and we both saw the plants and their labels. All the plants were linked to tribal land because we found his codes in a logbook."

"And he's confessed, right?"

"Yes, but that doesn't exonerate *you*."

"Then so be it. My granddaughter's father will defend me if Knight presses charges. But I think Knight will be too busy defending himself to do that. Especially if he's trying to bargain for a better jail cell."

Ella glared at her. "Mom, doesn't *anything* scare you?"

"Sometimes," Rose admitted softly. "But it's what we end up doing in spite of it that defines who we are."

Big Ed laughed. "Like daughter, like mother. Right, ladies?"

Ella sighed. "I give up."

Rose stood. "Unless the police are pressing charges now, I have a Song of Blessing to attend."

Big Ed shrugged, then shook his head, turning to look at Ella.

"Go see Lena at the hospital. If we have any questions, I know where you live," Ella said.

Ten days later, Rose, Maria, Willie, and Sadie gathered on Lena's porch for a visit. Although Lena tired easily, she was obviously well on the road to recovery, and had prepared dessert for all of them.

"I thought I was going to lose you, old friend. Don't you ever scare me like that again," Rose said.

"I wouldn't have made it if it hadn't been for all of you." Lena smiled at Rose and the others. "You kept searching and finally found the plants the *hataalii* needed. That's why I'm here right now."

Maria poured herself another glass of iced tea from the pitcher. "I heard this morning that the tribal council has asked the Navajo nursery to separate a section of land and dedicate it to cultivating the endangered Plant People. There, they'll increase in numbers until they can be reintroduced into the areas of the Rez where their kind have diminished or disappeared."

Lena smiled, approving.

"After you get better," Rose said, "you and I will go to the schools and teach both teachers and kids about the Plant People. They've become very curious about medicinal plants ever since they heard that a huge pharmaceutical company was interested in our herbs."

Lena chuckled. "Isn't that the way it always is? No one appreciates what they've got until someone else wants it."

"I've also suggested that the tribe work hand in hand with the mining companies' reclamation efforts, and the tribe has agreed that this should be done. All the Plant Watchers will be monitoring and reporting what the Anglo companies do from now on," Rose said.

Lena laughed. "Oh, I bet they just loved you for that."

Rose smiled. The afternoon with friends was just what Lena—and she—needed.

They passed the time pleasantly. Then, after the others had all left and only Rose remained, Lena stood up. "I want to go to my family's shrine. It's not far from here, just behind the house and up that canyon. Will you help me walk up there?"

"Are you sure you're ready for it?"

"Yes, if you're willing to help me."

"Of course I will."

Ten minutes later, Rose and Lena were a hundred yards up the narrow canyon. Rose's gaze swept the area automatically, always alert for the Plant People.

"Look over to your right," Rose told Lena, pointing to a plant with gray flowers.

" 'Mind medicine,' " Lena whispered.

"And growing beside it is 'cone toward water.' " Both plants were used to work spells—"frenzy medicine," they were called. "What if the kids get hold of those!" Rose reached down, intending on pulling them up, but Lena stepped in the way.

"No. Even these plants have a part in the path of harmony. Everything is interconnected. The absence of one plant can lead to the loss of others and we've all learned the hard way how one tiny plant can make all the difference in the world."

Rose nodded slowly. "You're right. Everything in nature has two sides, and accepting both is the only way to walk in beauty."

With the sun high over the Chuska Mountains far to the west, Rose and Lena continued their walk to the shrine.